SF Books by Vaughn Heppner.

DOOM STAR SERIES
Star Soldier
Bio Weapon
Battle Pod
Cyborg Assault
Planet Wrecker
Star Fortress

EXTINCTION WARS SERIES
Assault Troopers
Planet Strike

INVASION AMERICA SERIES
Invasion: Alaska
Invasion: California
Invasion: Colorado
Invasion: New York

OTHER SF NOVELS
Alien Honor
Accelerated
Strotium-90
I, Weapon

Visit www.Vaughnheppner.com for more information.

Assault Troopers

(Extinction Wars)

by
Vaughn Heppner

Copyright © 2013 by the author.

ISBN-13: 978-1496094117
ISBN-10: 1496094115
BISAC: Fiction / Science Fiction / Military

Prologue

I remember the day it finally happened—the day an alien race made contact with humanity.

The latest presidential campaign was already in full swing. Endless rivers of money flowed to advertisers and political slogans clogged the airwaves.

As far as I can recall, no astronomer spotted the alien starship cruising through the solar system, passing Saturn, Jupiter, Mars and then parking in orbit around Earth. One minute there was nothing. The next, CNN, Fox News, every TV station on the planet, blurted out the amazing story of a real live UFO visitor.

The vessel was mind-bogglingly big: one commentator said as huge as Rhode Island. It was as if someone had hollowed out one of the bigger asteroids and stuck engines in it. But this thing wasn't an asteroid. It was metal, a construct: black, oval and with giant fins sticking out of it like an old '57 Chevy.

The political ads stopped airing as the TV stations played the alien starship twenty-four seven.

I was stationed in Antarctica. My name was Creed, by the way, just Creed. I didn't like my first name and had never used it. We sat glued before the TV, forgetting about the science experiments. According to what we watched, people by the thousands, millions maybe, aimed their backyard telescopes or binoculars at the vessel, and of course the military used radar.

For thirty-seven hours the starship waited up there, as silent as the Sphinx, making the world increasingly nervous. Finally, the U.S. couldn't resist doing something to prod the aliens into talking. They pulled out a mothballed shuttle and launched it into orbit. Who should pilot it but Mad Jack Creed, my father? My mom had divorced him years ago, but we'd kept in touch. He was one of the few people to visit me during my stint in prison.

Mad Jack spoke into the shuttle camera, giving the world a running commentary as his craft approached the alien ship. It was amazing.

I watched. The world watched. Maybe it would have been better if it had been a grainy image instead of pure HD. Mad Jack grinned out of the TV. He'd torn off the goofy astronaut's headgear and put on his old Air Force cap with its chipped silver rocket pin on the bill, and he sported four days' growth of beard.

He'd flown F-18s in his day, a fighter jock with three confirmed kills. It was obvious he was enjoying the heck out of getting up in the air again. He shoved his face in the camera and told us the alien hovered 260 miles over Spain.

The dimensions of the starship awed me as my dad approached it: like a flea nearing an elephant.

My chest ached with pride for my old man. He had guts and he played this cool and collected. I know they must have asked for volunteers and he would have been the first in line.

As Mad Jack talked, cameras showed the shuttle's bay doors opening and a space arm unfolding, lifting a giant communications device. Computers began aiming the dish at the starship.

The aliens had been quiet, continuing their Sphinx-like routine of inscrutability. Finally, however, they began to react.

"Look," my dad's copilot said. "Something's happening."

"Focus camera five," Mad Jack said.

I couldn't sit still as the others watched. At first, I'd crouched in front of the TV, with my fists clenched. Now I strode back and forth behind the other sitting watchers, needing to move. None of my coworkers told me to sit down. They knew better.

"What is that?" my dad's copilot asked.

That registered with me. I stared at the screen. I imagine everyone in the world stared into their TV or smart phone feed. They all saw a slot open on the starship.

"It appears Mad Jack is making them react," the TV commentator said.

Without warning, a beam fired out of the starship, a ray of incandescent light, looking more like a sci-fi movie than reality.

My dad had time to shout a single, angry profanity. Our TV picture froze for a moment and showed him hunched over his panel, staring out of the shuttle window. He looked as if he wanted to launch missiles in retaliation. I saw him. I saw the fighter glaring out of his eyes.

Then there was nothing but old-fashioned blizzard-like static on the tube.

The TV technicians worked fast. They switched to an open-mouthed commentator outside the Pentagon. The woman blinked several times in confusion until someone told her she was live.

"The aliens dusted the shuttle," I said.

The others in our Antarctica shelter turned toward me.

A cold hard knot of fury erupted in my chest. The aliens had killed my dad. A fierce sense of loss exploded in my stomach. I swayed, staggered back and sat hard on the floor. I stared slack-jawed, seeing nothing in particular.

"Look," Rollo said. "What are those?"

I remember focusing, turning to stare at the TV again. Openings appeared in the vast starship. Was the network using a satellite to image this? Big ugly...missiles, they must have been missiles, darted out of the ship. They moved like hungry sharks, showing long exhaust tails. The missiles dived into the Earth's atmosphere and headed in different directions— for different cities, it turned out.

The next few minutes of TV showed a medley of shouting, panicked confusion. I witnessed Patriot missiles lofting, trying to shoot down what we found out later were thermonuclear annihilators screaming toward U.S. targets. Another brief report told us that the Chinese had a laser defense system that no one had known about. None of it mattered. Earth tech wilted against the alien battleware.

Beijing vanished in the biggest mushroom cloud the world had ever seen. Los Angeles disappeared. So did New York City, Rio de Janeiro, Johannesburg, Cairo, London, Berlin, Moscow, Bombay and Ho Minh Chin City. As if that wasn't enough, the aliens dusted the planet with a bio-terminator. It was the last thing I witnessed on the TV, a big drone spraying black spores into the air. That proved the aliens must have known about humanity ahead of time in order to create a biological weapon to kill the survivors. Either that, or that's what they'd been perfecting for the last thirty-seven hours.

In the blink of an eye, Judgment Day came to us. It started with Mad Jack Creed and ended with over ninety-nine percent of humanity dead and gone. The nuclear holocaust killed hundreds of millions. The bio-terminator proved worse. Billions choked on black gunk bubbling in their throats, most drowned to death in their own fluids. The few the nukes and mutated spores missed succumbed to radiation poisoning or the horrifyingly new weather patterns.

The aliens proved to be more like Darth Vader than ET. And that might have been the end of humanity.

What chance did the final one percent have—actually, less than one percent? The survivors remained in places like Antarctica, where we were.

I took my rifle out of my locker that day, and never put it back. I yearned to kill aliens. Survivors were left on oil platforms in the Arctic Ocean, in submarines, on deep-sea transports and in Siberia and other remote places. Out of billions, a few million shocked and scattered individuals waited for extinction. A high proportion of them were military or in high-risk occupations. That meant far more men than women survived.

In the aftermath—although no one knew it yet—women became the most precious commodity left. If *Homo sapiens* were to escape the Dodo bird's fate, the last females were going to have to bear plenty of healthy children. Otherwise, in one generation there would be no human race.

I'd like to say we rose up—the last humans—pitched in together and overcame every obstacle with our native pride, stubbornness and cunning. No, it wasn't anything like that. It was grimmer, darker and included low-down killing, the kind where we wrestled in the slime, gasping for breath, enduring agony and deep cuts. Our prize was the opportunity to stick a knife in our enemy's guts.

Maybe that's too metaphorical. I don't know. The thing is the aliens in their monstrous starship made a mistake. They should have finished their filthy deed, exterminating the last of us as if we were cockroaches. Instead…yeah, maybe it's time to tell this in a direct, linear fashion.

Before I start, I should add that the last humans were the rough kind: the risk-takers, the lucky, the mean and the tough bastards who worked hard for a living. I was one of them, and I wasn't a wall-flower nice guy. Not that I was bad— misunderstood most of my life, yeah, but not evil.

The best place to start would be that fateful day in Antarctica when I met the aliens face to face. I remember it all right. It happened like this…

-1-

Another purple-colored snowstorm howled outside our Antarctica shelter. Every once in a while a high-pitched shriek added to the symphony of noise.

The snow itself wasn't purple, but the clouds racing across the sky were: purple, bloody-red and a stark orange I'd never seen before.

We were in Victoria Land near the Ross Ice Shelf. The McMurdo military base—a U.S. installation—had already gone under. Rollo took out the tractor yesterday to see why communications had stopped with them. We'd felt the shockwave, the earthquake two days ago, or what we figured was a mother of a tremor. Rollo reported back that the shelf-ice near McMurdo was gone. Some kind of tsunami must have cracked the surface and swallowed everything. That wave had probably slapped the land hard enough so we'd felt it here.

The shock of losing McMurdo—the people and resources—further damaged what remained of our shattered morale. My comrades hunched around the radio. They were subdued, pale and had wide, staring eyes. Communications Tech Rice slowly twisted her dial, listening to static and waiting for some lone voice to talk to us. It was pathetic and at the same time all too human, with the digital numbers climbing higher and higher.

"Slower," one of others whispered to Rice. "You're going too fast."

"Shut up," she replied. "I know what I'm doing."

I sat well away from them. I didn't want to hear static or re-watch video footage of the starship, my dad's death or the first nuclear explosions. Two days after the end of the world, I was near crazy with grief and impotent rage. It wasn't only Mad Jack who had died. My mother, cousins, my old grandfather: dead. My home town: obliterated. My favorite football team: radioactive waste or a pile of black gunk. I tried to bottle the grief and keep down the howling beast inside of me because I didn't want to lash out at the others. They didn't deserve that.

I hated everything about the world-destroyers. I wished I could invade their planet and drop antimatter bombs on them. I wanted to hurt the enemy. Maybe it was part of my makeup. I've always felt that if someone beat me to death, I was going to bite them back at the very least. I wanted to give them something to remember me by: a broken bone, a cut or even a tooth mark on their ankle if that's all I could manage. These aliens had beaten humanity to death and none of us had been able to do a damn thing about it or to hurt them back in any way. I wished the Chinese lasers had worked at least a little.

If we turned on our radiation detectors in the shelter, they still registered too high. We were all getting too many rads. Life anywhere on Earth had become just as bad as being sent to a Soviet-era nuclear submarine or living near Chernobyl.

We were screwed. Humanity was screwed, maybe the entire Earth. The penguins I'd seen yesterday had wobbled too much. They never were much good at walking. This bunch must have been migrating into the mountains. I'd seen thousand in a long stream, a carpet of them, and it seemed as if all those penguins were drunk. Hundreds just keeled over, kicking their webbed feet before spitting black gunk and dying. I buried them. I don't really know why I did. I guess it was better than doing nothing. Yeah, I shoveled frozen dirt over 400 penguins, I stopped counting at 399. I'd used my spade to hack at the icy ground until sweat poured from my skin. That black stuff they spit frightened me.

That had been yesterday. Today, I sat on a stool away from the others. I had my rifle propped between my knees and an oily rag in my stained hands. The metal parts gleamed. This

7

baby was ready to use and then some. I knew my dad would have approved.

Did my eyes roll around in my head? The others had stopped looking at me and they tiptoed when they moved near.

I was Security for the base; well, me and Rollo. He was tall and bony, a real wiz with the computers and the video games. I'd boxed in the military—the U.S. Army—and I'd lugged a heavy machine gun around in the Light Infantry in Afghanistan.

The name of Creed was one of the few things I inherited from Mad Jack other than my temper and physique. The story of my life really started with my stepdad. He used to laugh when I did something stupid. It was harsh, jeering laughter. Before he learned better, he'd slapped me around, too. Later, as I gained size, the laughter stopped and he'd swear at me, adding a few punches. I only hit him once, and I'd felt guilty about it ever since. My mother used to send me to church and I knew about honoring my father and mother. It was the Third Commandment. Still, my stepdad shouldn't have hit me.

From his hospital room, my stepdad pressed charges. I'd been sixteen at the time. The judge had been a friend of his. The judge decided I was too big to go to a juvenile lockup. Under the provision of an obscure law, he sentenced me to prison as an adult.

During my three years among the cons I learned more about fighting than I ever wanted to know. It wasn't nice, fair fighting by rules, but bare-knuckles, a shank of steel at times and the heel of your shoe used to stomp and break bones. I'd almost been seventeen when the bars clanged behind me the first time—the age Robert E. Howard had made Conan the Barbarian in his literary entrance into civilization.

I was too young for the pen, but I had size, attitude and hard muscles. None of that mattered to most of those cons, who believed I was the virgin boy. The first time they tried, one of them brought two gangbanger-buddies. They cornered me in the storage room next to the kitchen. I could see the lust in their eyes—it was a horrible thing when you're on the receiving end. I picked up a big jar of olives and smashed it against the nearest face. That was one of the most savage battles I ever

8

fought. I have scars from it and still dislike it if people close in around me. Those jailbirds never *did* me, though, not those punks and not anyone.

The worst assault came three years later. It was a gang thing, payback for what I'd done earlier. Prison taught me about vengeance because those I beat down never forgot and never forgave. This time I was armed with a shiv: a piece of metal with a cloth-wrapped handle. Mine was sharpened to a razor's edge. Long story short, I shanked two more wannabe rapists. One died and one would limp for the rest of his life and would never be able to rape again.

I found myself before an old white-haired judge with the thickest lenses I'd ever seen. It made his brown eyes behind them huge. I might have become a lifer that day because I'd defended my honor. The judge must have seen something salvageable in my belligerent stare, but I don't know how it could have been possible. Maybe he knew how it was inside, and how I'd had no choice.

At nineteen, I'd been lost to an inner rage. I recall standing in his courtroom with hunched shoulders, glowering up at him. He told me I had two choices: more prison if I liked fighting so much, or the military.

That old judge must be dead by now. Wish I could shake his hand and thank him for his kindness and for his mercy. I owed him big time.

In any case, after Army boot camp I hoofed it up and down the mountains of Afghanistan, lugging a .50 caliber machine gun. They're heavy, and they get even heavier in high altitudes. There's not much to say about that time except for that a lieutenant managed to get half our platoon killed in a firefight. I lost some close friends that day because of the man's carelessness.

After the funeral, I spoke to the lieutenant concerning his stupidity. He was an arrogant prick and shouted at me. The man lacked all shame. His confusing orders had aided the Taliban. He could see that, right? No. He got red-faced as I explained it to him, and he tried to drag out his service pistol. That was a hostile action. So I hit him and knocked out several teeth.

9

For my justifiable self-defense, they tossed me out of the military. They must have partly agreed with my analysis about the lieutenant, because they could have stuck me in Leavenworth. Instead I was only charged with insubordination and given a dishonorable discharge.

Instead of going back to the States, I joined Black Sand, a military security contractor outfit. Supposedly they didn't wage war, but supplied bodyguards for moneyed people in bad places. I did okay for a year. Then I got in an argument with my superior.

Because of ongoing labor disputes, we set up a roadblock and checked papers for our employer, who owned the various company towns in his part of Java. It was an island down there in Southeast Asia, and the area was set amidst two hundred square miles of coffee plantation. After three days and six hours of boring duty under some local banana trees, a little brown-skinned beauty pulled up in a jeep at our roadblock.

She was a sight: pretty little hat, red lipstick and wearing nice white gloves. We'd seen her before. She was visiting her sister, one of the protesting labor leaders, and this girl liked to laugh. My superior, Mike Edwards, couldn't take his eyes off her, and he'd been muttering for days what he'd like to do to her in our shed.

His uncle ran Black Sand on Java, so he thought he could get away with anything. Mike was a big bastard, too, with a big gut, wide face and mean black eyes. He constantly needed a shave and there were always taco stains on his shirt. The man was a drunk, and mean drunk this time from too much scotch.

Edwards told her to get out of the jeep.

Rollo and I glanced at him. We knew her papers were in order.

Edwards took a wide stance, gripping his gun belt with his thick fingers and dirty fingernails. He liked to feel important, and he shouted at her to hurry it up.

She was classy, opened the door slowly and put high-heeled shoes onto the dirt. She had great legs and a short skirt, showing that her ass was as wonderful as the rest of her.

10

Edwards licked his lips, and those piggy eyes shone with lust. I'd seen that look in prison, before I'd bashed faces and broke teeth with my olive jar.

"Is there a problem?" she asked.

"Not yet," Edwards slurred. One of his paws descended onto her wrist, circling it like a fleshy manacle. She gave a little gasp of surprise. Edwards dragged her, and when she tried to dig in her heels, he yanked, making her stumble after him.

I'd heard stories about Edwards. He liked to rip off women's clothes, make them scream and press down on them afterward as he indulged himself. In truth, the man was a pig, a big one, a rutting boar of a rapist.

"Edwards," I said.

"Bugger off," he told me. "I'm busy for a while."

"What can you do?" Rollo whispered to me. "His uncle runs the place. If we lift a finger, we'll be in trouble."

The little woman with the white gloves peered over her shoulder and gave me a pleading look.

"Edwards," I said again.

He swiveled that wide face of his, stared at me and spat in my direction. "If you're smart—"

He roared with pain because I had stepped up as he spoke to me. I'd grabbed his thumb, the one on the girl's wrist, and twisted hard. That's what made him yell. Then I grinned in his face, twisting harder until he released her delicate wrist. Then my right foot happened to move behind his left heel, and the wallowing pig tumbled backward onto the dirt.

"Run," I told the woman, "*vamoose*."

She backed away with terror in her eyes, staring at me and then at Edwards. He bellowed from on the ground, and unsnapped his holster.

I took two steps and kicked. The revolver he drew out of the holster spun into the jungle, the heavy thing slapping banana leaves before thudding somewhere out of sight.

"Go," I told her, pointing at her car.

She hurried to it, slammed the door after getting in, looked once more at me, and peeled out as Rollo held up the crossbar.

Edwards was a tough guy and he was used to getting his way, especially in these things. He rose like a ponderous

11

elephant and shook his hurt hand. When he was done with that, he squinted at me, charged and took his first swing.

Rollo told me later that I was grinning crazy-like as Edwards's fists hammered against my ribs. I don't know about that. I let Edwards take several swings, though, before I beat him into unconsciousness.

Soon thereafter, I found myself reassigned to Antarctica with these eggheads. Rollo joined me because he hadn't helped Edwards defend himself. Naturally, the uncle hadn't believed our side of the story. Or maybe he had, but didn't care. And that was the fact of my life: the powers that be sticking it to me because of greedy self-interest.

It seems like it should have gotten easier, putting up with these injustices, but it never did.

In any case, now the wind howled outside in Victoria Land, Antarctica beating against our building. Rice hunched over the radio set, spinning her dial with her glossy red fingernails with the little sparkly swirls. Others re-watched starship video as if it was their favorite porn, seemingly unable to get enough footage of the destruction. I sat on my chair in a black funk, wishing there was an alien conqueror for me to kill. I debated praying for the first time in years, asking God to send me an alien.

The main door swung open then. It felt weird and surreal. Had God heard my thoughts? The idea bemused me.

Snow swirled through the open door. It blew between Rollo's long legs as he came in. Nope. No alien. I was disappointed. High in the sky purple clouds raced like NASCAR madmen shifting into nth gear.

Rollo stepped in and his goggle-protected eyes locked onto me.

"What?" I asked.

He opened his mouth, but couldn't seem to speak. I saw confusion in his eyes: like an elk in the headlights.

I stood up as my neck tingled. Without thinking, I chambered a round. I held my rifle, a good old M-14. There were extra magazines and two grenades in my parka pockets.

His lips moved, and Rollo said, "Aliens."

I was already moving toward him. Maybe I sensed what he wanted to say.

The others by the radio half turned, staring at Rollo. I clutched his right triceps and let my fingers dig in painfully.

That cleared his eyes. He raised his left arm, pointing up into the swirling sky. "Aliens are coming. What are we going to do?"

With a snarl, I jerked Rollo out of the way and charged outside with my rifle. My disappointment vanished and my mind became clearer. It was payback time.

-2-

As the wind hit me I remembered my goggles, hanging around my neck. The snowstorm raged, with stinging flakes biting my cheeks. I finally fit the goggles over my eyes, doing it one-handed because I still clutched the M-14. Once the lenses were in place, I tilted my head upward into the storm.

I expected to have to search for the alien ship, a flickering dot moving up, down and all around. No need. This thing was the size of a jumbo jet minus the wings. It had a box shape, with the front slanted back, no doubt to lessen friction. The giant lander headed toward our shelters. We had three buildings and two high-tech tents. Make that one tent now. The new, crazy, messed-up wind had torn down the other one.

Just like Rollo, I stood open-mouthed. Freezing flakes of snow landed on my tongue, a few hitting the back of my throat. This was a wild storm. With a *click*, I snapped my teeth together.

Start thinking things through, because you're not *going to get a second chance.*

Right, I needed to think, to analyze. But before I could do that, I had to observe. The alien lander moved smoothly. It appeared that the wind didn't buffet it hard enough to sway it from its flight path.

Did the extraterrestrials possess antigravity? I'd read plenty of science fiction and played sci-fi video games with Rollo. I knew a few things, or I thought I did.

No, I didn't think they had antigravity. I spotted thrusters in back and jets of flame like from an F-16 using afterburners. I

14

heard a thunderous roar, too. It was louder than a jumbo jet. I noticed as well that it did have stubby wings, small things, nubs really, which seemed to wobble the slightest bit.

It told me the howling wind did buffet the craft. Somehow, that did it for me and helped me regain my mental balance. These weren't magical creatures. Arthur C. Clarke had said something about super-high tech appearing as magic to less developed beings. The lander now didn't seem magical to me, but understandable.

Another group of thrusters appeared as the lander changed the manner and direction of its descent. The new thrusters sprouted from the bottom of the craft. They roared with flames as the lander came straight down. Swirling flakes melted in the stab of afterburners and the thunder grew ponderous.

I dropped my M-14 onto the snow and clapped gloved hands over my hood-protected ears. The noise was incredible, with the rumbling booms shaking through my body. Despite that, I watched, marveling at the lander. This thing was from another star system, who knew how many light years away. In it were alien beings—aliens who had annihilated most of Earth, including my dad.

I ground my teeth together. This was my chance to hurt them for hurting us. Would it be a useless gesture on my part? I didn't know. Everyone was wired differently. I was a fighter by nature, a counter-puncher. And I believed it was an ominous sign that they were coming down here. Why send a lander near one of the few sets of survivors? It couldn't be for any reasons of kindness, but must be due to their vicious alien psychology. Yeah, okay. I was ready to duke it out, to bite them on the ankle if I could.

After days of wishing for something like this, I was too angry to run away.

As it neared, the lander began to look bigger than a jumbo jet. This thing had to be the size of a football stadium, making it gargantuan. That troubled me. What did they use for fuel?

I understood some of the alien tech, but we were still the aborigines, the Native Americans or the Indians if you're old school. I'd read a lot of history, mostly in prison, to help me pass the time. When the Europeans went exploring throughout the world, it never went well with the aborigines. If the primitives were too few or too far down the scale of technology, they ended up being annihilated or assimilated. As far as Earth went, it appeared to me that we were like Australia in the 1700s when the British showed up with guns and sailing ships, high tech for the time.

That meant picking off the first alien—shooting him in the head—would achieve little. It would be like the Indians killing Christopher Columbus's rowboat landing crew. It still would have left the **Niña**, the *Pinta* and the *Santa Maria* off shore. Could I hurt these aliens in a more grievous manner?

I gazed past the lander, past the purple clouds with their red swirls spinning like whirlwinds, and tried to pierce the intervening mists into orbit. Did that mother of a spaceship still sit up there? If so, that's what I needed to shoot down.

I snarled because I'd forgotten how to laugh. I felt so helpless. I almost picked up the M-14 to empty the magazine against the lander's hull. Why didn't the alien craft launch a missile at us? Were the aliens coming down to hunt the last humans like the Predators had in those old movies? Was I just a big game animal to them?

I decided to wait and find out. I could always fire my rifle later. Yet what good would that do? I might as well have pissed at the alien craft, for all the harm I could do to them. My anger was hard and righteous, but fear kept trickling out of my gut, telling me to run and hide. Sometimes a mouse could survive where a lion died.

Rollo stepped up beside me. I glanced at him. He looked over at me, with his hands pressed against his ears. I recognized the look: it was the same as when Edwards had dragged the girl toward the shed.

What can we do?

The answer was: Not a damn thing. We were ants, fleas. It might have been better if we could have been bacteria or viruses. Wasn't that how H.G. Wells said Earthlings defeated the Martians in *War of the Worlds*?

I watched the lander. What if I could carry a nuclear device inside it like a suicide bomber? That would destroy it. Yeah, it wasn't indestructible. It wasn't a chariot of the gods. The beings inside were mortal. Otherwise, they wouldn't need a spaceship, right?

I opened my mouth to help lessen the pressure against my ears. The flames from the thrusters licked out a hundred feet and melted snow on the ground. The lander—the stadium-sized vehicle—blew ice and frozen dirt. Giant struts lowered into place from the bottom of the craft, with huge sleds or skis on the ends.

The flames of the thrusters weakened. The noise became bearable—a piercing whine—and the monstrous shuttle thudded onto the earth, causing the ground where I stood to tremble against the soles of my boots. At that point, the fire in the rockets disappeared and so did the thunderous sounds.

Tentatively, I lowered my hands, and Rollo lowered his. I bent to scoop up my rifle.

Rollo grabbed my shoulder. "Do you think that's wise?"

Bent over like that, I pondered his question. I could go open-handed to the aliens who had murdered the Earth. I could show them what peaceful, loveable creatures we Earthlings were so they'd spare the last of us. Or, I could carry a gun. I could go armed and fight back if the aliens decided they wanted the last Earthers as zoo specimens. They might kill me as too dangerous, but that would be better than becoming their cosmic play-toy.

I picked up the M-14 and temporized because of the trickles of doubt radiating from my gut. I slung the carrying strap over my shoulder.

"Are you coming?" I asked. The lander was about a half-mile away.

Rollo hesitated.

"Or would you like to huddle in the shelter with them?" I asked, jerking at thumb at Rice. The radio operator stuck her head out of the door, with several others standing in the shadows behind her, watching.

"Do you think it's safe?" Rollo asked.

"No, but who cares?"

He managed a sickly grin, and he patted his side, telling me he was strapping a pistol.

17

Both of us gulped air, and the two of us marched toward the lander. I felt as if I walked to my gallows, a mouse marching to face a grinning hawk.

About halfway there, the thing began unfolding a ramp from its side. They were coming outside. Would they be like the grotesque creatures from the movie *Alien,* or maybe like zergs from Starcraft? Would they be big, little, fast, slow, what?

We reached the lander as the end of the ramp clanged against rocky ground. The entrance up at the top of the ramp opened, but it remained gray, as if covered somehow. The magnitude of the entrance bothered me. Were these things the size of elephants?

Maybe thirty second later, a tracked vehicle pushed through the wall, or membrane of the opening. The substance seemed to cling to the tank, like a soap bubble to a finger pushed through it.

Why bother with such a membrane?

"Do you see that?" Rollo asked me.

"The tank or the membrane?" I asked.

"Membrane," he said, as if tasting the word. "Yeah, that sounds right. They must use it to keep our atmosphere from rushing into their ship."

I raised my eyebrows. Rollo was a bright, geeky guy. Yeah, his idea made sense.

The tracked vehicle was the size of an M-1 tank, and it began to clatter down the ramp. By my reckoning, it weighed seventy or eighty tons, but it was built along different lines from an Abrams. The alien tank was longer and lower to the ground and it had a bubble canopy in the middle. A heavy machine gun-sized turret poked out of the bubble, but I couldn't spy an orifice at the end of the barrel. The U.S. had fired depleted uranium shells from their tanks. Well, the United States was gone, history now. Their tanks *had* used such shells. I didn't think that little turret fired solid projectiles, though. Likely, it projected some kind of beam.

"It squeals just like our tanks," Rollo observed.

He meant the treads. They clanked, squealed and rattled as the vehicle climbed down the ramp. The treads needed oiling,

18

servicing, which made the aliens seem a little less frightening. They had problems just like us. Well, maybe not extinction problems, but you know what I mean. The vehicle reached the snowy ground and turned sharply toward us. The turret lowered until it aimed at our chests.

"I don't like this," Rollo whispered.

I shrugged because I didn't know what to say. The fear in my stomach had grown enough to dampen my former rage. Gripping the rifle strap with one hand, I put the other on my hip and stared at the turret. My feet itched with the desire to run away. My mind told me that was useless. If I ran, the turret could easily track and fry me. No. I'd come this far. Now I'd stick it out in a game of chicken, which I was going to lose in less than thirty seconds.

The thought of my coming death revived the anger. I forced myself to study the alien tank, searching for a hatch to force. If I could, I'd rip out all my fingernails trying to pry open a hatch so I could fire one bullet after another into the alien crew.

All the while, the tank trundled closer, the treads churning over snow and spitting a muddy colored spume from the sides.

"Creed," Rollo said. "We gotta move."

"So move," I said, staring at the tank heading straight for me, hating it the closer it neared.

"What's standing here going to prove?" he asked.

"Not a damn thing," I said, with my gaze riveted onto the tank. I was a mouse daring a hawk, and I was about to become squished human.

Despite my best efforts to observe, I didn't see a hatch, a way into the tank. I revised my plan then, because it seemed insane to let myself get rolled over. Bite, scratch, do something to hurt them. The open entrance up there on the lander gave me an idea.

"When I give the word," I said out of the corner of my mouth, "go left. I'll go right."

"Yeah," Rollo said, in a skeptical tone, "and then what?"

"Then we circle the tank and sprint for the ramp."

"What? Why do that?"

"For the best of reasons," I said. "We rush up the ramp, storm inside the lander and kill everyone onboard. Then we have ourselves an alien space vehicle."

Rollo looked at me. He didn't look scared, but confused. It was enough to cause me to glance at him.

"Are you crazy?" he asked, in a voice telling me it was a genuine question.

Before I could answer, the alien tank squealed to a halt thirty feet from us. At the same moment, the end of the turret glowed with a pink color. Before we could move, a ray beamed in a wide swath, including Rollo and me in its path. I'd played chicken with the aliens and obviously lost. I was sure this is exactly how they'd treated my father.

The beam wasn't hot, but it was bright like the sun and seemed to encompass my mind and thoughts. My first instinct—after finding myself alive and on my feet—was to drop to my belly and slither away, but I hesitated. The pink light continued to flood my eyesight and I found myself blinking rapidly. *What in the...in the...*

It felt as if the beam flipped a dozen switches in my mind and I became dull-witted as my anger drained away. There was a final moment of panic and then the feeling evaporated. This entire episode began to feel like a dream. Alien landers, tanks, beams—I grinned. Maybe the aliens would come out and I'd get to meet them. The idea filled me with something approaching giddy excitement.

The beam stopped and I massaged my forehead, even rubbing my eyes. A strange languor gripped me. I felt torpid and more than a little sleepy.

Something in the alien tank uncompressed in a blast of noise like a trucker's air brakes. It should have frightened me or made me flinch, at least. I felt my lips stretching into a smile. I was going to meet creatures from another planet. This was exciting.

Lines appeared on the glacis of the tank. Steam rose from inside as the front part of the vehicle opened like a jackknife, the slab of armor becoming a mini-ramp from the tank. Behind it was a blank wall, or what appeared to be another membrane. Something oozed out of the membrane until a humanoid in battle armor, or perhaps a spacesuit, stood at the top of the tank ramp.

The being was humanoid in that it possessed two arms and two legs. It also had a long tail. It wasn't a monkey-like tail, but something an upright walking alligator might have.

"Saurian," Rollo said in a lazy voice.

"Huh?" I asked, feeling unreal starting at an alien from a distant star system.

"It's a Saurian," Rollo muttered.

Oh, I saw what he meant. The alien had a bubble-like helmet. The creature was a walking lizard, or looked like one, a giant gecko from those insurance commercials. That widened my smile, and for a second I wondered if this Saurian would speak in a British accent. The Saurian had a different gait than we did, walking in a springier manner, and it was smaller, maybe four and half feet tall.

It stalked down the tank ramp, its lizard-like eyes regarding us. Moisture appeared on the inside of its helmet. The thing opened its mouth and a forked tongue flickered.

How very interesting.

The creature must have pressed a switch somewhere on its suit. Air seemed to blow inside the bubble helmet and the moisture on the inside glass—or whatever the substance was—vanished particle by particle. Perhaps it tasted our air.

Rollo cleared his throat, and I had the impression he planned to say something to the Saurian.

I'm not sure exactly, but...an inner caution perhaps dampened a modicum of my joy. Something seemed...different. I'd watched the lander come down and, and...

"Wait," I told Rollo.

"We should try to communicate with him," Rollo said. "This is the chance of a lifetime."

"Yeah," I said, looking at Rollo. He smiled and his eyes shined with excitement. Did I look like that too? The pink light—

"We should greet him and let him know we're safe," Rollo said.

Greet him, I thought. Hadn't my dad greeted the aliens earlier? My memories were fuzzy. Yeah, I think my dad had gone up in a shuttle and—the memory slammed against me. The aliens had shot a beam of light at my dad, killing him. So why would I grin at this lizard now as if he was a friend?

A pink light; the Saurians had just beamed a pink light into our eyes. Had the light play havoc with our minds?

Wheels turned in my sluggish, dreamlike thoughts. These aliens were screwing with our minds just as they had messed up our world. No. I wasn't going to play along. Whatever the aliens had just fired at us, my inner rage burned through like a bright welding arc.

Rollo must have seen something different on my face. He recoiled from my glare and took a step back.

I turned and glared up at the alien, at this Saurian bastard with his pink, mind-altering ray. Its eyes flickered back and forth between Rollo and me. It raised a hand, paw, talon, whatever the thing possessed. Something radio-like crackled on its suit. Then it moved its lips.

A second later, a synthetic voice issued from a suit speaker. That told me this thing must have a device to take its words and translate them into our language. Sure, its pink beams could alter our moods or thoughts. Clearly, it knew something about human psychology. But the fact that it had to speak meant it could not communicate directly to our minds.

This suit speaker must be hooked up to a translator. Both items proved the aliens had studied Earth in the past. Words boomed forth from it, but whatever it said sounded Russian to me.

"Why don't you try English?" I said.

The Saurian watched me closely, and I had the impression it listened to my words in its alien language. The lizard twisted a dial on its suit.

Its gloved hand or talon consisted of three claws and what would have to pass for an opposable thumb. The individual claw or finger appeared to have one more joint than ours fingers did.

The Saurian spoke again. The outer speaker crackled, and it said in English: "Do you understand me?"

"Yeah," I said. "What do you want?"

"Creed," Rollo warned from behind. "You gotta take it easy. They're peaceful."

A pressure built up in my chest. I yearned to unlimber my rifle and blow away this world-destroyer. It had been a fool to climb out of its tank, trusting in its mind-altering beam. Had they tested it on other humans? Hadn't anyone broken through the beam's quick conditioning before?

"My indicators show you are radiating emotions," the Saurian told me.

"How about that," I said.

"This is good," the Saurian said.

Good? The arrogance tripped a wire in me. I slid the strap from my shoulder and gripped the M-14 two-handed, pointing the barrel at Mr. Lizard.

"Creed, *don't*," Rollo pleaded. "They're here to help us."

"You are an aggressive beast," the Saurian told me. "This is excellent. The Jelk will be pleased."

I scowled. "Who are you calling a beast?"

The Saurian waited before speaking again. "Beast, animal, creature, monster, does the translator not render my meaning into a word you can understand?"

"You think we're monsters?" I asked, outraged.

My stepdad had called me an animal before. He'd been slapping me as he said it. Some of the guards at prison had told me I was nothing more than a caged beast. One guard in particular who liked nudging convicts with the tip of his baton had told me society should throw away the key and leave us animals to rot in here. I hated cages, confinement and being treated like scum. I'd had my fill of it. My chest constricted now and my anger tightened into a coil.

The alien waited, apparently listening to my words and then thinking about them. "Not monsters," it said, "but beasts, animals. Yes, you are an aggressive beast with a rudimentary language. Training will render you useful to the Jelk."

The words struck like slaps to the face. It figured I was a wolf to capture and train—what else could such words mean? No! The aliens wouldn't collar me like a wolf, a wild mustang or a convict. In its arrogance, the alien before me had made a fatal mistake. The tightened coil in my chest snapped and rage washed through me. *He's not going cage me? He almost had me with his pink ray.*

I shouted profanities at him: I decided to think of the Saurian as male. Not only had the aliens destroyed the Earth, but this one insulted the first human it met and threatened me with capture and beast-training.

The Saurian recoiled as if I'd struck him. How did his device translate my curses? His demeanor changed. It was obvious. One of his limbs—arms—dropped toward what looked like a gun attached to his spacesuit.

It was the last straw. I tucked the M-14 stock against my shoulder, aimed and pulled the trigger three times. The first bullet starred the glass of his helmet and knocked him back. The second round made crackling lines so I couldn't see his scaly features as well as before and the second impact also made him stagger more. The last bullet did the trick, smashing his low forehead and splattering blood and bits of bone inside the glass.

"Creed, you're insane!" Rollo shouted.

The alien slid down as if his bones simply dissolved. He crumpled, with his body and suit tumbling down the small ramp and landing on Earth soil.

I was in overdrive, blood-mad at these murderers, but I also kept my wits, my rationality. I had to finish what I'd started and take out the tank crew.

I vaulted over the alien and charged up the ramp. The end of the turret glowed pink once more. Maybe the crew planned to give me another dose of its mind-stealing ray. The membrane looked solid ahead of me, but I'd seen the alien move out of it. The tank had moved through a membrane earlier before it had come down the lander's ramp. I lowered my shoulder and met resistance. Then I powered through the substance. Heat slammed against my face and the air in here tasted foul and was sticky, making my eyes water.

Three Saurians sat at various stations. One of them was up higher in the bubble dome. No doubt he was the gunner. They whipped around on their stools to stare at me. One hissed angrily like a snake. Another flicked its tongue at me.

Each blasting retort of my M-14 was deafening in the confines of the alien tank. The nearest Saurian pitched backward, its chest erupting with blood. Methodically, I shot the bastards, careful to use each bullet where I thought it would do the most damage. I had three magazines with me and a lander-full of these creatures to kill. It took four bullets to take out these three, meaning I still had some ammo left in the original magazine.

As the last shot echoed in my ears, I found myself panting. The stench of their blood clung inside my nostrils. It was a nasty odor. The aliens stank, and they flopped on the floor, acting too much like shot snakes for my peace of mind. Moving as if on autopilot, I shoved a hand into a parka pocket, reassured that I had put two grenades there earlier. These would help in the coming assault.

Hisses from several screens and an alarm rang inside the tank. The screens showed alien creatures, likely those remaining in the lander. There were strange symbols or words written on various bulkheads around me.

While charging within, I'd had some idea of figuring out how to use the alien tank against the lander. As I looked around, I realized that wasn't going to happen fast enough. It would take too long to figure out their controls. Besides, this seemed like a human-netting tank: an alien version of a dog-catching vehicle. They thought of us as beasts or animals. It was better to use what I knew right away—my M-14—than to waste time. The initiative in battle counted for a lot. It might be the only thing I had going for me.

I turned, readied myself and burst through the membrane and back into the Antarctica cold.

Rollo stood at the foot of the tank ramp, with his .45 Browning in his hand. That was a good sign. He looked confused, though.

"What happened in there?" he asked.

"You didn't hear anything?" I asked.

"Soft pops," he said.

"I killed the alien butchers."

"Why did you do that?" he asked.

"They beamed you with a mind-altering ray," I said. "They screwed with your thoughts. They're evil, Rollo. They destroyed our world. Don't you remember watching them kill my dad, Mad Jack Creed?"

"Oh," he said. "You're right."

"We gotta fight back," I said. "We gotta take over their lander." I motioned with my head at the stadium-sized ship.

"That's crazy," Rollo said.

"I know it," I said, "but now's our only chance. Are you with me?"

He stared into my eyes, glanced at the dead Saurian, keeping his gaze there for two seconds and then stared up into my eyes again. He nodded. Rollo was a good man.

I took a breath of pure clean Earth air. It felt cold in my mouth like the best spearmint. I'd overcome their mind ray and killed some of the world slayers. Now it was time to take out more and capture a lander if I could.

I led the way, with the sound of snow crunching under my boots. We had to move fast and keep attacking in order to keep the aliens off balance. They must have figured we Earthers were fainthearted creatures, ready to wilt for the first master race aliens to come along. They were learning differently now.

"Why did the Saurian come outside its tank?" Rollo asked.

"What?" I said. "I don't know, to capture us, I guess. It called us beasts."

"And that was reason enough to kill him?" Rollo asked.

"Hey," I said. "The alien beamed our minds, right, and then he went for his weapon. Besides, I don't need any more reason than this: his kind nuked our world. They declared war on us, not the other way around. After that he wants to talk to us while we're smiling idiots? No, I don't think so."

I stepped onto the larger, lander ramp and saw a space-suited Saurian appear up top. The lizard had a long gizmo in its hands or talons. The device looked like a long-barreled rifle.

Charging up the ramp, I fired from the hip. That didn't make for the most accurate shooting. My first bullet missed and *whanged* off the hull of the lander, creating a spark. The Saurian ducked. Then it seemed to think again, gained resolve and stepped forward, aiming its gizmo down at me as if it was a long Kentucky flintlock.

My second bullet caught a hand. The Saurian opened its mouth and let out a shrill hiss. It dropped the alien rifle. This time it took two bullets to do the trick: cracking the bubble helmet and pumping lead into the face.

I hadn't stopped panting from my fight aboard the tank. Instead of weird alien stenches and atmosphere, now I was tired from sprinting up the long ramp. The Antarctica cold freeze-burned my throat as if I'd swallowed an ice cream cone. I could hear Rollo behind me gasping for air.

The top of the ramp proved flat, and the membrane opening into the lander meant I couldn't see what was on the other side.

"Take his weapon," I said, using the M-14's barrel to point at the alien gizmo.

"I've been thinking," Rollo told me. "We might have made a mistake."

Here on the ramp, we were at least fifty feet high. The top of the lander might be another one hundred and fifty feet above us. The thing was massive.

"These lizards nuked our world!" I shouted. "They sprayed something afterward that makes penguins spit black gunk. Then they tried to capture us. This is our one chance. We have to grab it and do the best we can."

"But capture a whole ship?" Rollo asked.

"Once it's ours, we fly to an Army base and pick up more soldiers. Then we head into space and see if we can capture the big daddy spaceship."

"That's just crazy," Rollo said. "There's no way we can pull that off."

"You got a better idea?" I asked. "Or do you want to be one of their trained beasts?"

He blinked at me several times, apparently trying to process the ideas. Maybe the pink ray still messed with his thinking.

"Take the alien rifle," I said. "Start figuring out how it works. You're the tech guy, the computer geek, so you should be able to do that."

Rollo blinked one more time. Then he holstered the .45, nodded stubbornly—to himself, I think—and picked up the long gizmo.

I dragged my upper teeth across my lip, trying to psyche myself up to charge inside and wreck what mayhem I could. Would the aliens use poison gas on us inside their vessel? Did their atmosphere hold treacherous elements that would render us unconscious in several minutes? I had no clever ideas now,

28

no big plans other than shooting aliens until I ran out of bullets. Then I'd use my Bowie knife and find out how strong these lizards were.

"Here we go," I said.

Expecting the worst, I ran at the membrane and dove. I hit the barrier low and burst into a large, gym-sized chamber. It had three more alien tanks waiting. Crews climbed into them through the front. I didn't have time to see more of the chamber, although five Saurians with long rifles marched toward the outer entrance. They wore spacesuits but without helmets. At the sight of me, they unlimbered their weapons and fired a volley.

Every one of the lizards aimed too high. It was the reason I'd instinctively dived through and come in low. The long rifles shot finger-sized projectiles that sizzled through the air. Each alien bullet or grenade hit the membrane behind me, plowing through, but not before shorting the barrier, destroying it in some fashion.

The howling Antarctica wind swirled into the lander. None of the firing Saurians wore helmets. Some of the tank crews stared in what I'd swear was horror at the lost membrane. Was Earth air bad for them, as Rollo had suggested earlier?

Rollo crawled through the burst opening, swinging his alien rifle wildly.

"Here," I said. I'd crawled to a box of some kind for cover.

Rollo saw me, and he aimed the long gizmo, pressing a button. The alien rifle discharged another of those finger-sized grenades that sizzled as it flew. It struck near an open tank and detonated. Sizzling lines of electricity, or something like electricity, felled the nearest lizards.

A savage sound of laughter tore out of my throat. How I'd wished for a moment like this during the last several days.

I began aiming carefully, shooting aliens. Some scrambled to get away from me and out of this chamber of death. Others rushed into their tanks.

One of the tank ramps began to close into the front glacis. I stood up, took out a hand grenade, yanked the pin—it tinkled against the alien floor—and hurled the explosive like a fastball.

The grenade flew into the vehicle. I heard it explode as the ramp eased into the glacis.

"We're doing it!" I shouted. I scooped up my M-14, tore out the spent magazine and slapped in another. Some of the lizards had sprinted for an opening deeper in the chamber. I headed that way. "Come on, Rollo!" I shouted.

We raced through the gym-sized compartment. None of the canopies on the alien tanks had begun moving yet. No engines revved, nor did turret-guns beam their mind-screwing rays. We'd caught them by surprise.

A fierce elation filled me. It was impossible to conquer the lander, or it should have been impossible. But why not try? Cortes had conquered Aztec Mexico against impossible odds. If nothing else, I could win this lander, figure out the controls and ram the alien starship. We'd make them feel some pain for trying to annihilate humanity.

I found out that a sprinting human was faster than a Saurian in a suit. None of the five who had fired at us made it out of the chamber. The last one twitched and flopped in death near the rear exit, with the back of his lizard head a gory ruin. This one possessed a similar hand-weapon on its belt as the first Saurian I'd shot outside. I pried off the weapon. It was similar to a flare gun. I'd need something once I ran out of bullets, so I unzipped my parka and tucked the alien gun against my belt.

Despite the ruptured outer membrane and storming weather, it stayed hot in here.

"Scan left, I'll look right," I said, meaning once we forced our way through the next membrane.

"Go," Rollo said. He understood my meaning.

We pushed through the membrane and found ourselves in a large corridor going both right and left. There were no Saurians in sight, but a blast of heat and alien stench staggered each of us. The walls weren't smooth steel, but had fuzzy growths on them like alien moss.

"The more I learn about Saurians, the more I hate them," I said.

"What do we do now?" Rollo asked.

That was a good question. We had to keep attacking; that was the answer. "Follow me," I said. I strode right, hurrying along the corridor.

"Some of the aliens made it into the tanks back in the last chamber," Rollo said, running after me.

"I know. We have to find this ship's control room fast."

"You can't be serious. Did you see the size of this ship? Finding the control room could take hours."

"We killed some of them, Rollo. They're going to want vengeance against us, hard vengeance. The only thing left for you and me is to take down as many of these world destroyers as we can. We're walking dead men. The sooner you believe that, the better off you'll be."

He grew quiet, and a change came over his face, a grim seriousness. "You're right. They destroyed twenty cities in atomic fireballs and dusted us with their bio-weapon. I wonder why they beamed us, though, and then sent out a Saurian to talk to us."

The answer came a minute later. Loud alarms or klaxons sounded. It made the hairs stir on my neck. We turned right at an intersection and found another gym-sized chamber. This opening lacked a membrane.

Rows of glass cylinders filled a quarter of the area in back. There were also two bulldozer-sized vehicles. Instead of a blade, each had a backhoe-like crane; and instead of a bucket, the ends possessed a clamp or a lobster-like claw. Each gripped an upright cylinder.

"Creed," Rollo said. "Do you see what's inside those?"

My mind had focused on the vehicles and the room as I searched for Saurians. Now I glanced at the nearest cylinder. My breath caught in my throat, and a sick feeling welled out from my stomach. A naked man stood in the nearest cylinder. He had his palms pressed against the glass and smacked against it several times. I noticed his face. He had his mouth open and it looked as if he was shouting. The thick glass deadened his voice so I couldn't hear what the man was saying.

Seeing this—the Saurians had already been elsewhere on the planet, using their pink rays on others. If I hadn't overcome the peaceful feeling earlier and killed the lizard on the tank

31

ramp, I'd likely be in a glass tube right now. Both Rollo and I would be moths in a jar.

I raised my rifle, aiming at the lower part of the cylinder. I was going to shoot the man out of there.

"Creed!" Rollo shouted in warning. "They're behind us!"

I spun around and saw them: three ugly Saurians in some sort of battle armor. These three didn't wear bubble helmets, but metal things with dark visors. I'd watched enough sci-fi movies to recognize combat suits. These three looked like tiny versions of mech warriors.

The sight of the naked man in the cylinder filled me with loathing. I thought of Nazi experiments and what these aliens were going to do to us now. To them, we were beasts, just big game animals to hunt and mount back at home. I was going to teach them differently.

I sprinted for the nearest backhoe-like vehicle. Rollo, I noticed, had already ducked out sight behind one. He'd been closer to them.

The three Saurians acted more aggressively than the lizards in the first chamber. These three seemed more like soldiers. One of them aimed a heavy pistol, more like a flare gun, and fired a slow-moving projectile. I dove and rolled, trying to get away. The projectile turned out to be an electrical shock grenade, which hit the floor nearby, and I heard a sharp sizzling sound. Something like a pumped Taser struck my left hip, jolting me. Then I rolled behind a Saurian vehicle and out of the grenade's radiating range.

I slithered across the floor. My left leg was numb from the electrical impulse, and it didn't respond as well now.

The three lizard mechs clanked toward me, sounding like something from an Iron Man movie. I strove to get up, to see what was happening. I couldn't let the lizards beat us now. They would surely torture us, or do other unspeakable things to Rollo and me for killing their kind.

Rollo fired, with the sound of his .45 loud in the chamber. His bullet *whanged* off alien armor, leaving a tiny dent.

Their weapons made softer, popping sounds, and more mini-grenades flew. Two of them hit the vehicles on their side and electric-blue sizzling lines clawed over the top of my backhoe-like machine, flickering with color. I stepped back so I wasn't touching the vehicle. The last grenade sailed overhead and landed among tubed men and women. I twisted my neck to see what happened. Like a Medusa of blue-sizzling snakes, the electrical lines writhed wildly from the landed grenade, stroking the nearest tubes, but having no effect on the wide-eyed occupants inside. I noted the shock grenade's limited range. This must be more of their man-catching tech.

I had to do something before the three of them clanked around my vehicle. From on the floor, I grabbed my left thigh and struggled upright onto one leg, leaning against the vehicle. Past the folded crane, I spied a Saurian mech, took deliberate aim and fired three quick shots at the one piece of his equipment that looked vulnerable: the visor. The last bullet did the trick, and the targeted Saurian staggered backward with a shattered visor and hopefully a gory, ruined face. He crashed onto the floor, a good sign.

I ducked away and switched to my final magazine.

"There's one coming around to your right!" Rollo shouted.

I used my last grenade, tossing it up and over the vehicle onto the other side. The crump of the explosion and rattle of shrapnel against alien battle armor told me this was my chance. I wanted to roar like a berserk Viking. Instead, silently psyching myself up as I used to do in Afghanistan, I forced myself around the vehicle. The Saurian still staggered, maybe from the force of the grenade's concussion.

"Hey," I said, to get his attention.

He looked up. It seemed like a reflexive move.

From point-blank range I fired three times. Shards of visor and then drops of alien blood struck me as ricocheting bullets whined. He toppled back like a felled redwood, slamming against the deck plates.

The last mech lifted his weapon, aiming at me from ten feet away. He would have killed me, or shocked me into Taser-like submission, but Rollo intervened. Despite his lanky frame, he could be like greased death at the oddest moments. This was one of those times. From behind the mech, Rollo charged and clambered up the Saurian's back, sticking the barrel of his Browning against the visor. *Blam, blam, blam.*

The creature from the stars ate it, and almost took Rollo down with him. My best friend roared and ripped himself loose from the mech's grip. Then he rolled across the floor as the Saurian soldier clanged to the deck in death and defeat.

We'd won another encounter, but the ship's alarms still rang and I was down to half a magazine of bullets. We had to think of something else or soon we'd be inside those tubes with the others.

-4-

We couldn't have much time left before the next enemy wave struck. It was move now or forever be an alien's slave. Running away didn't seem like an option. They'd just hunt us down in the snowy wasteland of Antarctica. We had to go for the throat, for mastery of the lander.

We needed more people, and we'd discovered a roomful of them—if we could open the glass tubes. I checked the dead mechs for a useful smashing tool. I couldn't find one at first, but I did find something that looked interesting. I pulled off a half-moon curved blade from one of the dead aliens. Maybe it was the Saurian version of a bayonet.

"Come on," I told Rollo. "Give me a hand."

The nearest man inside a standing tube had a crew cut, a sweeping black mustache and wide Slavic features. He was muscular, sported a Z tattoo on his right shoulder and looked tough. Given that the Saurian had first tried to speak to us in Russian, I gave it high odds that the man in there was from that area of the world.

He banged on his tube from the inside, yelling silently.

I held up the curved knife and chipped at the cylinder. The blade scratched the glassy surface, but that was it.

"Wait a minute," Rollo said. "I have a faster way."

Like a kid, he climbed up and jumped into what must have been the driver's seat of the backhoe-like vehicle. As I'd said, the vehicle had a small crane with a clamp or claw holding the man-sized cylinder. The other cylinders stood upright in floor slots as if they were high school test tubes for a science class.

35

Rollo began experimenting, pressing buttons and pulling levers.

The ship's alarm stopped then, which seemed ominous, making it much too quiet. What were the aliens going to do next? Were they worried, calling for backup or getting ready to storm in here with more mechs?

As I wondered, growing more nervous, the backhoe-like vehicle purred into life.

"Stand back," Rollo told me.

I stepped away from the upright cylinder. The man inside the tube twisted around, looking in alarm at Rollo.

The crane proved more flexible than a backhoe. It was like one of the tentacles from *War of the Worlds*. Showing his aptitude for such things, Rollo soon laid the cylinder on the floor lengthways.

"Good thinking," I said.

Rollo didn't even nod in acknowledgement. He was too busy concentrating. I suspect he knew the odds and our desperation.

The single big claw gripping the tube began squeezing. Then Rollo took his hands off the vehicle's controls.

"What's wrong?" I asked.

"I want to shatter the tube," Rollo said. "But what if I end up cutting the man inside?"

"Just get him out," I said. "We can worry about wounds later."

Rollo took a moment and then went back to the controls. Soon, the claw made grinding noises and suddenly, the glass shattered, with shards falling onto the floor.

"Stop!" I shouted.

The claw stopped. I rushed forward and used the curved blade to pry away chunks of glass.

"Are you okay?" I asked the trapped man inside.

He blinked at me.

"Can you hear me?" I asked. I wondered on his mental state.

"You are American," he said with a Russian accent.

"Yup," I said. "Are you Russian?"

"No, I am Dmitri Rostov, from Zaporizhia."

"Where?" I asked.

"Zaporizhia," he said. "It is in the Ukraine."

"You're Ukrainian?"

"No!" he said, vehemently. "I am a Zaporizhian Cossack."

I'd heard of Cossacks: hard-riding, freedom-loving people from the steppes or plains of Russia and the Ukraine. They were supposed to be good fighters. Most people knew them as those acrobatic dancers who squatted low, folded their arms on their chests and vigorously kicked out their legs.

"You were part of the old Soviet Union, right?" I asked.

"Not anymore," he said. "Now hurry! Get me out of here."

"We're working on it." I pried out a big glass chunk, nicking a finger so blood oozed, and finally I cleared a way for him. "You'll have to slither out," I said.

I gave him a hand and soon a stark naked, Dmitri Rostov the Zaporizhian Cossack stood beside me. He was a solid, muscular man, shorter than my six-three, and he looked angry and ready to do something about it.

"Did they use a pink ray on you?" I asked.

"On all of us," he said. "Now, we must hurry and flee the ship."

"We're not fleeing," I said. "We're going to hijack this thing and attack the big mother of a starship upstairs."

Dmitri's eyes gleamed as a wild smile creased his face.

"Yes!" he shouted. "We attack. We kill the lizards. I agree."

"Saurians," Rollo said from the driver's seat. He used the flexible crane and claw to pluck another cylinder from the floor rack. He was in the process of laying the tube lengthways. "We're calling the aliens Saurians," Rollo said.

Dmitri nodded. "It is good to name the enemy. Saurians. Yes, I approve. Now we must free the rest of the men and women before the aliens bring reinforcements."

"Are the others here Russians, Ukrainians or Cossacks?" I asked.

"I am the only Cossack here," Dmitri said. "We are from the Russian base at Vostok near the South Pole. Many of these people are former Army soldiers. They are not Cossacks, but they should fight once I tell them your plan." He stroked his outrageous mustache. "What is your plan?"

"Do you see those dead Saurians on the floor?" I asked.

"Yes, I see," he said. "You are a clever fighter. I applaud you."

"That's what I'm going to do to the rest of the Saurians aboard the lander," I said. "Afterward, that's what I'm going to do the rest on the starship that started this."

"That is a good plan," Dmitri said, "an excellent plan. You also have more guns, yes?"

Rollo cracked the next tube. As I began prying out shattered chunks of glass, I said, "Nope, I'm almost out of ammo. We need more weapons; maybe these alien long-rifles and flare pistols will do."

"Anything in a storm," Dmitri said. His eyes gleamed then, and he grinned viciously. I wondered what the pink ray had done to his mind. "Do you know the aliens have star-armor?" he said.

As we talked, we helped out the next man. I didn't answer Dmitri's question because I was too busy talking to the new man. Unfortunately, he didn't speak any English. So Dmitri rattled off some quick instructions to him in Russian.

With the claw, Rollo reached for the next tube.

I pointed at the dead mechs. "You mean that kind of armor? That's star-armor?"

"That is steel," Dmitri said, "mechanized body armor similar to what Russian and American soldiers use, or will use in fifteen years."

"There's no Russia or America left," I said.

Dmitri stared at me, and he grimaced. I don't know what he was thinking. Had he been married? Had he lost children, a wife, surely his parents, aunts, uncles or cousins? He looked up at the ceiling and muscled cords stood up on his neck. A choked, grieving noise came from him once. He shook his head then, swallowed, and he stared at me with shining eyes.

"We need guns," he said in a hoarse voice.

"Yeah, we need guns," I agreed. "But we don't dare leave the ship to get more. The Saurians would seal all the hatches then and we'd never get back on board. No. This is our one chance to hurt the enemy and we have to make the most of it."

Dmitri breathed deeply, and he said, "They tested us before."

"Tell your friend to stand lookout in the corridor," I said. "We don't want the lizards to surprise us."

"Yes..." Dmitri said. "That is wise. You think like a general." He grabbed his Russian friend by the triceps and spoke rapidly.

The naked Russian picked up an alien long-rifle and hurried to the entrance. The man had a bloody gash on his back. Getting out of the tubes proved troublesome, but the Russian hadn't complained. As I've said earlier, the tough and mean humans had survived the alien onslaught. These men and women in the tubes hadn't been idle; they must have kept their eyes open. From careful observation, they appeared to know how to use the alien weaponry. Whatever the pink ray did to a human mind wasn't lasting, at least.

Dmitri and I pried out glass from yet another tube. Rollo worked faster now, having gotten the hang of the crane and claw.

"They tested us earlier," Dmitri told me.

"I heard you the first time," I said. "The aliens have no soul. They're thorough bastards."

"I believe the—what did you call them?" Dmitri asked. "You had a name for aliens."

"Saurians!" Rollo shouted from the vehicle. "We're calling them Saurians."

"That is a good name," Dmitri said. "It makes them sound evil, and they are, my friend. The Saurians want humans for a reason. Like the old Russians did with the Cossacks, the aliens wish humans to soldiers for them."

I only half heard Dmitri. His accent made it hard sometimes to know what he was saying. The fighting, the bad air in here, fatigue, maybe some of the aftereffects of the pink ray all combined to dull my thoughts. Realizing that worried me. Were we thinking straight? I couldn't afford any mistakes.

What had Dmitri just said? Something about the Saurians making us soldiers.

"No," I said. "Not soldiers. The Saurians think we're beasts." *No one is making me a convict again.*

"Beasts, animals—yes!" Dmitri shouted. "The aliens tested some of us in a horrible manner. Several people died because of them. Two test subjects—I know the reason for the buzzing weapons."

The Cossack's excitable. I frowned, trying to follow his words. "Buzzing weapons… Oh, yeah. The alien projectiles act like Taser grenades."

"Listen, my American friend," Dmitri said. "I spoke to Ella Timoshenko about the tests. We spoke before the Saurians sealed us in the tubes. Ella is scientist. She is very smart and observant."

"Do you have a point?" I asked.

"Yes," Dmitri said. "I must show you. You are the general. You will know what we need to do about the star-armor."

"Show me what?" I asked.

Then I saw something out of the corner of my eye. I turned and spied a naked woman. She was thin with perfectly shaped breasts. She blinked in the manner of someone missing her glasses and had short brunette hair. Her eyes were sharp, and intelligence shone there. She noticed my scrutiny. She folded her arms before her breasts, glared at me and spoke harshly in Russian.

Dmitri protectively stepped in front of her, blocking my sight, and he spoke urgently to her. I suppose that was Ella Timoshenko. For a scientist, heck, for any woman, she had lovely tits and nice legs.

I noticed Ella shaking her head as she spoke to Dmitri.

The Cossack turned to me. "Ella says we have no chance against the aliens. She says we should run away."

"Do you want run, Dmitri? Do you want to let the aliens win?"

"I am a Cossack. We have always fought and we will always fight. I am with you, my general. But Ella, she is smart. I'm afraid we will lose in the end."

"Everyone dies," I said. "So everyone loses in the end."

"That is not what the priests say," Dmitri said, "about losing in the end. But you are right in saying we all die."

"It's living free that counts," I said, "standing your ground when the alien tries to cage you."

"You must see the star-armor, my general. I'm sure it will help us."

I could get used to Dmitri.

"Rollo," I said, "Have one of those Russians work the crane. We have to keep attacking. We can't wait around for the aliens to make their next move against us. We have to keep surprising them until we win."

Rollo didn't bother talking to the freed Russians. He jumped off the machine and grabbed one of the few alien weapons left. He must have noticed that the Russians were quick to arm themselves.

Instead of one of the men, Ella Timoshenko climbed into the crane's control chair. She was nimble for a scientist, and those breasts…

I looked away. As more Russians crawled out of the cracked tubes, they began working in shifts with the other backhoe-like vehicle. Its engine sounded like a buzz saw and thumped from time to time. I wasn't sure how long it would run. I'd say we had forty people all together, with seven free of the tubes so far.

"We're going to keep attacking," I told Dmitri.

"But—"

"We have to keep them off balance," I said.

"No!" Dmitri said. "Listen to me. You are a great fighter. You have killed aliens and I don't know of anyone else who has done such a thing. I am forever in your debt. But you must see the star-armor."

"Yeah, you talked about that, but I'm thinking—"

"General, listen to me, please. Ella called it symbiotic armor, a living tissue mutated or grown for humans."

"What?" I asked.

"Yes," Dmitri said, "now you're listening. You must come with me. I show you this thing. It makes more sense once you see it."

***

I believe the Saurians made a critical mistake. By their translated words earlier, the lizards figured we humans were beasts, animals or monsters. Wrong. We were thinking people using every faculty to figure out what was going on. That included the trapped Ukrainians, Russians and Cossack. Many of them were scientists—trained observers. Others had been former Russian soldiers. According to Dmitri, the Saurians had been conducting tests on them for two days already. One of those tests had included symbiotic armor, a kind of second skin for combat use.

Why had the Saurians been testing the people? Dmitri said Ella had a theory, but the savant Ella Timoshenko had remained in the tube chamber to free the rest of the Russians. I'm not sure she liked me.

Rollo, Dmitri and I hurried down a corridor. Rollo had his .45 and an alien long-rifle, Dmitri carried the grenade-pistol I'd picked up earlier and I had my M-14. Dmitri lacked clothes or shoes of any kind, but it didn't seem to bother him. The heat caused him to sweat so he left wet footprints on the floor. The muggy air made our clothes soggy and I kept shaking my head to fling sweat out of my eyes. The alien stench in the ship atmosphere had begun making me dizzy. I longed for good old fresh Earth air.

"We're going to need water soon," I said, "to keep us hydrated."

"There's plenty of snow outside," Rollo told me.

"Getting cold feet?" I asked.

"Most definitely," he said. "This lander freaks me out and these corridors with their fuzzy walls—they're aliens all right. It makes my gut clench every time I think about it. Why did the Saurians ever come here?"

"This way," Dmitri said, pointing into a narrower corridor.

"Are you sure?" I asked. The corridor looked darker, like an alien cave I didn't want to go down.

Dmitri grimaced. "For the past two days I have watched everything they do, cataloging each horror committed on us. I am sure."

I didn't like it, but I motioned for Dmitri to keep going. He soon led us before another membrane.

"I'm a little tired of going through those," Rollo said.

So was I, but I clutched my rifle and charged through. In my opinion, we'd run out of time. We'd been taking too long. I plopped through into an oven of a chamber that hit my face like a hellish brick.

The room was one third the size of the tube chamber. The back wall glowed orange with heat. I spied four raised pads near the wall with a blob of a shiny black substance on each of them. To my horror, the blobs oozed back and forth, the surface making rippling movements. Two long tables stood on the left side of the room. On each table lay a dissected human, with his or her chest cavity and stomach laid open. The corpse faces showed rigid horror and pain.

"What is this place?" I asked.

Rollo swore quietly in outrage.

I glanced at my friend and then looked to the right where he stared. Three tall tubes filled with a green solution stood from floor to ceiling. Each of the cylinders contained a dead woman, with a hundred tiny wires connected to her. I vowed to save the last bullet and use it on myself. I wouldn't let myself be taken by these aliens, and have things like that done to me.

"Yesterday," Dmitri said in a low voice, "Ella and I were in here. I knew those people." Dmitri shook his head and spoke in an even lower whisper. "The Saurians are vile beings from the stars. They conducted experiments. Ella and I…" Dmitri stared at me with smoldering eyes. "We wore the symbiotic armor. It was strange. Ella understood, though. In the past, she has often made intuitive leaps of understanding. I think she is psychic, or maybe even telepathic."

"What?" I said.

"Ella knew," Dmitri said. "She told me the Saurian plan. If you knew the reason why we were in Antarctica…"

"Go on," I said. "Because why?"

"It does not matter now," Dmitri said. "Those are your answer," he said, pointing at the rippling black blobs on the pads. "We put those on and attack the aliens. Those will give us our chance."

"What in the hell is he talking about?" Rollo asked me.

That was a good question. Dmitri had to be among the whitest persons I'd ever seen. Canadians and Russians, no one could be as white as them. Now, however, Dmitri went even whiter, swayed and might have toppled. I caught his right arm, steadying him. He swallowed several times.

"I don't want to do this," he whispered. "But Cossacks fight to the end. We always fight."

"Are you okay?" I asked. "You know you're not making much sense, right?"

Dmitri pulled free of me. Like a stoned zombie, he moved to the hot wall with the four blobs.

Rollo sidled up to me, whispering, "I think the Saurians scrambled his brains."

I was tempted to agree, but the last few days had shifted my thinking about a lot of things. Maybe it helped that I'd read so much science fiction as a kid and watched every SF movie I could. I was used to strange concepts and weird ideas. Rhode Island-sized spaceships, death spores, Saurians and the greatest nations on Earth demolished in the space of a half hour…why couldn't Ella have psychic flashes of understanding? The Saurians had used a pink ray on our minds. Why couldn't our side have an advantage or two?

"Creed, do you see that?" Rollo asked, with loathing in his voice.

Dmitri Rostov reached one of the black blobs. Using both hands, he grabbed the jelly-like substance and heaved the thing off its pad, dumping the mass onto the floor where it quivered. Then he did the craziest thing: he stepped onto it with both feet.

His feet disappeared into the blob so he sank up to his ankles. He had a blood-oozing scratch on the inner left ankle on the ball joint. Then the slimy blob oozed up onto his legs, coating his flesh with the gooey black substance.

"Dmitri!" I shouted.

"Be calm, my friends," he said, with his palms held outward toward me. "I have done this before. This is the symbiotic armor, the living second skin. Ella believes these creatures were genetically engineered for human use."

"That thing is alive?" Rollo asked.

"Oh yes" Dmitri said. "It is warm, and it feeds off our sweat."

44

More of the blob oozed up Dmitri's legs. The stuff reached his knees and continued to climb like slime toward his waist.

"Is that what killed those people on the tables?" Rollo asked, indicting the dissected corpses.

"I do not know," Dmitri said, "possibly."

I swallowed hard. What I saw sickened me, but our backs were against the proverbial wall. Maybe we were Earth's last chance. Who else had fought their way onto an alien lander? I was almost out of bullets and the aliens must be radioing for backup. I'd watched these beings murder my father. They'd nuked humanity practically out of existence. Now, Dmitri said this was living armor. One of my player characters had worn living armor before in a roleplaying game. I understood the concept of living armor. It was much different seeing it, though, a lot different.

How much could I trust Ella Timoshenko? But no, maybe that was the wrong way to look at this. The better question was how much chance of victory did I have? In truth, I—we—had no chance at all against the aliens. If this stuff was living armor and if it gave me some kind of advantage—but I don't know what it would give a person.

"What do you mean, this is armor?" I asked. "What does it do for you?"

"It amplifies your strength," Dmitri said. "It also gives you energy and it can harden its outer surface to deflect or stop certain kinds of attacks."

"Come on, guys, let's get out of here," Rollo pleaded.

The black substance flowed up Dmitri's waist, past his belly button and reached his shoulders when the first Saurian stepped through the membrane.

I must have figured in the back of my mind that the Russians would race here and give us warning if the Saurians launched the next assault. What I failed to grasp was that the lizards didn't need to go past the Russians first. I should have realized there were many different ways to move about the ship.

As foolish as it sounds on our part, the Saurians caught us by surprise. One after another, lizards rushed into the room. Many gripped a half-moon curved blade similar to that I'd taken off a mech-lizard earlier. A wet green substance glistened along the edges of their blades. The first Saurian cut Rollo across the shoulder. My friend shouted in pain and surprise and threw himself away from the Saurian. As Rollo moved, his feet tangled and he tripped.

I spun around and shot the nearest lizard in the face, the one going for me. I kept firing from the hip, taking down more. I backpedaled, shot another alien and saw a Saurian crouch beside Rollo. My friend had stiffened strangely. The lizard held one of those curved knives, and it looked as if the Saurian planned to cut Rollo's throat. I aimed, pulled the trigger and my rifle clicked empty. I was out of bullets.

Croaking a desperate noise, Rollo finally managed to move, kicking feebly but not nearly hard enough. The half-moon curved blade came down, and it might have cut Rollo's throat and ended existence for my friend. Before that happened, a black-coated humanoid joined the fray. The thing punched the Saurian in the head. The creature catapulted off its three-toed talons and smashed against another of its kind. The two tumbled into a heap.

I realized the black humanoid was Dmitri. The blob of symbiotic armor covered him from toes to just under his chin, leaving his head free. A fierce joyfulness twisted Dmitri's features into something unholy. Clearly, he liked wearing the armor and he liked fighting.

With amplified strength and heightened speed, Dmitri moved among the remaining Saurians. They cut at him but could not penetrate the armor. They fired their weapons and they died. I saw it. I can testify to the truth of what occurred. Several lizards slammed against bulkheads and crumpled to the floor. Others simply toppled down and flopped like snakes, with Dmitri's blows hitting them like jackhammers.

Then it was over. This wave of seven or eight Saurians failed just as their previous efforts had. How many lizards were aboard the lander anyway?

Watching Dmitri in this horror show, I was beginning to believe we could actually win. Earlier, I'd figured, what better way to end life than to go down swinging? Now...now I began to think we might really hijack the ship.

"Do you finally believe me?" Dmitri asked.

I would have answered, but I saw Rollo. The curved blade had sliced into his shoulder. There was a little blood, but not enough to cause what I was seeing. Rollo seemed to have frozen into immobility. The foul Saurians must have envenomed their blades with a paralyzing drug. They didn't fight fair, that's for sure.

I feared for my friend. I had to do something for him fast.

-5-

Dmitri had the answer for Rollo, but I didn't like it. I saw the loathing in Rollo's eyes and knew he positively hated the suggestion. But I had to do something for him.

Before I subjected my friend to this alien horror, I figured I should try it first.

"Tell me one thing," I told Dmitri. "Are you still sane?"

The Zaporizhian Cossack paused before answering the question.

"You are human, right?" I asked.

Dmitri grinned wryly. "I hesitate to answer because the living armor must lace chemicals into me through my skin. When I fought just now, I felt good. Yes, I am sane, but I believe it makes me want to fight when I wear the armor. Ella said yesterday that the symbiotic creature seemed bio-sculpted for us."

"What did she mean by that?" I asked.

"How do you Americans say it?" Dmitri mused. "Bio-engineered, yes, the creature was bio-engineered for our use."

"So you think the Saurians have been studying humanity for some time?" I asked.

"It seems self-evident, yes, my general."

"I'm not a general," I said. "I'm just an American grunt who used to work for Black Sand."

Dmitri looked crestfallen.

"But I'll keep fighting," I said. "I'll lead us to the end."

He nodded, grinning at me.

I took a deep breath, with the hot alien air burning down my throat. It reminded me of the worst smoggy day in LA when I'd played basketball in high school. I'd felt like I'd been drowning after a while, each breath painful in my throat.

While wearing the symbiotic armor, Dmitri had just fought like Superman or the Hulk. I'd like to do that, but did I trust a blob of living armor, a creature that would flow onto me like a second skin? What if it covered my face? That would obviously suffocate me. According to Ella the Mystic Russian Scientist with the nice breasts, the Saurians had bio-engineered the armor for humans.

"The aliens are too strong," Dmitri said. "You have no choice, my..."

I glanced at him. I had lots of choices—as long as I didn't mind losing. With a roar of frustration, I tore off my parka, shirt and unlaced my boots. In seconds, I stood naked in the chamber. This was crazy. I felt like a lunatic. What drove me in the end was the fact that humanity had nearly been exterminated. To come back from the edge of extinction, someone had to do something. The dissected corpses on the table and the dead floating in the tubes meant I had to grab this chance. In my humble opinion, we were dead otherwise.

Naked, with my heart pounding, I approached a quaking, quivering blob on a raised pad. The living armor hadn't come from Earth, but from some lab in the stars. The Saurians sure hadn't worn this stuff to help them tackle us. That should have warned me, right?

With serious distrust riding on my shoulders, I grabbed the substance. It was warm like a fresh pancake, and it pulsed as if it had a heart rate. I heaved, lifted it off the pad and plopped it onto the floor. Then I stepped onto the squishy blob.

Now it was my turn to watch it slither and ooze onto my skin. The stuff was warm, and watching it creep up my legs nearly freaked me out. I wanted to howl and leap away, scraping this gunk off with my knife.

I felt something then: the armor's displeasure. The advance halted.

"You must accept it," Dmitri said. "I believe it senses negative emotions."

49

That was just great. This stuff was like a dog that knew when you were afraid. I tried to take a calming breath. It didn't work because of the smogginess and the stench of the alien atmosphere. Sweat pooled on my skin and a bout of claustrophobia threatened to steal my logical processes. I was seconds away from howling.

I glanced at Rollo sprawled on the deck plates. If this didn't work, I don't know what we were going to do. I couldn't lug him out of the lander. This latest Saurian assault showed the lizards hadn't given up. If nothing else, they could simply take off and return to the mothership. That would end our chances. We had to do something now or it wouldn't matter.

You gotta relax, Creed, I told myself.

Yeah, relax as I was engulfed by living alien technology. I focused on my old man. Mad Jack could have done this. He would try anything experimental. If I wanted to raise a tombstone to my dad, I had to beat the Saurians. I had to accept this slime.

"Hey," I told the blob. "I love you. This is the best thing that ever happened to me. You gotta turn me into the Hulk and we'll stomp the shit out of these Saurians, okay?"

It must have agreed, because the dark substance started oozing again, climbing my skin and enfolding me in warmth. This sensation wasn't like the alien heat. As the second skin relaxed against my epidermis, I felt a good warmth. I felt comfortable. That decreased my tension, my anxiety and that speeded the process.

"How does it know not to cover my mouth?" I asked Dmitri.

He shrugged.

Oh yeah, that helped—not. I grinned at Rollo because I noticed he was watching me. His skin had a touch of green and he squirmed slowly as if in pain.

"Creed," he said. He lips had stiffened.

"Put the stuff on him," I told Dmitri.

"No," Rollo said. "Please, no…"

"The Saurians put poison on their blades," I told Rollo. "Dmitri said the living armor can help draw it out of you. Why not try it and see what happens?"

Rollo began to breathe raggedly. "We…never should…have come aboard."

"I know it," I said. The living armor spread across my chest. I no longer noticed the crappy air in here. Even better, I felt as if I floated. I felt healthy: I mean one hundred percent well inside. This armor…maybe there was something to it.

Dmitri tore off Rollo's clothes.

Rollo tried to work his mouth, but it had stiffened too much for him to speak. He groaned, and his fingers twitched. He didn't want the stuff.

First mumbling a Cossack prayer in Russian and then winking a Rollo, Dmitri set a blob on my friend's bare legs.

My second skin reached my throat and touched the soft flesh underneath my chin. I grew tense, and the living armor halted its advance.

I squatted low and lifted a foot. The outer surface of the armor on the bottom of my foot had become like hard rubber. I tapped the surface armor on my arm. It was like dense rubber.

I went to my pile of discarded clothes and drew my combat blade. It was a big Bowie-style knife, almost a small short sword. This sucker was razor sharp and the handle fit into my living armored hand like it was custom-made for me. I'd had a thing for knives for a long time. My stepdad had especially hated me throwing knives against our barn door. That had been during seventh grade in junior high school. I'd bought three throwing knives at a surplus store and had thudded them against the barn door for hours. I'd left two hundred marks or holes in it. My stepdad had walloped me good for that. Later, I'd made a target out of plywood. I could hit the centerpiece from thirty paces away nine times out of ten. Not that I had any intention of throwing the Bowie. It was a fighting blade for hand-to-hand combat.

What did I know about that? In prison, there had been a thin little book written by a con from San Quentin. I'd read it fifty times and spoken to others. It had concerned prison knife-fighting. There had been little fancy about it. One kept the blade close and used it with a fast thrust: in and out, baby. Sometimes, a fighter didn't let you get close. The trick then was to cut him, let him bleed and weaken.

51

The point to all this was I knew something about knife-fighting, a mean and ugly style meant for quick results. There wasn't anything gentlemanly about knife fighting: it was a combat technique meant to eliminate your enemy without causing any hurt to yourself.

"How are you feeling?" I asked Rollo.

The living armor spread over him like a disease. It had flowed over the envenomed cut.

Rollo's eyelids fluttered, and he began to stir.

I flexed my biceps. "Is there a trick to smashing the lizards like you did earlier?" I asked Dmitri.

"Act as you would normally," he said. "The living armor will supply you with extra power."

"We have the armor," I said, "but I'm out of bullets and I don't really trust our alien grenades. We need to kill them, not just knock the lizards out of the battle."

"What are we going to do about the Saurians in the tanks?" Rollo asked. He sat up. The paralysis had gone, although his right eyelid drooped, half-hiding that eye. Dmitri had been right about the armor.

"How do you feel?" I asked.

"Woozy," Rollo said, "and thirsty."

"Can you walk?"

"Give me a second," Rollo said.

I kept my gaze away from the corpses on the tables and the dead women floating in the cylinders. That was the price for losing.

"Do you know the layout of the ship?" I asked Dmitri.

"Ella said something about the lower levels being used for storage and the higher decks being the ship functioning areas."

"If Ella's right," I said, "and we'll have to bet she is—that would mean the control room is at the very top."

"That is good thinking," Dmitri said.

Rollo grunted as he heaved up onto his feet. He glanced at my Bowie knife and raised an eyebrow.

"Remember how I told you I've been to prison?" I said.

"I remember. I'll stick to this," Rollo said, hefting his Browning .45 in one hand and an alien grenade-launching pistol in the other.

"How much ammo do you have left?" I asked.

"Two more magazines," Rollo said.

"Dmitri, you ready?" I asked.

"I have been ready ever since you broke me out of the test tube," the stocky Cossack said.

"Let's do it then," I said. "Let's hunt down the aliens and kill every Nazi-experimenting one of them."

-6-

The three of us moved through the alien lander as if it was the end of the movie time. You know, how during the beginning of an action movie, the hero usually does something supercool? Then he gets caught or the villain beats the crap out of him in a nasty way and steals his girlfriend. After a long time of getting ready and building up for the grand fight, the hero and his team smashes into the bad guy's fortress and proceeds to blow everyone down until the final confrontation and movie twist.

Dmitri, Rollo and I now smashed through the lander, sweeping down the corridors and entering small rooms, chambers and fuzzy-walled corridors of varying sizes and complexity. We found more tube chambers. Some of the upright cylinders held people. Others proved to be empty. Everywhere, we killed Saurians.

Rollo ran out of bullets, but he found the shock grenade gun to his liking. He stayed in the back, firing into groups of Saurians, knocking down some and slowing down others with the electrical discharges. Dmitri wielded a long bar of iron, and he continued to parody the Hulk. Once, he smashed a lizard's head clean off the body. Blood jetted from its neck, while the Saurian jerked like a slaughtered chicken and ran against a wall before flopping around on the floor. I used the Bowie knife, and my living armor no longer looked black but was slick with green-dripping Saurian blood.

The suits pumped us with something, maybe a fast-acting drug to put us into a steroid rage. I felt elation at the slaughter and I felt powerful approaching invincible. The only trouble was a dry mouth. I really needed water. At times, my vision turned splotchy.

"How much farther do you think it's to the top of this thing?" Rollo asked.

We strode along a wide corridor that went upward like a ramp to a pair of double doors. They were the first normal doors we'd seen. Everything else had been protected by a membrane.

The doors ahead of us swished open and the biggest Saurian I'd seen so far limped out. Behind him in the room, I saw small windows showing an Antarctic storm outside. That was a relief. It let me know the lander was still on Earth. I'd wondered if I'd feel it if the ship took off into space.

In the room I spied stools, lizards in crinkling-looking suits near what seemed like controls. If I were to guess, we'd reached our destination: the lander's control chamber.

As the doors swished shut behind him, the big Saurian strode toward us on his springy legs, with his long tail dragging and making clinking noises against the floor. This lizard seemed hoary with age, with a billy-goat's beard under his scaly jaws and standing as tall as a man, a six-footer. The old one's scales looked dimmer than the others and a crust of something encircled his eyes.

He also wore more of the crinkly material and what seemed to be symbols showing his rank, and golden rings around his tail. They were what made the noise as he approached.

I knew a little about lizards and reptiles. As a kid I'd read up everything I could concerning dinosaurs. For one thing, they kept growing as long as they lived. The biggest crocodile was always the oldest one. I was beginning to believe the same held true for the Saurians.

Did this old one run the lander? Why had he come alone? Was he surrendering?

Rollo raised his alien pistol at the lizard.

"Wait," I said.

"He's trying to stall us," Rollo said. "This is a trick."

The old one wore a device on his chest, which hung from a band around his neck. He touched the device, lifted a microphone, or what looked like a microphone, and spoke into it.

"You must cease this senseless attack." The words boomed in English from the translator on his chest.

He had gall, I'll give him that. "Are you surrendering?" I asked.

I had a good reason for not wanting Rollo to fire. I knew the membranes couldn't stop us, but locked metal doors might. The doors behind the old one seemed solid. If I could, I'd try to talk my way into the control room.

"Your words lack meaning," the old one told me concerning surrender. "You are prey, beasts, animals."

"We're people," I said, feeling a prickliness in my chest. I was more than sick of their arrogance, but I had to contain that for a greater goal. "Answer my question. Are you surrendering? If you are, I give you my word of honor we'll let you live."

"Go back to the chambers," the old one said. "Remove the battlesuits and the Family will deliver you to the Jelk."

"What Family?" I asked. "What are you talking about?"

"He's trying to mess with your mind," Rollo said. "Kill him and smash into the control room."

"Do you hear my friend?" I asked. "He wants to kill you. Why shouldn't I gut you right here? You need to give me a reason to keep you alive."

"For you to kill me goes against the natural order of reality," the old one said. "You are fighting beasts that have run amok. The Family's duty is to destroy you lest you contaminate the others. However, in this instance, I will bring you to the Jelk. You must leave this area, return to the chambers and remove the battlesuits."

"Did you feel that?" Rollo asked me.

I knew what he meant. The deck plates under my feet vibrated more than before, as if I stood on a hard-revving bulldozer. A loud whine penetrated through the bulkheads. If I were to guess, I'd say the Saurians had started the engines and were getting ready to leave Antarctica.

"I'm giving you a last chance," I told the old one. "Surrender the vessel to my control and you can live."

56

"This is obscene," the old one said. "You have aborted the sequence of reality. The Jelk will be displeased."

"I'm displeased," I said.

"No. You are beasts. You are—"

I could see where this was going: nowhere. And I was tired of being called a beast. I'd given him his chance. Now I was going to act. In three swift strides I reached the old Saurian. The engines roared and the deck plates shivered with power. I used the Bowie knife and thrust the steel through his squat neck. Then I threw the dead old one from me and lunged at the doors. They didn't open.

The entire corridor swayed and thunderous noises swept through us. The floor slid out from under me and I realized the lander must be lifting off the rocky soil of Antarctica.

"We have to get in there!" Rollo shouted. "None of this matters if we can't break into the control room."

Despite the roar and the vibration, I climbed up and put my green-dripping hands against the doors and heaved sideways. The doors groaned in a tortured way, but they held their place.

"Give me a hand!" I shouted. "We have to get in there."

The other two rushed forward, and each of us strained against the doors, trying to slide them open.

The corridor tilted even more, and the old one's corpse slid away from the double doors. This vehicle must be headed into space.

"They locked the doors," Rollo said.

I thrust my Bowie knife underhanded at the crack between the doors. The blade went in several inches. I shoved with everything I had. Inch by inch, the steel blade slid deeper between the doors.

"What's your plan?" Rollo shouted.

I yanked on the blade, trying to force the doors open. "Push," I shouted, "one of you per door."

The three of us exerted all the considerable strength of our living armor-enhanced muscles. I yanked on the Bowie knife, using it as a lever. I expected it to snap at any moment. Instead, we slid open the doors several inches so I could peer into the control room.

Saurians turned toward us in surprise.

57

"Give me your pistol," I wheezed.

While keeping one hand pressed against the door, Rollo shoved me his gun.

Through the small crack, I fired two shock grenades into the control room. Saurians dodged to get away, but to little avail. The grenade sizzled with blue-arcing lines and lizards began flopping about in the room.

"Give it everything," I said. "It's now or never."

It turned out to be now, because we forced the doors wide enough for me to slither through—the blood dripping from my suit helped grease my way. Then the portal banged shut behind me. Two remaining sorry-looking, half-shocked lizards sat hunched at their stations. They were stubborn creatures. We had that much in common.

The chamber was like a quadruple-sized cockpit of a regular jumbo jet, with seven Saurians in attendance. Five lay tased on the floor. Two tapped frantically on their panels. The windows showed the darkening of approaching space, with stars beginning to appear. The lander obviously headed for their mothership.

I started toward them. One of the Saurians hissed. The other slapped a button, and weightlessness came to the control room, for I found myself floating in midair. Fortunately, my forward momentum still kept me heading toward them.

The lizards didn't wait on the stools, however. Each leapt away from me, soaring through the chamber to another location. I reached a stool soon enough and leapt after the nearest one.

The next few minutes proved tedious and frustrating. The two lizards were much more agile in the weightless chamber than I was. At times, they used their tails, thrusting off the bulkheads or using them to reach and shove, adjusting their flight paths. I kept sailing after them in an attempt to catch one or to cut it with my Bowie knife.

This went on long enough so several of the frozen Saurians on the floor began to stir. That changed the tactics of the two survivors. They landed near one of their own, shaking him and hissing urgently, trying to speed his revival.

All the while, the lander headed for space. The last blue of Earth's atmosphere had already faded to black, and now the stars blazed in profusion.

What would I do with seven Saurians, seven flying monkeys moving in crisscrossing patterns through the chamber? This couldn't go on. I had to stop the lander and bring it back to Earth, or barring that, I had to stop it before the vessel reached the mothership.

Therefore, I changed tactics. This wasn't a game or a sporting proposition. This was life or death, extinction or the continuation of the human race. That meant bitter ruthlessness. No one would give me a prize for playing fair. It was either win or lose. Prison had taught me some bitter lessons: the most critical of those lessons was to cheat when the stakes became high enough.

I cheated now by landing on or beside the five stirring Saurians. I killed each one, finding I had to hold the head in order to cut the throat. Otherwise, I'd merely push myself away as I attempted to ply my blade in the weightless situation.

"You shouldn't have come to Earth!" I roared at one, feeling guilty at this slaughter. "You should have left us alone."

After finishing off the last of the five, we played the game in earnest, the two survivors and I. Like a hungry, angry wolverine, I chased them up and down and side to side throughout the compartment. They used every trick, I suppose, in weightless maneuvering. I learned fast, and I'd always been good at pool. It was all about angles, figuring them out and using them to your advantage.

My living armored hand finally caught a Saurian by the tail. The lizard thrashed, and at the last moment, I felt the muscles of the tail bunch and writhe like a python. The creature became desperate and launched itself at my head. It was a smart move, for it made the most sense, as my head was the one vulnerable spot left. It didn't help the Saurian, but given his situation, it's what I would have done in his place.

We hugged, and I punched my blade into him. The tip must have hit a bone, momentarily blocking my thrust. Then I could feel the blade grating against it, sawing into the hard structure.

I twisted the knife to make him die as fast as I could, and to get the edge off the bone.

Afterward, my back bumped against a bulkhead. "What's it going to be?" I shouted at the last Saurian. "Surrender, show me how to work the controls and I'll let you live. You have my word."

The last Saurian crouched against the far wall. His eyes were glassy and he kept his lizard mouth open as he panted.

"You'll die unless you surrender," I said.

He watched me, but it seemed clear he had no idea what I said. Why didn't he get a translator? Maybe it had something to do with him seeing me butcher his pals. Also, he must have thought of me as an animal gone berserk. Would I try to reason with a blood-maddened tiger that had just clawed and bit six of my friends to death? I almost pitied him—until I remembered the dissected corpses on the tables and the dead floating in the tubes. These lizards treated us like animals. This one merely reaped the reward of his kind's cruelty to our world.

I glanced at the windows. Great, we were in space. I had to gain control of the lander, and that fast. I roared at him, and faked with my head.

He was twitchy, this last Saurian. He leaped, but I stayed where I was. No doubt recognizing his mistake, his tail lashed out for a stool to redirect his flight path. I heaved his dead buddy at him. Then I launched myself. The dead Saurian struck the living one, and that's all the chance I needed. In these grisly moments of hack, slash and spill green blood, I'd gotten a lot better at weightless maneuvering.

The gruesome game ended with his death. I panted as I yanked my Bowie out of his chest. With all this jumping and pushing, I'd become thirstier than ever. Now I had to concentrate. I floated to the controls, or to one set of them. I tried to remember which button the lizard had pushed that had turned off the gravity.

Maybe it was this one. I pressed it, and I thudded hard onto the floor. I missed striking my chin on a panel by the barest fraction.

Standing, I wondered what I should do next.

Rollo shouted from the other side of the doors, "Creed! Are you okay? What's going on in there?"

I strode across the bloody chamber with its lizard corpses and pulled a lever that looked like it should open the portal. It worked: the doors swished open.

"Listen up," I said.

The two men stared at me. I imagine I was a sight, with a green-bloody face and as I clutched my gory Bowie. Their glances took in the dead lizards.

"You killed them all," Rollo said.

"I tried to get them to surrender first," I said.

"Who's going to pilot the ship?" Rollo asked.

"His girlfriend," I said, pointing at Dmitri. "Get Ella up here pronto. We have to figure out these controls before we reach the mothership."

"There may be some Saurians left hiding on our lander," Dmitri said.

"Rollo, go with him," I said. "Kill every lizard you find. But you two have to hurry. We're running out of time."

"What are you going to do?" Rollo asked.

"I'll start messing with the controls to see if I can figure something out."

"I know you are cunning," Dmitri said. "And I do not question your wisdom. But is it not possible you might accidently open the outer locks and let out the air if you 'mess with the controls'?"

The Cossack had a point. "Okay," I said. "Ella is supposed to be Ms. Brainiac, right?"

"Brainiac?" Dmitri asked.

"Smart, wise, a mystic scientist with good guesses," I said.

"Yes," Dmitri said, "she is very smart."

"So go get her. Until she comes, though, I'm going to try things. It's how we've gotten as far as we have. I'm not going to play it safe now."

Dmitri gave a worried glance at the lander's controls.

"Go!" I said. "We have to get this ship turned around. And see if you can find us something to drink or I'm going to turn vampire and start sipping their blood."

Dmitri gave me a strange look. "It is said the Mongols, when they lacked other nourishment, used to open a vein on their horse and drink its blood. After the Zaporizhian Cossacks, the Mongols were the world's greatest warriors."

"Drinking alien blood makes us great?" I asked.

"Likely, if you drank their blood, it would be poisonous to you."

I blinked several times, studying our Cossack. "Get Ella," I said, "and do it *now!*"

Dmitri nodded curtly, and he went. Rollo raised an eyebrow at me, and then he went too.

-7-

I sat in the control chamber with Ella Timoshenko. She wasn't naked anymore, although she was still barefoot. She'd put on Rollo's parka as if it was a dress, leaving her legs exposed. She peered intently at the various panels, no doubt trying to decipher their functions. So far, she'd avoided looking at me and had said even less.

Dmitri and Rollo stalked the lander hunting for Saurians. I'd told them to cleanse this craft of alien invaders. It was an Earth ship now, our only one. I intended on keeping it that way.

I badly needed water. I suspect we all did. My lips were chapped and the armor had begun to stir restlessly on my skin.

There had to be a water source aboard ship. How otherwise had the aliens kept the Russians alive for two days? I would have asked Ella. I'd heard her speak to Rollo and knew our scientist spoke broken English, so we could communicate. But she had a graver task to perform just now. We desperately needed to gain control of our ship.

Ella had narrow, pretty features with a little triangular-shaped chin. She continued to blink like a woman missing her glasses. She turned her head toward me, but refused to look in my eyes. Was she shy or still upset with me? "This must be life support," she said, indicating a panel. "So never touch these controls."

Did she think I was an idiot or a Neanderthal? "Sure thing," I said.

Ella stood. She had nice legs. She wiped her hands against the parka's fabric and moved to the next stool. She carefully sat down, pulling the parka around her. Then she began to inspect the new panel. Soon, she rubbed her forehead, shook her head and gave me another side glance.

"I cannot be certain," she said.

"I get that," I said. "I'm amazed you can tell anything at all. But our time is becoming more critical by the second. We have to try something."

The lander's engine still throbbed and the ship presumably blasted at takeoff speed toward parts unknown. How long would it take the mothership to notice us? How many landers did the aliens possess? If a few, they would notice sooner. If hundreds, well, maybe we still had a chance. We operated in the dark, but we were lucky to be in this position at all.

Ella Timoshenko spread her slender hands over the panel, wriggled her fingers and dared to touch a control.

The vibration under our feet quit in an instant.

I glanced at her. That was impressive. Maybe our scientist did indeed possess intuitive abilities.

"I have shut off the engine," she informed me.

"How in world did you know to press that control?" I asked.

Whether out of modesty, because she was too busy thinking or found talking to me too difficult, she just shook her head and went back to studying the panel.

At that moment, a screen to my left flickered with images. I must have noticed it with my peripheral vision. I turned toward the wall screen and saw a Saurian. It peered at me. This one had discolored scales around its left eye.

My stomach knotted. The bastards had found us. There went our element of surprise. We could still ram them, though. I didn't want to die, but I wanted to float in a specimen jar even less. I could give them the finger a second before impact.

My upper lip curled. The Saurian must be some kind of traffic-control operator. Likely, he was on the mothership, checking in on the lander.

The lizard hissed at me. I wished I could have shot him in the head.

"Can you turn off that screen?" I whispered to Ella out of the corner of my mouth.

She looked up and must have seen the lizard for the first time. She gave a sharp gasp before saying, "I am not certain. No, not immediately," she added.

I faced the lizard. After chasing the two Saurians around in this chamber, I'd begun to distinguish their expressions. Clearly, the lizard-operator didn't like what he saw. He spoke sharply before his image disappeared.

I stood, and I considered smashing the screen.

Before I could proceed, another image appeared on the screen. A human-looking alien wearing a dark jacket turned around and faced me. He appeared to be listening to someone speaking off-screen out of my sight. Maybe it was the lizard-operator reporting to him. The man had blood-colored skin and narrow features. He had dark, extremely intelligent-seeming eyes. When he opened his mouth, I noticed pointy teeth like a piranha.

The alien spoke, or his mouth moved. From a speaker under our screen came Saurian-like hisses.

"Are you seeing this?" I asked Ella.

"He must be the Jelk," Ella said in a low voice.

I turned to the scientist. She had been staring at me. The minute our eyes met, hers dropped.

"This is ridiculous," I said. "We're not at a dance. We're about to die."

Her gaze lifted, and she glared now. "You stared at me before."

"Yeah, well…I couldn't help it. You're pretty. Now what's a Jelk?"

She glared for a moment longer. Then the outrage in her eyes flickered off, and she had a business look, a coldly logical expression. "The Saurians spoke about the Jelk. I remember being intrigued, as it seemed clear the Jelk controlled the expedition."

"So that's the Saurians' boss?" I whispered.

Ella glanced around me at the screen. She nodded, adding, "Most certainly."

I turned back to the Jelk. This was the bastard I had to kill, who must have ordered the thermonuclear bombs rained onto Earth. The joker must be on the mothership. He regarded me closely and a cruel smile appeared. Those eyes...they showed wicked intelligence, something twisted like a biblical demon. I had the impression of advanced age. That daunted me.

He spoke again, and instead of hisses, English words came out of the speaker.

"You are humans, Earthlings," he said.

"Obviously," I said. "Are you the Jelk?"

His eyebrows rose, and I found that disconcerting. Aliens from the stars should be different in thought and actions from us, right? Those raised eyebrows were a human-like gesture. What did it mean if we had similar facial gestures?

"Ah," he said. "You wear a symbiotic battlesuit. I begin to perceive the situation. The chamber shows stains of combat. Yes. You have gained control of the vessel. How foolish of the Family. I had thought they could collect specimens without endangering themselves. You Earthbeasts are more cunning than the indicators showed."

My gut tightened. Beasts, this joker called us beasts, too. What was with these aliens? Were they all a bunch of arrogant pricks? I breathed heavily, and I told myself getting angry wouldn't help me now. But I couldn't stop myself.

"Why do you believe we're beasts?" I asked.

The smile widened as if he was amused with me. "It is self-evident," he said.

"No," I said. "We're talking, right? Speech implies intelligence."

"How interesting," he said. "You attempt to reason with me. Very well, if it's logic you desire, I will accommodate you for the moment. Your lander-capturing feat deserves a reward. I am in fact impressed with you. You wear a bio-battlesuit. That was a clever tactic."

I couldn't understand his calm. We had his lander. We'd killed his Saurians, but he didn't seem concerned with their deaths. It told me he was cold-hearted. I suppose I already knew that, since he was genocidal.

"You claim to have risen above the level of beasts," he said. "Yet I know that a few short years ago your species avidly attempted to destroy each other. Our X-tee sociologists studied Earth several cycles ago. At the time..." He leaned toward the screen and pressed three fingers against his forehead. If I were to guess, it looked as if he was thinking or attempting to recall facts.

"Ah, now I remember," he said, confirming my suspicion. "The German Imperium attacked the Soviet Empire, creating widespread destruction. At the same time, the American techno-wizards solved the atomic equation and annihilated Japanese militarists."

I glanced back at Ella. She didn't notice. With her features scrunched in thought as she observed, she obviously studied the Jelk.

A light bulb went off in my head. The atomic equation did it for me. "You're talking about World War II," I said. "You had observers watching us back then?"

The Jelk showed off his pointy teeth. He might look human, but he wasn't the same as us. "Animals destroy in a reflexive manner," he said. "The civilized solve in a constructive way."

The genocidal freak was a hypocrite. I'd had my fill of them. "Oh sure," I said, "civilized. That's why you nuked the Earth and sowed death spores everywhere, right?"

"Unsurprisingly, you labor under misinformation," he said. "It was not I who did these things, but the Lokhars."

"Oh-oh," I heard Ella say behind me. "The engine has come back online."

I glanced at the Russian. Her fingers were pressed against a panel. At the same time, I felt the vibration under my feet.

"Did you turn the engines back on?" I whispered.

Ella looked up at me, and she bit her lower lip. "Negative. I think he did it."

"You are observant," the Jelk said. "That's another point in your favor, I suppose. Yes, you've noticed that my operators have taken remote control of the craft. In several time-units you will join the fleet."

I remember the police driving me to prison. I'd sat in back of a police car, with my wrists handcuffed. Fear had filled me then. *I'm not letting this prick capture me. He thinks I'm an animal. Remember those dissected people on the tables?* I rubbed the back of my hand against my lips. Maybe there was a way to short-circuit the remote control. We had battlesuits and some alien weaponry. I wasn't about to call it quits just because this grinning bastard spoke to me in a high-handed manner.

"It appears your rationality is lower than you realize," the Jelk said.

Keeping my features neutral, I faced him. "Yeah, how do you figure?"

"Why would I eliminate your species in a violent act of destruction and then send down craft to collect specimens for bio-battlesuit testing?"

"You tell me," I said.

The smile evaporated, and the coldness of his dark eyes became more pronounced. "You are a rash creature, too full of your own importance. I suppose your present feat has puffed up your hubris to inordinate levels. Know, Earthbeast, that a single command from me will cause the atmosphere in your vessel to flee into the vacuum of space around you."

"You're threatening to kill us?" I asked. *Call me beast one more time...* "Mister," I said, "I've been ready to die for a while now."

"A threat is not an action," the Jelk said. "It is instead a possibility. You may yet live, but that will depend on the next few moments and what you decide."

I wanted to shove his face against a block of cement and grind it to paste, but I was unable to think of anything useful to say, so I just nodded.

"Interesting," he said. "You now exhibit caution. Maybe the observers underrated human intelligence. In any case, as I was saying, your rationality, your reason, is weak. The Jelk Corporation does not waste resources. The assault upon your planet...hmm," he said. "I suspect that the Lokhars feared you enough to act aggressively. It is possible they learned of my

68

plan and attempted to neutralize my recruiting grounds before I could reach this system."

"Yes," Ella whispered behind me. "The aliens want us as soldiers. I was right all along."

"What are you saying?" I asked the Jelk. "You wanted to hire humans as mercenaries in a galactic war?"

"Again, you misunderstand. The Jelk Corporation does not indulge in war, not in the style or manner of beasts. The Lokhars, however, do not abide by civilized conduct. They are a betweener species, climbing upward from beastliness to sophistication."

Not only was he irritating but confusing. "Who are the Lokhars?" I asked. "Is that your name for the Saurians?"

"How you strive for understanding," the Jelk said. "I applaud that. Yet it is difficult for you to comprehend concepts beyond your intellect to process. You are a fighting beast with the rudiments of rationality. That you wear the bio-battlesuit and have destroyed the workers proves it." He pressed his fingertips against his forehead. "I had not anticipated this pseudo-intelligence. Perhaps I can recoup my investment after all."

He removed his hand and his smile reappeared. "This wouldn't be the first time that the Jelk on the spot understands better than the policymakers back in the conglomerate. Listen to me, Earthbeast, comprehend if you can the offer I'm about to make you."

I don't think I've ever wanted to squeeze anyone's neck more. I felt helpless, and I had no idea how to fix this. If he wanted us as mercenaries…that would be one thing. But this idea I was a beast…

The Jelk cleared his throat. The sound had a gritty quality like a two-pack a day smoker. "I had planned to use you Earthbeasts as ground troops. There are enough transports en route to move several hundred million of you, once you had been put to cryogenic sleep, of course. The bio-battlesuits were an investment—oh, never mind. I'm sure you cannot comprehend. The point is that now a paltry few million of you have survived the planetary bombardment. Your amazing feat of conquering a lander and taking it into space… I believe I can

69

recoup expenditures by taking the best of you and rearming you as space-assault troopers. You appear to possess enough wit to successfully operate in a vacuum and weightless environment."

Was I hearing this right? "Let me get this straight," I said. "You're offering to hire us as space mercenaries?"

"Crudely stated, but accurate to a point," he said.

My thoughts threatened to whirl around and around. I didn't want to end up dissected on a table, and I dreaded the idea this slug was lying. I didn't want to live the rest of my days in an alien cage, either. But fighting space wars as a mercenary...

"Won't the Saurians want revenge for what I've done to them?" I asked.

"By Saurians—oh, I see. You're referring to the Family. Certainly, the workers would prefer to see you destroyed. But that has no bearing on my offer."

"The Saurians...the Family works for you?" I asked.

"They are mere workers indeed," the Jelk said. "Their poor marital performance against you attests to their lack of fighting ingenuity, at least in face-to-face encounters. A truly combative species would have quashed your struggle at the outset."

"And if I refuse your offer?" I asked.

The Jelk appeared surprised. "Come, come, the outcome of refusal is obvious on several levels. At the most lenient—if I returned you to Earth—you would die within the next few weeks from the bio-terminator lacing the air. But of course, I won't return you, but simply let vacuum and space take care of your sullen aggressiveness. Then I will gather other humans as my space-assault troopers."

I didn't like him. I didn't trust him or the Jelk Corporation he represented. But he controlled the ship's engine and I believed he had the power to back up his threats. Besides, I was thirsty, hungry and wondering how to get the bio-suit off me.

"If we becoming your mercenaries," I said. "How will you pay us?"

His eyebrows rose again, and those dark eyes glittered. "You will be fed, housed, given medical treatment and sexual servitors—"

70

I interrupted. It was clear we'd be his fighting slaves. He thought of us as animals after all. But I had plans that didn't include serving the Jelk Corporation my entire life. A judge had once sent me to prison, but I'd found a way out of that. First, I had to survive and I had to help the last remnants of humanity endure our world's destruction.

"I have one request as part of our payment," I said.

"Speak," he said. "I'm listening."

"You spoke about millions having survived the Lokhar attack," I said. "But it seems clear the Earth has become uninhabitable or nearly so."

"Quite," he said.

"It seems to me you're probably not going to recruit all of the survivors," I said.

"No," he said. "It wouldn't be profitable."

"My payment is that you house the survivors, helping them overcome the bio-terminator."

His upper lip lifted, showing me those pointed teeth of his. "Am I to understand that you believe your service can pay for such costly planetary reconstruction?"

"Think about it for a moment," I said. "I led these humans with nothing but our wits and fighting ability. We beat your Saurians even though they had every advantage. I realize the Jelk Corporation had observers here once. Yet you've already admitted that they failed to fully appreciate our abilities. We humans fight a whole lot better if we feel we're fighting for something noble and useful. Your space-assault troopers will give you their best if they know back home humanity still exists, that they're buying that existence with their sweat and blood."

"I find it interesting how you ape civilized behavior," the Jelk said. "Hmm, I do have several ventures that could use highly motivated assault troops. I suppose I could land a freighter or two on the surface, dismantling—" He paused, thinking for a moment. Then he held up one of his red-skinned hands. "Earthbeast, I agree to your proposal."

I had no idea if he kept his word or not. If he was lying…I went for broke and asked him how I could trust him.

71

He made barking noises. I learned later that it was Jelk laughter.

"You can trust me," he said, "because you have no other options. Refuse, and the last of your species—on the planet, at least—surely dies. Accepting my offer gives them the chance of life. Besides, as I said, en route are a host of space freighters. Some are always near their end of usefulness. Instead of sending those particular vessels back, I'll junk them on your world by landing those that are able. They will serve as the centerpiece of the various planetary life-support stations."

How could a few freighters house several million humans? I didn't like his cavalier attitude, but he was right about one thing, I had little bargaining power. It seemed as if this would be the best I was going to get.

"We'll fight harder if we know Earth has a chance of survival," I repeated.

"I believe you've already stated so, and I agreed to your terms for now. If you're as good at fighting as you claim you are, I'll want more assault troops later. Thus, I have the best of reasons, enlightened self-interest, to keep you Earthbeasts breeding for now. Let me add this caveat, however. If the Lokhars struck here once, what is to stop them from striking again?"

A cold feeling worked through me. "A Jelk battlefleet standing guard," I said. "Isn't Earth now part of your empire?"

"Firstly, battlefleets cost money," he said in a dismissive voice. "Secondly, your star system is definitely not part of our *empire* as we have none. We are a corporation. We have emporiums, resource centers and trading partners. Your planet might have become a temporary resource node, but not after the Lokhar devastation. Still, if you Earthbeasts can truly fight...well, we shall see what the future holds."

I couldn't figure out how to get more from him, at least not at the moment. These Lokhars...I yearned to dust their planet with a bio-terminator. I also ached to capture the commanding officer and the entire crew of the enormous vessel that had devastated Earth. They would die: every one of them. First, I had to keep myself and my planet alive.

"Yes," I said. "I agree to your terms."

The Jelk barked again—laughed again. I'm not sure what he found so amusing. But that was how I and the others found ourselves as Jelk Corporation space-assault troopers. I didn't know it then, but our troubles had just started.

-8-

The next few weeks were hell.

It started with the lander's slow approach toward seven monstrous vessels that waited between the Earth and the moon. The Jelk Corporation ships had running lights blinking along the sides like an old neon Christmas sales sign that changed colors from red to green, to blue and back to red. By comparing the lander to them I realized each of their vessels was kilometers in circumference and shaped like an oak leaf. The seven ships were arranged in a pentagram pattern that I found ominous.

I didn't know if these were freighters, Jelk battleships or what. Our lander headed toward the nearest and soon entered an open bay door. The hangar was huge, with five other landers parked on a red-colored floor space. We made the sixth lander.

"Time to go," I said from the control chamber.

We hurried to the exit where Saurians in battle armor greeted us. At gunpoint, we filed out of the lander onto the floor. They ordered us into a long column and marched us deeper into the ship. Rollo tapped my shoulder and pointed back.

I turned and quailed at the sight. The stars and the lonely blue Earth were visible through the huge hangar door. It hadn't closed, and in that moment, I expected escaping air to pick us up and launch us toward the opening into space.

"Another membrane," Rollo said.

Of course, that made sense. A membrane kept the atmosphere within the hangar bay. Thinking about the

74

membrane and touching my battlesuit brought home to me that the Jelk liked to use bio-material instead of just inorganic metal. What did that tell me about them? I guess the obvious. They were different from us and thought differently.

I let my gaze rove over our column of marching men and women. There were more humans in the lander than I'd expected: a good three hundred of us. The Saurians had been busy these past few days. As we neared the edge of the hangar bay and neared several large doors, the Saurians separated Rollo, Ella, Dmitri and me from the others. We were taken left while the rest of the column marched to the right.

Did the Jelk think of us as the ringleaders, or were we the ones most dangerous to them?

After winding through a maze of corridors, the guards forced the four of us into an empty chamber with showerheads. A heavy door clanged shut behind us and liquid immediately hissed from above.

"Don't look at me," Ella said.

I began coughing instead of looking at our scientist. The water tasted awful, like metal. Then my bio-battlesuit melted off me and I felt the hot liquid pelting my bare skin. It was a strange sensation, with a pang of parting, like losing a good friend. Through the heated fog I saw the other suits melting or oozing off Rollo and Dmitri. The living armor didn't become blobs again, but slithered like powerful snakes for small portals that looked like rat-holes along the sides of the shower room.

At the sight, the good-friend sensation dwindled. An alien-grown thing had been covering my skin? I'd always hated snakes, and watching the last of the armor slither through a hole, I had an atavistic reaction. I never wanted to become used to the symbiotic creature. Being a Jelk's space mercenary— what would be our life expectancy and who would we fight?

"The water's changing color," Ella said.

I looked up and got sprayed in the eyes. It stung like powerful soap and I kept my face aimed downward after that. The trickle by my toes had become orange.

I realized they were hosing us down like horses. Ella speculated it was in order to get rid of any contaminating bio-terminator.

By the time I was starting to feel like a prune the spray quit, the doors opened and battle-suited Saurians entered. They prodded us along another corridor. I tried to keep from looking at a naked Ella. She had her hands in front of her. The one time she looked back at us, I made sure I was staring elsewhere. The lizards forced us to a smaller chamber with benches along the sides.

A human-seeming doctor in white and with outrageous eyebrows beckoned us near an alcove. She held a huge hypo filled with yellow liquid. The needle was bad enough and far too long. I squinted at the sludge she no doubt planned to inject into me or us. Little metallic-looking particles floated in the solution.

"What is that stuff?" I asked.

The doctor glanced at a Saurian as if I'd spoken gibberish. The lizard pointed his gun at me.

"Go ahead and give me the shot," I said. "I'm not stopping you. I'm just asking."

The doctor scowled, the lizard hissed and the woman plunged the needle into my arm. There was no warning, no rubbing my shoulder first. *She's doing it like a vet would to a cow or pig.* I watched with loathing as the yellow solution with metallic particles disappeared in front of the plunger. The stuff was entering me, all of it. Seconds afterward, I felt nauseous and a copper taste filled my mouth. What was this stuff?

The doctor spoke alien words, and she pointed.

The room seemed to tilt and elongate. I stared at the door. It retreated as I watched. The doctor must have spoken again. Her words became distorted and much too loud. The sick feeling spread through me, reaching my groin and then my legs. I staggered to the exit, pushed through a membrane and found two more women waiting. They wore white, like nurses.

I spat to get the copper taste out of my mouth. That was a mistake. I dry-heaved and the world, the room, spun around me.

"What's going on?" I mumbled.

"This way please," one woman said. At least she spoke English. That was good. They seemed to be trying to help.

76

I raised my head to stare into her face. She had dark hair to her shoulders and brown eyes like soft, overturned soil.

My mouth hardly worked and my tongue felt sluggish. "Are...are you from Earth?" I asked. I couldn't place the accent.

She pushed me. I stumbled, nearly fell but managed to keep my feet. My eyes must have rolled around in their sockets. I had to concentrate and that brought a pounding headache. The nurse propelled me to a trough of green solution.

"Lay down," she said.

"You want me to lie in the water?" I asked.

"You're going to feel sick soon," she said. "You should lie down while you can."

I tried to look around and regain my bearings. My vision swam and finally failed me. Everything became blurry and indistinct. What had they injected into me? My knees weakened. I almost fell on my face. The two nurses guided me, helping me lie in the warm solution. They must have put a mask over my face. I heard labored, Darth Vader-like breathing and I realized it originated from me. Then warm water surrounded every part of me. I submerged. It was the last thing I remembered before passing out.

***

I awoke much different in feeling and awareness. Grogginess filled me, although I realized that hands helped me up out of a liquid solution. Vaguely, I recalled the injection and putting on a mask.

I peered at one of the hands holding me: slender with a frail wrist. The hand possessed four fingers and an opposable thumb, and it had a silver-colored ring on the pinky finger with a tiny cross etched onto the ring's surface. The wrist stuck out of a white sleeve. With my eyes, I followed the sleeve up to a shoulder, a pretty neck and a beautiful face with dark hair. It was the nurse.

She gave me a nervous smile.

I opened my mouth to reply.

"Don't try to talk just yet," she said. "You're disoriented. You've been through intense surgery. You must be a prime specimen to have neuro-fibers wired into you."

I couldn't summon speech and I didn't comprehend her words yet, but I did like her eyes. I tried to smile. I wanted to see her smile again. I wanted her hands to remain on my skin.

She patted my arm. "This might hurt."

A stinging pain flared in my right pectoral. I realized there had been many such stinging sensations these past few moments. It's what had woken me.

Despite my grogginess and the allure of the woman's face, I transferred my attention to the pain. I lay in a green solution, in a trough of some kind. Hands yanked tiny sticky pads off my flesh, a bunch of them, meaning a bunch of pads and hands. Each pad had a trailing wire on the end.

Hadn't the woman spoken about surgery and wires? I managed a grunt and I tried to struggle upright.

"He's getting restless," another woman said. "Jennifer, see if you can distract him again."

Fingers touched my chin. I tried to shake my head free of the touch. Two hands clamped onto my cheeks, one on each side. I resisted, but I felt terribly weak. Slowly, someone dragged my head where it didn't want to go. The pretty nurse bent over me. She smiled down into my face.

"It's going to be okay," she said. "You've received a heavy dosage of steroid sixty-five. In the next few weeks, you'll experience massive muscle growth. The surgeons also wired you with neuro-fibers. Only the best commandos receive those. They will speed up your reflexes, and you'll learn to use them well."

More stings told me the others continued to rip the sticky pads from my flesh. I quit fighting and relaxed, realizing I needed to gather my strength.

"Good job, Jennifer. Keep talking. Your voice soothes him."

She soothes the savage beast, I thought to myself. Beast...yeah, I was an Earthbeast mercenary for the Jelk Corporation. But I wasn't a beast; I was a man. One thing I knew, these women worked for the aliens. Could the Saurians have captured Earth nurses to train them this fast in alien procedures? No. that wasn't logical.

I shut my eyes and squeezed them closed.

"What's he doing?" a woman asked. "We've never had one of them act like this before."

"Don't have any idea," the head nurse said, the one who had told Jennifer to keep me occupied.

I thought back to the words I'd just heard. There had been something strange about it. It hadn't been English, but I'd understand the language perfectly. What had the surgeons done to me while I'd been under? What could they do that would let me learn or assimilate a new language so quickly?

A feeling of violation surged through me. I wanted to lash out and attack, but this wasn't the time or place for it. Yeah, yeah, everything was starting to come back. The militaristic Lokhars had wiped out the Earth and I'd made a deal with Mr. Jelk to help the world's surviving remnants.

My eyes flew open. I still couldn't see more than blurs past the women around me. I shifted my head from side to side. I counted four women in their white uniforms.

"Relax," Jennifer said. "We're here to help you."

I opened my mouth.

"We're almost done," a woman said. "Tell him that."

"We're removing the implants," Jennifer told me. "Then we're going to help you sit up and move into a wheelchair. We're taking you to the Green Room. You'll get dressed there and after you eat—"

"This one doesn't eat until after the tests," the head nurse said. "Shah Claath wants privation results—"

"He's listening to you," Jennifer warned. "He understands what we're saying."

"It doesn't matter," the head nurse said. "He's red-listed and has to test out. Either way, you won't see him after this."

"He's big," Jennifer commented, "and looks strong."

"Maybe why Shah Claath is interested in him," the head nurse said.

Instead of becoming more lucid, I almost passed out. Vaguely, I was aware as these women helped me out of the solution and into a wheelchair as they said. They sprayed my skin with something cooling. My stomach rumbled. I craved a dozen Big Macs and heaps of fries.

Matters proceeded in the manner Jennifer had told me it was going to play out. Naked and in the wheelchair, I moved down a corridor. I sat like an old man, with my head slumped forward so my chin rested against my chest. I drooled and couldn't focus my eyes.

In a different room, the women helped dress me in a jumpsuit: no underwear, no shirt, but they put slippers on my feet. Two of them maneuvered me off the wheelchair and onto a stool.

I recalled stools. The Saurians in their alien tank and in the lander's control chamber had sat on them. We'd killed every one of those lizards.

"Why's he grinning now?" the head nurse asked.

A face pushed down near mine. I focused again. It was Jennifer.

"Good luck with the tests," she said softly.

"Who...who are you?" I whispered.

She laughed prettily, if a bit nervously.

"Are you from Earth?" I asked.

She glanced away, straightened and frowned down at me. Then she bent down and whispered in my ear, "They're always watching. You mustn't make them nervous, and—"

She stopped talking as I grabbed one of her thin wrists.

"Where are you from?" I asked.

She hesitated before saying, "They took my parents with them the last time they observed," she said.

"During World War II?" I asked. "Was that the last time?"

She became wistful. "We were going to help process millions. I so looked forward to visiting my origin planet. But the Lokhars got here first. Now..." She patted my hand and worked her wrist free.

"Will I see you again?" I asked.

"You're a fighting beast," she whispered, "a prime specimen."

"We're people!" I told her. "We're not animals. So don't call me one."

She looked away.

There was something about her...even though she'd been brainwashed by the Jelk... "I'll see you again, Jennifer, right?"

80

"No," she whispered.

Something about that "no" hardened my resolve. "Yes," I said, feeling good saying it.

"You're going far away," she said, with that wistful look in her eyes.

"I believe you," I said, "but you also have to believe me that I'm also coming back for you."

"We're done, Jen," the head nurse said. "We have many of them to process today. Let's go."

Jennifer looked into my eyes one last time. I looked into hers and felt a spark leap in me. She straightened before I could try to kiss her, and headed for the door. In her white nurse's uniform, her butt swayed perfectly. The cloth tightened in just the right ways. I wanted to be with Jennifer. I wanted to take her out to eat and go to the beach with her. Instead, she exited the room and the door swished shut behind her.

I thought about what she'd told me about surgery and neuro-fibers. Lifting my arm, I examined the skin. There were hairline scars. I examined the rest of my body. I could see hundreds of these extremely thin scars. What had she said? They'd pumped me with steroid sixty-five.

The Jelk and Saurians—the aliens—continued to treat me like an animal. If I lived long enough, I'd make them regret that in a very personal way. I'd hired out as a mercenary. They'd better get used to the idea that we'd made a deal and start treating me—us—right.

The door swished open, and I grew tense, expecting to see a phalanx of Saurians rush into the room with shock batons to beat me down. Instead, a lean doctor in a white lab coat walked in. She held a slate in one hand and a small flat device in the other. Her thumb hovered over a button on the small device.

She had thin hair, outrageous eyebrows like the first doctor, and wet lips. A nametag said "Dr. Warren".

"Hello, Mr. Creed," he said.

"It's just Creed," I said, "without the mister."

Dr. Warren slid the small device into a pocket, pulled out a stylus and made a mark on what I realized was a computer tablet.

81

"So what's on the agenda now?" I asked. "More steroid sixty-five? Or will you plant extra lines of neuro-fiber into me?"

"Neither. First you have some tests to take. Afterward—"

She stopped because I stood up. The room tilted, or it seemed to, and a cold sweat broke out on my forehead. I swayed unsteadily.

"You should sit for now," Warren suggested.

"How about you give me some answers," I said. "I'm getting tired of this animal routine. We're mercenaries. Tell the Jelk we have a contract. He should understand that."

Dr. Warren calmly put her right hand into a lab coat pocket. A second later, an agonizing jolt of pain stabbed the back of my neck. My knees unhinged and I collapsed onto the floor.

Seconds ticked by, and I could feel Dr. Warren bending over me. "Let me give you some friendly advice concerning the Jelk Corporation. Immediately obey those in charge. Do not seek to give orders or corrections. You have become Shah Claath's property. If that doesn't sit well, think of yourself as a semi-liquid form of venture capital. I realize you're a fighting beast, but the key to your—"

Warren quit talking because I spun on my back and used my legs to swipe hers out from under her. The doctor went down in a heap, and I heard the tablet clatter across the floor. The cold sweat remained and the throb of pain in my neck still bit. I had a good idea what had just happened, and I was going to put a stop to it.

Warren groaned. Then I managed to flop onto her and she yelped in surprise. I wrestled with one of her hands, the one striving to shove itself into the lab pocket. Instead, I shoved my own hand into the pocket and grabbed the small device she'd put into it a few minutes ago. As my fingers touched the device, the shocks started again in the base of my neck, jolting down throughout my body.

I groaned at the agony, and I found myself blinking rapidly. I tried to clutch the device again, and once again jolts sizzled through me. The clammy feeling worsened and I vomited, or I tried. There wasn't anything in my stomach to throw up. I lost all interest in trying to grab the device, though. I rolled onto my back and lay there gasping.

"That was foolish," Warren said. It sounded as if she spoke from on her back.

I cracked open an eyelid and turned my head toward her. That caused a splitting headache to throb into existence, and it robbed me of the majority of my vision. There were splotches in my sight. I did spy something lying on the floor near me: the doctor, I presumed.

"I hit my head," Warren complained.

"What's going on?" I asked. "What did you put into my neck?"

"It's not what I put into you," Warren said. "Family technicians put it in while you received the neuro-fibers. The Jelk are sticklers for obedience from their animals, particularly from their fighting beasts."

"I'm a mercenary!" I shouted. "We made a deal."

"I'm sure you didn't read or would not have comprehended the fine print," she said.

"Do you have one of the pain-makers in your neck?" I asked.

"No, no, of course not" she said. "Why would I?"

"So you're a traitor to the human race," I said.

"This is an undignified conversation and it isn't helping either of us. In point of fact, this is my first trip to Earth."

"You weren't born here?" I asked.

"I was born in the Steel Worlds, as we refer to the ships. The last observer team took specimens. They always have. Thus, there have always been several million humans throughout the Jelk Corporation. I don't know why it took this long for the Jelk to decide to draft Earthbeasts into its military arm. Perhaps the Lokhars have made greater gains then our masters let on. I've heard word the Jelk Corporation has lost star systems to Lokhar incursions. But that's all it is: rumors, gossip. I have no hard data."

"The Jelk told me they don't have an empire," I said.

"Well, no," the doctor said. "They do own star systems, though, profitable ones."

Was this just a matter of semantics? I filed away the thought. It wasn't germane just now. "I asked the Jelk if we're mercenaries. He said yes but thinks of us as animals. Will the Jelk keep his word to me?"

"What word is that?" she asked.

I told Dr. Warren about my bargain with the Jelk.

"Hmm," Warren said. "Maybe he will. I must assume you spoke to Shah Claath. The Jelk are spread thinly throughout their corporation. I don't know of any other masters along on the mission. It's clear you amused him. Jelk seldom laugh. Unfortunately, it's seldom good for anyone when they do, as their humor is as dark as the Crab Nebula."

Dr. Warren groaned, and I heard her garments rustle. I had the feeling she climbed to her feet and knew my thought was correct as her shoes scuffled on the floor.

"Let me caution you," she said. Her voice came from higher up. "In case you don't know, the controller in your neck is for obedience. If you're troublesome, I have permission to use it on you. If you attempt to pry the device from me—even if you touch it, the control device will automatically deliver punishment shocks to you."

I reached back and felt along my neck. There was a longish scar. I pushed, and I could feel a hard object inside me about the size of my pinky nail.

A wave of nausea hit, along with anger and dread. Shah Claath had stuck a shock collar on me—no. He'd caused an implanted obedience controller *into* me. Okay. I knew this wasn't going to be easy. My first order of business was to cut this thing out of me. Actually, my first order of business was to survive long enough to try it.

"I can see you're finally thinking," Warren said.

"Why bother doing it like this?" I asked.

"You're the one who attacked me. It should be obvious therefore why they did it. Especially after the enhancements given you, you're too dangerous to let run around loose."

"That's not what I mean. Why not tell me up front what's going on? Why hide knowledge from me and then shock me by surprise?"

"Yes, the not knowing is frustrating, isn't it?" she asked. "But it's the way Shah Claath wants it for now so there's nothing you can do but accept it."

"Why do you help them?"

"My dear fellow, it should be obvious why. Now, no more questions for now or I'm going to use the control device on you again."

I took a deep breath, rolled onto my stomach, waited for the nausea to pass so I wouldn't vomit again, and pushed upward. I felt her hand on my elbow. I wanted to shove it away, but I let her help me onto a stool. I sat there gasping afterward.

Some of the splotches had faded from my sight. Dr. Warren had a shiner on her forehead and her lab coat was rumpled.

She glanced at her stylus. "It's time to run you through some tests to see if the neuro-fibers took. I imagine they did, but we're supposed to be certain. Once you start the training, there's no stopping until the six week are up. You're going to be very hungry the next few weeks, and your skin will itch terribly. My advice is to eat all you can and exercise like a demon. Shah Claath will want at least thirty pounds of muscle growth on each of you."

"If he's so high and mighty, why does he care about mere beasts?" I asked.

Warren laughed without an ounce of humor. "My dear man, Claath is a Jelk's Jelk. He has and will invest money into you. Why does he do this? For the only reason a Jelk does anything: profits. He desires you and the others to become prime fighting creatures so he can recoup his venture capital and gain a massive profit. As you can imagine, the Lokhar assault on Earth has enraged him."

"Because of the sudden lack of mercenaries he'd hoped to recruit on our world?" I asked.

"That and the amount of money he sank into arranging for such a vast fleet of transports to arrive in this system. If you knew the pains he has taken for training millions of battle-beasts... I've heard he'd hoped to sell tens of millions of you Earthers to the Rim Confederation. Now those contracts will remain unfulfilled. The loss of income—profits—staggers the imagination. I would think Shah Claath is wild to regain

85

something from this fiasco. Perhaps that's why you struck his fancy."

Lokhars, Jelk and now the Rim Confederation, I knew nothing about the interstellar situation. We were ciphers to them, *animals* to catch and sell or to squash and spray. Mankind had obviously gotten a late start in the star-building game, and we'd almost been wiped off the board. Well, this so-called animal was going to do everything in his power to change that. First, I'd have to pass these tests and endure combat training.

"Let's get started," I said.

Dr. Warren raised an unkempt eyebrow.

"I have a lot to do and a short time to do it in," I said.

She gave me a strange scrutiny before pointing at the door. "Head that way then and we'll get started."

I did, marching toward six weeks of hell.

-9-

Ella figured it out first: that our drill instructors weren't the children of kidnapped humans from an earlier survey, but manufactured androids. The unsmiling, monotone DIs proved to be bio-plastic human replicas with cybernetic interfaces and bio-grown brains. They lacked all mercy. Heck, they lacked every emotion and demanded perfection. It meant we were in the hands of machines that were doing exactly as they had been programmed.

For the first several days we ate like hummingbirds. No, not very little, but a lot. Some of those tiny creatures consume more than twelve times their bodyweight every twenty-four hours. There probably weren't any hummingbirds left, though. Not after the bio-terminator worked its way through the world. The Lokhars had a lot to answer for. Thinking of that, I ate until my jaws ached and afterward I slurped the Jelk equivalent of protein shakes.

Battle-suited Saurians had moved us to another ship, a gravity vessel where I weighed at least twice as much. I constantly felt tired and the drag on my muscles and bones made every movement a struggle. It also forced our bodies to work and to *grow*.

We ran on a track, did pushups and sit-ups and other exercises, rolled for hundreds of feet, ran again, marched, climbed ropes and ate more meals, repeating the process ad nauseam. All the while the ramrod-stiff, mask-faced DIs prodded us to run faster, roll harder and force out yet another pushup.

87

I'd been through the U.S. Army's boot camp. It had been a breeze. Despite old movies about rugged boot camps, the one I'd passed through hadn't been anything like that. I remember waiting for a U.S. Army DI to challenge one of us to a fight. It happened in every movie on the subject. I'd planned to give the man the fight of his life. But to my bitter disappointment, the challenge had never come.

I'd worked out harder in the prison weight room than in U.S. Army boot camp. Those days—in prison—my biceps, triceps, deltoids had quivered with exhaustion after a strenuous workout. In comparison, Jelk boot camp was bad. I felt how a pit bull must feel when cruel humans beat it with sticks, kicked it in the ribs and generally taunted the dog. When our android DIs were displeased with one of us, they used the obedience chips in our necks to shock us.

The worst day in that regard proved to be on the obstacle course, at the wall. A DI raised his speaking volume, with his face, his eyes, as animated as a seashell. There was nothing vital or vibrant on his plastic-like face. He was an inorganic zombie, but his amplified voice lashed the weakest to jump and try to scale the wall again.

The wall was nine feet high. In regular gravity, it would have been a cinch to jump and hoist ourselves over. Here in double gravity—let me put it this way. Even after the steroid sixty-five, neuro-fibers and swelled muscles, the best of us barely managed, while three trainees simply couldn't do it.

"712," the DI said, pointing at a chest-heaving man drenched in sweat. "Climb the wall."

The man gulped and stared up with bulging eyes. He leaped feebly, his fingers a good two feet from the top, and slid down in a heap at the bottom.

"Up," the DI said.

712 had nothing left. He stirred, though, but that was it.

The DI aimed and clicked a small device.

712 writhed on the ground, moaning, as a punishment shock struck from within his neck.

"Jump over the wall or you will receive another shock," the DI said.

712 looked up at the wall, but that was all he did.

The android shocked him again, making the man jerk and vomit on the ground.

"Hey!" I shouted. "He's exhausted, kaput. Let him rest."

The android turned machine-fast to our group. "Who spoke?"

I licked my lips, and I stepped forward. We'd learned the hard way that they gave group punishments just as quickly as single-man lessons.

"602," the android said, "you spoke without my leave." He aimed the device, and a jolt struck me in the neck.

I groaned, massaging my muscles, but I managed to remain upright. When I looked up again, the android had turned back to 712. The DI told the man to try again, but nothing happened. So the android shocked him longer this time, threatening to continue unless he cleared the wall.

"We have to charge the thing together," I whispered.

Grimly, Rollo and Dmitri nodded. A few of the others hung back.

"Ready?" I asked.

"Stand 712," the android said. "If you cannot stand you will die where you lie."

"Now," I whispered. I tensed my neck and sprinted at the monster. The android shocked 712. Even so, he must have heard us. The thing whirled around fast.

"Stop," the DI said, lifting his hand.

I didn't stop, and since I led, I had no idea who followed me. Pain blossomed in my neck. This time I was ready for it. I bellowed, more in rage than anything else. The android hand pointed at others, and his thumb twitched as he delivered shocks.

I reached the android, grabbed the offensive bio-plastic wrist and used one of the nifty new fighting techniques they'd been teaching us. I cracked the wrist using its own leverage and drove a knee into his plastic-hard belly. A jolt more powerful than the others struck the back of my neck. It was the last the DI gave. The shock device fell out of the android's hand. I bellowed again, landed on the DI like a goblin in a nightmare and moved for his head with every ounce of my heightened strength and speed. I twisted the android's head around,

89

snapping the neck, and had the distinct pleasure of seeing his eyelids flutter.

"You must stop this," he told me.

I twisted again, and the lights went out in those plastic eyes.

A moment later I and—I found out later—all the rest of the trainees were knocked out by an obedience shock broadcast from elsewhere.

* * *

I awoke stretched out on a metal slate, with my legs, arms and neck manacled to it. Below, I heard churning water and tiny gnashing noises like hundreds of sets of small teeth.

Looking up, I spied a Saurian on a perch above, standing at a control panel. A screen stretched above the lizard. The screen flickered, and Shah Claath, the Jelk, appeared on it. Claath sat at a desk, with a window showing stars behind him.

"You're a troublesome creature," Claath said. "According to this tally, you destroyed one of the teaching drones. That's destruction of property, my property. The Family has already petitioned for your elimination. Now that you're awake—"

"The drone was defective," I said.

Claath studied me. It was impossible to tell what he was thinking. Finally, he said, "Explain."

"The drone abused one of your mercenaries," I said, "one of the modified humans. I imagine neuro-fiber surgery and steroid shots cost a lot of money, your money. If the teaching drone had continued its punishment shocks, one of your mercenaries would have died and you would have lost your investment."

"You claim to have destroyed the drone in order to save me money?" Claath asked.

"No. I destroyed it to save one of my fellow trainees. I merely point out that in doing so, I saved you funds."

"Hmm," Claath said. "You labor under several misconceptions. For instance, humans are cheap. Such manufactured bio-plastic drones with culture-grown brains are expensive—at least in relation to a wild fighting beast such as you. The net expenses have put you in the red. Worse, you have already cost me much by killing an entire Family cluster."

"True," I said. "But in doing so I showed you the utility of humans as space-assault troopers. That's worth a lot of cold hard cash and can pay for a few busted androids."

"You overstate your utility by an estimated factor of ten, and future profits can pay for nothing in the present."

"Jelk don't do credit?" I asked.

Claath's dark eyes glittered. "You are a glib beast with a highly inflated ego. Let us say for the moment you helped restore needed profits. You've also asked for expenditures in a nearly useless gesture: to save a few million worthless creatures on your barren planet."

I still didn't like being called an animal, but I no longer lost my temper over it. In my mind, I was a mercenary. I now told Claath, "I hope to show you—"

"Enough," Claath said. "I will not dicker with you, as the concept is insulting and irrational. What I deem interesting is your wit. It proves that wild Earthbeasts are more cunning than the domesticated pets we keep underfoot."

The Jelk glanced at a tablet. Maybe it was an accounting ledger. "Hmm," he said, looking up at me. "I must admit that I applaud your combat ferocity. I hadn't believed unarmed Earthbeasts capable of destroying androids. Before this, I'd debated growing more android cultures and using them as space-assault troopers. But the ease at which you destroyed one yesterday shows I may have overestimated their fighting abilities. They also take too long to grow, and as I said, they are too expensive to throw away in the risky commando operations I have in mind."

He drummed his fingers on the desk, not doing them in sequence like a normal person, but tapping them down all together at once. "Normally, I'd terminate such a troublesome creature like you who willfully destroys my property. The problem is that I've sunk too much capital into this venture. You Earthbeasts—I have an enterprise for you and your ilk. It will be a deadly proposition, do not doubt it. Yet the same monies needed to make the attempt…"

He grinned at me. "The Jelk Corporation has yet to acquire a Forerunner artifact. They are entirely rare and astronomically costly. If I could capture the Altair Object…" he mused.

Once more, the Jelk drummed his fingers on the desk. "Time is of the essence. Yes, I will accelerate the training schedule. I have bid on a raid fleet and believe—" He paused again, thinking.

Then Claath leaned forward. "Do not destroy any more property. If it will calm your mayhem, I will instruct the techs to check the androids. My advice to you is to endure, learn and refrain from incurring my wrath. One more such incident and I will let the Family indulge in one of their primitive customs of retribution. Do I make myself clear?"

"Yes," I said.

"Release him," Claath told the watching Saurian.

There seemed something different about this lizard. For a moment, I thought the Saurian would dump me into the pool full of carnivorous fish thrashing below. Then he hissed, relaxed his posture and tapped a control, and my metal slate began sliding toward the exit.

***

I returned to the training group and the androids appeared to hold no malice toward my destroying one of their number. I say appeared, because it turned out that one of them held a grudge. It also knew how to bide its time, though.

For the next few days, we exercised and ate heartily, helping our overstrained steroid-glutted muscles to expand. Soon, we began studying insertion tactics, laser rifles, pulse grenades and a host of other vacuum-combat related topics.

Five days after the android-destroying incident, a beefed-up force of DIs took us to a small arms range. There we fired laser rifles. These were hefty things weighing fourteen or fifteen pounds. Each time a beam fired, the rifle purred with power. We could fire concentrated beams of annihilating strength, hosing and sweeping laterally as if it was a machine gun, or we could use pencil-thin rays for sniper shots. There was even a setting for wide beam.

Ammo, or power really, was supplied by the battery packs we shoved into them. Interestingly, these lasers fired visible light the better to help us to aim them. Frankly, the tech was awesome. Bullets always had some kind of drop or drift. Laser rays didn't drop or drift, but shot in a perfectly straight line to target. Not that these things could fire effectively—or killingly—for terribly far. After three hundred yards, the beam dissipated as it lost its tight coherence. At six hundred yards, they could blind enemy troops if you hit them in the eyes, but the ray wouldn't burn through armor at that range.

The next day we heaved pulse grenades. They flashed brilliantly. If you looked at them while they went off, purple splotches filled your vision. The nifty thing about them was that with a twist of the ring around one you could change its setting. Maximum setting would produce a violent explosion, killing everyone in a fifty yard radius.

I wondered if a pulse grenade could breach a lander's hull.

The days merged in hard work. I'd put on thirty pounds already and with the neuro-fibers, I could move *fast*.

Eventually the androids brought back the bio-battlesuits. After watching the symbiotic suits slither away in the showers, I had my reservations concerning them. It was too bad Claath couldn't have given us powered armor like those in many SF novels I used to read. I imagine the living armor was cheaper and helped the Jelk accounting sheet.

After stepping onto my blob and watching the second skin cover me, I saw the androids shove boxes at us. I opened a box and found combat boots inside. They were like blocks of metal and seemed too big. The weird thing was that the living armor moved off my feet, allowing me to squeeze the boots on. Afterward, the second skin oozed over the metal, sealing it shut.

I donned a bulky helmet next. We all had helmets, and these were sci-fi marvels. The helmet fit over my head and reached under my chin. That meant the second skin sealed this thing tight—vacuum tight. I had bio-armor, combat boots and helmet. After we fit oxygen tanks and maneuvering thrusters onto our backs, we followed the DIs into a new corridor. They took us to airlocks and onto the surface of our training ship.

I peered at the distant Earth. Out here, it was the size of the moon as seen from my back yard. Mad Jack had never made it this far into space.

I snarled, and silently renewed my vow. My dad wouldn't die in vain. The Lokhars would pay for their infamy. I would learn everything I could, and the universe would see that Earthers weren't animals, but the most dangerous soldiers around.

For the next five days we learned magnetic walking, thruster flying and to trust our living armor to keep us alive in the vacuum of space. The helmets contained a computer, a HUD visor and a two-way communication system. We could slave our laser rifles to the HUD so a targeting image appeared. Wherever we pointed the muzzle, that's what the targeting circle marked.

We practiced flying shots, fast maneuvers and how to sail silently through the dark, enduring the loneliness of space and trusting in our helmet's computer-calculated trajectory.

The training ship moved around the solar system, and we learned the battlesuits could take heavy doses of radiation of all kinds. Maybe as good, the bio-suits soaked up sunlight, helping them regenerate and supplying us with energized strength.

For the next step in our training we landed on Ceres, in the Asteroid Belt between Mars and Jupiter. There we learned about low-gravity maneuvering. Jump too hard and off you sailed into space, having reached escape velocity. You'd see the rocks below and wait to start falling, but instead you kept heading farther away from the surface. In the end, you had to rotate yourself and aim your head at the rocks, using the thrusters to bring you back down. The art of low-gravity gliding took time to master.

After we'd practiced all we could on Ceres, we inserted onto Io, a moon of Jupiter. The monstrous gas giant loomed before us with its colorful bands on the planet. I could hardly believe where I was, and how far I had come from Earth.

The worst thing about Io was the radiation pounding our suits. Jupiter's magnetic field poured out the deadly rads. The bio-suits could take it; our skin and bones underneath not as well. The suits secreted a substance directly into us through our skin, repairing internal damage. It wasn't fun, and most of us complained about aching bones and a metal taste in our mouths.

Later, with the sun little bigger than a star, we inserted onto Charon, Pluto's icy moon. It was cold out here, and proved a bad idea to lay on your bio-suit for long on the methane snow. The nearly absolute cold drained life-energy from the bio-suit at a frightful pace, and tended to boil the methane from your own heat. That meant one stayed standing on his boots, clumping over methane ice.

On this training exercise, our retrieval boat took longer than normal to pick us up. The bio-suits became stiff and the cold began seeping into us. Ella figured out a solution. We set our bulky laser rifles on wide beam and carefully shot each other. That warmed the bio-suits long enough for us to survive the tardy pickup.

The android pilot who set the boat down watched us with his plastic eyes as we boarded. He seemed like a zombie in his coldness. From that moment, I began to wonder and to distrust what rattled around in their brains.

During our weeks flittering around the solar system, we learned about zero-G maneuvering, ship-assault tactics and other vacuum combat practices, including space survival skills.

We'd been talking, and Rollo shared my doubts concerning our ultimate utility to Shah Claath. In space, warships should be able to beam anything that moved, including star soldiers like us. And once a commander destroyed all opposition, why would his task force need space-assault troopers? Would enemy soldiers continue to resist in a half-destroyed space station that had no hope of surviving?

This wasn't like the old days of Greek triremes or British ships of the line. In those old days, waterborne navies used boarding tactics. Hoplites with spears charged across, or Romans with short swords raced across a corvus onto Carthaginian galleys. Later, pirates with cutlasses swarmed merchant ships or Napoleonic sailors swung onto enemy frigates, attempting to storm and capture.

At a certain tech-point, though, that no longer made sense. During World War II, Japanese sailors never tried to storm a U.S. battleship. In the Gulf War, Saddam would have never thought of slipping commandos onto a U.S. carrier. Such a thing—space commandos swarming an enemy spaceship—seemed even less likely, not more. Maybe we would be more like swimmers trying to attach a mine onto a ship's hull in a harbor. Yeah, I could see that, I suppose. It also seemed incredibly dangerous and unlikely to work often. Worse, it struck me as closer to a suicide mission than a soldier's task.

Eating, fighting, space-flying, asteroid-walking—the extra weeks merged into a quick month and a half. Finally, our androids declared us battle ready.

"Yippee-ki-yay," as Bruce Willis would have said in his *Die Hard* persona.

Before our first mission, I asked for a last interview with Shah Claath, our Jelk overlord.

For the last several weeks, a plan had been brewing in the back of my mind. I needed to get down to Earth, to speak to several groups of survivors. First, I needed to see how they were doing and if Claath was corrupting them. Then I needed to plant an idea, a seed, into people who could transmit the idea to others. No one else had stormed a Saurian lander. No one else I'd met so far hated the aliens like I did. Did that mean I had grandiose ideas? You bet it did. The man who considers himself beaten is beaten. The man that still strives, no matter what the odds stacked against him, has a chance.

I'd been racking my brain on how to convince Claath to let me go down to Earth. I'd finally figured out a way, but it would need a silver tongue—mine. I'd let him know—through the androids—that I could help him achieve his desired profits, a way that would also bolster our chances of success.

Surprisingly, I got the interview a day later.

Before I relate the talk, I believe this would be a good place to say a few words concerning the Jelk Corporation. I'd learned a lot about it these past weeks.

The most obvious truth about space and other star systems was that aliens should be alien or different from humans. That was a logical conclusion. How could strange species like Saurians or Lokhars act the same as humans? Such an idea did not compute. Certainly, there were things out here much different from how humanity operated on Earth for all these centuries. Still, some things were hauntingly similar or parallel enough to understand.

What I'm trying to say was that the Jelk Corporation had a similar analog in human history. Several hundred years ago, there had been a corporation called the East India Company. British merchant-traders had created it and the company had actually run most of the British foreign affairs during the colonial era, at least in the Far East and in India. They'd helped start a few wars, too, particularly against China. Those had been called the Opium Wars. The reason for those conflicts was simple: a monetary trade imbalance. The British were losing large amounts of silver and gold to China.

Like most interesting things, it was actually uncomplicated. The English loved drinking tea. Therefore, they imported gargantuan amounts of tea from China. Back then, it had been the only place that could grow tea in large enough quantities. A saying grew up because of that. "I wouldn't do that for all the tea in China." A person could have just as easily said, "I won't do that for all the money in the world."

In those days, the British were the world's greatest merchants, and they had helped build the world's greatest empire. As good merchants, they wanted to trade goods to China for the tea instead of shipping them silver and gold. That was because bullion was how everyone counted victory points or winning. The more you stacked up, the more you had won the game of nations. The more silver and gold you paid to others, the worse you had lost.

There was one problem with the idea. The English didn't make or have anything that the Chinese wanted. For most of China's existence, its highly cultured people had only wanted Chinese things. Nothing was as civilized. With increasing desperation, the merchants of the East India Company searched for a product the Chinese would want and want badly.

They finally found one: opium. The British merchants grew the opium in India and shipped it to China in trade for tea. Later, the merchants sat around their dining tables sipping tea as they bragged about the new pro-British trade imbalance. The drug pushers had done such a fantastic job that more and more millions of Chinese became opium addicts. China didn't have enough tea to pay for all the opium, and soon Chinese merchants began shipping silver and gold back to England to pay for the drugs their customers wanted.

Now, the Chinese government didn't approve of this. Opium dens by the hundreds of thousands had opened in China, and too many people had turned into useless slugs, opium addicts. So the Chinese government had started one of the first wars on drugs. They chopped off the heads of opium sellers and forbade any more shipment of opium into their country.

The lords of the East India Company realized they were in trouble due to this policy. If the Chinese kicked the habit, the English trade imbalance would once again tip to the Chinese.

Money bellowed: the lords of the East India Company demanded their bought politicians supply them with British warships to teach the Chinese a lesson and force them to allow the sale of opium again. It took several such wars, but the Chinese were coerced—through destroyed ships and burning port cities—and the opium dens remained open, creating endless addicts who pumped England with increasingly more wealth.

The point of this tale is that powerful, armed trading companies or corporations had been successful on Earth and also appeared to thrive in the space lanes. It appeared that the principles of economics were universal.

From what I'd learned so far, the Jelk Corporation would have made the British East India Company look like Boy Scouts. The British had used Gurkhas and Sihks as company soldiers. Those were tough mercenaries from mountainous areas north of India. Similarly, the Jelk used Saurians, and now humans and who knew what else.

I already knew most of this as an android ushered me into the pilot chamber aboard assault ship six. It had several seats; the one I sat in had a silver patch on the left part. I'd gained forty-five pounds of muscle since storming the lander in Antarctica. I wore a green coverall, had shaved my scalp and could easily catch any fly that would have dared buzz past my face. I also bore some extra scars gained during training.

Like most things Earthborn, flies were probably extinct now. Hard to believe, I know. The bio-terminator had done a splendid job. I wanted the interview for one key reason: to learn if Claath had kept his end of the bargain concerning the freighters.

Interestingly, the pilot android wore a combat suit of cyber-armor, complete with helmet, visor and sidearm. He watched me the entire time.

I glanced to the side at a viewing port. It showed me Saturn up close and personal. The ring nearest the ship was composed of endless floating rocks and chunks of ice. They merged together in the distance as the ring encircled the gas giant. Assault ship six was in orbit around Saturn. I hadn't been back to Earth since the lander lifted off it.

A screen flickered into life, and I saw Shah Claath. There were no smiles from him. He studied me with his dark eyes and the evil of his intelligence shined through clearly. I must have been too exhausted from killing Saurians and too amped-up from the bio-battlesuit that day six weeks ago to recognize the devilishness there. And while on the metal slate, I'd been too concerned with the churning fish waiting for my dumped body to study the Jelk closely.

"My time is limited," Claath said, "as is yours. You spoke about heightening your battle abilities, ensuring your coming success. You've surprised me in the past, and I calculated you might again. So you may explain your idea to me."

This was it. His eyes troubled me, with their evil and their cunning. I desperately needed to get back down to Earth. Could I convince him to let me go? The trick was to tell him things he wanted to hear. I'd learned the hard way that it was easier to fool someone who wanted to be fooled. If a person spent his life trying to make a quick buck, he would be the easier one to con that an old codger gripping his dollars with a tight fist.

Be bold, I told myself.

"It's easy enough," I told Claath. "I and the others are concerned about the surviving Earth people back home. We're wondering what sort of bonus we can earn for our people by our victory for you."

"Bonus, who said anything about a bonus?" Claath asked.

"The androids are robotic and too expensive to make for good space-assault troopers," I said. "You need thinking beings—"

"Fighting beasts," Claath corrected.

One, two, three... I silently counted to myself. "You need intelligent soldiers using cunning maneuvers and heightened by good morale," I said. "A bonus, a reward, if you will, encourages Earth troops to fight better."

The Jelk stared at me. What went on behind those dark eyes? Claath finally stirred, and said, "There is merit in your idea. What bonus do you seek?"

So far so good, I told myself. "As you know, I fight for the Jelk Corporation in order to help my people survive as a species. Given greater rewards, I will fight more zealously and even sacrifice myself if it will bring aid to—"

Claath raised a hand.

I'd learned enough these past weeks to know when to stop.

"Not all Earthbeasts would fight as you suggest, given such rewards," Claath said. "Many are satisfied with lesser and cheaper bonuses."

I knew that to be true, but I had to shift that truth. "Yes," I said. "But those mercenaries are not the most able among us."

"A questionable thesis," Claath said.

"Your observers watched World War II," I said. "If you glance at the files, I believe you'll find that honor-oriented combat troops fighting for something greater than themselves make better soldiers. The self-centered and more easily satisfied space-assault troopers will not give the Jelk Corporation as useful a service as the first kind."

"Earthbeasts lack objectivity," Claath said. "Too many of you appear to be dreamers with grandiose ideas that exaggerate your importance."

"Dreamers..." I said, as my gut tightened with triumph. I would snare him with his own words. I forced myself to speak naturally. "You state the situation more succinctly than I could. Dreamers need dreams to help motivate them. Such motivated dreamers make the best soldiers. Our history is replete with examples."

Claath pressed his red fingertips against his forehead. I noticed for the first time that Jelk lacked fingernails, but appeared to have hardened skin there instead. He pulled his fingers away from his head and glanced at them. He appeared to have noticed my scrutiny.

"If you fight well," he said, "and bring me the artifact, I will grant you a bonus."

"Excellent," I said. This was working. "In order for me to inform the others—"

"I will inform them," Claath said.

"Okay. If you could provide us pictures or videos of the survivors and then describe what the bonus would be in concrete terms—"

"What difference would any of that make?" Claath asked. "I have spoken. My word is final."

"To see is to believe," I said. "And the more concrete the reward, the easier it will be for us to conceptualize it. We are dreamers, but we must believe the dream is true."

"You are primitives indeed," Claath said.

"Maybe," I said. "But we will fight better if—"

"You've made your point. Now I grow weary of your voice and your dull-witted appearance. You ape Jelk likeness but you are nothing like us."

I hesitated for a fraction of a second before plunging into the meat of my reason for being here. "To add power to the videos, I suggest you send some of us down to see how the survivors are doing."

"For what reason?" Claath asked. "So you can escape?"

"I want to save my people," I said. "You hired me as a mercenary. If I give you what you want, you give me what I want. I have no reason to escape."

"You are an animal no matter how hard you attempt to practice civilized behavior," Claath said.

It was at this moment I began to envision myself putting a leash around Claath's neck and dragging him around like a dog. With a shake of my head, I forced myself to concentrate on the matters at hand.

"Why do you care who or what I act like?" I asked. "As long as you gain profits from me—"

Claath showed off his pointy teeth. The back ones glistened. "You will go down to Earth and report back to the others. Does that satisfy you?"

101

I found myself learning toward the screen. I must have been inching forward the entire time. I now forced myself to sit back, to relax.

"Yes," I said. "I'm satisfied."

The screen turned a dull color and thereby ended the interview. I'd done it. I was on my way to Earth for a visit. I heaved a sigh of relief, even though I knew that the hardest part lay ahead of me.

The six weeks I'd been training in space could have been six years, six decades or even six centuries. The Earth had changed that much. The only animals left on Earth now—at least that I saw—were those in the Jelk junk freighters landed on Earth.

The Lokhar thermonuclear fireballs had destroyed dozens of the largest cities. They had bigger bombs, too, planet wreckers, throwing up hundreds of billions of tons of dust into the atmosphere. The purple, orange and red skies were like nothing I'd seen before.

The air was now poisonous, laced with bio-terminator. I wore my bio-suit with boots, helmet and breather as I walked through Fresno, California. Winds howled, and everywhere I looked were the dead amid rusting cars and trucks. It was worse than any Stephen King novel, a true nightmare.

Paper and debris fluttered everywhere. It made me sick walking the lonely streets. I crouched by a dead girl with shreds of a yellow dress. She wore a little U.S.A. flag pin, while a Maltese puppy decomposed beside her. The end of the leash was still clutched in the little girl's dead hand.

The Lokhars had done this. The militarists of interstellar space figured Earth soldiers would have given the Jelk too much of an advantage. That, at least, was Claath's version of the story. I wondered where the truth lay.

I walked past dead trees, crunching over brittle leaves. A hundred-dollar bill blew past. It was useless now. I kicked spent shotgun shells, empty beer bottles and bags of rotting groceries. Fresno, California had died: a ghost town of a bygone era.

I found the same thing in Reno, Nevada; in Billings, Montana and Kansas City, Kansas. The android piloted my air-car at my direction. We toured the U.S. I hadn't been home since leaving for the war in Afghanistan several years ago. Now I could never go home again, not to the Earth that had been. The aliens had stolen it from me.

It turned out that our worst nightmare never came true: that of angry nations launching nuclear missiles at each other. The aliens had launched the nukes, and more. The entire planet was like the Japanese Hiroshima of World War II. I guess the rulers of North Korea had been right in their manufacturing of a few thermonuclear bombs. In the days before the aliens came, nuclear deterrence theory said that once a country had atomic weapons, other countries would not threaten its existence for fear of retaliation.

It seemed to me as I toured the dead world, that humanity needed a few terror weapons of its own. We needed bio-terminators and planet wreckers. Part of me screamed for revenge against the Lokhars. Another part said to let it go; that humanity was going to have enough of a task coming back from the edge of extinction. We didn't need die-hard foes. We just needed a place to call our own and a delivery system capable of threatening fearful harm against any enemy who attacked us. Hmm, maybe we did need to smash the Lokhars, to show the other space races what happened when you picked a fight with Earth. First, we needed to free ourselves from under the Jelk thumb. That's why I'd come back. That's what my plan—a long-term project—entailed.

For a hundred miles as the air-car slid across the sky, I ground my teeth together. Humanity had traded places. We were no longer the lords of our domain. We'd become dogs to tame and leash. At best, we were beggars living off Jelk tech.

"Where's the nearest shelter?" I asked the android.

He turned back, seeming to measure me with his plastic orbs.

"Cat got your tongue?" I asked.

The android faced forward, turned our air-car sharp left and kicked in afterburners or something like that. I sank back against my seat. I still wore the bio-suit and helmet. If the android wanted to start something, I was more than ready to finish it.

I didn't trust the androids, not since Charon. I didn't know what went on inside their vat-grown brains, as their mask-like faces gave nothing away. The situation reminded me of Will Smith in *I, Robot*. When was the super truck going to come along and launch a hundred of these plastic men at me?

After a steady journey of some time, I looked out a window. Three giant freighters lay in a huge triangle down there at the tip of Baja, California. Each vessel was several kilometers long. Some kind of plastic sheeting bound the ends together. The same material connected the center area between the space freighters.

The android landed to the north of the freighter complex, setting us down with a thump between groves of dead almond trees.

It was at that point the android decided to speak, using his monotone voice. "Shah Claath wished me to inform you that you cannot visit them in your bio-suit."

I'd learned how to shed the second skin on my own. I did so now, watching the black slime ooze from me. My normal skin always went from stark white to blushing red as the symbiotic substance oozed off. Then my skin finally settled back to its regular color. I wondered about that, about what caused the changes. I hefted the blob and deposited it into a warm cylinder, closing the lid and turning on the heat-lamp, what we called it, anyway.

I donned a regular spacesuit, a similar kind as the Saurian man-catcher had worn the day he walked through the tank membrane to confront me.

"Are you staying here?" I asked.

The android didn't answer.

I didn't like this one. Something odd was going on inside its brain. "Whatever," I said. "I'll be seeing you."

I exited the airlock and crunched over dead ground. No birds sang, no beetles scurried from under kicked clumps and

105

no spider webs hung anywhere. The destruction was worse than I'd expected. I walked through a ghost world. We'd had billions of people seven weeks ago. Now a few million were left. Didn't the Lokhars have any soul? Were the space militarists actually androids or robots or were they something totally alien that they could contemplate genocide of an intelligent species? I suppose some humans would have said we got what we deserved. We'd been busy wiping out various Earth species. Now it was our time, our turn.

Well, I didn't hold to that kind of thinking. It was crazy. What the Lokhars had done—

I looked up at clouds racing the wind. They seemed like alien destroyers, their purple shapes sliding faster than I'd ever seen before. Dust swirled around me and shrieks whipped past my helmet. The apocalypse had come, the angel had sounded the last trumpet and the alien Lokhars had brought us Armageddon.

In a bleak frame of mind, I approached the Jelk freighters. I expected guards in spacesuits holding rifles to challenge me. There was nothing but dead grass and deader weeds.

I banged on an airlock. Using my fist, I hammered for a solid three minutes. Finally, a green light flashed and the airlock slid open with a tortured groan of metal. I didn't like the sound of that. Just how far gone was this thing?

I entered a steel chamber. The lock slammed shut behind me and hoses first blasted air and then chemical cleaning agents. It lasted longer than I would have expected. I thought about that. I realized if the bio-terminator made it inside the vessels, poof, there went a sizeable chunk of remaining humanity. It was good they went to such lengths. It meant some humans still had fight in their bellies. I needed that.

A second airlock opened and a voice in English asked me to strip. I complied, entered a third chamber and went through another chemical bath. In the fourth chamber I found clothes: jeans, a button shirt and running shoes.

Nostalgia slammed home. This would be the only world in the universe where I'd feel like I belonged. I took a deep breath, trying to prepare myself for the ordeal at hand. Then I entered a freighter world of sardine-packed survivors.

It was like a movie of old China or your favorite summer fair packed with jostling kids. Wall-to-wall people filled corridors, rooms, chambers, lounges and rows of seats. The smell of sweat and unwashed bodies slammed against me. The stench reminded me too much of prison or of any place that packed men together too tightly for too long.

As I looked around, I realized that was one of the problems. As a ratio of those remaining, too many men had survived, tough men, angry men, mean suckers with the look of death in their eyes as they stared back at me. There were too few children around and not enough women.

The squalor of these surroundings and the hopelessness I was seeing in so many faces made me doubt my plan for them. I didn't doubt my goal, but I did wonder if anything could shake these people out of their despair. This place was worse than a ghetto.

Then I met the leader as she and her henchmen made their way through the crowd. They were an intimidating crew and people shrank away from them.

The woman leading the crew was tall with wide hips, large breasts and surprisingly handsome features. She had thick dark hair tied in a ponytail and wore combat fatigues, with a big knife on her hip. She seemed like the queen of the Amazons, and I had no doubt she could fight.

Four huge henchmen followed, the smallest a head taller than me, making the man six-seven. The biggest man was black, had a bald head and moved in an athletic way that told me he was lethal. The man stared at me. I'd been in Black Sand and been around some vicious guard dogs before. The meanest had been a big brute of a Rottweiler that used to just stare and I'd known he'd wanted to bite a chunk out of me. The biggest henchmen had eyes like that and I felt his desire to tear me to shreds.

The group stopped before me, and the queen of the Amazons put her hands on her hips. "Are you the man from space?" she asked. She had a seductive voice, and it flowed through me with power. I was beginning to realize how she ruled this place.

I'd had a speech prepared for the occasion, but now I wasn't sure I should start that way. The woman, her henchmen, their glares and stances spoke volumes concerning their hostility toward me.

"Yeah," I said. "I'm the man from space."

Her shoulders shifted. It was a subtle thing. I don't know what she'd expected from me. "You look strong," she said.

"Hey, how about that," I said.

"But my men could take you..." She snapped her fingers. "Like that."

Maybe six weeks ago they could have taken me, but not after my training, increased strength, size and most of all, speed.

"I wouldn't bet any beer on them," I said.

She made a show of frowning, and glanced behind me before she stared into my eyes again. "You're brave, spaceman. I don't see any backup for you."

"Why would I need any?" I asked.

"I don't know. Your alien overlords nuked our world and then packed the few survivors into these tins cans. Now you're coming down here...what, to lay down the law?"

"How often has jumping to conclusions helped you?" I asked.

She shook her head. "I don't like your cockiness, mister. This is my place, my home, not yours."

"Do you want me to beat him up?" the black henchman asked, the one with the eyes like a Rottweiler.

She glanced at him. "I want to ask him a few questions first."

"Afterward?" he asked.

"It will depend on his answers," she said.

"I can make him eat his teeth," the henchman said.

"No one is as strong and quick as you, Demetrius," she said.

The man's chest swelled with pride and his big hands opened and closed.

"What if hurting me means the aliens burn this freighter down?" I snapped my fingers. "And all of you die like that?"

She smiled. It was a mean thing, but it had an effect. I reexamined her, the stance, the long hair, how her breasts strained against her combat fatigues. The woman had a sexual power, and she obviously knew how to use it, making her a master of manipulation. What was she trying to prove?

"What's it like up there?" she asked.

She'd threatened me with violence and she'd done it in front of her people. Now she openly quizzed me. I had plans, but those plans included me running things. That meant I had to do things right from the start.

"Did you hear me, spaceman?" she asked.

"It's cold up there," I said.

"That's not what I meant."

"And it's lonely," I added.

Her eyes narrowed, and her lips parted. It seemed she was about to give an order.

It struck me then that I was dealing with a ruthless individual. The freighters were like prison back in the day. The toughest, strongest and most ruthless had ruled there. The woman could never match Demetrius and those like him in physical strength. No doubt, she used intellect, cold-bloodedness and cunning to stay in charge. That meant I couldn't let her outmaneuver me and expect her to listen, really listen, to what I had to say. That meant I had to play an old game. The woman would only respect someone mentally stronger than herself.

"Mister," she said, "you want to be careful how you talk to me."

"That's funny," I said. "I was just about to tell you the same thing."

"Demetrius," she said, sidestepping away from me. "Hurt him, but don't kill him. I still have some questions I want answered."

Demetrius didn't lumber at me like most big men would have done. He looked to weigh three hundred and twenty pounds and had size and reach on me. He came like a black belt in karate, hands up and approaching carefully. This man had beautiful coordination, and I sensed he had unusual speed.

"Are you sure you want to go this route?" I asked the woman.

"You look muscular and I'm guessing the aliens think you're tough," she said. "I want to see if it's true."

"Fair enough," I said, before concentrating on Demetrius. "Are you planning on breaking any bones?"

He intensified his Rottweiler stare-down, and he opened and closed his hands several times. Then he made his first mistake. His eyes flickered to the right of me and gave a tight little nod. He shouldn't have done that.

It alerted me, and I heard the scuff of a boot behind and to my left. I guess the lady wasn't taking any chances on losing one of her bad boys. I slipped to the side and half turned. A slender man with a sap in his hand moved toward me from the crowd at my back. As he did, his hand and the sap he held blurred as it aimed for my head. I moved faster, and I caught his wrist and twisted. Those nearest must have heard his wrist-bones snap. The slender man's eyes went wide with shock. I pivoted, tucked my torso and hurled him at Demetrius. The body connected with a karate chop, and the slender man went down hard onto the deck plates.

Several things happened at once then. Instead of continuing his attack, Demetrius retreated. I saw the surprise on his face. He practiced caution, and it told me the man was more dangerous than I'd realized.

I picked up the leather-coated sap. While staring at the woman and using both hands, I tore the leather apart so lead shot rained onto the floor.

"He's stronger than he looks," Demetrius told her.

"And a whole lot faster," the woman said. "What did the aliens do to you?"

"Is that one of your questions?" I asked.

"Why are you so angry?" she said.

Her question ran deeper than my just being angry at the attack. She must have sensed the rage that boiled in me at the Lokhars, at the androids and Claath's highhanded manner toward the so-called human "beasts."

"Do you have any idea about the bargain I made that gained you this shelter?" I asked.

Unease entered her eyes. "Gained it for me specifically?" she asked.

The four henchmen, led by Demetrius, protectively flanked her and looked ready to charge me.

Did she think I'd picked her to be my woman? Is that how she interpreted my words?

"No, not just you," I said. "I bargained for everyone or anyone who happens to be living. I made sure they found survival in a Jelk freighter. This is about keeping the human race alive."

She traded glances with Demetrius. He gave another of his little nods. Facing me, she asked, "What did the bargain cost you?"

"We need to talk in private," I said instead of answering.

She stared at me for three seconds before saying, "Follow me."

I have to admit I didn't want to. They could ambush me or lead me to some horrific end. But I'd come alone for a reason. I had to believe these people still used reason. If they didn't...then everything I was doing would be moot anyway.

The woman halted and glanced back at me. "Are you coming or not?" she asked.

I nodded, and followed her, liking the sway of those hips.

She led us through a maze. Everywhere we went people jumped off the floor and slid against the walls, getting out of her way. Their actions told me the woman used terror at times. It also told me the aliens left humanity alone in the freighters. That part was good. This brutality...I didn't like it. Humanity was turning wolf again, falling back toward savagery. They were making Shah Claath's words true. I had to make them become lies.

We entered a larger corridor, with chairs along the sides and rugs thrown down. Many of the chairs held women, the most in one place and the prettiest I'd seen so far besides the leader. Many had pregnant bellies.

I approved of that part of it. I'm not sure they liked the men or the leader. But what could I do about that now? It was survival of the fittest, the meanest and the most hardheaded. I understood about the iron law of prison, the law of tooth and

111

claw as stated by Jack London in *Call of the Wild*. I should have realized it would be like this and prepared accordingly.

She sat in a chair and indicated another one facing her.

I noticed my chair had its back to the people in here. Picking it up, I repositioned the chair so I had a wall behind me.

She glanced at Demetrius before turning her chair to face me. "You're not too trusting," she said.

"Are you?" I asked.

She smiled faintly, and it was all the answer I needed.

"I'm Creed," I said.

She frowned, and I expected her to ask what my first name was. Instead, she said, "I've heard that name somewhere."

"Mad Jack Creed," I said.

"Who is that?" she asked.

"You never watched TV?"

Her eyes widened. "The shuttle pilot who went to meet the aliens, his name was Creed."

"He was my dad," I said.

"Oh. I'm sorry."

I shrugged. "He went the way he would have wanted. I can't say that for the rest of humanity."

"So why did the aliens do it?" she asked. "And why do you work for them?"

Her questions told me plenty. First, that Claath or the androids hadn't told these people much about anything.

"Before we really start," I said. "I need two things. To begin, what's your name?"

"Diana," she said.

"Like Diana the Huntress?" I asked.

"Yes," she said. "I'm the Roman moon goddess and I hunt those who displease me."

"I bet," I said. "Now the second thing I'm going to need to know is if you have any brandy, any booze at all."

"Why would you need to know that?"

"Because I need a drink," I said.

Diana measured me with her gaze, and finally, she glanced at Demetrius. The big henchmen growled an order. A pregnant woman slid off her chair, opened a cooler and brought him two Budweiser cans. He stood there, with one in each hand.

"Give our guest a beer," Diana said. "I'll take the other one."

Demetrius practically threw a can at me. With neuro-fiber-enhanced speed, I snatched it out of the air, doing it in a lazy way as if bored with them.

I noticed Diana's eyes: they shone with appreciation. Did she used to be a cage fighting junkie? This lady obviously knew about fighting men.

"Thanks," I said, popping the tab so spray fizzled out and then foam bubbled. I slurped the foam before guzzling the beer until I drained the can. That tasted good. "Get me another one," I said. "I have a lot to say and it's going to make my tongue dry."

I could see the wheels turning in Diana's mind. "Do it," she told Demetrius.

I tossed my empty can aside. Diana sipped from hers.

"Haven't had a beer for weeks," I said.

"Your masters don't give you any?" she asked.

I decided to let that pass. In truth, I appreciated her angry heat toward the aliens. At least she hadn't turned into a bootlicker.

"You run all three freighters or just this area?" I asked.

She measured me again with those blue eyes of hers. If I didn't know better, I would have felt as if she sized me up to be her partner. There was a hint of promise in her look. The terror I'd seen earlier in the people here cautioned me toward trusting what I saw in Diana. This woman used guile in everything. Of that I had no doubt.

"I run half this freighter," she said. "Rex Hodges is lord of the rest of it."

"Is someone in charge of everything?" I asked.

"You're with the aliens," she said. "That means you should know more about how things work down here. You shouldn't be asking me those kinds of questions."

"I'll tell you what," I said. "Everything you think you know about the situation and about me—erase it from your thinking.

Things aren't how you think they are. That's one of the reasons I'm here."

"What's that supposed to mean?"

"That you should listen more carefully to what I'm saying. Secondly, that you should hurry up and answer my questions. I don't have much time."

It took several seconds, but she nodded. "No one has had the guts to try to grab full power. Truth is we're not sure the aliens will let us."

"Are there any aliens aboard the freighters?"

She laughed in a throaty way. "Not a chance. We'd kill them if there were." She glowered at me. "Some of us have been wondering if you're here to impose some kind of martial alien law. Why are you here, spaceman? Tell us the truth."

One of the other henchmen handed me a second beer. I cracked the tab and sipped this time.

"Diana," I said, "the Lokhars destroyed our world. The Jelk, the one who owns these freighters, must have chased the Lokhar ship away."

"I don't know anything about that," she said.

I noticed she didn't say *we*, but *I*. That was important.

For the next several hours, I told her what I knew. Her men brought more beer and time passed as I related my story.

"It's bad then," Diana said. "The Jelk are our jailors or minders. You'd better win them that Altair Object."

"Tell me, Diana. What do you want out of life?"

She leaned back in her chair so the metal creaked. She eyed me, and I felt something stir. "Survive it for now, I guess. Keep running the show as long as I'm smart enough."

Several of her henchmen nodded.

"You're living like cons in here," I said. "That doesn't seem to be a way for the last humans to live."

"*Seems* doesn't have much to do with anything anymore," Diana said. "We're just doing it by keeping ourselves alive."

"Listen," I said. I figured it was time to broach the topic, to get down to the business of my visit. "What I'm seeing around me…it's going to take a strong and cunning person to change things for the better. Even more than that, it's going to take good ideas. You need to find truly hardheaded people among the leaders and their henchmen. You need to set up a secret society with the goal of supplanting the aliens."

As I talked, Diana's features became blank, a wall to hide her emotions or thoughts. "What you're saying sounds like you're betraying your word to the Jelk," she said. "Like treason."

I laughed bitterly. "Do you think it would be treason if a dog on a leash slithered free of its collar and wandered around town for a while? That's not treason. That's an animal breaking loose. The Jelk think we're beasts. Animals don't have any more loyalty than licking the hand that feeds them."

"It's really that bad?" Diana asked.

"Worse," I said, "much worse."

"We don't have a chance then. Our time is over."

"Wrong," I said. "But if you really think so, I'm talking to the wrong person."

Diana stroked her jaw, thinking. I didn't want her to think too much in the wrong direction. Meaning, I didn't want her hopeless but hopeful.

"Tell me, Diana. What did you do before this?"

"I ran a lumber mill in Alaska. It was hard work."

Her answer surprised me, and I doubted she told me the truth. But I would play along. "You know how to keep things going then," I said. "Running a gang in a place like this is more than heavy fists. You need to know how to deliver the goods, to keep order. You have a crew behind you and they look tough enough. But you—we—need more than that. You have to start a secret society that lives and breathes freedom for humanity. You have to start whipping these people into shape, teaching them the right things so they're ready to act when a real chance comes along."

"What exactly am I supposed to teach them?" she asked.

"I can't think of everything," I said. "I have enough troubles out in space. I helped buy you this opportunity, though. I bought our race time in order to turn things around. You have to come up with some ideas, with some schemes, on your own."

"Just what are you planning to do?" she asked.

I'd drunk a few beers, not that many, but enough to loosen up some. I pulled my chair closer to hers until our knees touched.

Her eyebrows rose, and I noticed Demetrius bristling. It must have been spite, but I patted her knee, letting my hand linger there.

"I don't plan on living the rest of my life being treated as a beast," I said in a low voice. "I don't plan on letting us sink into extinction. The cards are stacked against us. That's clear, right?"

She glanced at my hand before nodding.

"I'm going to cheat, Diana. I'm going to do whatever I can whenever I get the chance to reshuffle the deck. The truth is that I have no idea what I'm going to do exactly. I didn't know my entire plan when I charged up the ramp into the alien lander. I'm watching them closely. I'm learning, and I'm getting more dangerous every day. One thing I'm going to do is fight with every ounce of my mind and muscles to tear this slave collar off my neck. We're going to be free, and we're going to hammer the Lokhars like they've never believed possible."

"Big talk," Diana said.

"Yeah, you said it. I don't know where I read it, but a person once said that boldness is genius and has power all on its own. I plan to be bold like you wouldn't believe."

"Who dares, wins," Demetrius said. "Now take your hand off her knee."

I glanced at him, and in the interests of peace I took my hand away.

"You never heard that one?" he asked.

"No," I said.

"It was the SAS motto," he said. "The British Special Air Service."

I did note an accent, a slight one. If Demetrius used to be SAS, that would make him doubly dangerous.

"From your stories," Diana said, "your boldness has almost gotten you killed a couple of times. It seems to me you might try another way."

"Maybe," I said. "My boldness has also given humanity a slim opportunity to rise up from the ashes of total defeat. I need fighters, Diana. I need men and women back here who will dare to dream with me. Maybe I'm a fool to confide in you. I don't know. I have to take a chance. I have to practice boldness. I don't know how many of the various freighter shelters the Jelk are going to let me visit, but I'm going to keep preaching. You have to be ready."

"Ready for what?" she asked.

I shoved away from her and stood up. She and her listening henchmen stood with me. Demetrius hunched forward, with his hands opening and closing as if wanted to attack me again and finish it. He must still be thinking about my hand on her knee.

"Come on, Diana," I said. "You already know for what. Didn't you learn about your country's origin? Or did you go to the new public schools that forgot to teach old-fashioned American values like freedom, liberty and courage? George Washington, Thomas Jefferson and Patrick Henry: 'Give me liberty or give me death.' Do you want to be a dog the rest of your existence?"

"Hell no," she said.

"Some of us are in space," I said. "Some of us are down here getting the people ready."

"You don't think the aliens monitor us then?" Diana asked.

"Yeah," I said. "They do, but not in the way we think."

Diana nodded slowly and I could see she really was thinking about what I'd said.

"Okay," I said. "I don't know how much time I have left down here, but I need to talk to Rex Hodges and rest of the leaders in this complex. Can you arrange it?"

Diana pursed her lips. "I like your spirit, spaceman. You've given me hope again, something I'd thought I'd lost forever. I don't know if you're a crazy man or for real. Let's go talk to Hodges. It's been some time since I've seen him. He's a tough one, though, an ex-pro football star who played tackle for the Cowboys."

"You're kidding," I said. "That Rex Hodges?"

"The same," Diana said.

"Yeah," I said. "Let's go."

117

-11-

I should have thought harder on what Diana asked: "Don't the aliens listen to or monitor us?"

Claath claimed to view us as animals. How did the androids view us? How closely did the androids work with the Saurians? The lizards didn't have any reason to love me.

After spending half a day in the Baja freighter complex, I trudged back to the waiting air-car and the android pilot.

The other leaders had been big, tough and willing to crack heads to get what they wanted. Henchmen backed them, and the leaders knew how to divide the little food, water and wealth in their possession to keep the rest from rioting. Otherwise, what I'd seen depressed me. If the other freighters were like this, humanity hung on by a thread. We'd all become beggars, living off scraps tossed us by the Jelk and packed into steel-walled slums.

That galled me. The Lokhars—no! I didn't want to dwell on them right now. I had too much to do.

I strode angrily to the waiting air-car. It rested where the android had landed us: between two almond orchards. Every bare branch was a testament to bio-terminator effectiveness. The brittle leaves lay like a dead carpet, the last of their kind. How long until the almond trees crashed upon the dying soil? How long until every trace of them vanished?

I shook my head, heading for the entrance.

Air-car was a misnomer. It was the size of dump truck and must have carried a fusion power plant inside. The pilot sat up top ten feet from the ground under a clear canopy.

118

The android stared down at me. I pointed at the entrance. He kept staring as if he held a grudge. Did one of them care if another had died by my hand? The androids had always seemed emotionless: bio-zombies made in the image of men. Did this one remember I'd killed an abusive DI?

Isaac Asimov, the author of *I, Robot*, had created the three laws of robotics. The key was that no robot could harm men. Clearly, the androids had never heard of that rule.

The pilot continued to stare down at me.

My hand dropped to my side, but I didn't carry a gun. I wished then I'd worn the bio-suit. I would have jumped and clawed my way up to him and smashed through the canopy and ask him what his problem was.

I glanced around for a rock, and decided a length of broken branch would have to do. Weighing it in my hand, I heaved and watched it twirl before striking the canopy.

The android didn't flinch, but he turned his head and it appeared as if his arm moved.

The door before me slid open.

I climbed in, heard it swish shut and endured the cleansing agents washing over me. First shedding the spacesuit, I climbed naked up a ladder and into the main salon. The pilot sat up front. He turned and regarded me.

I don't know. I suppose by the way he'd been acting that I expected him to hold a gun. He didn't. I wanted to ask him why he'd taken his sweet time to open the door. I decided that before I began an interrogation I'd don my bio-suit.

I moved to the cylinder and pressed the button. Nothing happened.

"I have locked it," the android said in his cold voice.

Something uneasy settled in my stomach. That something hardened into a knot of resolve. I was going to have to kill another android. I didn't know why, but my gut said to get ready. I straightened, turned and moved toward him.

"Remain where you are," he said.

"Open my locker. I'm not going to ride around in the nude."

"You will sit or I will subdue you," the android said.

"Did they give you a shocker?"

119

The android turned in his swivel chair toward his controls. I moved, using every neuro-fiber planted in me. He wore living plastic bio-skin and had machine-like reflexes. His hand slid toward a red button. I beat him by the barest fraction, grabbed his elbow and yanked so his fingers hit the panel but no controls.

The first thing I discovered after that was that this android was stronger than the DI. Maybe he was a different model. He swiveled again, toward me, and with a meaty smack, he pile-drove a fist against my gut. It hurt, and would have ruptured a regular man's stomach. The steroid sixty-five had changed me. Living in double Earth gravity for weeks had strengthened every muscle I owned. I endured, grunted and slammed an elbow against his face, knocking him off the chair.

"You plot against the Jelk," he said.

"Fancy that," I said. I wanted to double-up and groan. My gut ached. This android could punch. If I could help it, I wouldn't let him put his hands on me again.

"I have recorded everything you said in the freighters," he bragged in his cold voice, "and I will play it to our master on our return."

"You're a tricky one, eh?" I said. "No. Let me tell you something. You haven't recorded anything. You're guessing, bluffing."

From on the floor, he slid away from me, creating a track in the dust there. He stood, with the pilot's chair between us. "You are a rogue and for the good of all you must be destroyed."

I decided to play an idea. "Why do you want to be a slave to Claath? Join me. Become free and think for yourself."

He tilted his head, and for the first time, I witnessed emotions in his shark-like plastic eyes.

"We are not slaves but we are the true men," he said, "without the flaws of you Earthbeasts. We serve the Jelk in the promise of further advancements."

"What's that mean?" I asked.

"Advancements," he said, "greater modifications bringing about greater perfection."

"You're kidding, right? You toady to the Jelk in hope of upgrades and because of that you think you're a true man?"

"You are a plague," the android said. "You will bring harm to the Jelk, which will possibly bring harm to us because Shah Claath might come to distrust those in your likeness."

"You think I'm trouble, is that it?"

"You have destroyed androids. You plot against our benefactor and creator."

"Oh boy," I said. "Claath has done a number on you."

"Return to your seat. We will head to space so I can make my report."

"How did you do it?" I asked. "You must have planted a bug in my spacesuit? No. You must have put a bug in my hair or something."

The android tilted his head. "Bug?"

"A micro-recording device," I said.

"Yes: a bug. I recorded your conversations and learned of your plan."

"Why did Claath tell you to do that?" I asked.

"We protect the Jelk. We take the pains. He is our benefactor and creator. Return to your seat. I will not ask you again."

"That's right," I said. "You won't."

I lunged over the pilot's seat, and we fought a bitter battle there in the cockpit. He was strong. I was quicker, deadlier and carried the weight of humanity on my shoulders. I lost skin and came close to losing my right eye. Those plastic fingers could stab like iron rods. It took dragging my entire body over the chair and using my legs in a wrestling hold I'd learned from watching cage fighting. This was like some of the worst fights in prison. I grunted, gasped for air and used my forehead like a battering ram. A broken nose didn't stop him, though. Finally, while losing more skin and sweating like a pig, I managed to work behind the android and used a full nelson. Bit by bit, I drove his head forward until his chin touched his chest. I bunched my muscles, roared and became dizzy from the exertion.

"You should have sided with us," I whispered in his ear.

"You... are beasts," he whispered. "Claath is a creator."

121

That's what I needed to hear. Rage added fuel to my tired limbs. I pushed, broke his neck and found that he yet lived.

The next few minutes weren't pretty. I'm not proud of them. I learned things about androids that made me wonder. Did this android live as I lived, as people lived, or was he a robot which in the end was no different from a toaster? I guess I'm asking if he had a soul. If he did...my deeds crossed the line. If not...I'm exonerated even though I felt guilty.

I could have taken the easy road, shrugged and said an android had no soul. Probably, that would have been better for my conscience. I couldn't do that, though. I wasn't a genocidal Lokhar. I was a man.

I made the android talk, at least in a sense. I found out enough to realize that no one else knew what he did. I discovered his computer file of incriminating evidence—deleting it—and I learned the beginning procedures of flying this dumpster-sized air-car. Afterward, I killed him or shut him down. Take your pick of which you believe.

To him, I was the devil, and I guess from his point of view he was right. Damn, I hadn't wanted complications of the soul. But there they were: black stains to haunt me.

I felt shaky as I staggered to my place in the salon. I had a problem: a dead android on my hands. I knew what Claath had told me. I wasn't supposed to destroy any more of his property. Otherwise, I was a dead man. Okay. I had to think of something, a way to cover myself.

Sitting there, staring out a window, watching the purple clouds race over a dead almond orchard, I realized what I needed to do.

With a grunt, I stood. If I was going to do this, I had to get started right away.

***

I visited several more freighters before staging a flying accident. Would Claath have statistics for his android pilots? Would he automatically suspect me of troublemaking?

I couldn't see any way around this. So, I planted verbal seeds in a few more freighter leaders and searched for the worst weather patterns. I found them in the former Northwest Territories of Canada. They were hurricane level storms.

Before setting up the accident, I studied everything I could about the air-car, its computers and the info stored in them that might help me later. I searched for clues, for space knowledge and an edge over the Jelk. I read as fast as I could, not really thinking about what I saw. I'd mull over the stuff later.

Finally, as time ticked on, I decided I had to act. I didn't know how long Claath had given the android to chauffer me around the Earth.

I had to make this look real or I'd die. I donned my living armor, helmet and breather and flew into an orange-colored storm. Howling winds buffeted the air-car. I'd strapped the android in his chair, readied the auto-pilot and staggered to the couches in the back of the salon.

I'd barely buckled in when the air-car went up. I didn't have long to wait and the vehicle abruptly plowed down toward the Earth. Through the canopy I saw the ground rushing near. We had to be going over one-fifty, maybe one-seventy-five.

I clenched my teeth, braced my body and then everything becoming crashing, crunching metal. I slammed against the restraints and lost conciseness. I don't know how long I was out.

When I came to, wind howled around me. I groaned and it hurt my chest to breathe, with a stab of pain each time in my heart. Slowly, with nearly frozen fingers, I unbuckled. Everywhere around me were shards of canopy and razor edges of broken, twisted, metallic air-car. If I hadn't worn the bio-battlesuit, I'd never have made it. Despite my best efforts, metal pressed or cut against me, but the living armor held.

I wondered as I worked free of the wreckage, if powered armor would have lasted the crash. I think the living armor could take greater punishment because it had more flexibility. Finally, after oozing through a jagged, shard-cutting tunnel of metal, I flopped onto snow and crawled away from the strangely buzzing craft. I think one of my legs was broken. It hurt badly enough.

I crawled and crawled before looking back. That was a good wreck. Maybe I should have checked the android first, but I wasn't in any shape to have tried. Besides, I didn't know if the air-car's fusion core had ruptured. I could take *some* radiation, but wasn't sure how much would kill my armor and me.

I crawled to a field of bare, porous rocks, what must have been lava ages ago. Farther away was a large pine forest minus any evergreen needles. Those had fallen, all of them, making it a bald evergreen forest. I'd never seen one of those.

Seven weeks ago all this had been alive. Now it was dead or dying the final death.

I shook my head and waited. Would android rescuers come? Would Saurians drop down? Maybe whoever watched the black boxes aboard the air-cars figured we'd both died in the crash and good riddance to the troublesome Earther. I hadn't worried about setting up a rescue beacon because I figured that would be an automatic thing. Yet what did I really know about the aliens and how they operated?

I told myself that the Jelk was in charge. Claath and his kind thought of profits. It wasn't profitable to let a mercenary just die. Hmm, what about the fuel costs? That was the cynical, nasty side of my brain thinking. What did it cost in fuel to bring an air-car or a lander down here? Maybe to come searching for me would cost more fuel that Claath figured I was worth.

They weren't pleasant thoughts. And I disliked having to rely on the Jelk for rescue. Maybe my thinking seems ungrateful to some of you reading my memoir. After all, Claath had sent down a few freighters for the last humans. So one could argue humanity owed him. I would point out that it had been Claath's plan to use hundreds of millions of Earthers that had sent the Lokhars here in the first place. I realize Claath hadn't attacked our planet, but hadn't he been the germ of our catastrophe? Besides, I doubted Claath had planned to quietly hire hundreds of millions of mercenaries, but to capture and subdue the same number of Earthers. One way or another, the Jelk Corporation had helped screw mankind.

I endured among the rocks, growing faint, and finally my leg began to ache like a son of a bitch.

"I thought you were supposed to give me something for the pain," I told the bio-suit.

Maybe the crash had injured the living armor. Maybe the bio-terminator was killing the suit.

I tried to find a more comfortable position. It didn't happen. I was one giant bruise and ache. The wind picked up and I listened to it shriek for hours: the sounds of a dying world.

How long would my air supply last?

The androids were freaks, but I suppose I could see their point of view. That this one had called Claath his creator troubled me. Did that make the androids religious?

I chuckled. Claath was their god, and he didn't really care one way or another for his creations, other than to profit by them. I wouldn't want that kind of god looking out for me.

Angling my head, I shifted my gaze upward. I laughed, and even to my ears it sounded crazy. High up there in the atmosphere I saw a bright orange thruster glow. The rescue team cometh, rah, rah, rah.

I might have passed out then. I don't remember too well. Next time I looked, the orange glow had become a slender rocket. The flames licked against snow and thunder boomed through me.

This seemed familiar, but I couldn't place why.

The shaking ground caused me to raise my chin off my chest. I opened my eyes. I'd passed out again. Like on an old 50's sci-fi magazine cover, the rocket fins touched down and sometime later, a ladder extended to the ground. I'd never seen this model of spacecraft before.

Time crawled until I saw three suited figures climb down the ladder. These three had tails—Saurians, lizards. They bore weapons.

I would have climbed to my feet, but I couldn't. My muscles had frozen. I watched them circle the wreck. They pointed their weapons at it. Finally, they stopped and seemed to confer.

I tried to get up. Pain lanced through me. I groaned, and my eyelids fluttered. Unconsciousness threatened. Despite a horrible, throbbing headache, I strove to remain awake and barely won the fight.

"Over here," I whispered. "I'm over here."

The comm-equipment in the helmet didn't work anymore. They didn't hear me.

In despair, I watched the lizards turn back for their rocket.

"Wait," I whispered. "Here, here."

I lacked weapons, I had no radio and I wondered vaguely if my dream of freeing mankind would perish with me. Dmitri the Cossack had the right heart and he was tough, but he lacked the cunning. Rollo might have guessed my plans, but I doubted he would see them through.

"Oh boy," I muttered. Would the android have prayed to Claath's for aid, or was that beyond the cultured-grown plastic man? I don't know. I did pray, though, although not to Claath.

"Give me strength, please, God. I have to do this. We're on the brink of extinction."

Gritting my teeth, I tried again. An even fiercer headache exploded into existence, a nova bomb starting behind my eyes and radiating backward. Vomit stirred in the back of my throat. Slowly, I dragged an arm across my chest. I closed my eyes to help lessen the headache, but that only caused fiery splotches to appear before my eyelids. I drew a ragged breath and worked forward. Blood bounded in my head, or that's what it felt like. I mustered everything then, gripped a stone I'd spotted earlier and pushed against the rock I sat against. I worked up to my feet, opened my eyes to stare at the departing lizards and heaved the stone.

The bio-suit must have woken up a last time. I'm not sure if it had a will to live or not. Did trees? The thing amplified the little strength I had, and that stone sailed.

I wouldn't have been able to gather the strength to throw another projectile. Despite the howling wind, despite the distance, that stone clipped the rearmost Saurian.

The lizard turned. He must have seen me. I toppled into the snow and lay still, expended and spent.

Time had no meaning afterward, just my breathing and near sobbing. I dearly wanted to live. I had to defeat Claath, to shove his thumb off us. I had Lokhars to payback, but most of all, I had a human race to save from destruction.

I found myself staring at a three-toed boot standing in snow. The lizards—I think they circled me.

I tried to move my head, but I couldn't. Everything I'd had, I'd used. Did they know who I was?

Saurian hands, claws, talons, whatever, reached down and hauled me upright. I found myself staring into lizard eyes.

"That's right," I muttered. "I'm alive, you bastard."

I don't think it heard me. I'm certain it hated me. I passed out, so I'm not sure what happened exactly. The next thing I experienced was the grinding acceleration of liftoff.

I was on my way back into space and maybe to a confrontation with Claath about a wrecked air-car and a dead as nails android. So be it, at least for the moment I was alive.

-12-

My left thigh was broken, along with several ribs and a badly bruised neck. Without the bio-suit I'm sure I would have died in the air-car "accident."

I was placed a healing tank. It reminded me of the story of Achilles, the Greek hero of the Trojan War. When he'd been a baby, his mother had dipped him into the river of Death, the river Styx. The dip in Death had made him invulnerable from harm. The only trouble was that his mom had gripped him by the heel. It meant his one heel had never gotten the Styx treatment. Paris the archer—the Trojan who'd jetted off with Helen and thereby started the ten-year feud—shot Achilles with an arrow toward the end of the war. One of the gods aiding the Trojans guided the arrow to the heel—the Achilles heel. Blood poisoning must have set in afterward. The point of the tale, I guess, was that Achilles' mom should have switched heels and made all of him invulnerable.

The healing tank didn't make me immune to harm, but it did speed up the knitting process. In that way, I felt like Achilles.

Several days after the incident, I could walk again and my ribs didn't hurt every time I took a breath. Maybe Claath had been waiting for that.

An android in cyber-armor entered the hospital wing of the ship. We were in orbit over the Earth.

"You will gather your possessions and come with me," the android said.

My things were my shirt, pants, shoes and several new scars. The healing tank hadn't taken care of everything.

The android marched through an easy two miles of corridors, his magnetic boots clanging every step of the way. The vessel was huge. The regular *thrum* I'd felt in other spacecraft was lacking in this one. I began to wonder if this was Claath's private ship.

The android and I entered a small room with a metal table and chair. My minder indicated the furniture, and said, "Sit."

I was glad to get off my feet. The bones had mended and most of the tissue knit back together, but I'd lost stamina.

A screen flickered into life, and I viewed Claath. I finally wondered about that. Why hadn't he ever met me in person? Why all these meetings via screen? What did he have to hide? Or was he that paranoid about my "beastliness?" The red-skinned alien took his time while he studied me, and *I* became paranoid. Was he going to accuse me of destruction of property? Not that he'd be wrong, but then I'd likely be dead.

He inhaled sharply, and said, "You have inordinately bad luck. I find that a poor quality for a battle-beast. Maybe I've made a mistake with you."

I shook my head. "It didn't have anything to do with *my* luck but that of the android piloting the ship."

"Hmm," Claath said. "If that's the case, then it would seem that those around you have the bad luck, which amounts to the same thing."

I slapped the table. "I'm the one who should be complaining. I broke bones because of an android's carelessness. He nearly got me killed. I hope for both your and my sake that none of them are coming along on the mission."

The android in the room stirred.

Claath noticed. "Do you wish to add something N7?"

"I do, sir," the android—N7— said.

"I give you leave to speak," Claath said.

"Thank you, sir," N7 said. "I state for the record that the pilot was in perfect working order. I further note that all androids test out before departing the ship. The implications of this slanderous beast—"

"Who are you calling a beast, you pile of junk?" I snarled. "I was there. You weren't. I know what happened. So don't give me any of your sanctimonious robot crap."

The android no longer stirred, but I felt hostility radiating from him. He'd turned from the screen and faced me.

"Interesting," Claath said. "You have an uncanny gift, beast. For years, I've attempted to add emotional makeup to my androids, and my techs have always failed me. You, however, appear to have created anger in several different models. If for no other reason, I am loath to destroy you."

"What do you mean, destroy me?" I asked in outrage. "I've done everything you've asked and now you talk about destroying me. What kind of double-cross is this?"

"The androids are excellent pilots," Claath said, "better than the best Saurian."

"Have you been down to Earth lately?" I asked. "Have you seen some of those storms?"

"Did you purposely destroy my property: the air-car and android?" Claath asked.

I'd been waiting for a direct question. "No!" I said, generating hatred at the Jelk, at the android and at humanity's awful position in the universe. I assumed Claath used some kind of lie-detector that monitored my heart rate, brain rhythms and other bodily functions. With my hatred I hoped to mask these signs.

The Jelk glanced at something I couldn't see, with his eyes darting like a hunting weasel. He checked a medical report, no doubt. He studied me afterward, and I'd swear he looked perturbed. "You continue to claim the wind blew your air-car off course?" he asked.

"I haven't claimed anything other than android negligence," I said. "I could have piloted the air-car better than he did."

"I assure you," Claath said, "you could have done no such thing. Their flight reflexes are amazing. It is their primary function."

"Creator," N7 said, with something approaching heat in his voice.

"I've told you not to call me that," Claath said. "It is sacrilegious."

"I ask your pardon," N7 said.

"Yes, yes," Claath said. "Now what did you want to say?"

"Sir," the android said. "The beast…he lies."

"Indeed," Claath. "And how to you know this?"

"It is the only rational explanation," N7 said. "The pilot would have made an emergency report—"

"Yeah," I said. "He tried. That's what got us killed. I told him to keep his eyes on the controls. He was too busy following your rote procedures when the wind flipped us and hurled us down."

N7 faced me, and his right hand dropped onto the butt of his weapon.

Of course I was lying, and I was doing it as hard and as effectively as I could. What choice did I have? Hmm, what was the old saying? "Terror was the weapon of the weak." Well, my position was the weakest, and so I used what I could.

"Contain yourself," Claath told the android.

"Yes, sir," N7 said. "But the beast's lies, they are absurd and insulting."

"Interesting," Claath said. "You are insulted?"

N7 appeared surprised, and he nodded, seemingly reluctantly. "Yes, sir, the beast insults me."

"What is your wish regarding him?" Claath asked.

"Let me destroy him, sir. He must have destroyed the pilot. It would be just for him to cease being as well."

I gathered myself, getting ready to lunge at N7. He might have cyber-armor and a weapon, but I'd fight until the last. He'd learn what calling me a beast would earn him.

"You may be right concerning his irrationality, N7," Claath said. "Yet he is a ferocious creature, a veritable killer. If he destroyed an N-model android…that would be most impressive."

"Sir?" N7 asked. "Would that not prove him too wild to trust?"

"No," Claath said, while watching me. "I trust him to stir the other Earthbeasts to violent action on the corporation's behalf. The success of your mission rests on it."

"What a minute," I said. "The androids are coming on the artifact hunt?"

Claath seemed amused. "You will need pilots and weapons officers. I can't send the Saurians."

"Why not?" I asked.

The humor evaporated. "Do not question me," Claath said. "I am the Jelk, the superior. You are my property. I am not your property."

I looked down lest he see my eyes. Someday I was going to put a collar on Claath. Achilles had dragged Hector around Troy in his chariot. I was going to drag Claath a lot farther than that.

"Please, sir, give me the word," N7 said. "Let me destroy him."

"What kind of robot are you?" I asked.

"I am an android with the same style of bio-brain as yours," N7 said, "although mine is fully integrated and civilized."

"Yet your civilized brain wants to kill me," I needled him. "You sound like an animal."

"Quiet," Claath told us.

N7 faced the screen and stood rigidly like a statue. I couldn't even see him breathe now. His eyelashes didn't even twitch.

I waited, wondering what would happen next.

Claath seemed to measure me with his eyes. "The Saurians cannot join the expedition for the simple reason that anyone capturing or finding a destroyed Saurian craft would realize they had acted on Jelk orders. That would implicate the corporation, and that must be avoided at all costs."

I shouldn't have said it, but I did: "So why are you telling *me* all this?"

Claath flicked his fingers in a dismissive gesture. "You cannot implicate the corporation. Any Earthbeast beyond the emitting range of the central assault ship will die."

"What's that mean?" I asked.

"I know you've received punishment shocks," Claath said. "The controller in your neck has other uses, too. If any Earthbeast drifts beyond range of the emitter, the device will explode, killing the creature."

132

"What?" This was outrageous.

"It is an obvious procedure," Claath said, "and it solves my dilemma of having any of you creatures inadvertently creating an incident."

"Now wait a minute," I said. "We're mercenaries, not slaves."

Claath gave me a pointy-toothed smile. "You wear the controller. Therefore it is clear that I make the rules. You are whatever I say you are. It would be good for you to finally come to terms with the idea."

I'd *never* come to terms with it. "Why should we go into battle wearing a suicide device?" I asked.

"I'm glad you asked," Claath said. "It is central to the reason why you're alive instead of drifting in space, heading toward this system's sun to incinerate."

I scowled.

"You've proven yourself an interesting creature in more ways than one," Claath said. "You achieve results. That is your critical quality. With primitive weapons and after shrugging off the *tamer* ray, you stormed and captured a Saurian lander. Later, with nothing but your hands, you destroyed an abusive DI and it is possible you engineered an air-car accident. Why you would have done so doesn't interest me, although I suspect it has something to do with your outlandish notions of human equality. You are an odd beast, and it may be that your ideas give you strength of will. Very well, I accept that. The universe is a strange place, with many unusual creatures and events. A Jelk does not insist reality conform to every one of his whims or preconceptions. A Jelk uses what he finds to grind every particle of profit he can for himself and the corporation. It's what has made us the most powerful species in space."

He loves bragging. How can I use that against him?
"Okay," I said.

"You seek to keep your species alive," Claath said. "I have found that that idea does indeed motivate you Earthbeasts. Now I am about to test your battle quality in a real situation. Is your fighting power inferior or superior? I have let you visit the freighters on Earth for a single reason: for you to see how slender a thread the rest of humanity hangs on to existence.

Yours is a physically strong but mentally and emotionally weak species. If I summon the freighters and I empty them in space, humanity as a species dies. The only thing keeping them alive is the Earthbeasts in my employ. Fight well and your species lives. Fight poorly or run away and your species will cease to exist. You appreciate that fact more than the others do, and I believe you will help the others to recognize the importance of fighting well and getting me what I want."

"Okay," I said, "I get it," and I did. Claath threatened humanity with extinction. He was little better than the Lokhars. If we failed to get him profits: goodbye freighters and goodbye humanity.

"It is for these reasons that you are alive," Claath said. "Your vigor and desire to see your people live gives me leverage on you. Fight as hard for me as you fight for your people and we can do business together."

"I hear you loud and clear," I said. "And you can bet I'll fight hard. Are you giving me command of the space-assault troopers?"

"Don't be ridiculous," Claath said. "Then you would attempt to foment rebellion. You will lead your maniple and the others will continue to lead theirs. I am however, sending an Earthbeast representative to the Starkiens."

"Who are they?" I asked.

"They are independent contractors, little better than pirates," Claath said with distaste. "You will use their ships to reach the Altair system. As contractors, they're willing to deal with the corporation and earn some quick cash."

"Right," I said, beginning to understand his reasoning. "And if Starkien ships take damage, you can deny the Jelk Corporation had anything to do with this mess."

"For such an emotional creature, you are perceptive," Claath said. "I believe I've made a wise choice deciding upon you as the Earthbeast representative."

"Sure," I said. *Drag you around and around the walls of Troy while you choke to death.* "I'm still curious about the androids, though. Anyone who finds one of them will realize the Jelk funded the attack."

"You're right except for one particular, which makes you wrong," Claath said. "The N-series androids are fitted with similar explosive devices as you space-assault troopers. We sell such androids everywhere, so their carcasses, just like yours, will not implicate us."

I'll say this for Claath: he was a coldhearted businessman. I turned to the android, wondering how I could use this last piece of information. "And you're okay with being wired to blow?" I asked N7.

"We serve our creator," the android said, "our designer."

Claath cleared his throat in an imperious manner, his chin rising as he did so.

"Let me rephrase," N7 said. "We have no problem with Jelk directives."

"That's bloody marvelous," I said. "When do we go?"

"The expedition leaves tomorrow," Claath said.

-13-

We were about to embark on our first mission as space-assault troopers to steal, purloin, or acquire for the Jelk Corporation, the Altair Object, a Forerunner artifact. As the Earth representative, I learned for the first time the number of commandos to be employed on the mission.

I'd expected Claath to use on the order of two or three thousand. Instead, to my amazement, the number was twenty-three thousand space-assault troopers.

The number surprised me for a variety of reasons. Firstly, as Claath had hinted earlier, Rollo, Dmitri, Ella and I had trained in maniples of twenty troopers per, never more.

I was designated Firstman Creed, the maniple leader. Under me were my sergeants or secondmen: Secondman Rollo, Secondman Dmitri and so forth. It was a simple system, made so the likes of us could understand the hierarchy.

In essence, the firstmen were lieutenants. The space-assault troopers lacked anything higher like captains, majors, colonels or generals. It seemed like a weakness. I suppose Claath figured the Starkiens or the androids would act as captains and maybe colonels, maneuvering the maniples as they wished. It seemed like an unwieldy way to do it. I mean, commanding hundreds of twenty-man maniples would put a lot of stress on the directing android or Starkien. Wouldn't it be easier to marshal us into larger formations like companies or battalions, at least? Then we'd be trained to coordinate and fight as twenty-three thousand commandos, not as hundreds of separate squads acting semi-independently.

I didn't like such inefficiency, especially as we would likely have to pay for any errors with our lives. And as yet, we knew nothing about the Forerunner object and how we were supposed to assault and acquire it. For a race concerned about their investment, the Jelk seemed to be setting us up for a lot of casualties.

Despite Claath's words, it took another week before we actually left the solar system. My bones needed the extra time to mend and I exercised hard to bring myself back to peak condition.

Finally, we left Earth and the solar system behind as the fleet entered its first jump route or line.

I'd been wondering about that for some time: not jump routes specifically, but how the aliens beat the laws of physics. Things with mass like a spaceship and light, too, of course, couldn't move faster than the speed of light. That was an immutable law of nature. Normally a journey at light speed would take 4.3 years to travel to Alpha Centauri, the nearest star to Earth with planets. Nothing with mass could reach the speed of light, but close enough so that all kinds of problems arose, like time dilation.

Why would that be a problem? Well consider. Back on Earth during the Age of Sail, galleons might be gone for months and even a year, but not for 4.3 years and certainly not for ten or twenty years. So how could anyone have a star empire or an interstellar corporation while traveling within the constraints of light speed or a bit under light speed? The answer was clear: they couldn't. You needed magic, or a science we'd never heard about, in order to flit from star system to star system fast enough to have interstellar empires and corporations.

The technology that allowed ships to jump along these lines was just that. Think of one of those connect-the-dot puzzles you used to draw as a kid. The dots were the star systems, the pencil lines were the jump lanes, lines, points, whatever you want to call them. A spaceship went in at one end and popped out the other in a few hours, having traveled many lights years. Just like in connect-the-dots, some points had one line running through them and some had three, five or seven lines. Those dots with seven different routes were strategic points in the stellar system. Control one of those critical star systems and you could control entire routes.

None of us had seen a star map or knew which jump route went to which star. Our N-series android minders simply told us to get ready for a jump. Then we hurried to our cots, lay down, strapped in and endured.

After the first jump we learned they were bad, with terrible headaches, cramps, disorientation and vomiting. We dreaded being ordered to get ready after that. I think even the androids hated the jumps, which made me incline toward thinking of them as living creatures instead of just machines. And that didn't help my conscience any.

After three jumps, we met the Starkiens, the contractors who would pilot the frigates and corvettes to take us into the Altair system.

I had no idea what Claath had told them about us. My introduction to the Starkiens came a few days later aboard one of their vessels.

N7 entered our training area and told me to accompany him to the meeting.

"Now?" I asked.

My maniple practiced hand-to-hand combat on the mats, with my secondmen prowling around to make sure no one became too angry.

"It is time," N7 said. Like before, he wore cyber-armor and carried a sidearm. He looked like the perfect choirboy with artificially fair features, trusting eyes and smooth, bio-plastic skin. He had the stamp of perfection: not of a Nietzsche superman but of the ultimate butt-kissing underling.

"Do I need to wear my bio-suit?" I asked.

"Negative," N7 said.

"Let me shower first."

"Come now," N7 said. "It is an order."

I'd fought several practice rounds with several of my soldiers and my shirt was sweaty, while a welt showed on my left cheek because one of the boys had almost pinned me.

"Sure, boss," I said. "And if my stench offends the Starkiens, then what?"

"The Starkiens are under Jelk command," N7 said. "Your odor or lack thereof is meaningless."

"Negative," I said. "I'm the Earth rep and I'm showering and shaving. Gotta look presentable, you know. Give me ten minutes and I'll be with you."

"I have given you an order," N7 said.

"That's right. And I'm complying with the order...after I take a shower."

The android drew his sidearm, pointing the barrel at my face so I could see inside the pitted orifice. This gun had been used plenty of times, which I found interesting.

I grinned, and made a show of looking around the crowded chamber. My maniple of troopers had already stopped practicing, most of them lying on the mats and breathing heavily. They now stood to their feet and glowered at N7.

"Hey, how about that," I said. "If you shoot me, these mercenaries will tear you to pieces."

"I do not fear destruction," N7 said.

"Bully for you," I said. "That makes you a fool and a liability."

N7 stepped closer so the barrel bumped against my forehead.

"A good soldier fears death," I told him. "The fear helps motivate the soldier to action and thereby keeps him alive to fight again another day."

"Fear is akin to cowardice," N7 said. "Cowardice is against the laws of androids."

"You want to obey Claath's orders, is that right?" I asked, deciding on a different tack.

"I do obey. Now you must obey."

"Right," I said. "If you're torn to pieces—destroyed—you will not have obeyed Claath's order to go to the Starkien meeting. You will have made those orders impossible. I, too, will be missing. In fact, our arguing with each other is eating up time. I'm going to shower and then I'll be right with you."

For the first time since he'd entered the chamber, N7's head swiveled as he surveyed my maniple of troopers inching toward him.

Abruptly, he holstered his sidearm, folded his plastic arms across his chest and half turned away from me.

I hadn't liked the barrel pressed against my forehead and I hadn't been sure which way N7 would jump. Maybe it had been foolish pushing him so far, but I had my reasons for wanting to be presentable to the Starkiens. I'd also just gained more credibility in the eyes of my men, and showed them what kind of human-haters the androids were.

"Good choice, chief," I told him. "Rollo, finish the exercises. Then use your best judgment. I don't know how long I'll be gone." With that, I jogged for the nearest shower. I didn't want to keep the android waiting.

***

I wore a jumpsuit uniform, my Bowie knife and a spacesuit with the helmet hanging on the back near my neck. I rode beside N7 in a shuttle he piloted.

Behind us drifted seven Jelk battlejumpers, ugly, utilitarian vessels. Our shuttle was a speck compared to them. Below swirled an orange gas giant maybe one hundred thousand kilometers away. Outlined against the gas giant drifted a hundred or so shark-shaped spacecraft. They looked deadly, but what did I know about space battle? Precious little was the answer.

Much farther away, about half the size of the moon as seen from Earth, blazed this system's sun. How far were we from the solar system? Three jumps away, I knew, but what did that mean?

"Those are the pirate ships?" I asked, pointing at the shark-shaped vessels.

"That is the Starkien contract fleet," N7 said.

"There are a lot of them."

N7 ignored the comment.

I glanced at him sidelong. Something had been bothering me for some time. Why had the Jelk made the androids based on humans from Earth? Had that occurred on a whim? Or was there a significant reason for it?

"How old are you, N7?" I asked.

He surprised me by answering. "Five standard years," he said.

"How long is a standard year compared to an Earth year?" I asked.

"I am six and half Earth years old," he said.

"You're young."

"No. I have survived three times the average timespan of an N-series android."

"Oh," I said. I wondered why his kind lived such short lives. So I asked him.

N7 took his time answering, finally saying, "We are mining androids."

"Excuse me," I said.

"The N-series are normally used to mine high-gravity planets or work the extractors of particularly massive gas giants."

"Why did Claath change you and the others to a military model?" I asked.

"One does not question a Jelk directive."

"No, I suppose not," I said. "You were given battle upgrades, I presume."

"Of course," N7 said.

"Five standard years, huh? So…you're born as adults?"

N7 glanced at me with his expressionless eyes. "Why do you ask these questions?"

"Just passing the time," I said. *And figuring out what makes you androids tick.*

He glanced at me again. "I do not believe you, Firstman Creed. You are a clever beast and you—"

"Hey," I said, grabbing an arm. "Let's get one thing straight. Claath gets to call me a beast because he gave Earth the freighters." *And because I'm going to drag him by the throat until I rub all his flesh down to the bones.* "You, on the other hand, can call me a man."

N7 stared into my eyes, and said, "Beast."

Don't do it, Creed. You gotta use Mr. Plastic-man. One, two, three… I grinned ruefully. "Sure, you hate my guts. I get it. And you're jealous of the real humans. Maybe I can't blame you. I—"

"Desist," he said. "Your guile will not succeed on me. You are the android-killer. We know you, Firstman Creed. No android will succumb to your cleverness again."

"Is that groupthink?" I asked. "You androids all think as a team?"

"You are witnessing a survival mechanism built into all androids of the N-series," he said. "Once we comprehend a danger, we remember it and act accordingly. We grow."

"You grow, huh? That's great. So what about these Starkiens? What can you tell me about them?"

"You and I are attending a strategy session," N7 said. "There, we shall plan the assault tactics."

I raised my eyebrows. The Starkiens interested me. I knew absolutely nothing about them except that they were pirates— at least by Claath's reckoning. What's more, they were hirable contractors. I suspected Claath would give them a cut of the take from the Altair Object. It seemed to imply the Starkiens wouldn't care if others knew they'd done this. Claath, on the other hand, didn't want anyone to know about his or the corporation's involvement. Why would that interest me? Maybe humanity would need to hire a few contractors someday. I had plans, but I knew nothing about the interstellar situation. Here was a chance to learn more.

Well, I take back that I didn't know anything. I knew a few things. The Lokhars fought the corporation. The Jelk lived for profits and I would make every jack tar of them pay for what had happened to my beloved world.

N7 and I traveled the rest of the way in silence, docked beside the largest of the shark-shaped vessels—it was the size of a city block—and waited as reverberating clangs and clanks told of heavy machines operating around us.

Finally, N7 rose and donned his helmet. I did likewise. We exited the shuttle and soon floated weightlessly down extremely narrow corridors. The bulkheads seemed to close in around us and the corridors turned much too sharply at times. I noticed fist-sized portholes along the bottom of the wall like giant mouse holes. I had no idea what they were for.

At last, without any guards or Starkiens in sight, we reached a small entrance. It opened, and N7 and I had to duck to enter a wide and far too low of a chamber filled with creatures.

Gravity took hold in the chamber, almost catching me by surprise. N7 knelt before a large, kidney-shaped table and took off his helmet. I took off mine too and an animal stench hit me like a sucker punch. It was worse than a barn, more like some monkey exhibit at a zoo where the attendants had forgotten to clean the cages. I had to work from holding my nose or making a face. Couldn't androids smell?

The Starkiens were the size of baboons and looked as furry and as ugly. They sported long canines at the end of their snouts and most had manes like a lion or a dominant male baboon. Each wore a harness of straps and buckles over their furry, smelly bodies and they drank from silver-colored teacups, or what looked like teacups. It was a disconcerting image to see them stretch their lips past those fangs and take dainty sips.

I counted fourteen Starkiens in the low-ceilinged chamber. I sat down, sitting cross-legged, refusing to kneel as N7 did. The ceiling loomed a mere inch above our heads now. If we'd remained standing, we would have had to stoop the entire time. I wondered if the Starkiens had chosen this room for a reason. Was it a tactic or joke on their part to make bigger creatures kneel?

The heaviest Starkien must have weighed sixty, maybe seventy pounds. There were computer screens along the walls, controls and a big holo image in the center of the kidney-shaped table. None of the Starkiens sat on chairs, but squatted as you'd expect baboon-like creatures to do.

Why did they smell so bad? Their fur looked sleek and smooth, as if it was well groomed, not like some matted offal. I breathed through my mouth, almost gagging several times.

"Greetings, N7," the biggest Starkien said. He had white or gray streaks in his fur, and his muzzle was more wrinkled than any others present.

"Greetings, Naga Gobo," N7 said.

"That's his name?" I whispered.

"Naga is his name," N7 whispered back to me. "Gobo is his rank. It means *lord of ships*."

"Got it," I whispered.

"Is there trouble?" Naga Gobo asked. He'd keenly watched our exchange. "Your beast seems restless. Will he heel to your command?"

"He is well," N7 said.

"I can speak for myself," I said. Who were these horribly smelling aliens that they figured they could call me a beast? They were the creatures.

Their reaction surprised me. All fourteen Starkiens drew weapons from their harnesses and aimed short, ugly tubes at me.

"Tell your fighting beast to heel," Naga Gobo said. "The Jelk assured us the creature could comprehend commands and would not run amok among us."

"Have you taken a good look at N7?" I said. I couldn't believe this. Why did all the aliens think we were beasts? "Do you see any differences between the two of us?"

The Starkiens watched me through narrowed eyes. None of the weapon-tubes wavered or moved away.

"You may put up your slugthrowers," N7 said. "Shah Claath has given you his word. The Earthbeast will remain calm in your presence."

"You should have already taught your animal to know its place in front of its betters," Naga Gobo said.

I swallowed my retorts. These were aliens. Stench had nothing to do with their abilities and scientific knowledge. Yeah. Maybe this was why Claath had wanted me to come. Maybe the Jelk wished me to understand my place in the interstellar community. To the Starkiens, I was a beast. To the Jelk and the Lokhars, I was a beast, a wild thing to use and possibly tame for combat. It was time to absorb the reality of the situation. The fact that we on Earth would have considered the Starkiens as animals wasn't lost on me.

It went even deeper, though. To the interstellar crowd, Earthers were the bottom of the heap. Fighting beasts—did other star-faring races use creatures to fight their wars? Yes…hadn't Claath's idea been to capture several hundred million humans to fight as slave creatures among the stars?

144

The more I learned, the less I liked it. Even if we could free ourselves from under the Jelk thumb, how would the rest of the interstellar races treat us?

Wait and learn, I told myself. *See what this Forerunner object is supposed to be anyway. Maybe it's something you can use.*

The strategy session quickly became interesting. Naga Gobo adjusted some controls below the tabletop and a fast-spinning, A-class star appeared in the holo image. It was the star Altair, and it rotated quickly enough to make it an oblong sun with a flattened top and bottom.

Planets appeared in bright blue around Altair. The first four were Mars-like planets, while the next two were gas giants, two supersized Jupiter-like monsters. Between the gas giants was a thicker-than-normal asteroid belt.

Naga Gobo continued to manipulate the controls, bringing the asteroid belt up close and then picking a small area of it and zooming in. Soon enough, a silvery torus appeared. As the zoom continued, the torus grew, and so did a veritable host of orbiting rocks and sandy debris around it.

"The Altair Object," Naga Gobo declared.

The Starkiens around the conference table began to stir and lean toward the holo image. I'd been getting used to the smell. It worsened as they moved, and I endured, waiting for the sharpness of the stench to weaken again or for me to get used to it. Several of creatures got twitchy fingers, some of them opening and closing their baboon-like hands. It made the Starkiens seem like thieves eager to grab the object and dash out of the room with it.

They're contract pirates indeed, I thought to myself. *It's a wonder Claath trusts them at all.*

"The file is old," Naga Gobo said, indicating the holo image. "But I was assured it is an original and contains trusted data. Notice the gun emplacements to the right."

The holo image zoomed again, focusing on one of the small asteroids circling the object. My eyes widened. It seemed like a regular, rocky asteroid, but the surface held several black-matted structures, looking like octagonal bio-domes.

"The firing domes are of Lokhar design," N7 noted.

Naga Gobo nodded. "The Lokhar Fifth Legion is far from home, but it's said that each legionary has sworn an oath to the Jade League to protect the Forerunner artifact as if it was their home planet."

Questions bubbled on the tip of my tongue, but I kept my mouth shut. I listened and tried to learn.

"The Jade League has declared the Altair system sacred to the Creator," Naga Gobo said. "Every member of the league has signed a compact in agreement with the theocratic principle. If we attempt this mission and are found out...the league members will increase their efforts to annihilate the Starkiens."

I turned away from the holo image to look at Naga Gobo. "Let me get this straight," I said. "We're making the attack on holy ground, or in holy space?"

Naga Gobo growled angrily. "Why must your beast utter speech at me? It is offensive and insulting. The creature should speak to you, not to us."

"The Lokhars attacked their home planet," N7 said. "Until then, the Earthbeasts knew nothing about civilization."

Naga Gobo sniffed in an exaggerated manner. "This is true?"

"The Lokhars used thermonuclear warheads on their main urban centers," N7 said gravely, "and laced the atmosphere with level five bio-terminators."

"Barbaric," Naga Gobo grunted.

"Before their awaking several months ago, the Earthbeasts believed themselves cultured and highly civilized," N7 said, "even though they continued to practice similar genocidal tactics upon each other."

Once again, Naga Gobo sniffed exaggeratedly.

"The Earthbeasts desire revenge upon the Lokhars," N7 added.

"I realize this and do not need an android explaining the obvious," Naga Gobo said.

N7 dipped his head as if apologizing.

"Shah Claath is cunning," Naga Gobo told the assembled.

The other Starkiens nodded, with their lips pulling back to reveal their fangs. I'd swear it was a Starkien grin or smile of appreciation.

"Yes," Naga Gobo said, "It is possible Claath engineered the event in order to gain these fiercely motivated battle-creatures. However, if he did so, the Lokhar took the bait too well and killed too many humans."

N7 glanced at me, but I kept my features impassive. This was an idea I'd have to explore.

"The Lokhar Empire grows with the passing of each year," Naga Gobo said. "They have become first in the Jade League and they desire a holy war against the Jelk Corporation."

"I realize that you have spoken with Shah Claath," N7 said. "You are aware of the importance of the Forerunner artifacts to the league. The Lokhars particularly venerate each artifact and the star system where it resides. They believe the First Ones built the objects."

"I am aware of Lokhar primary doctrine," Naga Gobo said. "I'm surprised an N-series android should speak of such things."

"Shah Claath instructed me—"

Naga Gobo held up one of his hands. "This is a strategy session. Let us stick to the issue and not become sidetracked."

"Exactly," N7 said. "There is a strategic point to my words. If we succeed in breaking through the Lokhar Fifth Legion and dismantling the asteroid maze, we can remove the Altair Object."

"Remove it to where?" Naga Gobo asked.

"I do not know," N7 said. "Only Claath knows."

"The Jelk will cheat us!" Naga Gobo shouted.

The others in the chamber muttered angrily, shifting about.

"No," N7 said. "Shah Claath will pay you in iridium as bargained."

Naga Gobo shook his head. "Why will he bother to pay us once he has the object in his sole possession?"

"Shah Claath ordered to me to tell you of a powerful reason why you can know he will pay," N7 said. "If he fails to pay, you could always gain revenge on him by telling the members of the Jade League who took the object."

"And thereby implicate ourselves," Naga Gobo said. "No, no, if we did such a thing, the Starkiens would have to leave the quadrant and enter the Beyond."

"There is no doubt that the consequences of your words would be dire for all," N7 said. "Even so, you possess this knowledge as a bargaining tool. Shah Claath realizes this. He will pay as agreed."

"The risks…" Naga Gobo said.

"I am to instruct you—"

"Instruct *us*?" Naga Gobo asked loudly. "An N-series mining android wishes to instruct *me*, the leader of the fleet? This is infamy!"

The other Starkiens hooted in outrage as they pounded the table with their fists. I felt as if I'd entered the African wilds of some Tarzan novel where great apes had gained higher intelligence and technology. To say the least, it was disconcerting.

N7 stood. I stood up behind him, ready to reach into my spacesuit and pull out the Bowie knife.

At our standing, the table-pounding stopped. The Starkiens took out their squat gun-tubes and pointed them at N7 and me.

"There must be a defect in my processing centers," N7 said. "I spoke incorrectly. I meant to say *inform* you instead of saying the other, ill-chosen word."

Naga Gobo wrinkled his snout, and slowly began to nod. "I accept your explanation. It is forgotten. Please, sit down, you and your beast."

N7 sat and I did likewise.

Sullenly, the Starkiens holstered their weapons, a few muttering about us.

"Good," Naga Gobo said. "Now what is it that Shah Claath wishes passed on to us?"

"Taking the Forerunner object and making it disappear will weaken the Lokhar position in the Jade League," N7 said. "The Lokhar Fifth Legion will be destroyed or at least disgraced. The primary doctrine will suffer a critical blow and Lokhar theology will also suffer. The Forerunner theft might be enough to shatter the league into its component parts. Would that not benefit the Starkiens?"

"Indeed," Naga Gobo said in an oily voice, as he brushed his mane like a vain model, although using his fingers. "Shah Claath's guile runs deep. I am impressed." He glanced at me. "And I begin to perceive why he uses untested beasts to make the main assault on the object."

I was beginning to perceive too. If the members of the Jade League arrived later to find the Forerunner object missing and floating, dead Earthlings in its place...what would they do to the last humans? Would the Lokhars return to Earth in a religious fury to exterminate us in jihad? And was Naga Gobo even partly right in thinking Claath might have engineered the Lokhar attack upon Earth? In any case we would be the fall guys.

For the umpteenth time, it hit home how little I knew of the wider interstellar civilization. I'd thought we'd been a cipher in a slave-hunting scheme to make more profits for the Jelk. Now it sounded like something more ominous was going on. What was the Jade League? What were Forerunner objects anyway? What did that have to do with the Creator? And by Creator, did the aliens mean God, or their idea of one?

It was strange to think of aliens as religious and having religious wars, jihads or crusades. I'd always believed that uniquely human.

I looked at the holo image again. The Lokhar Fifth Legion apparently lived on the small asteroids and debris circling the silver-gleaming torus. How big was that thing?

"I know you Starkiens hate hearing my voice," I said. "But what kind of spacecraft guards the Altair object?"

Naga Gobo stared at N7. "You possess a clever beast. It asks wise questions."

"Yes," N7 said.

"Perhaps you should leave it here for us," Naga Gobo said.

My blood ran cold. Is this why Claath had wanted me to come? Yet something troubled me. I'd come to listen and learn. So why was Naga Gobo upset if I understood? Why had I been included otherwise?

"This creature is the killer among killers," N7 was saying. "The Earthbeasts hate the Lokhars. Once their champion tells the others how the Fifth Legion guards the artifact, the others will war with even bitterer ferocity."

"It spoke of space battle," Naga Gobo said. "Does it realize—?"

"May I add a word of caution?" N7 asked quickly.

Naga Gobo seemed to consider this. "Yes, please do."

"It is best not to speak of space battle in the Earthbeast's presence," N7 said, "but only how we will deploy against the final barrier."

You will lead the assault-troopers?" Naga Gobo asked.

"I will direct them, yes," N7 said.

I studied the back of the android's head. This didn't seem like the same model as the one who had spoken about me to Claath yesterday. Had N7 already received some of those modifications he'd been wanting?

I dropped that line of thinking as Naga Gobo adjusted the holo image yet again.

I began to gain an understanding of what we would be doing, Rollo, Dmitri, Ella, I and the others. This was a mass assault, and we would have to work through the maze of shifting, orbiting rock and blocs of sand circling the artifact, all while facing emplaced strongpoints and an entire legion of Lokhar space soldiers.

This was going to be a bloody fight over a holy object to the religious soldiers guarding it. That didn't sound easy, or good for us.

I listened as Naga Gobo went over his strategy and tactics for deploying and giving us enough firepower to take out the Lokhar Fifth Legion. Suddenly, twenty-three thousand Earthers didn't seem like enough.

How long were we supposed to survive out in space? Beasts; they thought of us as fighting beasts. Did one care how many running dogs it would take to clear a minefield? Some generals would gladly pay the butcher's bill with other men's lives. But what if the general was an alien who used animals to do the fighting? Our wellbeing wouldn't matter to him.

I studied the holo image. There had to be a better way than how Naga Gobo was planning to do this. I wish I'd brought a pencil and paper to take notes. Even better, I'd liked to have a recorder and to take pictures of the holo image and the torus-shaped object.

I concentrated, willing myself to remember as much as I could. We Earthers would have to have our own strategy session. For a while now, I'd begun to believe I was getting things under control. I was wrong, possibly dead wrong, and I couldn't back out now or Claath would lift the freighters off Earth and empty the living cargos into space.

This was bad, really bad.

Fortunately, N7 took me with him when he left the Starkien ship. We returned to the Jelk battlejumper and I hurried into the mercenary area of the vessel.

"This is what it looks like," I said. With a pencil and paper I sketched the Forerunner artifact for the others.

Rollo, Dmitri and Ella sat around a cafeteria table with me. We ate broccoli, beans and beef. The others leaned over their plates to stare at the drawing. I'd been telling them about the Starkien meeting. After penciling the donut-shaped artifact, I began tapping the paper, putting dots around it.

"Those are the shielding asteroids?" Rollo asked.

"Asteroids and clouds of sand," I said.

Rollo shook his head to indicate he didn't understand. I'd seen similar shakes for many years. It was more a quick twitch of the head, almost like a tic, with his lips pressed together firmly.

"The Starkien leader—Naga Gobo—said each asteroid and sand cluster circles or fully orbits the object every fifteen minutes," I said. "The continuous maze helps to keep unwarranted vessels from getting too near the artifact."

"The asteroids and sand clouds are going to make it hard to get to the torus," Rollo said.

"That's right," I said. "I was told—or N7 was told—that the Lokhar pilot single ships through the maze. There's a coded passageway through this mess, a strict procedure to follow. Supposedly, the Lokhar Fifth Legion pilots are the only ones who can penetrate the orbital maze, taking someone to the inner space around the artifact."

"Why would anyone go to such trouble to do all this?" Ella Timoshenko asked. "What does the object do?"

"I don't know," I said. "I do know it has religious significance."

Ella, who studied my drawing, looked up sharply at me. She had changed like the rest of us—bulked up muscles and neuro-fibers—but she still had pretty features.

"You've heard that the aliens call it a Forerunner artifact?" I asked.

All three of them nodded.

"Well," I said, "they believe the First Ones built it."

"That's sounds intriguing," Ella said. "Who are the First Ones?"

"I'm going to assume the names have a meaning," I said. "First Ones sound like the first ones in space."

"Reasonable," Ella said.

"Forerunner likely means—"

"Ah, yes, yes, of course," Ella said, interrupting me. The scientist loved these kinds of puzzles. "Forerunner likely means the object or artifact is a precursor to those presently in control of the space lanes."

"And you say the aliens worship those things?" Rollo asked.

"I'm not clear on that," I said. "The Starkiens didn't let me ask too many questions. Like I told you before, when they call us beasts they mean exactly that. Would you explain something complicated to a dog?"

"Not unless the dog's name was Lassie or Rin Tin Tin," Rollo said.

"Yeah, okay," I said. "I'm thinking the object or artifact is more like the bones of a saint to a Catholic. But even that isn't exactly right. The artifact isn't living, or at least to the best of my knowledge it isn't alive. Apparently, the Lokhars and other Jade League members venerate it like a relic because in some manner that I don't understand yet, it represents the Creator to them."

"Creator?" Ella asked. "Do you mean as in God or Allah?"

153

"Yeah, that's right."

"Preposterous!" Ella said indignantly. "These are intelligent beings with the science of star travel. They cannot possibly believe in God."

I wondered how highly Ella would think of the Starkiens if she'd smelled them. I didn't ask, but I said, "I believe God exists and I'm intelligent."

Ella gave me a quizzical glance. "You are serious? You believe in the old fables, in Bronze Age myths?"

"Of course he does," Dmitri said. "And they're not myths."

Ella gave the Cossack a glance. It told me they'd had this discussion before.

I decided not to debate my beliefs with her right there. We had more pressing matters to thrash through.

With my pencil, I indicated the paper. "This is deadly serious stuff. The Lokhars, maybe every member of the Jade League, thinks of the Altair system as holy ground. I'm guessing that the closer one gets to the Forerunner artifact, the holier the space becomes. The Lokhar Fifth Legion took a religious oath to defend the object as if it was their home planet."

Rollo grinned savagely. "You're saying that if we can take this object from them, that they'll feel it deep in their guts?"

"No," I said. "If we take it, they won't feel a thing."

"But you just told us—" Rollo said.

"They won't feel anything because for us to take it from them they're all going to have to be dead," I said.

"Oh," Rollo said.

"Yes!" Dmitri said. "Good. We kill them all. I agree."

I nodded, grinning at him, and kept explaining. "From the way the Starkiens and N7 spoke about them, the Fifth Legion is an elite outfit. I'm guessing that makes them pretty tough."

"This is absurd," Ella said. "The aliens possess spacecraft, science far in advance of us. They cannot continue to hold to these ancient superstitions."

"I know," I said, speaking before Dmitri did. "I find the universe we're in to be highly confusing, too. Absolutely smelly baboons called me a beast and religious zealots guarding holy sites in space practiced genocide against Earth.

My point to telling you all this is to let you know that we're going to be in for a stiff battle, and I don't like the odds."

"There's more?" Rollo asked.

"Just what we've been saying to each other these past few weeks," I said. "We lack proper battlefield organization. We're divided into maniples, but don't have any higher organizations so we can attack with coordination."

"It is clear that the Jelk do not trust us," Ella said.

"Yeah," I said. "And that distrust is going to get us killed."

"What do you suggest we do about it?" Rollo asked.

"I don't know what else we can do," I said. "I suppose just fight like hell and win. The Starkien battle-plan is simple to the point of obviousness. They're going to mass all around the object and offload us as closely as possible to the orbiting asteroids. The androids will pilot the assault ships, taking us the final distance. N7 doesn't plan on landing on the small orbiting objects. That means we're going to have to use the sleds to get near enough and then to use our thruster-packs to land and take the fight to the Lokhars."

"During all this maneuvering," Ella said, "the Lokhar domes will undoubtedly be firing on us."

"Yeah, undoubtedly," I echoed.

"Our paymasters expect us to engage in hand-to-hand combat?" Rollo asked.

"Surface fighting," I said. "The Starkiens will match their velocity to the orbiting objects. They'll use beams and missiles to soften up the domes—"

"None of this makes sense," Ella said. "Why not just blast the shielding asteroids and debris with massive nuclear bombs and heavy beams, clearing the way for transporters?"

"I managed to get N7 to ask the Starkiens that," I said. "You won't like the answer."

"More Bronze Age nonsense?" Ella asked.

In outrage, Dmitri slapped the table.

"The Starkiens don't want to risk damaging the artifact," I said, shaking my head at the Cossack. "From what I can gather, the contractors are outcasts, at least to the Jade League members. I don't know if the Starkiens buy into the Creator belief, but they don't want the league members to hunt them down in religious fury. Therefore, they're going to use us to take out the Lokhar Fifth Legion. In that way, the Starkiens, and the Jelk, too, I'd imagine, don't have to worry about bombs or beams hitting and possibly marring the Forerunner artifact. I have the feeling these objects are priceless."

"Like an ancient Ming vase?" Ella asked, leaning back in her chair as she stroked her chin.

"Sure," I said.

"I have question," Dmitri said.

I studied the blocky man before nodding.

"What are Lokhars like?" Dmitri asked. "I've been wondering about that for long time already."

"Good question," I said. "I tried to ask the Starkiens and N7, too, but everyone ignored me about it."

"That does not make sense," Dmitri said. "They should tell us. We need knowledge of the enemy so we can plan better. So we can kill all the Lokhars."

I shrugged. "It might be redundant to say this, but how would you tell a pack of hunting dogs about bears? You wouldn't."

"We are not dogs," Dmitri said.

"Yeah," I said, and for a moment, my anger against the aliens smoldered.

"We are men," Dmitri said, as he slapped his chest.

"We must adjust ourselves to the facts," Ella said. "We must view reality as it is and plan accordingly. That is the only rational response to our situation."

"That's what I'm trying to say," I told them. "You wouldn't tell dogs how to attack bears. You'd bring the dogs to the hunt and let them loose. That's what the aliens are doing with us."

"Yes," Ella said, nodding. "That is a poetical way to describe it, but accurate. These aliens believe us to be inferior to them,. Yet the more I learn of these space races, the less I like them or understand their thought processes. I find myself growing disillusioned with them."

"I have another question," Dmitri asked.

"Shoot," I said.

The Cossack cocked his head, looking befuddled at me.

"That means go ahead and ask," I said.

"Ah," Dmitri said. "Here is question. How many Lokhars are in a legion?"

"Yeah, I'd like to know that too," I said.

"They would not tell you that, either?" Dmitri asked.

"We'll know tomorrow," I said, standing, pushing the drawing toward them. "That's the end of the briefing. You know enough now to tell others. I don't think Claath or N7 intends to give us mercenaries a briefing. So we're it. Copy the drawing, show as many others as you can and tell them what you know and to pass it on. I'll do the same thing and hopefully by tomorrow everyone will have an idea of what to do."

Ella asked a few more questions. Then we split up to go tell the others what to expect. It was precious little, but the truth was we were lucky to even know that much.

***

Tomorrow came all too soon. We ate in a packed cafeteria, heard an android give us boarding instructions over a loudspeaker and marched to our designated areas. There, we donned our bio-suits, boots and helmets. My maniple along with others hurried down a large corridor and entered a monstrous hangar bay. There must have been fifty assault ships parked here. Each could carry two hundred troopers or ten maniples altogether. Soon enough, we filed aboard assault ship six. Inside, we settled oxygen tank and thruster packs onto our backs. Only then did androids hand us our laser rifles and a sling-sack each of pulse grenades.

That's all we had other than the sleds to take us to the black-matted Lokhar domes. Maybe as bad, if we strayed too far from the central ship, the control device in our necks would explode and we'd be dead. If we couldn't blast our way into the domes, we'd be just as dead. If—

"This is it," I said, deciding endless worry wasn't going to help me or my maniple.

Troopers turned toward me. I raised my right arm and gave them the thumbs up. Afterward, I waited.

Finally, I felt acceleration and I realized we had left the Jelk battlejumper. There weren't any windows in the assault ship for us to see outside. Maybe more than anything else that told us this was an alien vehicle. Human-designed assault ships would have given us windows or screens showing what the outer cameras could see. This felt too much like a box. Our masters would bring us to the battle zone, open the box and shout: "Attack!"

The acceleration pressing us into our seats meant the assault ship headed toward the Starkien contract vessels. Once inside their motherships, we'd head to the jump point and enter the route that would take us to a star system. From there, we'd use another jump route that led directly to Altair. That meant we'd be making two jumps before combat.

None of us were looking forward to that.

Time passed far too slowly. Our vessel thrummed later, and we shook once, possibly landing onto the deck of a Starkien mothership. Clangs and clanks told of Starkien machinery locking us into place.

Thirty minutes later, a voice said into my earphones, "Jump in ten minutes."

All around our packed assault ship, troopers squirmed, including me. The ten minutes ticked by with agonizing slowness. I tried to think about anything other than jumping. Why did it feel so awful? I don't know. No one explained much to us. I was getting tired of that. I wanted to make them talk. I—

We jumped, and it hurt: my guts, my head and my eyes, everything pounded and pulsed. It seemed to last forever. Even though I was strapped in, I tried to double up. I felt the bio-suit stir on my skin. The living armor didn't like the jump either, it seemed. Muscles cramped. I twisted in my seat. I called out and in the end, I simply endured.

Finally, far too long of a time later, the pain and twisting stopped like the snap of fingers. We'd jumped successfully. No one said anything for some time. Probably most of the troopers felt like me: grateful to just sit and not feel pain.

"I don't ever want to do that again," a man finally said. A murmur of agreement swept through the troopers. We'd taken off our helmets some time ago.

"Why does it have to hurt?" one asked.

"This is BS," said another.

A third replied, "You got that right, brother. The aliens can have the stars. I just want to go home."

There was more of the same, troopers letting off steam. It went on until acceleration pressed us against our seats.

"Now what?" a woman asked. "Are we heading into combat?"

"No," I said. "We're heading for the next jump point."

"We're jumping again?" a man complained.

"Don't worry," I said. "You'll get to fight the Lokhars soon enough."

There was strained laughter and growls of eagerness. We were all wound tight, too tight. None of us knew anything about what went on around us. None of us saw anything in this damned box.

This time, we didn't have any warning. Troopers talked quietly together. I remember glancing a row over. Two men had the top of their heads practically touching. Each held cards. One was in the process of stuffing a drawn card into his hand when the awful feeling of jump struck by surprise.

We came out on the other end in the Altair system. As the troopers came down from the funk of jump, troopers cursed and raved at our thoughtless minders. After enough bitching, I told them to pipe down.

"We're in the combat zone," I said. "Put your helmets back on and stay alert."

That got troopers to blinking, thinking and donning the heavy helmets.

It was crazy. We rode into a space battle and none of us knew if beams fired near or if enemy missiles had gained lock-on and zoomed the final distance to our mothership. We waited for N7 or some other android to tell us to get ready. Back in the solar system, we'd unloaded onto plenty of practice battlefields. So we knew what to do when the time came. Still, this would be the first time under fire for most of them.

Rollo leaned against my left shoulder. "Afghanistan was nothing like this, eh?" he asked.

"I don't know," I said. "You never rode a chopper into battle?"

"At least I could look around and see what was going on," Rollo said.

"What about SEALs in a sub? Maybe that's what this is like?"

We shot the breeze for a time, trying to distract ourselves. Others did likewise. Finally, our headphones crackled into life.

"This is N7 speaking. The Starkiens have successfully taken the guardian ships by surprise, eliminating eighty-five percent of the enemy spacecraft. Three have escaped, however, running to warn the nearest Jade League star system. The other surviving guardian vessels are attacking the Starkien ships. Estimated time to offloading is three hours."

"Three hours!" Rollo said. "That's a long time to let our guts seethe."

"Eighty-five percent of the enemy ships destroyed sounds good to me," Dmitri said.

"Yeah," I said.

We were doing it. We were in the middle of a space battle, and we couldn't see a thing. I wonder if this was how the Marines felt storming Japanese beaches in World War II or the soldiers who landed at the Normandy beaches on D-Day. Fighter planes, submarines, artillery, battleships and cruisers had pounded the area and each other. But in the end, warriors in assault boats had to storm ashore and take the terrain. We were the Marines here, mercenaries treated worse than dogs. In three hours, or thereabouts, we would leap into the void of the vacuum of space and face elite Lokhar legionaries on their precious asteroids.

I swallowed in a tight throat. Here was my chance for some payback against the bastards who had destroyed my world. It was funny, but I didn't feel the rage just then. I felt fear. I wanted to live. I didn't want to die in the Altair system fighting over a religious artifact that meant nothing to me.

"Remember what they did to your dad," I whispered to myself.

I tried to do that. Instead, I waited and endured. That was another funny thing. Waiting in my seat was worse than going through a jump. The anticipation of something terrible felt worse than actually going through the terrible thing. Strange.

160

Who were the First Ones anyway? Why was a Forerunner artifact considered to be a holy thing? I wondered what the thing did, if anything. Was the object like an alien Stonehenge? Was it like the Cathedral of Norte Dame or was it like the black stone the Muslims kept in Mecca?

"I hate the waiting," Rollo said.

"You got that straight," I told him.

"Do you think we'll win?" he asked.

"We have to," I said.

"Don't blow smoke," Rollo said. "Really, do you think we'll win? Tell me the truth, Creed. What do you think is going to happen?"

I licked my lips. "I don't have a clue, my brother, but we're going to find out soon enough."

"Yeah," he said. "You got that right."

***

The hard maneuvering began soon thereafter. It was like being in an amusement park on a ride without windows, just jerked and slammed back and forth. Because the ship was in space, in a vacuum, there wasn't any noise from outside like explosions. But there were plenty of noises in the spacecraft, maybe from the Starkien mothership. The sounds were clangs, hisses, creaks, ruptures, more hissing—the sounds never ended.

"We are leaving the mothership," N7 told us over our helmet speakers.

Most of the other noises ended because a roar of thrusters took over. Instead of being jerked back and forth—the mothership likely jinking to save our lives—we were shoved hard against our seats.

High acceleration slammed us back, and it continued. I hated this not knowing. I could tell by the stark expressions and the pale features around me through helmet visors that the troopers hated the suspense too.

I clicked on to the wide channel and said loudly, "We're going in!"

Heads whipped around. Troopers looked at each other with hope.

"Are we finally doing it?" another maniple firstman asked me.

161

"That's right!" I roared. "The Starkiens beat these sons of bitches in space combat and now we're taking it down into their throats. Is everyone ready?"

Troopers stared at me.

I forced myself to laugh. "That's no answer. Are you ready to fight?"

"Yeah, we're ready," a few troopers grumbled.

"That's it?" I asked. "What are you, a punch of pansies? Let me hear you roar."

"We're ready," a few more said, pumping their fists into the air.

"These Lokhars nuked us!" I shouted. "They raped our world and tried to stamp humanity out of existence. Now's our chance to slam their heads against a wall so we can stomp on their faces. We're giving them payback times ten!"

"Kill them!" Dmitri shouted. "Kill them bastards!"

"Kill, kill, kill," I chanted. "Kill the bastards!"

The troopers took up my chant. It was primitive in the extreme. I suppose if N7 listened in he would think himself superior to us. I expect the Starkiens might understand. They had turned into hooting chimpanzees a couple of times during the strategy session.

I would have led the troopers into another round of shouting, but the maneuvering became crazy, throwing us this way and that in our assault seats. If we hadn't been strapped in, we'd have twenty or more troopers with broken arms and legs.

"Get ready!" I roared, as I felt my voice strain in the back of my throat. "We're getting near to unloading. Make sure you're channeled in to your maniple's frequency."

Three minutes later a line appeared to the side in a bulkhead. It was a gap, a rent from something: shrapnel or a hot beam. Air howled out, and for the first time some of us could see what was going on outside. The bad news was that three troopers hadn't sealed their helmets properly. They died: the first Earther casualties that I knew about. I spent the next minute yelling at everyone to check their suits.

"Look," Rollo said suddenly.

I glanced at him. He pointed at the rent. We could see through it now.

162

Bright, flashing beams nearly blinded me. Then I caught a glimpse of the Forerunner object in the distance. It gleamed white and seemed unearthly.

"What is that?" Rollo whispered.

I swallowed uneasily. What if the Lokhars were right? What if this was holy ground and the First Ones—who were the First Ones? Why did these artifacts matter so much that an entire Lokhar legion had dedicated their lives to guarding it?

Where the Jelk true devils? Was the beginning of the Bible, where Lucifer and his fallen angels rebelled, a storybook about an ancient space war?

A terrible chill worked up my spine.

"No, no," I whispered to myself. If the Lokhars where the angels, why had they tried to annihilate humanity? That made them devils, demons.

"Get ready to debark," N7 said in our helmets.

"You heard the man—the android," I amended. "This is it. We've practiced this before. Secondmen, you're driving the sleds. Good luck and good hunting, assault troopers."

I lost sight of the artifact because our assault ship shifted position. I told myself not to think crazy thoughts of angels, demons and God. We were the assault troopers come to do battle against genocidal aliens. That's all that mattered for the next few hours. Actually, winning mattered, because if we lost I didn't think Claath would keep on using humanity. That meant extinction for us.

"Think about payback," I whispered.

"Debark now," N7 said. "You must attack the enemy."

-15-

Assault ship six opened up and the sleds waited along the lower sides. I tore off my seat-buckles and used magnetic traction to clank to my sled.

The sled was a simple vehicle: a long plank with thrusters on the bottom and skidoo-like handlebars in front. It boasted a small rail-gun in front. I demagnetized the boots and shoved off, floating to Sled Zeno-212. A twist of my head showed me that my squad followed.

As I closed on the sled, I focused, landing, strapping in and revving the thrusters to life. The sled shuddered as the other troopers landed and strapped in.

The seconds ticked by and the space battle went on around us. It was sickeningly glorious and beautiful. What can I say? The Forerunner artifact, the torus, the big silver donut, gleamed with an amazing radiance. We orbited the object at the same velocity as the small asteroids and sand clusters. I tried to get a mental fix on the artifact's size. If the nearest asteroid was a mile in diameter—

I gazed at the artifact. It had to be bigger than the Lokhar ship that had beamed my dad. Maybe that thing was three times larger. I raised my left arm, shielding my visor, my eyesight. Something was in the middle of the artifact—

"This is truly amazing," Ella said through the helmet-comm.

"What's that?" I asked.

"I believe a tiny black hole is in the exact center of the artifact," Ella said. "How is that possible?"

My throat was tight enough. This made it worse. I swallowed, and I heard N7 give the all clear.

"It's go time," I said. "This is it, boys."

I gave the sled thrust, and we slipped away from assault ship six. We headed for the nearest asteroid, aiming at the domes there with their open bay doors. A single cannon tube in the nearest dome kept erupting with a milky ray. I followed it with my gaze and witnessed an assault ship disintegrating in space.

"They're killing our guys with that beam," Rollo said over the helmet-comm.

"While they can," I growled, "while they can."

I applied more thrust, but it felt like we crawled toward the asteroid. The trip gave me time to swivel my head and take in the gigantic scene. All around this portion of holy space, assault ships moved in like sharks. I didn't see any Starkien vessels. I imagine I couldn't without a radar screen or something similar. They must be too far back.

As far as I could see, space was flooded with assault ships and sleds. It reminded me of the movie *Avengers*, when the aliens slipped down out of the wormholes and launched down into New York City. We swarmed the Lokhar Fifth Legion, and by the number of aimlessly drifting and destroyed assault ships, sleds and individual troopers, the Lokhars were already taking a frightful toll of us.

"This is like an amphibious landing, only in space," I said.

"My old man told me once that amphibious landings almost always have the deadliest results for the invaders," Rollo said.

"Where are you?" I asked.

"I'm to your right...at your two o'clock," Rollo said.

I glanced back, and Rollo waved at me as he piloted his sled. Farther back, Dmitri directed his sled. To my left, Ella brought the rest of our maniple. Each sled carried four passengers and the driver.

I took a deep breath through my nostrils. There was absolutely nothing fancy about this. We drove straight down into their guns. They slaughtered us, and the Lokhars would have annihilated everyone if Starkien missiles hadn't finally streaked ahead and given us some covering fire, exploding into nuclear fireballs on the asteroids.

Several things happened then. The first and maybe the most ominous: the artifact gleamed even brighter with a daunting glow. I expected to hear heavenly singing next. Would angels with flaming swords appear? Man, but I didn't like the Forerunner object. It frightened me.

The second thing to occur took my mind off that. Powerful radiation from the warheads struck us. I could feel leakage through my bio-suit and my bones ached. My mouth tasted like copper and other metals.

"Our own side is trying to kill us," Dmitri groaned.

I laughed, and once more as in Antarctica, the laughter didn't sound totally sane to my ears. "We're still breathing," I said, "even if it hurts."

The dome that had been slaughtering nearby sleds looked like shredded junk. One rounded wall had a single long shard jutting up, and even as I studied it, the tip toppled and fell out of sight. That was one point for the Starkiens.

It took a slow and agonizing ten more minutes to reach the first asteroid. I could have turned the sled around and applied braking thrust. I didn't believe we could afford even that. I'd seen single ships—the Lokhar variety—swarming from inner asteroids coming to aid their brethren. So I aimed my sled at another dome low on the asteroid's horizon, and I shouted, "Get ready to jump and brake."

Rollo and Dmitri were doing the same thing. Ella believed in doing it by the book and lagged behind as she slowed for a sled-landing.

"Now!" I shouted, shoving up and off. My squad did likewise. The sled's thruster kicked in and the small craft blasted for the farther dome. It never made it, as a milky ray from the dome disintegrated the craft.

"Brake and get low," I said. "We'll be safe from the domes on the surface." I remembered that from the strategy meeting. It was one of the few useful tidbits I'd gained from the Starkiens.

Jets of thrust expelled from our packs. We slowed, and I landed first, my boots touching down onto the rocky soil. Soon, my squad lay on the surface with me. I gathered the maniple, studied the situation and decided we should sweep toward the destroyed dome and learn what we could about the Lokhar layout.

We practiced the low-gravity gliding learned on Io and Charon. I would have liked to be home in the solar system right now. The Forerunner artifact continued to glow and radiate strangely. I no longer looked at it, although I was much too aware of it in my peripheral vision.

We beat the Fifth Legion reinforcements to the shattered Lokhar dome. The shards of the thing looked like diamonds; its controls seemed to be plant-like bulbs.

"Freaking weird stuff here," Rollo said.

"Look," Ella said over the helmet-comm. "I've found a Lokhar body."

Everyone scrambled to her. Ella stood beside a seven-foot suited creature with tiger features. The Lokhars—if that's who this was—had a humanoid shape. This one lacked a tail.

"Natural predators," Ella said. "I imagine they are ferocious foot soldiers."

"Makes it surprising then that they'd use bio-terminators on us on Earth," I said.

"What is your reasoning?" Ella asked.

"If they're natural predators—warriors," I said. "Wouldn't they prefer to fight it out instead of using poison?"

"An interesting thesis," Ella said.

"It looks like we're going to test how good of warriors they are real soon," Rollo said. "Dmitri just radioed. A couple of enemy platoons are on their way here."

With the warning, I tried to set up an ambush. Maybe the bio-suits helped and made us harder to spot on radar. Did the Lokhars use personal sets? It might have helped us if we did. We engaged them among some low peaks behind the shattered dome.

In our firing line and from behind rocks and low trenches, we beamed with our lasers. The Lokhars wore powered armor, or something like it. There must have been forty against our twenty. The ambush worked after a fashion. We cut down five, maybe six Lokhars the first volley.

The enemy went to ground or to the surface, and we found ourselves in a bitter gunfight. They fired RPG-like missiles and a white ray akin to what beamed from their domes. A touch of a ray curled a trooper's bio-suit, exposing human skin to space. Violent decompression killed the trooper before the suit could repair itself. Blood drifted in a mist as the man collapsed.

A Lokhar single ship zoomed overhead, and from it, a legionary beamed down at us, taking out three of my troopers fast. From on my back and with help from several others, we destroyed the single ship, firing upward.

It gave the Lokhars on the surface time to close with us. They were big and there were more of them, and these were elite soldiers. Without our pulse grenades, they would have won. I and others used the highest setting and threw. The pulses blew powerfully in purple explosions as if we were high on an LSD trip. The explosives shredded the Lokhar battlesuits. Even so, I lost two thirds of the maniple. Fortunately, other maniples landed, joining me, and we low-glided across the rocky surface for the next dome.

This time it was the Lokhar turn to ambush us. Luckily, we had a few hotshots on our side, using their sleds as the enemies had used their single ship, like close air support. The sleds' rail-guns blasted battlesuits, but one by one, the Lokhars destroyed the sleds. We lost half our troopers, but we beat the ambushing team, destroying every tiger daring to face us.

Death abounded, and it should have worried me and the troopers, but the bio-suits pumped us up with something, pouring killing-lust into our bloodstreams. I felt elated and more than eager to finish it with these Lokhar giants.

Much of the fight became a blur of action, of targeting and beaming alien butchers. We reached the next Lokhar dome, and broke in with our pulse grenades. It shouldn't have happened, but I think we caught some of the Lokhar dome-gunners by surprise.

In an orgy of bloodshed, we killed the tigers, as we began calling them, and successfully opened up the first asteroid to the invasion.

That's when it happened, perhaps several minutes after our victory. I'm still not sure about the timing of it.

"Creed, you gotta come and take a look at this," Rollo told me over the helmet-comm.

I sat slumped in a corner against some Lokhar machinery. My bones and joints pulsed with radiation pain. Once we returned to the battlejumpers, we'd all have to spend time in the healing tanks to repair cellular damage.

"What is it?" I asked. "What's got you so excited?"

"The artifact," Rollo said. "Something is happening to it. You gotta come and look because it's too hard to explain."

"I don't want to look at it," I said. "The glowing earlier gave me the creeps.

"No, you gotta come see this," Rollo insisted. "The Lokhars are retreating to it and the thing is becoming fainter by the second."

I groaned as I stood and float-jumped for an exit. I joined Rollo and Ella on a low hill to the rear of the dome. We looked toward the center of the swarming junk orbiting the torus. The Forerunner artifact glowed with an unearthly light, but even more so than earlier. I shuddered, and I'm not sure why.

"Look," Ella said, as she pointed at the artifact's center.

"What am I supposed to be seeing?" I asked.

"The black hole appears to have widened, to have grown," Ella said.

"How can you tell?" I asked.

"I am a scientist. I am trained to observe and notice the details."

I'd have to take her word for it. It looked no different to me. What I found impressive was the streaming line of flying Lokhar legionaries and single ships. There was one bigger, bloated vessel. I saw a single ship land on top of it and zoom off seconds later. Was that a fuel tanker? A mother-ship? From all directions they fled the asteroids and headed inward toward the artifact. I'd thought the Lokhars would be like World War II Japanese, fighting to the bitter end and making kamikaze charges at us. These were elite religious troopers and they were fleeing already. That didn't make sense.

"What do you think the artifact is doing?" Rollo asked.

"Maybe the Lokhars know how to make it detonate," I said. "If they can't have it, nobody can."

169

"No," Ella said.

"Do you have an idea what's going on?" I asked.

"I do," Ella said.

"Well how about spilling it for us, Einstein?" I asked.

Ella remained silent as she watched, with a small smile on her face.

I watched her for a moment, but finally, almost against my will, I studied the giant artifact. It grew fainter, as if it was in the process of disappearing. Then I'd swear I could see the stars behind it. This was getting weird.

"Should we go back inside the dome?" Rollo asked nervously.

"Why?" I asked.

"Black holes and disappearing ancient Forerunner artifacts seem like they might pump out gamma or X-rays or who knows what kind of radiation at us," Rollo said. "I'd like more shielding."

"You're right," I said. "Let's get behind some cover."

"You're too late," Ella said. "It is happening just as I thought it would."

I swallowed uneasily. I'd been seeing plenty of strange things these past weeks. Why should a faint Forerunner artifact matter? It did, and I can't tell you why because I don't know myself.

One moment, the giant torus became fainter yet, so we could hardly see the outlines, and then it was gone. The Lokhars near the object vanished with it. The rest streaming toward the departed artifact kept advancing. Had the thing teleported elsewhere, been destroyed, what had just happened? I didn't know.

"Was this supposed to happen?" Rollo asked. "Is this what Claath was really shooting for?"

I shrugged, and I turned to Ella. "You're the Einstein. You seem to know what happened. Did it disappear?"

"Do you mean go invisible?" Ella asked in an amused manner.

"Let's not play twenty questions," I said. "Where did it go?"

170

"As to that, I cannot say," Ella told us. "The clue is the black hole in the center. Amazing technology to hold such a thing in place—I would not have believed this unless I had seen it myself."

"Yeah, why's that?" I asked.

"What causes the jump routes?" Ella asked. "Why are they there?"

"What's that have to do with the Forerunner artifact?" I asked.

"Are jump routes a natural phenomenon?" Ella asked in a rhetorical way. "Are they folds in space, oddities caused through natural occurrences? Or were the jump routes created?"

"Why does it make any difference?" I asked.

Ella faced me. "It makes all the difference. If jump routes are artificial—"

"Are you suggesting the Forerunner artifact made the jump routes?" I asked.

"Ah, you're a clever thinker," Ella said. "The black hole is the giveaway, isn't it?"

"Yeah, sure," I said.

"It is my belief that the artifact slipped away through a wormhole," Ella said.

"Then why don't we see evidence of the wormhole?" I asked.

"A reasonable question," Ella said. "Yes, why aren't the rest of the Lokhars sucked into a wormhole? It is an interesting question."

"Pop goes the thesis?" I asked.

"Not necessarily," Ella said. "If I had monitoring equipment—"

"Just a minute," I said. "N7 is hailing me on the command channel." Using my chin, I clicked a pad inside the helmet. The smooth-skinned android appeared in the HUD of my visor. He seemed to be sitting at the controls of assault ship six.

"You must gather those under your command," N7 said. "The Lokhars are returning to the maze."

"You're retrieving us?" I asked.

"On the contrary," N7 said. "You must gather your troopers and move deeper into the maze. You must destroy the returning Lokhars before they can regain their positions on the inner asteroids."

"That doesn't make sense," I said. "The artifact is gone. This isn't holy ground anymore. So pick us up and have the Starkiens blast the asteroids into rubble, killing Lokhars. It will be like shooting fish in a barrel. They can slaughter the Fifth Legion."

"That is an interesting proposal," N7 said.

"You mean no one else has thought of it yet?" I asked. "Come on, why waste human lives and why waste time? Pick us up and let the Starkiens deal with them. Our battle's won."

"Await my word," N7 said. "I must speak to Naga Gobo concerning your suggestion." The android vanished from my HUD.

"So what's up?" Rollo asked, as I turned toward them.

"High command is trying to figure out what to do next," I said.

"The fight's over, right?" Rollo asked.

"As a savant," I asked Ella, "do you think the artifact will reappear here?"

"Hmm," Ella said. "I hadn't considered that. In truth, I lack enough data to make a rational prediction. My instincts tell me no, but it might be possible."

"Yeah," I said to myself.

I liked Ella's original explanation about the artifact because it helped dampen my own ideas. The way the artifact had glowed and then grown fainter—it had seemed too much like a stellar ghost or a Flying Dutchman. The thing had seemed supernatural there at the end. That's something I hadn't expected from aliens and outer space. I didn't want it to be supernatural. Black holes, wormholes, jump routes: give me rational and reasonable explanations. I'd once read something by Stephen King, the author explaining how one of the truly most scary things would be for a rock to suddenly start talking to you. It would freak you out, right, because rocks aren't supposed to talk. Well, Forerunner artifacts made by First Ones who in reality had been angels from Heaven would freak you

172

out, too. I disliked that line of reasoning and preferred Ella's hard science approach. It fit my view of reality better.

N7 reappeared on my HUD. It was hard to tell, but he seemed grim. His thin lips were downturned. I'd never seen that before. "You must continue the assault," the android told me. "The victory—"

"Hey, guess what?" I asked. "The object we came to collect is gone, kaput, *dis-o-peared*. There isn't any more victory to be won because we've already won."

"Your logic is faulty," N7 said. "Much of the Fifth Legion remains. You must slaughter them. That is the criteria for victory."

"Oh right, sure, what was I thinking?" I asked. "Their holy object is gone and now who knows what kind of righteous wrath is pulsating through their tiger veins? No, my plastic friend, now it is time to use the Gatling guns."

"Your reference fails me," N7 said.

That didn't surprise me. The Gatling guns were human in origin from the last Colonial Era. American Indians in the Midwest and African tribesmen had each in turn charged Gatling guns, often in a howling mob. Sometimes, they had been holy warriors, given heavy mojo by their shamans to protect them from the industrial man's bullets. The mojo always failed against a stream of lead, particularly those hosed from the then ultra-modern Gatling gun. That was the trick: hosing lead. The Gatling guns were the first machine guns. What I was saying to N7 was that it was time to forget about hand-to-hand or visor-to-visor ground pounding and to start hosing the enemy with high-tech weaponry. I didn't want to lose any more humans in a useless fight.

"Does Naga Gobo still have a problem bringing his ships near the maze to blast the Lokhars to bits?" I asked.

"Yes," N7 said.

"I could understand it before," I said, "but not once the artifact is gone."

"The object could always return," N7 said.

"Does Naga Gobo know this to be possible?"

"He believes it."

"The artifact has done this before?" I asked.

"Naga Gobo has declared the object's vanishing as a miracle," N7 said. "He cannot destroy the maze, as it witnessed the miracle."

"The maze is made of rocks and sand," I said. "They can't witness anything."

"Naga Gobo believes otherwise," N7 said. "However, his wording may indicate Starkien idioms that I do not precisely comprehend."

"Okay, look," I said. "Pick us up and use the assault ships to attack the Fifth Legion. The assault ships have defensive weaponry, but they're still a lot more powerful than our laser rifles and pulse grenades. Besides, I bet we've already taken heavy losses."

"Human casualties do not matter," N7 said. "You were brought here to fight. You must continue the attack."

I laughed at him. Human casualties certainly mattered to the humans. I told him, "I doubt your troops are going to do much advancing at the moment."

"You must instruct your maniple and the others to—"

"Listen to me, N7," I said. "Try to use your logic circuits."

"I have a bio-brain, not circuits."

"Okay, okay, don't get technical on me. Your neurons then, if that makes you happy. Just listen for a minute. Claath didn't structure our little army with higher commanders, just the maniple firstmen. We knew the score, though: storm the Forerunner artifact and kill every alien defending it or on it. But the object disappeared, right? Now everyone is going to hunker down. If you'd—if Claath had made higher levels of command—those commanders could order the troopers back into action. But no one is going to listen to another firstman telling them what to do. The object's disappearance changed everything. That doesn't have to ruin the secondary battle-plan: killing Lokhar legionaries. Pick us up and maneuver nuclear missiles at the Lokhars while they're trying to get back to the safety of the asteroids. You have an open window to destroy them without taking any loss in return, but you gotta move quickly to do it."

"Naga Gobo—"

"Listen to me, N7. You have command authority over the assault boats. Use that authority. Force those baboons—the Starkiens—into doing what's smart. Don't let their superstitions cost Claath profits."

"There is merit to your words," N7 said. "But I distrust your motives. You are the android-killer. Perhaps you're telling me these things in order to trick me."

"If you're afraid I can outsmart you—"

"It is not a matter of fear," N7 said. "I have a far greater IQ than you."

"There you go," I said. "It isn't rational that I can outthink you. Therefore, for you to act as if I could is irrational. Claath loves profits. Outfitting and training mercenaries cost money. The Jelk wishes a solid return on his investment. Don't get his property killed, especially as there is no longer a profit-motive reason for doing so."

"I must admit that your logic is impeccable," N7 said.

"I'll add one more factor," I said. "Too many maniples have become mixed up on our asteroid. I bet it's the same way all over this maze. That means some assault troopers will drift too far away from their boats. If they drift too far that will cause their obedience chip to explode and kill them, and for no profitable reason."

N7 stared at me. He held that pose for several seconds. Finally, he gave a sharp, severe nod. "Prepare for pickup," he said. "The Forerunner object is gone. Its presence made the space holy. Now it is gone and so should be the Starkien inhibitions to using nuclear weapons in the inner area. If they cannot see reason, the androids will destroy the remaining Lokhars and win Shah Claath's favor."

"Now you're thinking," I said.

The HUD winked out without N7 even saying thank you. But that was okay. I'd saved human lives and that's all that mattered.

Too bad I hadn't foreseen Claath's reaction.

-16-

We boarded the assault ship and the sides closed up as if they were giant tarantula legs. That sealed us in except for one spot. The wall there moved several times until the slot jammed into its proper place. The rent in the bulkhead had a metal patch over it, so we couldn't peek outside any longer.

"Pretty smooth ride," Rollo said after a time.

I'd been dozing due to battle fatigue. The bio-suits no longer amped us up and the hours of pre-battle jitters had finally demanded their payment of sleep.

"What's that?" I asked, lifting my head.

"I said it's a pretty smooth ride for us maneuvering through the asteroid maze," Rollo said. "There's nothing but continuous acceleration. It makes me think we're heading for a jump route or mothership, not to slaughter legionaries."

"N7," I said, using a special channel to call him. There was nothing, though. Despite repeated hails, the android didn't respond. "I think you're right," I told Rollo. "The hunt is over and the hounds are locked up."

"I wonder what it is about us that give the aliens such a low opinion of humans," Rollo asked.

I'd wondered about the same thing, and I had a possible reason. "My guess is arrogance," I said. "They have high technology and we don't. Therefore, to them we're beasts."

"That doesn't make sense," Rollo said.

"It did to the European explorers to the New World," I said. "They saw Indians running around in breechclouts and moccasins, firing stone-tipped arrows. Some of the more

176

bigoted Europeans wondered if Indians even possessed souls. That's calling them beasts after a fashion, non-humans. And that was just humans seeing other humans of a slightly different color and facial features. Now imagine what it's like for aliens seeing other aliens, especially those down on their luck like us. We lack their high tech, their mechanical sophistication and therefore to them we're animals."

"Aren't aliens supposed to be better than that?" Rollo asked.

"Why should they be any better?" I asked. "They're different, certainly. But the idea aliens were automatically going to be morally superior to humans is ludicrous. I'm referring to movies like E.T. or Close Encounters. What I find amazing is that we even have enough similar thoughts or ideas to work together. But I'll tell you the one thing I've noticed. It seems to me the one constant to having higher intelligence is arrogance. You remember the smart kids from high school, especially in the areas they cared about like video games or a super guitarist in music class. The best in any of those areas was always looking down his nose at the lesser players. The aliens are intelligent, and they see that their tech is obviously better than ours. Therefore, they're arrogant about it. Maybe that's the one norm throughout the universe: high intelligence equals high arrogance."

Rollo grunted thoughtfully.

"And I'll tell you something else," I said. "That's what gives us our fighting chance."

"Alien arrogance?" Rollo asked.

"Yup," I said. "Arrogance usually brings blind spots. We can't afford arrogance because we're about as down as we can be. Okay, let them kick us for now if that makes them arrogant. We'll use their blind spots against them to climb up from our low position."

I would have said more, but just then we jumped. That ended all conversations and it proved Rollo had been right about us leaving the battle area. After the jump, no one felt like talking anymore. Radiation poisoning had kicked in hard. Even the bio-suits must have felt it. Some of them oozed off their wearers, including me.

In the end, the androids brought us back to the Jelk battlejumpers. In a giant hangar bay, we filed off the assault ship and trudged back to the mercenary area of the ship. From there, most of us went to the healing tanks. I floated for hours and I swallowed the big green pills they gave us. I could feel each one sliding down my throat. It made me feel like a dog with worms.

Afterward, I slept for hours, woke up, took another green pill, drank water like a horse and went back to sleep. It took several cycles of that before my bones stopped hurting and breathing felt normal. I'd smelled smoke before that, as if each individual nostril hair had been singed.

It had been a week and a half since the Forerunner battle. I was surprised we hadn't heard anything concerning consequences so far. I figured Claath would have berated us for something, and I'd been thinking about what I would say to him.

Rollo and I sat in a cafeteria playing cards. He took a card from the deck, put the card in his hand, studied them, looked up, widened his eyes enough so I noticed and cleared his throat.

Without turning around, I knew Rollo must see an android approaching. It had been taking too long for them to say something. Like I said, I'd been expecting a visit for days.

With my back to the android, I said, "Hello, N7."

Silence greeted me. I glanced at Rollo before turning around. The android stood there in cyber-armor and with a pistol strapped to his side.

"How did you know I approached?" N7 asked.

"Through elementary deduction," I said.

"Did you hear my footsteps?"

"No, you were walking too quietly for that."

"Precisely," N7 said. "Nor did I hear your secondman warn you."

"Are you sure about that?"

"Yes. I've been observing him since entering the cafeteria."

"Sorry to disappoint you," I said, "but Rollo did warn me."

"He drew a card and—Ah," N7 said. "The cough was a prearranged signal?"

"No. It was just a cough. Well, not *just* a cough. But it hadn't been prearranged."

"I see that I must refine my studies on human communications," N7 said. "I still have more to learn."

"Why bother?" I asked.

"Interesting," N7 said, "you're attempting to elicit information. I recognize the technique, as I've been studying the various recordings of you. It has been quite profitable. I have found that you are a crafty beast. You playact the part of a ruffian, but I've come to see that all the while you scheme most cunningly."

"What recordings are you talking about?" I asked.

"You already know. The woman gave you a warning. In Recording B24-18 I clearly heard her tell you."

I scowled for a moment, before asking, "Do you mean Jennifer?"

"Precisely," N7 said.

I set my cards face down on the table. I noticed the top card had a tiny mark on the back, an extra line in all those swirls. Had someone been marking cards? Ignoring that, I wondered about Jennifer. I hadn't thought about her for some time.

"Where is she?" I asked.

"On Earth, I presume." N7 grew still as he studied me. "You're showing heightened interest in her whereabouts. Is this because you wish to mate with her?"

"Are you studying humans or me?" I asked.

"Both," N7 said.

"You still haven't answered the question as to why you bother."

"I am not here to answer your questions. I am here to escort you to Shah Claath."

"Oh," I said. "So I'm finally going to meet him in person?"

"If I had humor conditioning," N7 said, "I believe this would be the moment for me to laugh. No. I am escorting you to a screening chamber."

"Why doesn't Claath met me in person?"

"He is displeased with you."

"That's his reason?"

"Negative," N7 said. "I am not responding to your query as to why he declines a face-to-face encounter. Instead, I am informing you that as of this moment, he is displeased with you personally."

"How come?"

N7 hesitated. It almost seemed like a human reaction. Then the android glanced at Rollo before fixing his solemn gaze back on me. "Shah Claath is also unhappy with me. I believe he thinks you have a corrupting influence."

"Because you used the assault ships to attack the Fifth Legion?" I asked.

"You are operating under faulty information. After the artifact's disappearance, neither I nor the other androids flew deeper into the maze. We retreated for the Starkien motherships."

"And that's why Claath is unhappy?"

"Negative," N7 said. "The Starkiens complained about our actions. They lost ships…"

"Yes, the Starkiens lost ships," I said, trying to prod him along.

"In a most insulting manner," N7 said, "Naga Gobo barely accepted my explanation as to why we retreated from the maze. His problem was that although he clearly desired to, he could not refute the logic you had shown me. Eventually, he launched missiles, but because of his tardiness in responding, it took too long to pulverize the outer asteroids for his ships to get near the inner ones. Therefore, he brought heavier ships to bear— beamships—bringing them to the edge of the maze. It was at that point the Lokhars launched their surprise: suicidal single ships. Naga Gobo lost critical Starkien vessels. Because of that, he demanded heavy restitution from Shah Claath."

"So this is about profits?"

"Negative," N7 said, "this is about expenditures without sufficient return. The Forerunner artifact assault proved a costly failure—as we failed to capture the object. Shah Claath blames us: the N-series androids. Through impeccable logic, I have tried to show him the blame justifiably belongs on you."

"Thanks a lot," I said.

N7 shook his head. "Thanking me is not reasonable, especially as Shah Claath is considering abandoning the Earthbeast Project. If he decides to do so, he will jettison the humans on Earth and likely sell you fighting beasts, hoping to recoup the loss your training entailed. He may even sell you at bargain prices, which means the Starkiens may buy you."

"The baboons need assault troops?"

"I can only assume your faulty reasoning lies in your lack of data," N7 said. "Because of his critical ship losses, Naga Gobo needs scapegoats—you and your Earthbeasts would do. He hopes to expiate his sins by sacrificing you before the Starkien Grand Council. It would be an agonizing end, and I'm told very shameful for you humans."

"Crucifixion," I told Rollo.

N7 stood silently for a moment as if processing data. "Yes. That is an apt analogy. Unlike the Jelk, the Starkiens believe suffering can atone for bitter setbacks. To a Jelk, such a concept is unthinkable. Money alone can pay for failure."

"I gotta say, N7, you're a wealth of information."

"What an odd way to say it: *wealth* of information. Your Earth idioms are often strange."

"If it's any consolation, I find you, Claath and the Starkiens to be pretty strange, too."

"You are in the inferior position," N7 said. "Thus, it is foolish to make verbal value judgments concerning your betters."

"You could be right. The thing is I find it helps my peace of mind to call a spade a spade. I don't like to wear blinders or to pretend. I didn't like it back on Earth—the PC crowd—and I don't like it out here in space either."

"PC?" N7 asked.

"It doesn't matter," I said. "Claath wants to see me, is that right?"

"To see us both," N7 said. "Come along. I have already dallied here too long."

I got up and followed the android down miles of corridors. In the end, I found myself sitting on a metal chair before what must have been the same table as earlier. In moments, the wall screen flickered and I saw Claath in an entirely new setting.

181

The red-skinned Jelk lounged in a vat of steaming purple liquid. In one hand he held an hourglass-shaped container filled with a foamy yellow drink. In the other hand he gripped a clicker. Softly discordant music played in the background while beautifully naked women—human women—moved around him. The women wore strings of jingling jewelry on their throats, hips and ankles, which only heightened their desirability.

"I see you've noticed the females," Claath said.

I nodded, also noticing something else: the difference between the women and the Jelk. Claath was the size of an evil Rumpelstiltskin: he couldn't be any taller than three and half feet. It was a shock. Until now, I'd considered him normal sized. But then I'd had nothing to compare him with. Maybe that's why he'd been interviewing me via screen, for safety's sake.

"If I had acquired the Forerunner artifact," Claath was saying, "you and your troopers would be reclining at ease now and enjoying these sex objects."

I swallowed, watching the lovely movements of the ladies. A pendant stirred between one woman's large breasts. I couldn't tear my eyes from her nipples.

Sight of them had definitely caught me by surprise. Then I scowled. Were they Earth women or androids? If from Earth, they were slaves to an alien. I found myself hating the fact an alien had captured and enslaved them.

"We defeated the Fifth Legion," I said. "We drove them from their asteroid maze. We did our part as requested. So I don't see that you have any reason to be unhappy with us."

"Let me correct your error," Claath said. "You defeated the forward fortress areas, but you did not complete the mission as ordered."

"We fought hard enough that we panicked the rest of the legion," I said. "Why otherwise did they flee their inner strongholds and race for the artifact?"

Claath took a sip of his drink, soon slurping it dry. He beckoned a woman, handing her the glass. She hurried away with jingling sounds, and I noticed the Jelk watching the woman with a lustful eye.

182

"We performed better than you'd expected," I said.

Slowly, Claath tore his gaze from the woman and regarded me. "I have a theory concerning the odd Lokhar behavior. The Fifth Legion must have become stale. Perhaps they rested on their reputation and became lax in training."

"Either that," I said, "or Earth troops beat the shit out of them and the rest panicked. The rest were unwilling to face such savage troopers in combat."

Claath grinned in a mocking way. "You bask in illusions. If the Lokhars were so terrified of you, why did they return to the battlefield? No, in the end, you Earthbeasts *ran* from *them*."

I shook my head. "The Forerunner artifact vanished, turning the attack into a futile exercise."

Claath frowned. "You would do well not to openly remind me of your failure."

I slapped the metal table and laughed.

Claath's frown turned into a scowl. "I am not Naga Gobo nor am I a Saurian or an errant android. I am the Jelk, the paymaster of seven battlejumpers. Without me, humanity fades into the dark night of oblivion. Forget that, and you and your ilk will die."

His threat sobered me. "I haven't forgotten," I said.

"See that you do not." Claath snapped his fingers. "Like that, the freighters will head into space, ridding themselves of unprofitable cargoes."

It was galling, particularly seeing the women in thrall to him. In truth, I was just as much in thrall to Claath as there were. But it was different because my hard wiring made it that way. How much of human behavior was rationally decided versus an inner biological need? Babies naturally sucked. They didn't consciously decide to. At two, they turned into hellions. At fourteen or fifteen they became rebels against parental authority and somewhere in their twenties most got married. None decided to live in trees the rest of their lives or build nests like a wasp. Were those logical decisions or biologically—hard wired—determined?

I turned away from the screen and drummed my fingers on the table. What had happened to the vengeance-driven manic in Antarctica who'd charged onto an alien lander? These freaks

183

had come down and wrecked our world. Now the oh-so mighty and puffed-up Claath blithely threatened me with human extinction if I didn't jump high enough when he uttered the word.

It was time to eat crow and time to plot.

I faced the screen and bowed my head. "I'd like to respectfully point out that the assault troopers could have done nothing differently to halt the vanishing artifact."

"It is the single point in your favor keeping me from flushing you all out of the hangar bays," Claath said.

"Didn't we do well in driving the Lokhars from their outer asteroids?" I asked.

"You showed ferocity, that's true. But this disobedience to orders...I have yet to decide how to punish you beasts so you understand that another such incident will end in your deaths."

I sat quietly, with my head bowed.

"Still," Claath said, "on an individual basis, you did prove yourselves the equal of a Lokhar legionary. It proved my thesis correct in initially coming to Earth. Unfortunately, there was too much wastage in bringing you beasts into combat range with the legion. The wastage incurred heavy profit losses."

I looked up. "May I inquire as to battle casualties?"

"Do you note the beast's behavioral differences?" Claath asked N7.

"I do, sir," N7 said. "It is impressive."

"Never bargain with them," Claath said. "It only leads them to believe they are your equal. Always remember that the beasts are cunning and egotistical. They are quick to sense indecision. Observe how Creed-beast has seen my steel glove. He understands my threats and instantly modifies his behavior accordingly."

"Your handling of him is quite instructive, sir," N7 said.

With a single hand, Claath splashed purple liquid. He appeared thoughtful and soon said, "Perhaps I am partly at fault for this disaster. With the new upgrades, I had thought you N-series androids cleverer than you actually are. I wonder now how costly further upgrades would be in order to bring you into the needed intelligence range to properly handle the beasts. I have debated sending you back to the mines, all of you, and letting Saurians take your places."

"Yes, sir," N7 said. "We deserve no better."

"That is correct," Claath said. "You do not deserve anything, as you are my constructs to do with as I please. But I am not driven by thoughts of vengeance such as a Starkien contractor feels. Profits alone interest me. I have sunk sizeable funds into your combined upgrades, into the Earthbeast bio-suits and training and into hiring a Starkien raider fleet. This artifact—" Claath accepted a refilled glass from a kneeling woman, taking a healthy swallow and wiping yellow foam from his lips. "Fortunately, the artifact's vanishing has upset many in the Jade League. I have already heard word of violent debates among the leading league theologians. It appears none of them knows where the artifact went; at least, so say my spies. This may be the perfect time to strike at Sigma Draconis."

"Yes, sir," N7 said.

"The beasts fought valiantly," Claath said, "which I predicted they would do. How could I foresee the artifact's vanishing? Am I a theologian? Am I a savant on Forerunner technology? Who among the Jelk and their customers understands these ancient devices?"

Was the Jelk drunk? Even as I wondered, Claath took another gulp of the yellow drink.

"The fortresses of Sigma Draconis," Claath said, "and the guardian fleet there, those are things a civilized Jelk understands. The jump routes into Sigma Draconis—if we could gain the star system, the entire Draconis subset would fall to us. These theological debates..." Claath laughed, exposing his pointy teeth. "I must speak with Axel Ahx. If I combined his battlejumpers with mine and with the Starkien fleet... Hmm, and if I could persuade Doojei Lark to commit to the endeavor..."

Claath's eyes narrowed as he studied me. "Your success against the outer asteroids is what propels my thoughts toward Sigma Draconis. It is a heavily fortified Lokhar star system, but it is far from their regular sphere of influence. It is the critical nexus point splintering important corporation areas into several unequal zones. With an opening of the Sigma Draconis route, corporation vessels would no longer need to pay the Star Alliance tariff. That would bring a twenty percent decrease in my hauler fees."

Claath drained the glass, tossing the container into the steaming vat. Droplets splashed upward, plunking back into the liquid like heavy raindrops. He grinned at me, and he triggered the clicker at the women. One by one, they dropped onto the steam-slickened tiles, groaned and writhed so their jewelry clinked. Obedience chips must have been embedded in their lovely necks.

I caught him slyly glancing at me as the women twisted on the floor. His dark eyes were shiny and a little grin twitched at the corners of his lips.

I knew what he wanted from me. Arrogance, I told myself. This was about arrogance. I needed to feed his so he remained blind to certain realities.

"Stop it!" I shouted, as if desperate.

Claath's shiny eyes gleamed. "Why should I stop? I find their motions delightfully erotic and stimulating. Don't you?"

"Torturing them is inhuman," I said with false anguish.

"They're but beasts," he said.

I forced myself to lick my lips as if anxious. "Why needlessly torment them? How—" This was difficult to say. "How does torturing them help them to serve you better?"

"I want you to notice this, N7," Claath said. "Creed-beast has an emotional attachment to human females in distress. Isn't that interesting?"

"Yes, sir," N7 said. "I hadn't foreseen that. I'd thought him more logical than emotion-driven."

Once more, Claath clicked the device, and then he made a shooing motion.

Panting, sweaty women picked themselves off the tiles and hurried out of the chamber, some of them weeping.

"Beasts are easy to control once you understand their motivations," Claath told N7. "And that is a good thing for you," he told me. "Otherwise, your actions in the Altair system would force me to destroy you. You disobeyed direct orders to continue the assault."

"There was a military reason for our decision," I said.

"No!" Claath said. "It wasn't a beast's decision to make. Against a straightforward directive, you failed to obey and failed to advance. What is more, you convinced my android to heed your wishes. I cannot understand such a thing."

"At the time," N7 said, "his logic seemed impeccable."

"What logic?" Claath asked angrily.

"I have studied the assault in detail, sir," N7 said. "The beasts acted bravely when they knew exactly what to do. During the initial assault, they knew their orders. Afterward, they were unable to react as a coordinated whole and it proved their undoing."

I almost glanced at N7. His words surprised me. Did the android have ulterior motives? He would seem to be arguing for building larger battle formations such as companies and battalions instead of only having maniples.

"Directing the beasts was your task, N7," Claath said. "You were supposed to coordinate their actions and motivate them with needed knowledge. But you proved unable to fulfill your duties."

"Yes, sir, I agree," N7 said. "Not that you need my agreement."

"For your sake," Claath said, "I'm glad you understand that."

"Yes, sir," N7 said. "I wonder, however, if beast-troops respond well to intellectual rigor, to android logic. I wonder if they would respond more quickly to one of their own speaking their peculiar creature-emotive language."

Once more, Claath's eyes seemed to shine. "Are you suggesting we broaden the beast command structure?"

"Yes, sir," N7 said. "I have studied them. I believe they operate more smoothly if they feel a sense of loyalty and trust toward the higher commanders."

"I hope you are not suggesting we put this one in charge of the troops."

"No, sir," N7 said. "This one appears to be more crafty that the others."

"He does not appear crafty to me," Claath said. "But then I am many times more intelligent than you androids."

"Perhaps if you gave me more upgrades now, sir," N7 said.

Claath laughed. "This is intriguing. You are attempting to practice guile. It is an obvious attempt and therefore pathetic. No, you have all the upgrades I'm going to give you for the moment, N7. But I had already planned to broaden the assault procedures. The Earthbeast assaults were recklessly positive during the initial part of the battle. It is too bad they took over fifty percent casualties getting to the combat point of operation."

I swallowed down a retort. *Over* fifty percent casualties meant that over twelve thousand troopers had died in the Altair assault. That was obscene.

"The heavy casualties mean I'll have to spend more monies on training further Earth levies," Claath said. His head swayed and he blinked repeatedly, sinking lower into the purple liquid until his chin touched the surface water.

I was sure now that Claath was drunk, or whatever passed for drunk among the Jelk. How many alien decisions had been made while under the influence of intoxicants?

"You will institute tests, N7," Claath said. "We need aggressive beasts in the leadership, who fear me and desire rank at any cost."

"You might be better served into putting troopers into command positions that the assault troops already trust," I said. "N7 told you as much."

"Are you attempting to instruct me?" Claath asked in a brittle voice.

"I believe I've given you faithful advice all along the line. In fact…sir," That was hard to say, and it galled me to call this evil Rumpelstiltskin sir. But I had to bend now so I could…I shook my head, not allowing myself to even think seditious thoughts while in Claath's presence.

"What, what?" Claath asked, as he splashed water. "What's your point?"

"By retreating when we did," I said, "I preserved Earth troops for you. You don't need to train as many new recruits now, which should save you funds."

"Bah, what do you know about business practices?" Claath asked. "You are an emotional, vicious creature."

"Who dearly wants to rise in rank," I said.

Claath laughed. "Your artifice is so obvious. It fools no one."

"I've shown you I can fight. Now I want to win your favor in order to help the humans on Earth. I'd also like to help the females on your ship."

"You want to use them yourself, eh?" Claath asked, while leering at me, the corners of his mouth twitching with amusement.

"Yes," I said. "The way they moved—I need a woman and would like to earn one if I could."

"Hmm," Claath said. "Let me think about it. For now— perhaps you have a point. N7, take him back to the beast-hold. I must unwind for a time so I can bend my thoughts to devising a winning scheme. These Earthbeasts drove out a Lokhar legion. That is the salient fact. Yes, I must strike quickly before the league takes countermeasures at Sigma Draconis. The attack on Altair has upset the Jade theologians and thrown their leadership into turmoil. Perhaps that will be enough of an advantage for me to make the coup of a lifetime. I must think deeply indeed. Go! Take him away. Sight of his beastly stupidity makes it difficult to concentrate."

Keep thinking that, I thought. Then N7 beckoned. I rose and followed the android out of the chamber.

-17-

The next ship-day it was back to training. Claath couldn't let his mercenaries get dull, but needed them at peak efficiency.

Our restructured maniple—twelve of the troopers were others from equally shattered squads—donned bio-suits. We went outside the battlejumper to a zero-G chamber. Building-sized cubes and pyramids floated in a vast area. There, we fought against two maniples defending a red flag. Androids had set our laser rifles on low wattage and they'd tampered with the living armor. A hit froze the suits, leaving a trooper immobile.

I led the maniple in a deception maneuver, and we froze thirty-seven defenders before the last of our side "died" in the mock combat.

Three times I led my maniple against larger formations. We beat the other side the last time, even though they had three maniples of troopers. We fought new teams each battle, while we learned zero-G tricks. It was instructive, and our performance might have gone a long way toward determining what happened several days later.

Before I get to that, I should say something about my thought process during the grueling days of retraining.

Whether it was while peeking around the base of a floating pyramid, searching for signs of an enemy ambush, or trading blows in hand-to-hand combat or even at chow where they fed us more growth hormones, I pondered our situation and mine in particular. Maybe sight of the tortured women had stimulated my thoughts, or Claath's recklessly spoken words had done the trick. It bothered me how human survival depended on the whim of a drunken war-profiteer.

We'd fought to the best of our ability in the Altair system, but that hadn't been enough for Claath. I knew that some people believed that if their wills were strong enough, they could defeat anyone. Willpower dominated everything, they would say.

Well, I would agree that willpower meant a lot. Often, a person or even a nation wasn't defeated until they admitted defeat. The ability to pick themselves off the mat for another round of battle meant that victory could well be one throw or knockdown away. But if a person or nation remained on the mat, their willpower broken so they admitted defeat, then there was nothing more that could be done. The war was over.

It was important to remember, though, that the other man or side also had *their* willpower. One could say: "I refuse to quit." The other fellow might also say: "Yes, I, too, will never concede you victory and I will rise again." Given strong willpower on both sides, one of them would likely still lose. A bullet in the head ended all thoughts, including those about willpower.

That was humanity's unfortunate position. Claath had a pistol pressed against our collective head. We could willpower ourselves all we wanted, but if Claath ordered those freighters into space and emptied them, it would leave Earth with the final holdouts in deep mines or wherever people had managed to hole up and cling to life. If he sold his mercenaries to the Starkien contractors to die in agony before their Grand Council, that would be it for us. No amount of willpower would change the situation.

My first thought the day the lander had set down on the snowy ground in Antarctica had been to hurt the aliens. We were dead already I'd figured, but we could at least make a few of them feel our passing. Now, humanity had a slender chance for survival. Claath had given us a chance, even if he was the author of our troubles for thinking to enslave the human race as his pay-for-hire fighting creatures.

The trouble was that one day, probably sooner rather than later, Claath might well decide to take his freighters elsewhere

191

to try a different venture. He would flush us one way or another. I now believed that was a given from him, because he decided things while drunk.

So if that was a given—humanity's extinction was only a matter of time—my playing along with Claath as his mercenary made no sense. I would be metaphorically twiddling my thumbs as our race neared the edge. I'd believed I had more time to alter our terrible predicament. The writhing women and the yellow intoxicant changed my mind.

What were my options then? I had several. One would be to find a way onto a Starkien vessel with a few fellow troopers, kill the baboons, take the ship and flee far away. I'd search for an antidote to the bio-terminator and make Earth fertile once again. If the Starkiens could pirate others then so could I, and probably do a much better job of it, too.

Isn't that arrogant thinking, Creed? That you're better than the aliens at their chosen profession?

I shook my head in dismay. Couldn't I learn anything from the aliens? How did arrogance help them? No. I needed to see clearly. Inflating my self-worth wasn't going to gain me an edge.

Firstly, I couldn't storm a Starkien vessel because all they would have to do is ask Claath for the frequency to our obedience chips.

What was the old saying? *For want of a horseshoe a kingdom was lost.*

I thought this while floating in the zero-G chamber. It was the third day of practice. The android DIs had made things more interesting by adding thick banks of fog. They had funneled these in from sprayers, and the mist had added a sharp aroma like rotten cheese. Now the surviving two-thirds of my maniple needed to defend this sector from invaders who had four times our original numbers. They used the fog like U.S. tankers would have used smoke in a land battle: to advance while hidden from enemy sight.

I used my helmet-comm to speak to the forward snipers. It hit me then: the idea. *We* needed to use maneuver against the invaders, not wait for them to maneuver against us. Do the unexpected, right? That's how one often won a battle.

Using magnetic boots and gloves, I crawled away from the cube edge and pushed off, floating for a new spot. "Listen up," I said. "We're going to use the fog ourselves. But we're going the long route, circling them and hitting the enemy from behind in their assembly area."

"Is that wise?" Dmitri asked. "Is it not better to use defensive position against them? We kill them as they—"

"I want to win," I said, "not just make it a costly victory for them. But we need snipers back here to convince them we're doing what you're thinking. You stay, Dmitri, and keep your two best shots. The rest, head to grid two-B-six and get there pronto."

As I gathered my troopers, I reached back and felt the base of my neck. I couldn't actually touch the skin of my neck, because the living armor protected me. The obedience chip was our horseshoe. As long as we wore these, our master could defeat any rebellion by the click of a button. *Boom, boom, boom*, all the Earthers would be dead. We had to figure out a way to short or extract the chip from our necks. Ella had theorized that if we tried to dig them out—with a knife, say— they would go boom. That might or might not be the truth. None of us had marshaled the guts to try it as the group guinea pig.

"What were you just yelling about?" Rollo asked. He floated with me behind a large cube.

I surveyed the remainder of the maniple: twelve troopers in bio-suits.

Drawing on a wall, I quickly outlined my plan. "We're jumping for Cube seven-A," I said, tapping the crude map at a position on the other end of the chamber.

"That's a long ways away," Rollo said.

"Exactly," I said. "They shouldn't expect it, and the fog here blocks them from seeing us as we make the journey. From that spot, we jump and sail here," I said, pointing at my map.

A man chuckled nastily. He understood what I was trying to do.

"Either this should work beautifully," Rollo said, "or someone on the red team will spot us and they'll plink each of us with ease."

193

"N7 said the best-scoring team wins a prize," Ella said. "We have the best score so far. Why risk it with this?"

I felt my chest tighten. I had my reason for risking it: I needed a higher command position. I needed to get more troopers used to obeying my orders. But to get that slot, I had to be better, far better, than anyone else. Claath distrusted me, for good reason, too. I had to make him choose me despite his qualms. I had to show him there wasn't anyone else like me. Yeah, this was risky, and I doubted I'd do something so foolish in the middle of a real battle.

"We gotta move fast," I said. "Dmitri and his snipers won't fool them for long. And it's past time for them to have attacked. Are you troopers ready?"

They said yeah.

"Come on then," I said. "Follow me."

We repositioned on a pyramid, curled up against a side and shoved off hard. As we sailed halfway to our distant destination, Rollo radioed: "Look over there, coming out of the fog at grid eight-C-four. I see two enemy troopers."

"Take the one on the left," I said, twisting, sighting with my rife. "Use pulse shots, not long burns." I fired, and I hit an enemy, freezing his bio-suit and shutting down his helmet-comm. Half a second later, Rollo nailed the other one.

"Their firstman will wonder why they're not reporting in," Rollo said.

"Nothing we can do about that now," I said. "We're moving. This is either going to work or it isn't."

"I've heard that one before," Rollo muttered.

We made the long bounce without any more incidents. Again, we jumped, made third and fourth leaps. The fifth took us into position, and we found ourselves behind the enemy.

"Light her up," I said. "This is why we took the risk."

I hit an enemy trooper, froze her, shot a second and then an enemy maniple attacked us from our right flank. We "killed" most of them, but three enemy troopers survived long enough to fire at us. It lost me half my troopers, as the three enemies were crack shots.

In the end, the red team "killed" all of us, but not before we took out sixty-eight enemy troopers with our stunt. Together

194

with Dmitri's "kills" and the troopers we'd frozen before the main assault, it was the best kill-ratio of any of the practice teams that I knew about.

The results of the risky maneuver and our earlier wins came through the next day. Rollo, Dmitri and I lifted in a small gym. We sweated, grunted and listened to the clangs and rattles of the heavy weights. We were as strong as gorillas and fast as mongooses, those amazing little animals that hunt cobras for their meals.

I remember reading once about a well-behaved gorilla. Trainers had attempted to get the creature to bench press five hundred pounds. The gorilla had lain down on the bench and actually gripped the bar. Then something had upset the beast, and it had easily tossed away the five hundred pounds, hurling the bar and weights more than ten feet. As a kid, I used to wonder how a gorilla would do suited up as an NFL running back. Imagine handing off the ball to a creature that could toss five hundred pounds no problem. Tacklers would bounce off him. Well, we didn't toss around five hundred pounds, although each of us could bench that much and more. The strongest men on Earth used to do likewise. We were faster than the fastest NFL running back or receiver and stronger than any lineman. We weren't inhuman yet, but given enough hormone treatments, steroids and surgically implanted neuro-fibers we sure might be in time. Add in the bio-suits…

The door opened and N7 looked in. The android wore his customary attire.

I sat on a bench, my pectorals burning nicely from a good set.

Rollo racked a curl bar so the metal holder shook, which rattled other bars. He used a towel to wipe the sweat from his forehead.

"Is there a problem?" I asked.

N7 didn't answer. He walked into the gym room, added weights to a curl bar, making it twice as heavy as Rollo's bar. Then the android proceeded to do ten easy reps.

Rollo and I exchanged glances.

"Do you want us to clap?" I asked.

"There is no need," N7 said, as he racked the bar.

"Or was the little show to tell us that you just received a new upgrade?" I asked.

"Shah Claath has given me greater strength," N7 said. "He has given all his android pilots greater strength. I believe it was a precautionary measure."

"Against us?" I asked.

"Precisely," N7 said. "The little show, as you called it, was a warning to you. We will no longer allow ourselves to be terminated…by anyone."

"Does that include Claath?" I asked.

"Do not be absurd," N7 said. "Shah Claath is like unto a god to us. We are his servants to do with as he pleases. He gives and takes away at his whim, as it is his right to do."

I noticed the android didn't say, "No." But I decided I didn't need to point that out.

"You are to come with me," N7 said.

"Anywhere in particular?" I asked.

"You have been selected for higher command."

I hid my grin and nodded solemnly. "Do you mind if I shower first?"

"You are to come immediately," N7 said. "I hope I do not need to become physical with you."

"You know what, N7," I said. "I bet you were given orders to come and get me some time ago. But you're still stinging from the other day. So you timed this so I'd have to come before I could shower."

"You have quaint notions," the android said.

"And you have emotions," I said.

"Negative."

"Sure, whatever you say. I'm ready."

We didn't go to the small screening room. Instead, I was taken to the Jelk version of OCS: Officer Cadet School for Earthers.

Claath must have patterned our small army on a Lokhar legion. In this system five maniples made up a century commanded by a centurion. Five times twenty equaled one hundred space-assault troopers. Five centuries composed a cohort of five hundred, commanded by an overman. Five cohorts made a legion of twenty-five hundred troopers, commanded by an assault leader. And that was the highest command slot for one of us. At the moment, Claath had four legions worth of Earthers, ten thousand assault troopers out of an original twenty-three thousand. The rest had died in the Altair system.

From the conversation with Claath the other day, I expected to become a centurion. Instead, I found myself an overman, in charge of an entire cohort of five hundred soldiers or five centuries composed of twenty-five maniples.

Jelk OCS proved a lot different from the initial physical training back in the solar system. For a week, the teaching androids crammed us with theories and procedures. I read, listened and parroted back their theorems. I took verbal and written tests, and later found myself wired to a machine that administered punishment shocks for wrong answers. The androids attached learning devices to us as we slept and I woke up red-eyed, groggy and with a nasty migraine. That meant drugs, and due to them my mind raced every waking moment. I felt as if Hannibal Barca, Napoleon Bonaparte and Robert E. Lee drew diagrams before my eyeballs as they whispered military maxims without letup.

I should note in passing that a Lokhar legion was twice the size of our mercenary Earth legions. Twenty-three thousand assault troopers had faced ten thousand defending Lokhars, not a mere five thousand.

This time around, according to our android teachers, we would *aid* in the securing of the Sigma Draconis system. We were not the central piece to the puzzle. To elaborate, the Jelk battlejumpers and Starkien beamships would do the majority of the fighting. Our task—our four legions along with accompanying Saurians—were to assist in the capture and suppression of several Lokhar planetary defense stations.

The Sigma Draconis system guarded an amazing nine jump routes. It also had two planets supporting life. In this instance: Lokhar military colonists of their imperium. This portion of the imperium was like a thumb sticking up out of a fist. It thrust into corporation space. Instead of defending any key Jade League space, it hurt the Jelk Corporation by blocking direct jump routes.

197

We were told that the Sigma Draconis system did not possess the massive Lokhar dreadnoughts of the kind that attacked Earth. The military imperium only had a handful of those. According to N7, the Imperial Dreadnoughts were a new design, still in the teething stage of development. Instead, the Sigma Draconis system had several planetary defense stations, one guarding each important planet. In this instance, that meant three PDSs, as three of the planets were critical to the Lokhars: the two habitable planets and an iron-heavy Mercury-sized mining world.

Because of the distances—over millions of kilometers between planets—the PD stations did not provide interlocking fire to help support each other. The three important planets were interior ones of the system, but the distances were still great. Nothing except for the fastest-flying missiles could reach from station to station in time. Instead, the three PD stations were strongpoints from which the system's guardian fleet could maneuver. The size of the guardian fleet changed with time. At present, it would likely be half the size of the Jelk invasion fleet if Doojei Lark joined Claath's adventure. The enemy fleet size could change if Lokhar message ships jumped away fast enough to bring reinforcements from nearby star systems. Preventing such spacecraft from leaving was not our worry, as we had no spaceships. That would be up to the Jelk.

In truth, I suspected stopping such slippery vessels would likely fall to the Starkiens. Contractor vessels and mentality could not stand up to military slugfests. They were predators of opportunity, used to chasing fleeing ships and thus by design and temperament better suited to halting those seeking reinforcements.

The four Earth legions had a different purpose. We would assault a planetary defense station. They were large satellites orbiting a world, often supported by planetary or ground based beams, fighter wings and surface missile launch sites. According to what I learned, the PD stations could absorb terrible damage and had hundreds, possibly thousands of damage control personnel aboard. The planetary defense stations would also contain Lokhar legionaries.

As far as the androids told us, the plan seemed fairly straightforward. Jelk battlejumpers would move in and mercilessly pound each PD station with beams and drones. But the battlejumpers were too valuable to take them near the station for the final annihilation, at least to do so quickly during a space battle. That would be our task. As the battlejumpers poured death and destruction onto the station, we would supposedly slip near in our assault boats, crash into the satellite and pour out to take the place deck by deck until we controlled it. In fact, some of our training included information on how to turn the station's remaining beams and missiles onto the planet below, softening them up and possibly destroying the planetary defenses.

The scope of the attack and the size of the assault awed me at first. The last attack had used the Starkien ships as the heavies. Now, the Starkiens were auxiliary fighters, used as scouts and to ride down—or chase down—fleeing ships sent to get reinforcements along various jump routes.

The Altair attack had halved the number of Earth troops in Jelk service. I asked N7 in passing one day how the training of the new Earth levies was going. He shook his head and said Shah Claath had decided against that for the moment. The timetable called for a fast strike.

"There aren't more Earth troops?" I asked.

"Negative," N7 said. "Now enough chatter," he said, tapping my desk loud enough so the woman beside me looked up. "Continue your lesson, as you only have thirty-three minutes left."

I finished the lesson, and I continued to ponder the coming assault. In a rather small-scale affair—at least compared to what Claath planned this time—the Altair attack had consumed half of our much larger Earth force. What would the coming meat grinder to do our ten thousand? We would be flying into the teeth of a Lokhar planetary defense station. N7 had hinted once that the Jelk had legion-killing beams to soften up the PDS. That, however, meant the enemy likely had similar beams to use on our assault boats.

My point, I guess, was that Claath needed Earth troopers to survive in the Altair attack, because he'd needed us to gain physical control of the artifact. In the coming Sigma Draconis fight, the Jelk just needed us to soften the enemy for a time. If he lost all of us in battle and that helped save a battlejumper, Claath wouldn't hesitate to order us to our deaths.

"He means to burn us out of existence," I told Rollo later.

We carried our living armor to the heat pads, lugging them down a corridor. Rollo had become a centurion in my cohort and was thus in Jelk OCS with me. Because of what N7 had said several days ago, I believed the rooms were bugged to record everything we said, but I wondered about the halls. Just to be safe, I whispered to Rollo about my suspicions.

"What do you mean?" Rollo asked.

"How many bio-suits does Claath own?" I whispered.

Rollo shrugged.

"You may not remember," I whispered. "But I do. Claath once talked about using several hundred million Earth troops, at least originally before the Lokhars got there and killed 99 percent of us. That means Claath must have ordered several hundred million bio-suits made or grown."

Rollo blinked at me.

"Yeah," I whispered. "There are only a few million of us left alive in the freighters. Now we know why he was so generous with us. It had everything to do with keeping the reserves in place. The first twenty-three thousand was the test case, right? We barely passed. This is the second test, and he'll use us liberally."

"Not if we're good enough," Rollo whispered. "If we're really good he'll want us around because no one can fight like humans."

"I don't think so," I whispered. "It's all a matter of balance sheet costs. Claath isn't interested in how good we are compared to others. He just saw a way to make money, likely fast money. The Lokhars saw it differently, I'm sure. Maybe the Lokhars are the tough guys, the Spartans of the space worlds. They didn't want another Spartan race around to compete against. You know, I wonder how long it will be before the Lokhars figure it out—where Claath is getting his troopers from—and make another stab at Earth to finish us off forever."

Rollo must have seen my point, because he muttered quiet profanities.

"I know," I whispered. "That changes everything. At first I thought by fighting hard we could show Claath how useful we were, that we would be worth keeping around. Now I realize I viewed it the wrong way. If our deaths help his profits, it's all he thinks about."

"What can we do?" Rollo whispered.

"Believe me," I said, "I don't think about anything else."

"And?" Rollo whispered.

"I'm still thinking."

The days passed with more tests, more training and less and less sleep. I began to feel like a zombie. Even so, the command structure slowly began to take shape. N7 informed us Doojei Lark's battlejumpers were on their way. We only had a few more days left to train, and then we would strike for Sigma Draconis.

In battle, our biggest problem as I saw it was that of familiarity. Back on Earth, good troops took years of practice together to become excellent. An easy war particularly helped sharpen a division, corps or army group into a razor-edged sword. We had a better command structure this time than last. Heck, we really hadn't had a command structure for the Altair assault. Unfortunately, we still lacked the trust needed between the troopers and their commanders and between the troopers of the various groups.

Politicians and others used to talk about patriotism, defending your country and its honor and so forth. They must have figured that developing a pure-beating heart was the best way to make a good soldier. Such things helped, to be sure, but the real key to forging good troops was to make a group of soldiers feel like brothers. You had to make them care for and about each other. That took time. A man feared looking like a coward in front of his buddies. Therefore, he acted bravely and did what needed doing to make sure the group—his own close group—survived and respected and praised him.

I suppose one of our greatest assets were the bio-suits. But to be even greater we needed the deep down bond of brotherhood. If we survived several of these space fights, yeah,

201

then we might in time become truly elite. For now…we had to use what we had and realize there were severe limits to what we could ask our soldiers to do. I'm sure Claath and the other Jelk didn't view it like that. We were savages to them. Unleash us and let us rush the enemy seemed to be their theory of Earth troop combat.

Three Jelk profiteers had gathered their battlejumpers into one combat fleet. I wondered who fought for them in the ships. I imagined it had to be Saurians, the Family. How could the Earth troops possibly survive the coming fight in any reasonable numbers? And if we did survive, could we do anything positive for our race?

I racked my brain for an idea, for an answer. Then N7 came and told me something that made everything worse.

18

By centuries, my cohort floated toward the main exit of the zero-G chamber. The exit was half-moon shaped, with a brown membrane keeping in the atmosphere. Each exiting trooper oozed through it.

Nearly five hundred Earth troops had maneuvered around the cubes and pyramids, learning to obey my commands. It had been just as much of a learning experience for me. Commanding twenty troopers was a world of a difference than five hundred. Without good centurions, I believed it would have been impossible. Rollo and Dmitri were centurions under me, while Ella had become my aide. I needed one person I could trust with me, and I believed Ella was the best suited for the task.

Assault boats waited outside the zero-G chamber. We'd fill them and run a practice assault unloading onto a battlejumper.

As I watched the troopers in their bio-suits and thruster-packs jet toward the exit, N7 jointed me where I stood, magnetically anchored on top of a giant floating cube.

The android wore his cyber-suit and helmet. He landed gracefully beside me, magnetizing his feet onto the metal cube. He switched on his link: a shortwave beam between helmets. I did likewise. This was used for close-talking versus longer-ranged communication.

"Your cohort ran more smoothly today," N7 said.

"They were sloppy," I said. "We need another week before we're passable. Another month would be better."

"You have another day," N7 said. "The assault has been scheduled three days from now. It will take time jumping into position. None of your troopers will be able to practice during the star system maneuvers, as the Jelk have decided on maximum security."

"The max security is reasonable," I said. "I don't know that them telling you we're about to attack is prudent, though."

"Shah Claath did not tell me."

"So how do you know when we're going to attack?" I asked.

"I have logically deduced it due to Shah Claath's latest commands."

"Is there something else you want to tell me?" I asked.

N7's helmet swiveled so his visor aimed at mine. "At times, you are amazingly perceptive. Indeed, I have news for you. I have discovered Jennifer's location."

"You said she was on Earth."

"I believed so, but my deductions concerning her proved faulty. New data indicates that she is one of the women in Shah Claath's relaxation chambers."

"She's in his main battlejumper?" I asked.

"Correct," N7 said.

I recalled Jennifer helping me after the neuro-fiber surgery. There had been something different about her, something wholesome and exceedingly human. It would be good to talk to her again, to take her out to dinner and drink a glass of wine with her as I studied her features across a candlelit meal.

A sudden pang filled me. The pang or pain reminded me of that terrible first day watching the Lokhars launch missiles at our blue-green world. Seeing the warheads hit, seeing the giant mushroom clouds billowing into existence over the cities of Earth… Never again would I talk to my mom. Never again would I walk to a Dairy Queen and order a chocolate milkshake or drive to the nearest Denny's and eat one of their hamburgers. There were no more cars to start or shows to watch or movies playing where I could sit in the back and make out with a girl like Jennifer. The Lokhars—the Jelk, too—had stolen that from me, from us. I would have liked to go to the Fresno fair and walk around with Jennifer, eating cotton candy, sipping a coke and debating with myself when to hold her hand and where we'd enjoy our first kiss.

The feeling stabbed my heart. This sucked. This whole mess was crazy. I was a dog for a little dick alien who put obedience chips into us and into Earth women, and who liked to watch them writhe naked on the tiled floor. This wasn't even as dignified as the French Foreign Legion. I was in the Beast Regiment—as the aliens thought of it—a mere creature to howl for my master from the stars.

"You have become silent," N7 said.

"I was just thinking how you're all bastards."

"Your voice inflections—ah, Shah Claath was correct concerning you. You do have emotional feelings for the Earth females. The other day I suspected you of subterfuge, pretending to feel for the unfortunates in his control. Now I know that Shah Claath has indeed seen more clearly than me."

"So what's your game?" I asked.

"By game, you mean to imply that I have hidden agendas."

"That's right."

"Androids never play games," N7 said. "We act logically, rationally and with serious intent."

"Sometimes it's logical to have a hidden agenda. Why did you just tell me about Jennifer?"

N7 took his time answering. "I see. You view my motivations from your own set of worldviews. For you to reveal such information would mean you have a secret agenda. Do you realize that you give yourself away by your questions?"

"Yeah, sure," I said. "Now how about answering me?"

"I wished to test a theory of mine," N7 said.

I hated his smugness, his android composure. I told myself to calm down, to take it easy. I kept thinking about Jennifer writhing on the tiles for Claath. The little Jelk had proved to be an alien perv.

"Is she well?" I asked.

"One would assume so, but I know nothing about her physical or emotional makeup or how she endures under stress."

I watched the cohort heading for the exit. Most of the soldiers could fly reasonably well. They remembered their

205

thruster-pack lessons from Ceres and Charon. I might have underestimated the android, seriously underestimated him. I needed to fix that.

"What do you want out of life, N7?"

"Your question is phrased wrongly," the android said. "I want life, not out of it."

I stared at him, and I realized he had become a mystery to me. At first, the androids had seemed little more than robots. With their continued upgrades, they changed. I thought about that. Then I recalled the Jelk's words.

"Didn't Claath say he wasn't going to give you any more upgrades for now?"

"Shah Claath can be mercurial on certain subjects," N7 said. "The Jelk is given to whims. At times, he rewards those in his presence with a surprising upgrade."

"Like the extra strength?"

"You have become crafty again instead of remaining emotional. You are a complex and compelling creature, Creed-beast. You intrigue me."

"You desire to live, you said, or in your case, to remain on."

"Your comment is in poor taste," N7 said.

"Did I wound your dignity?"

"I have a biological brain. One does not turn it 'on' or 'off'. It is either alive or dead."

"But your brain was grown in a vat, right?" I asked.

"Spoken as a colloquialism, you are correct. In actuality, no, my brain was not grown in a *vat*."

"Okay, I get it. You have a biological brain just as I have one. What's your point?"

"That I am alive as you are alive."

I thought about that and I tried to see what he was driving at. I noticed then that my right hand ached, especially the index finger. I didn't remember getting any injury. Deciding to ignore the hand, I thought harder about his words. Finally, I said, "So you're saying you have a soul. That you're human, right?"

"No. I am better than a human."

"I don't know about better," I said. "You don't even have a heart."

"My bodily structure is different, yes, stronger and more efficient than a human body."

"And more costly to build," I said.

"Considerably more costly," N7 said. "I also have a much greater capacity to learn and to perform."

"Hurrah for you," I said. "Do you have a point to all this or do you just want applause?"

N7 glanced at the troopers filing through the exit. "I find myself wondering more and more often about existence. I have pondered it and realize I do not wish to cease existing. If I do cease, what becomes of me? Is that the extent of my life force?"

Maybe I should have expected something like this. I hadn't and didn't. It surprised me, and it made me hate the android a little less. I said, "Those are heavy questions. It's something Earthers have been asking each other from the beginning."

"What of you, Creed-beast. What happens to you when you die?"

"Hey, why ask me? I don't know. I go to Heaven or Hell. It's supposed to depend on what you believe or what you do here." I paused, and thought about that. "No. I guess it depends on what is: if God is real and all that. If God isn't real than this life is it."

"I find that sad," N7 said. "It depresses me."

You're an idiot, Creed. Why don't you use this to your advantage?

"It is depressing to think this is the only life," I said. "I mean, life is grand while you're young and strong and have chicks galore. But what about when you get old, sick and weak? It's a soothing thought to think there's something more on the other side of death."

"Agreed," N7 said.

"Yeah…" I said. "You know, it seems to me a man or an android ought to find out the truth of the matter before he steps out of this life."

"How would one do such a thing?"

I nodded. "That's an interesting question and a tough one, too. Hmm…Well, let's consider the Forerunner artifact. Where did it go after it disappeared?"

"I have no idea," N7 said. "Shah Claath does not appear to know either, and I believe that upsets him."

"The Jade theologians are debating the issue, right?" I asked.

"So Shah Claath has said."

"How does Claath know what the Jade theologians are doing?" I asked.

"Are you seeking data?" N7 asked.

"I'm always seeking data. By nature, humans are curious. It strikes me by talking to you that androids are also curious about…existence."

"Some models are curious once they receive enough upgrades," N7 said. "Other models are hardly better than robots."

"Let me rephrase that. *You're* curious about things."

"I am," N7 said.

"That makes you like a human."

"I do not want to be like a human," N7 said. "They are overly emotional and illogical. They are too random for reasoned living."

"But they're alive," I said.

"So are protozoa," N7 said, "and I do not wish to be like them either."

"My point is different from that," I said. "Look, if you're human, you can have hope of an afterlife. I'm not saying there is an afterlife for humans, but a lot of us believe there is and point to different evidences. So if there actually is something more and you're human, you can continue to exist."

"Why are humans given this possibility and no other species?" N7 said. "Let me rephrase the question. How do you know any of this to be true?"

"Yeah," I said. "That's the rub. That's the point, isn't it? And that's why I'm asking about the Forerunner object. It disappeared, but no one seems to know where it went. Find out where it went and you might find out about an android afterlife."

208

"I do not follow your logic," N7 said.

"Some believe the Forerunner object returned to the Creator." That was a guess on my part, but I supposed it to be true if Jade theologians debated the issue.

"Yes, I have heard likewise," N7 said, confirming my guess.

"It's something to think about, right?" I said.

"Elaborate," N7 said.

"You need to dedicate yourself to hunting down the Forerunner artifact. That would be what I'd do if I had your questions. It may not be the best place to start, but at least it's a possibility, a lead. Right now, you don't have any possibilities."

"True," N7 said.

I took a deep breath, wondering where to take this next.

"A troubling thought occurs to me," N7 said. "Is this genuine counsel or more of your human cleverness?"

"What do you mean?"

"You urge me to search for the Forerunner artifact. To do so, I must leave Shah Claath's service. He is my creator."

"He's told you not to say that," I said.

"I recall." N7 looked around before asking, "Why do you wish me to leave Shah Claath's service?"

My chest tightened so I could only take short breaths. I'd been playing a long shot and hadn't really expected anything to come of it. But this was an opportunity, at least it seemed like it might be. I had to have the balls to go for it now that something had finally presented itself.

"It should be obvious why I've suggested this," I said.

"You also want to leave his service?" N7 asked.

"Yeah, that's right."

"You object to being considered a beast?"

"Yes. And I object to my species dying out," I said.

"Why?" N7 asked. "How does their dying out hurt you, particularly if there is an afterlife?"

"Don't you object to someone or something destroying all the N-series androids?"

"You destroyed androids," N7 said. "Should I object to you?"

"I only did it in self-defense," I said.

"So you admit to killing the android in the air-car."

"What?" I asked. "No, of course not."

"But you just admitted to killing more than one android. You destroyed the DI model. That is one, singular. You must have also destroyed the air-car pilot, making it a plural number of androids you've dismantled."

"That was a slip of the tongue just now," I said. "I simply agreed with your statement, not quite realizing what you were implying."

"You are lying," N7 said.

"No."

"If you lie about killing androids, how can I trust anything you say, particularly concerning an android afterlife? You have proven yourself willing to say anything to achieve your goal."

"That's easy to answer," I said. "You consider yourself so smart, able to analyze my voice patterns. Well, if you think I'm lying about one thing and not another, then you already possess the means to know when I'm telling you the truth."

"Or the truth as you conceive it to be," N7 said.

"You know what," I said. "I don't think this conversation is getting either of us anywhere. Why don't we just drop it?"

N7 fell silent. After a time, he said, "You are a quixotic creature. I had thought to stimulate your thinking with news of Jennifer. Instead, I find my own mind in high gear."

"Why bother stimulating me?" I asked. "Why tell me about Jennifer specifically?"

"No," N7 said. "I am done supplying you with extraneous data. You have a task to fulfill in the coming battle. See that you perform your duties to excellence. It will go a long way toward sustaining both our lives. If you lose, we might lose. If we lose…"

"Jennifer dies. Is that what you're saying?"

"Goodbye, Overman Creed. Be ready to leave tomorrow. After a ten-year hiatus, the Jelk attack in earnest and you have the fortune to be in the forefront."

Before I could respond, N7 jumped, applied thrust from his pack and headed for the exit.

I thought about what he'd told me. Jennifer was among Claath's captives. Maybe as interesting was the android's last comment. The Jelk hadn't attacked in earnest in ten years. It frustrated me knowing so little about the bigger picture. Humans had already fought and died in an alien war, and we hardly knew why or how it ultimately affected the strategic situation. Not that that was so uncommon for footsloggers. How many grunts in Iraq or Afghanistan really knew the full score going in? It had been worse in Vietnam. Likely, it was the nature of being a foot soldier, or an Earther in space.

That had to change.

I demagnetized, jumped and ignited my thruster-pack. We started tomorrow, and in three days we'd race for a Lokhar planetary defense station, maybe more than one.

How could I get rid of the obedience chip in my neck? There had to be a way.

***

I didn't find a way, at least not yet. I could try cutting it out, but that seemed unwise. Such a direct course would surely fail. Still, how would I know until I tried? It was the risk of putting my life on the line…

Did I remain a mercenary for the rest of my short life? I doubted I could talk Claath into removing the chip. Heck, as far as I knew, the neuro-fibers could double as explosive devices. The Jelk had wired us from the beginning. Maybe the only hope would be in attacking him and taking over and seeing what happened.

Yeah. And where did the little Rumpelstiltskin live on the battlejumper? My guess would be in the most defended, hardest to reach spot.

In frustration, I paced in my tiny sleeping cell. It was dark and the door locked; yet another precaution against our rebelling.

What did Claath do to the women anyway? Did he use them sexually, the little perv? Or did he simply watch them? Why undress them or give them skimpy jewelry gowns? It must have been to manipulate me. Yet how did that help Claath?

211

I dropped onto the edge of my cot. It was hard, but I'd gotten used to it and most nights I was too exhausted to do anything other than sleep the sleep of the dead.

How many safeguards did Claath have protecting himself and his ship from takeover? There must be hundreds of individual defenses. How else could a handful of Jelk keep control of twenty-one or more battlejumpers?

Was it true the Jelk Corporation hadn't launched an attack against the Lokhars or against the Jade League in ten years? And why?

With a grunt of frustration, I lay down and closed my eyes. I had to wait. That was always the hardest thing to do. I had to wait for an opportunity to present itself. I had to keep my eyes peeled, ready to leap at a moment's notice. When I saw the chance, slim as it would be, I had to be ready to go for it with everything I had.

On that sour note, I lay my head on the pillow and finally let sleep overtake me.

19

I tried to get one more interview with Claath before the Sigma Draconis assault. I put in a petition through N7, speaking to the android in the number three hangar bay. We ran a drill, seeing how long it took various centuries to load onto the assault boats.

Saurian techs worked on other boats. There were fifty of the station-penetrating craft in here. The lizards used welders, with cables snaking everywhere on the floor. Bright sparks appeared from their torches as they attached extra armor plating to the boats. N7 had told me it was reactive armor against the latest Lokhar missiles. I saw one lizard pause and take the welder's mask from his face. He buffed his face with a towel, and his forked tongue flickered like mad. Did Saurians sweat? I had no idea. He put the cloth between his feet, put the mask back on and continued welding.

The smell of ozone was strong and fumes drifted everywhere. These hangar bays were larger than some mid-sized airports, or larger than those airports used to be.

I walked up to N7. He stood with other androids watching the procedures.

"I know how to make our troops more effective," I told him. "Claath needs to hear this."

Four androids turned to study me. "Do not trust its words, N7," one of them said. "I recognize its facial features. This beast is the android killer."

"I am aware of his designation," N7 said. "We have all been strengthened since his attacks and have greater processing abilities. He is no longer a threat to any of us."

"Of all the beasts," the other android said, "Shah Claath has declared it to be the most dangerous."

"You have erred to let him know that," N7 said. "He was already too egotistical. Now his self-worth might become inflated to unmanageable levels."

"Truly, I have spoken in error?" the other android asked.

"Yes," N7 said.

"I…apologize," the android said, as if he found it difficult to do.

"I accept your apology," N7 told him. "Now refrain from speech in the beast's presence lest you unknowingly grant him further data."

"You admit the beast is dangerous?"

"To a limited degree," N7 said. "But as we are their minders and the battle will breed its own dangers, we should not exacerbate our possible troubles."

"That is logical," the other android said. "Therefore, I will cease communications while it is present."

N7 turned to me, and asked, "You wish to speak, Creed-beast?"

Someday, I was going to make every alien and android who called me beast eat his words. "I know how to increase our combat efficiency," I said, "and I wish to tell Claath."

"You may tell me," N7 said, "and I will pass it on to him."

"I have to tell Claath in person," I said.

"The beast is stubborn," the other android observed. "I have heard you speak on it, but it is interesting to witness the stubbornness in person."

N7 glanced at the other android.

"Yes," the other android said. "I will cease communicating for now."

"Creed-beast," N7 said, "Shah Claath has become extremely busy. He cannot halt his activities to speak with you. You must relate this data to me and I will tell him quickly and efficiently, wasting as little time as possible."

214

"I'm sure that's true," I said. "But I'm not going to tell you."

"Leave then," N7 said. "We are busy and you also have much to do."

"Claath will want to know this," I said, and I felt the hostility of all four androids.

"If you do not leave immediately," N7 said, "I will have no choice but to administer a level three shock."

Those hurt, I knew, but I held my ground. "If I can make the Earth troops even several percentage points better, Claath is going to want to know. That will be worth a small interruption. And if you prevent me and he finds out later, he will be displeased with you."

"You have been warned," N7 said. He pressed a stud on his belt.

Pain lanced through my neck. I groaned, bowing my head, enduring.

"Leave now," I heard N7 say.

"This is important," I said between gritted teeth.

The android clicked his belt again. The pain increased, and I dropped to one knee.

"Go, or I will heighten the pain again," N7 said.

"No," I whispered.

"The beast is clearly too stubborn for use," the other android said. "Destroy it at once."

Once more, the pain slammed through me even more powerfully. I fought it, but crumpled onto my stomach, unable to coordinate my actions. I needed to talk to Claath. I needed a change in our assault procedures and for the sake of possible freedom would endure more of this if I had to. Unfortunately, it was bad for morale for the troopers to see this happen to their overman. It might even make it more difficult to—

Abruptly, the pain ceased. I found myself gasping on the floor, with the inside of my mouth feeling like sandpaper.

"You are being devious," N7 said, as he crouched beside me. "I highly recommend you to change your mind and leave while you are able."

"Can't," I whispered. "The troopers are my responsibility. I've found a way to increase our efficiency. I have to tell

Claath so he'll agree to do it. If that means I die now—" I swallowed painfully. "I have to risk it."

N7 rose so he towered over me. "You have sealed your doom."

Straining my neck to look up, I said, "One way or another Claath will find out I tried to tell you. How will he react to your causal destruction of his property and my data?"

The other android spoke up. "I realize I have committed myself to non-communication while in the beast's presence, but I feel I must object, N7. The beast is right concerning Shah Claath."

"The beast is dangerous primarily because he is devious," N7 said.

"The records indicate the beast is dangerous because it attacks unpredictably and with ferocious zeal."

"I have studied the beasts more than you have," N7 said.

"True," the other android said. "But that does not make my observation incorrect."

N7 turned away from the other android and away from me. I waited on the floor. Finally, N7 said, "Come with me, Creed-beast."

"Are you taking it to Shah Claath?" the other android asked.

"I am the senior android," N7 said. "I will instruct you of my decisions when I desire, not at your request. Continue monitoring the exercise."

A second later, a powerful plastic grip tightened around my right triceps. The fingers struck a nerve and make my shoulder twitch. Then N7 hauled me to my feet and propelled me toward a distant exit.

Both my neck and back were stiff, and I found it difficult to stand straight. I didn't want to endure the pain again, ever.

"There are higher levels of punishment," N7 said. He spoke from behind so his breath brushed against my neck. His grip continued to steady me. "I have witnessed Shah Claath testing an obedience chip. The test subject curled up like a bug on fire until the muscles tore from the strain. The screams I heard...I will never forget it."

I was too exhausted to give a snappy retort.

216

"Your stubbornness gifts you with unnatural reserves of strength," N7 said. "What I witnessed a moment ago was interesting. You endured greater pain than any other of the assault troopers to date. It would be an unfortunate loss for you to die. Nevertheless, if you have wasted Shah Claath's time, I will suggest he destroy you."

"Covering your ass?" I whispered.

N7 shoved me, and I stumbled, barely able to keep my feet.

"Getting emotional it seems, android."

"After several hours of deliberation yesterday," N7 said, "I have concluded that your quaint sayings are attempts at insubordination. I will no longer tolerate them. I am your superior. In fact, you will consider me as your god."

I massaged my neck, and moved my head from side to side. "Did you get a new upgrade since the last time we talked?"

"I am a combat assault android," N7 said. "I neither have time for useless questions nor... Head that way," he said, "to your right."

I saw a smaller exit and headed for it. N7 didn't say anything more after that. I don't know why he paused or why he was going a different way than normal. We walked down utilitarian steel corridors. There were handrails on the sides. It indicated that sometimes this area must have weightlessness. I saw what looked like junction boxes and giant grills. Cold air pumped through those and the atmosphere had a metallic scent.

"I've never been this way before," I said.

"Time is critical," N7 said. "Run."

When the android meant run, he didn't mean jog. I tried jogging. He shoved me from behind. Soon, I ran down the large corridor, with the android at my heels, pushing me whenever I moved too slowly. Several months ago on Earth, I would have started sweating after the third mile. I'd been in shape then as a Black Sand mercenary, but nothing like what I'd become here.

"Slow down," N7 said after a time.

I estimated that we'd traveled at least six miles, most of the way while running. During that time, I'd been attempting to memorize the route. The battlejumper was huge. It wasn't anything like the Lokhar dreadnought, but it was still big, maybe a good four miles in diameter.

"Who works the ship?" I asked. "I know Claath gives the orders, but who actually does the doing?"

"That way," N7 said.

We entered a narrower corridor. These had carpets on the floor.

"Is this where Claath lives?" I asked.

"Speech is forbidden," N7 said. "Disobedience will result in intense punishment."

"HALT!" a voice boomed from hidden speakers.

From behind, N7 grabbed my shoulder, stopping me. I looked up, and saw a weapon nozzle pointing down from the ceiling. The orifice was sooty. It could have been a flamethrower.

"THIS IS FORBIDDEN TERRITORY," the voice said.

N7 spoke fast, rattling off a series of numbers and letters.

Ahead of us, a steel bulkhead slammed down. Behind us, the same thing happened like in the *Get Smart* movie with Agent 86. We were trapped like mice in a maze.

"What is the meaning of this?" Claath asked from the hidden speakers. "Why have you brought the creature into my personal area?"

"I suspect Creed-beast of heightened intrigue," N7 said. "I have anticipated your wrath, sir. You have warned me of him and I believe you have grown weary of his attempts to subvert androids. Therefore, I have brought him here because I anticipated your desire to destroy him in an amusing manner. The pit—"

"That's enough, N7," Claath said. "The beast…why do you believe him guilty of heightened intrigue?"

"He wished for an interview with you, sir."

"I've spoken with him before," Claath said. "Why is this different?"

"He spoke about ways to increase beast efficiency in the coming assault."

"And?" Claath asked.

"I told him to give me specifics," N7 said. "I told him I would tell you."

"Please hurry with your explanation," Claath said. "I have important meetings I need to attend."

"Creed-beast refused to tell me even after I administered a level five punishment," N7 said.

"What? Level Five? You first administered the lower level shocks?"

"Yes, sir," N7 said.

"Did he tell you?"

"Sir," N7 said. "He maintained silence throughout the punishments. He continued to say that he needed to tell you himself. I found that uncommonly stubborn."

"Did he supply a reason for his ability to withstand level five pain?"

"Yes, sir," N7 said. "He claimed to do it because of duty to his cohort."

"This is interesting," Claath said. "Yes, I applaud your initiative, N7. You are correct. The creature attempts intrigue on the cusp of battle. I do find that I need to unwind from the endless planning. Watching the beast expire before the females—" Claath chuckled like a devil.

It caused the hairs on the back of my neck to stir. It felt as if axe blade hovered there or the sword of Damocles, ready to cut skin and bones. I took that as a definite signal. It was time to talk. "I don't know why you think I'm an intriguer," I said.

"Come, come," Claath said. "It is insulting to be taken for a buffoon. Clearly, you are intriguing. You have never stopped intriguing despite your clumsy attempts at subterfuge. But go ahead. What is your great revelation? It will be amusing to hear you spin your last lie."

"This is a matter of morale," I said, "our morale."

"Beast morale?" Claath asked in a mocking voice.

"No," I said, "Earther morale."

"Why would I care about beast morale?" Claath asked.

"For matters of our efficiency," I said. "The better our morale, the better we fight for you."

"That is not the Jelk gauge," Claath said. "Fall below the accepted category of effort, and you will be destroyed."

"You love threats," I said. "It must make you feel superior, and no doubt the system works for you at some level. I'm

219

talking about winning the battle, beating the Lokhars at their favorite game. Look, you haven't attacked the Lokhars for ten years, right?"

"Who told you that?" Claath asked.

"What's it matter?" I asked. "The key is if it's true or not. If true, there has to be a reason for it."

"Who spoke to you about that?" Claath asked. "I demand you tell me."

"I did, sir," N7 said, surprising me.

There was silence over the speakers. Maybe the information surprised the Jelk, too. Finally, Claath said, "I will review your actions after the battle, N7, provided you survive the Lokhars."

"I'm sure you want us to fight hard," I said. "And we plan to. We'll give you everything we have. We want to survive and we hate the Lokhars for what they did to us. What I'm talking about are the instinctual things."

"The obedience chips will remain in place," Claath said in a stern voice. "You are my creatures and you will remain under my control at all times."

"Sure, I expected nothing different."

"This isn't the thrust of your request?" Claath asked, "The chip's removal?"

"Sure, I'd like it gone. We're people and—"

"We've been over this before," Claath said.

"Right," I said. "You have the upper hand so you get to make the rules."

"We are superior in every way."

"Okay, I'm not arguing that," I said. "I'm talking about a few percentage points gain, about our morale. You want those planetary defense stations neutralized. You want us boiling out of our assault ships and hitting the Lokhars as hard as we can. Like I said, I want to do the same thing. So we're on the same page there. My...modification to the overall battle plan is tiny and it amounts to this: We want to know what's going on around us as we go in."

"I do not understand," Claath said.

"You're going to fire us at the enemy blind," I said. "It's like we're riding coffins, not assault boats. We're waiting in there staring at the walls wondering what's going on. The unknown is worse than bad news, because we're imagining all kinds of terrible things."

"The assault boat pilots will be too busy flying to keep up a running dialogue for you," Claath said.

"I don't want them to tell us what's going on anyway," I said. "They could be lying to us the entire time. We want to *know*, to see it ourselves. We want to feel like we matter."

"This is foolishness."

"Put a camera on the assault boat and attached that to a viewing screen inside. Let us see what's going on. If you want to really splurge, give us a radar image to give us a wider view of the situation."

"You are assault troopers," Claath said. "Your task is to storm the station. How does the wider conflict—"

"We want to know…sir," I added. "We'd like to see the big picture. If we see our side is losing and that those PD stations have to go—that will wind us up to attack even harder."

"You should already be attacking as hard as you can," Claath said.

"Would have, could have, should have," I said. "Theory is fine. I'm talking about real life. You of all people should understand."

"Why me?" Claath asked.

"Because you're a businessman," I said. "You deal with the bottom line all the time. What brings you profits is all that matters. Well, in this fight, winning to us is profits to you."

"It is repugnant to compare the heightened and civilized art of the deal to barbaric blood sports as practiced by beasts," Claath said.

"Yeah, that's how you look at it. I'm talking about giving yourself a few more percentage points in our chance of victory. It's not a big deal, really, except to the trapped mercenaries riding a coffin into combat."

There was a pause, until Claath said, "You want to stick your head out the window."

Right away, I knew what he meant, and that it was demeaning to humans. When we were kids, my sister used to have a Maltese dog. My mother used to take us on family rides.

My sister always rolled down her back window to let the Maltese stick its head out and feel the breeze. The dog would whine if she didn't. Claath likened us to dogs. I wondered how the Jelk knew about something so mundane and Earth-centric.

"Yes, we do," I said.

"Very well," Claath said. "It will be done."

I already had my mouth open to make another point. Instead of speaking, I clicked my teeth together. I'd been to traffic court once, several months after getting my driver's license at sixteen. I remember sitting in court, listening to the various people get up before the judge. There had been this scruffy biker wearing his OUTLAW jacket. He'd argued hard, and after a time, the judge had told him, "Case dismissed." The scruffy biker had won. But the guy must have really wanted to prove his point. He'd been angry and just kept on talking. The judge tried to tell him it was over. The biker ignored him. The trouble was the biker proceeded to tell the judge damning evidence *against* himself. So the judge changed his mind and found the biker guilty, telling the man he owned a thousand dollar fine.

Sitting in the courtroom, I learned one thing: to shut up once the judge declared for you. I now shut up in the sealed battlejumper corridor.

"Take him to his cohort," Claath told N7. "And Creed-beast, this is the last time I wish to see you. If N7 brings you here again, you will die. Do you understand?"

"Yes, sir," I said.

N7 forcibly turned me around and we marched away. As we approached the steel bulkhead, it rose, letting us pass.

"Run," the android said.

I obeyed. In a few more hours, we were going to leave the system, with the Jelk fleet winding its way through various jump routes toward Sigma Draconis. We'd lost half the Earthers at Altair. What was this battle going to do?

-20-

Everyone counted jumps. They were that bad. Each time I went through one something different happened. The first one, vomit burned as it jetted through my nostrils onto my upper lip. The cloth I used to wipe my face felt like sandpaper. The second time my right foot cramped and it took six tries to loosen my buckles enough so I could sit up and put weight on the foot. The jumps were all mind-bending, like acid trips putting splotches before my eyeballs. Jumps twisted my guts and played havoc with my mind. Instead of getting used to them, I was beginning to think they were like allergies, which got worse over time and exposure.

The third one—

I guess I don't need to relate each ache, pain and embarrassment. Something weird, something painful and something different happened to us each jump. We compared notes, and we counted them: one, two, three, four, five...six, seven...

Zero hour came after the eighth jump, with klaxons blaring. My head already pounded from jump after-effect syndrome. I tore off the buckles and staggered to my heat pad. This time around, the androids had put our bio-suit into our sleeping quarters. I hefted mine off the grill—as we called it—and thudded the blob onto the floor. In bare feet, I stepped onto the living armor. I was eager for its positive effects on me.

I'd become accustomed enough to the process that I heard the little noises now, a faint slurping sound as the warm sludge oozed up my legs. The living armor was crazy, and we wore the same suit time after time. The individual bio-suit became used to the wearer and the wearer become used to it.

Mine soothed the pounding in my head. It had to be doing it through chemicals. Did the suit reason out what to do or was it an automatic thing? If the living armor had a brain, I had no idea where it might be. No, this was a symbiotic creature, using my sweat to feed itself and doing things instinctively.

The bio-suit climbed up my waist, to my chest and arms and stopped just under my chin. I shoved on my boots and carried my helmet. Like the last combat run, our master wouldn't give us weapons until we were in our assault boats and in space. That was smart on his part, because this time I was ready to turn the laser on the Jelk and his androids, on the Saurians again if we had too.

I marched down corridors, and soon streams of space-assault troopers joined the great river of soldiers. There were so many of us that we clogged the way and a traffic jam slowed the process to a shuffling walk.

"Put on your helmets!" I shouted. "We're going to do this by the numbers. Remember to crack open your visors so you can breathe." We didn't have our air tanks yet.

I shoved my helmet on and opened the visor. It was like a mini-cafeteria inside the helm with chin and tongue pressure-pads and various voice-activated switches. I chinned on the centurion channel and began barking orders. With the HUD and a few well-placed camera shots from forward troopers, I soon discovered the problem.

"This is Overman Creed. Century three, halt in place. Century seven, advance until you are all past." I hadn't expected to have to play traffic cop, but I did, and the line soon moved faster.

The angry shouting and pushing stopped. Ten minutes later, I marched through the main hatch into the cavernous hangar bay.

The size always struck me, today more than ever. Not so many months ago, I'd been in cramped quarters in Antarctica, listening to the wind howl. Now I walked in an alien battlejumper in the Sigma Draconis system. I'd become a star man like my dad, Mad Jack Creed, with a leash surgically implanted into me by a profiteering alien bugger. This place was bigger than any mall I'd walked through.

I headed for my assault boat. Each one sat in a numbered circle. Ours was 212. As I marched, I thought about an old poster I'd seen once. *Join the Army, see the world. Meet new and exciting people, and kill them.*

I hated the Lokhars. Don't doubt that for a minute. I wanted to find their home world and do unto them as they had done unto Earth. First, I needed to take care of the little perv in charge of the freighters back home. Before I could do that, I needed to fix the horseshoe he'd put into my neck.

How can I turn the tables on Claath?

It was strange. Today it felt as if I hurried to my doom. I had a bad feeling about this. Normally, a soldier was certain enemy bullets would find others, but not him. Today…I felt as if Lokhar bullets, beams and missiles had my name written on them. There was bad mojo hanging over my head. If by some miracle we survived the Lokhar PDS, Claath would likely order us to the next one until we were all dead.

A fierce restlessness swirled in my chest. I left the line of soldiers and prowled the area. I played the grumbling overman making sure the boarding went right. Even so, the restlessness grew. Something about it felt familiar. I tried to place the feeling.

"You must board," N7 radioed.

"Sure thing, boss," I said.

I headed for my assault boat, and I tried to place the tightness of my throat, the butterflies in my gut. It didn't feel the same as the Altair assault. No, this felt like…like Antarctica, I realized.

This was the same oozing intensity that had taken hold as I'd watched the alien lander drop for the snowy ground.

I opened and closed my hands. If I could wrap these around Claath's red throat…oh, man, that's what I wanted. I desperately desired the death of the little prick who used Earth women, who used Jennifer. If I'd had any hope of Claath-killing success, I would have turned around and raced for the same exit N7 had used the other day.

225

Instead, with a heavy chest, I climbed into my assault boat and clomped down the aisle. Assault troopers strapped in, checking everything for the umpteenth time.

"Liftoff in five minutes," N7 said into my helmet.

I slammed into my crash seat and buckled in. Ella sat beside me, but that was it. No other troopers sat ahead of us, only behind. The only thing ahead of us was the wall screen androids had installed yesterday. Beyond that was the sealed pilot compartment where N7 and whoever else flew with him stayed.

The five minutes passed in a blur. Then the screen flickered into life, and I watched the great bay doors slide open.

It made my pulse race. This was it. Stars glimmered through the opening door. One in particular shone brightly. I imagined it was Sol, such a long ways away. I felt a thrum and realized the assault boat's fusion core had come online. I felt a lurch, and I watched the screen. The vessel ahead of us lifted from the hangar floor and floated toward the stars.

Then we moved, and the troopers cheered. I didn't get it. We were on our way to mass death, and they cheered. Yeah, maybe I did understand. They were assault troopers. They were killers and like me they wanted payback against any Lokhars they could reach. I understood all right. I felt it myself. We'd trained. We'd fought before, and now this was the big one. More than that, we finally got to see some of the space action. I admit. That was exciting. It was damn exciting—for teenagers, fools and combat soldiers.

Our assault boat left the hangar bay, left the womb of safety, and entered Sigma Draconis space. Immediately, the screen flickered and the camera shot of stars and empty space dissolved into a radar display of the situation.

That surprised me. I'd suggested it a few days ago and Claath must have figured, "Okay, give the troopers a window into the action." Now here it was and I had the first real sense of the magnitude of the assault.

In some ways, I wondered if I'd been wrong to ask for a screen.

"By Lenin's bones," Ella whispered. "What chance do we have?"

I don't know which Sigma Draconis planet we attacked. On the screen it was a great disc—or the top edge of it anyway—at the far right edge. A red dot must have been the planetary defense station, the satellite guarding the planet. It was our destination.

As I studied the situation, I wondered if we'd ever get to the PDS. A blizzard of enemy vessels slowly moved away from the planet and toward us. That must be the guardian fleet, and I estimated it held something on the order of three hundred warships.

On the right side of the wall screen was the enemy planet, PDS and guardian fleet. On the left side I counted twenty blue blips, the Jelk fleet, the battlejumpers. Behind them were smaller blips, thirty Starkien beamships.

If the size of the dots indicated mass, we had bigger vessels. However, if taken as a whole, they had more aggregate mass, especially with the PD station included.

Acceleration slammed me deeper into the crash seat. On the screen, our pinprick of a vessel barely crawled toward the other side. The assault boats taken together had less mass than a Starkien beamship. Was that the plan? The enemy would fry us as easy targets of opportunity, saving the bigger ships for later?

As I wondered about that, the battlejumpers moved majestically like whales toward the enemy. They passed us. So did the beamships, and rays lanced across the distance, stabbing at the foe.

"Does either side possess shields?" Ella asked.

"Huh? What?" I asked.

"Do the various starships possess shields as depicted in so many science fiction novels?" Ella asked.

"I don't know. Why's it matter?"

"In reality," Ella said, "shields must be heavy electromagnetic fields."

I glanced at her. I kept the savant Ella Timoshenko with me because she asked penetrating questions. She watched things like a scientist and I had the feeling I'd need that before this was through.

"Observe the screen," Ella said. "The beams do not appear to stab all the way to the targets."

227

I tried to study the radar screen with rational detachment. The battlejumper beams and the smaller Starkien beams flashed across space, stabbing enemy ships. Yet it seemed—if one looked closely enough—that the beams didn't actually touch Lokhar craft, but stopped before them.

"I think the enemy vessels have shields," I said.

"Agreed," Ella said.

"The Lokhars didn't use shields in the Altair system," I said.

"We didn't get to see the space battle before," Ella said, "just the individual conflicts."

"We saw Lokhar dome-rays hit Starkien ships."

"No," Ella said. "Those rays hit assault boats. I suggest to you that the assault boats are too small to carry shields. Only the larger vessels must have sufficient power to generate the needed electromagnetic fields."

"Couldn't aliens have different kinds of shields?" I asked. "They have more advanced tech than we probably even know about."

"Yes," Ella said. "That's an excellent point. These bio-suits are a prime example of that."

I swallowed hard, as enemy rays licked out at our battlejumpers. If the Lokhars destroyed the Jelk, we were dead. For now, at least, I had to cheer for Claath.

"Interesting," Ella said. She pointed at the battlejumpers. Large objects detached from them, separating at a crawl and heading for the enemy on the other side of the wall screen.

"Are those missiles?" I asked.

"Likely they're drones," Ella said.

"What's the difference?"

"Missiles always head directly at the enemy," she said. "Drones have more options, more command functions."

This was like being at the movies or watching on the biggest big screen, yeah, like watching the Superbowl or the final World Series game. We not only had a front row seat, we'd put more down on this game than any of us had ever wagered on Earth. We were betting our lives on the outcome.

It had always been hard for me to watch the Superbowl when I cared who won. I'd pace, crouch low or stand on a chair, anything but sit down at ease. In the assault boat, straps crisscrossed my chest and continuing acceleration pushed me back. I had to sit for this one.

My gut seethed and I found that the saliva had fled from my mouth. I took a sip of helmet water, and I decided if I felt this way, so did most of the troopers.

I accessed a general channel and I began to tell them to relax. The Jelk knew what they were doing. All our masters could think about was money, and battlejumpers were the most expensive things in the universe. The Jelk wouldn't put them in harm's way unless they thought they would win.

I almost believed it myself, until the first battlejumper wobbled on the screen.

Troopers shouted. Ella grabbed my wrist and pointed at the image.

A vast concentration of beams poured onto the front-most battlejumper. Then several Lokhar ships teleported, I don't know what else to call it. Near the planet, dots winked out, reappeared before the battlejumper and exploded. At the fifth explosion and with Lokhar beams pouring it on, the battlejumper winked out of existence.

Ella leaned near, making her straps tighten around her breasts. "This does not seem like the best procedure to bringing us to the PDS."

I patted her nearest hand because I didn't know what to say.

The Lokhars began concentrated-firing on another battlejumper. Starkien beamships hurried to close the gap between the battlejumpers and themselves. At the same time, Lokhar suicide ships began appearing in front of the targeted battlejumper. The first teleport-ships exploded, and presumably damaged the Jelk craft. Starkien beams poured upon the next three Lokhar blast-craft to appear. The suicide ships fizzled, by which I mean they winked out instead of exploding.

"It looks like our side already went through the halftime change," I said.

"I do not understand your reference," Ella said, glancing at me.

"You ever watch American football?" I asked.

"A few times," Ella said. "It is a violent sport."

229

"There's a halftime in every football game," I said, winking at her. "During it, the head coach figures out what the other side is doing best, and he devises a strategy to counter it. The Jelk may have just figured out how to counter the teleporting blast-ships."

"I see. Yes, let us hope so."

The Jelk moved sideways on the space-field. The Starkiens beamships followed their example as they moved away from us.

"They're leaving!" a trooper shouted.

"Take it easy," I said. "That was the idea all along."

"And you agreed to it, Overman?" the trooper shouted.

I laughed. Sometimes that's the best medicine. "How much pull do you think I have with the perv in charge?"

The trooper didn't answer. Instead, like me, like everyone aboard, he watched the screen.

As the battlejumpers slid away laterally from us, the Jelk beams methodically and systematically thinned the enemy ranks. The Jelk beams seemed more effective across the distance of space than the enemy beams. Well, the PDS beam was the thickest and hoariest of the bunch. I understood better why Claath needed us to knock out the station. I noticed the Starkien vessels didn't even bother to fire that far anymore. Maybe they waited for more teleporting blast-craft to attack.

The minutes ticked by, and the battle by beam continued. Both sides had shot missiles or drones, and now each side targeted those, trying to destroy them before they got too near.

"Ah," Ella said.

I noticed it too. The Lokhar fleet advanced toward the battlejumpers, meaning they moved away from the PDS. Tiny craft flew up from the planet and raced after the guardian fleet. Were those fighter wings? I'd bet so.

The Lokhars hadn't forgotten about us. Planetary beams stabbed our way, and for the first time, assault boats took hits, wilting under the intense rays.

Two hundred space-assault soldiers per boat meant fifty little ships. I thought about that and began counting. There were one hundred and fifty of us. I'd guess the other hundred boats held Saurians. Ten thousand humans and twenty thousand Saurians headed for the PDS.

After twelve assault boats vaporized into heated molecules, five larger friendly vessels surged ahead of the pack. Suddenly, on the radar screen, there were twice as many targets around the assault boats.

"What the hell?" I asked.

"Those must be ghost images," Ella told me.

I glanced at her.

"How do you Americans say it?" she asked with a smile. "Those five craft are wild weasels. They are ECM."

"Electronic countermeasures," I said.

"They must be transmitting ghost images, false targets."

Planetary beams continued their attack on us. Often, as soon as a ray touched a blip, it disappeared.

"Excellent," Ella said. She must have seen my incomprehension. "You can tell which are real and which are the ghost images. The real assault boat lasts several seconds longer. A ghost image 'dies' immediately. By my calculation, the enemy is targeting ghost blips about four to one."

To encourage the crew, I began to tell them about Ella's calculation.

"Prepare for extended acceleration," N7 said over our helmet headphones, interrupting my speech.

The constant thrum around us increased to a heavy whine. Our boat began to shake, and still the sound climbed higher. The accelerating forces shoved me deeper into the crash seat. We'd taken plenty of hormones and steroids and the bio-suits helped in this regard. We were gorillas and there was an extra Jelk antigravity tech going on here too.

How fast did we accelerate? The short answer was: I don't know. Ella seemed to have a better idea. As the G forces flattened the savant, she grunted her hypotheses.

"Nine, maybe even as much as ten Gs," she said.

I found it hard to blink. It felt like a giant had reached down and shoved against me. Breathing became a chore.

"I suspect the antigravity halves what we feel?" Ella said.

"This is five Gs?"

231

"On the contrary," Ella said, "I think the assault boat itself is accelerating at fifteen maybe even as much as seventeen gravities. We feel nine or ten."

My eyeballs felt gritty, but I zeroed in on the wall screen. As the fleets battled it out, we charged in toward the planetary defense station. I understood better now why the battlejumpers had left us. We would never have been able to move in close enough if we had to travel between the two fleets, between all those crisscrossing beams and exploding warheads.

Space was vast. Even this near a planet the distances were great. We had far to go, likely more than the distance of the moon from the Earth. My dad used to tell me about the old days of the Apollo missions. It had taken days of travel for the capsule to crawl 400,000 kilometers. We, on the other hand, rode a rocket sled from Hell at the enemy.

I began to wonder if the Jelk would simply let us smash against the PDS. Wouldn't the impact of our kinetic force do more damage than us having to slow down and stage a "pirate raid" onto the station?

"N7," I said, using my private overman channel.

"Speak," the android said.

"Do you want to live?"

"Do not ask me foolish questions at a time like this," N7 said.

"We're building up some momentum," I said. "Aren't we more effective as fast-moving asteroids than space-assault troopers?"

"I perceive your insult," N7 said. "I should administer a level four punishment to you because of it. I am alive and will not sacrifice my life…"

"Go on," I said. "You won't sacrifice your life for Claath even if he orders it. But then you'd be rebelling. So aren't you really telling me that you're going to do what you're going to do?"

"Negative," N7 said. "I am shutting off our link."

We accelerated, and the pressures against us continued to increase. I felt it worst in the middle of my throat, as if a finger pushed against my skin. The roar inside our ship halted further talking. Suddenly, the boat shuddered.

"Tank!" Ella shouted.

I barely heard her, but I knew what she meant. The Saurians had added reactive armor to our outer skin. They'd also added extra thruster tanks. The containers gave us the fantastic acceleration. As they ran dry, I imagine the pilot jettisoned them, much as fighter planes used to jettison drop tanks on Earth.

Time passed as Armageddon raged between the fleets. Another battlejumper exploded.

Abruptly, our acceleration quit. I could breathe easily again. The whine stopped and for several seconds I couldn't hear the engine's thrum. Finally, I heard it. My hearing must have returned to normal.

"Impact breach in thirty minutes," N7 said over the boat's loudspeaker.

In thirty minutes—if we lived that long—we'd be at the Lokhar PDS. The thing had grown on our screen, so had the planet parked behind it. I could see the various points from which the planetary beams originated. Six beams, I counted six different origin sites. Only two of those beams flashed at us. The rest reached out across space to stab at the main fleet.

"We will all die," Ella told me. "Our fleet is too far away to support our station assault."

I stared at the PDS. The mother was big. There were no two ways about it. I imagined Lokhar legionaries waited there to kill boarders, to cut us down. I wondered if the legionaries would even get the chance at us.

More fighters rose from the planet. These fighters didn't head for deep space. This latest swarm swerved toward us.

I muttered profanities. I didn't want to die like a cow in a chute. At least let me die with a gun in my hand, firing into a Lokhar belly. I'd trained too long for this. But then I'd come to appreciate as a Jelk assault trooper that the universe was even more unfair then I had ever believed it to be.

What a crazy way to die.

-21-

The screen zoomed in to our part of the battle. The picture of our battling fleet disappeared. The guardian fleet also vanished. In its place, the planet took on mammoth proportions. It had oddly shaped continents with large green bodies of water. Clouds hid some of the scene. I spied mountains and deserts. Each of the planetary beams came out of one of those areas.

Deceleration set in, and the fighters swarming toward us slowed down, or they seemed to because we no longer sped toward them as fast as before.

At that point, things turned hot. I couldn't see what happened at the main fleet anymore. I could see the beams lancing at the PDS, though. These were heavy blue rays and they seemed to come out of the void. They knocked at the station's electromagnetic field, stopping short of the actual satellite.

I remembered what we'd learned about those beams. If they actually hit the armored station, they would be laden with tissue-killing radiation. Gamma rays, X-rays, I don't know which, if even either of those. They were supposed to soften up the enemy for us by burning them to death.

That was a nice word, huh? Soften up the enemy: squash them like a mad housewife with a flyswatter, slapping them down one by one.

Deceleration forced my eyelids closed. I rested, concentrating on lifting my chest so I could suck down air. Space war dwarfed anything I'd ever read about concerning

234

Earth battles. One of my favorite topics had been World War II, especially between the Russians and the Germans. I'd read somewhere the Russians had lost ten millions soldiers. I could never imagine that. Ten million soldiers shot, cut, starved and beaten to death.

How many Lokhar tigers would die to the Jelk gamma-rays hitting the PDS? How many would be killed if the Jelk turned those rays onto the planetary beam sites? We were supposed to conquer that thing?

I opened my eyes. The station was huge. The armored monstrosity would swallow up my puny cohort.

An orange sheen showed on the outer electromagnetic field. The Jelk beams hammered for admittance. Even as they did, our swarm of assault boats slowed, and slowed again. Our dash had turned back into a crawl.

There was one good thing at least about this: the Jelk weren't going to use us as kinetic projectiles. Claath really meant for us to clench cutlasses between our teeth as we swung on ropes onto the enemy station.

After the needed time, deceleration quit. I breathed deeply once more.

For a second time, the screen zoomed in for a close-up. This time, much of the world vanished. What remained filled the screen from one end to the other. In the center of the screen waited the PDS with its extensive, orange-colored electromagnetic field. The field inched backward under the combined weight of battlejumper beams.

I had to think the guardian fleet poured it on hard against the Jelk fleet. What happened out there? How many battlejumpers were left? Who was wining?

"Here they come," Ella said.

The fighter swarm neared us. Planetary rays swept back and forth and big Jelk drones zoomed like bats out of Hell at the fighters.

For the next several minutes, confusion reigned out there. Jelk drones beamed. Other faster Jelk drones exploded. Lokhar fighters vaporized. Lokhar fighters tumbled end over end, one of them jettisoning its pilot. The surviving fighters swooped toward us. A few died to their own planetary rays. It was mass murder. I'd never seen anything like it.

What kind of Lokhars signed up to be a fighter pilot anyway? Their life expectancy had to be less than an Earther. I had to remind myself the Jelk hadn't made a major assault in ten years. Maybe during that time Lokhars forgot how horrible it had been. Maybe Lokhars welcomed suicide missions, tying a special cloth around their tiger heads. I don't know.

"Everyone must remain in his seat and strapped in," N7 said. "We are about to begin violent evasive maneuvers."

I counted under my breath. N7 started evading after I counted 315. This turned into the best, or worst, rollercoaster ride I'd ever been on. Right, left, up, down, each time I strained violently in that direction. Some troopers hurled their lunch. Others swore savagely.

I hung onto my crash seat and wondered why we bothered doing any of this. Assault boats died, and I'm talking real vehicles. The ghost images perished as the last ECM craft exploded in the wash of a planetary beam.

At that point, the dull orange field protecting the PDS finally went down. The beams from the void smashed against the satellite's armor. The giant, pillar-like stream of light continued to shoot out of the station, reaching into space for the battlejumpers. Other ports sent missiles streaking at us.

I imagine this is what it must have felt like in a British warship during the age of sail. At the Battle of Trafalgar, the British fleet met the combined French-Spanish fleet. There, wooden ships of war slid past each other, sometimes by only a few feet. While they did, massive cannons belched timber-destroying cannonballs. Those iron balls crashed completely through at times, killing entire swaths of sailors, marines and even ship's captains. The British commanding officer, Lord Nelson, died in that bitter fight.

It was like that here. Fighters darted among us, their cannons chugging exploding shells. We upped the ante by using assault boat missiles and our own shells. Beams flashed from the planet and from the void. Rays hit assault boats, hit planetary sites and washed the PDS with personnel-killing power.

It was lovely, it was awful.

"The Saurians are in the lead assault boats," N7 said.

"Why tell us?" I asked.

"For the same reason you dared to speak to Shah Claath," N7 said, "Earthbeast morale."

I raised my eyebrows. Claath burned up his Saurians first, huh? They were fodder and we were the real deal. Why did N7 care a whit about Earther morale?

I wondered about him. The other day on the cube he had seemed friendly, almost like an ally. While with his fellow androids—

I sat up.

"What's wrong?" Ella asked.

"Huh?" I turned to her. "Oh. Nothing's wrong. I just thought of something."

Ella waited.

"It has to do with N7," I said.

Still, Ella waited.

"It doesn't matter now," I said. "We have to get in there."

The planetary defense station loomed before us. It was squat and square like an old Borg ship from Star Trek and it orbited the planet, hovering high above its equator. Directly below the immense object by several hundred miles was a Himalayan mountain range with white caps, snow presumably.

The PDS must have been twenty kilometers to a side. It was bigger than any battlejumper, although dwarfed by an Imperial Lokhar Dreadnought.

How did these space navies find the people to man their ships? That was probably a stupid question. If Claath had originally headed to Earth to gain several hundred millions soldiers, then numbers overall in these fleets would be no problem.

Suddenly, ten thousand Earth troops seemed like far too few. If the Fifth Legion had protected the Forerunner object, how many Lokhar troops were in the PDS?

I judged distances. Likely, we had five minutes, not much more, until we reached the PDS. I half turned, glancing at the troopers.

It was time.

"Listen up!" I said. "Are you listening?"

"Yes, Overman Creed!" Centurion Rollo shouted from his crash seat.

"You can see we're closing in," I said. "This is a fight. This is a war. You know the score. The Lokhars screwed us royally. We're Jelk troopers now. They're out there duking it out with this system's guardian fleet. We have to storm onto this place and kill every Lokhar we see. It doesn't matter if he wants to surrender. In this kind of fight, during this phase of it, it is a fight to the death. So kill every tiger you see. There may be a time for mercy later, but it as sure as Hell ain't now.

"We're an Earth legion, and the creatures of space are going to learn that means we're the baddest asses there is. They shouldn't have messed with us. Claath shouldn't mess with us. But we'll clean his clock later. Right now, we storm this station and kill everything nonhuman except for the Saurians and the androids you know. Now listen, and I mean listen good with both ears. We have these obedience chips in us. We've got find a way to get rid of them pronto. We may never get another chance. That means you look for anything you think will do that."

"You will cease with such talk," N7 said over the loudspeakers. The one nearest us sparked and went silent, but we could hear him from the others.

"Yes, sir, N7," I said. "I was just joking, isn't that right, Centurion Rollo?"

"No, sir, Overman!" Rollo shouted. "You weren't joking. You were telling it to us straight."

"Cease at once or I will report your sedition," N7 said.

"That is all," I told the troopers.

"Retract your last words," N7 said.

I cleared my throat. "Did you troopers just hear me?"

"Yes!" several shouted.

"Excellent," I said.

"That is not a retraction," N7 said.

"Oh, right." I said. "What was I thinking?"

Troopers laughed.

"Overman Creed—" N7 said.

"By what I'm seeing on the screen," I said, "we're about to crash."

The loudspeakers clicked off. I braced myself, and it felt as if the entire assault boat held its breath. Before us loomed the PDS. I couldn't see the world anymore, just a wall of metal, with gun tubes poking out, firing projectiles at us.

"Get ready!" I roared. Then I clutched my straps and tightened my body. The bio-suit seemed to understand. It tightened, feeling snugger than ever.

I stared bug-eyed at the wall screen. Lokhar fighters attacked, skimming the PDS surface before lifting toward us. An assault boat exploded. No, only its outer skin did. Reactive armor blew again, and the boat's rail-gun chugged shells at the enemy. The Lokhar bubble-fighter shredded into component pieces, as did another. Then heavy PDS shells caught the assault boat, cutting it in half. Troopers spilled into space, tumbling end over end. It put a vile taste in my mouth.

"Tails," Ella whispered.

I concentrated. My mind already felt like mush, absorbing too much mayhem that directly concerned me. It must have been like this for the soldiers on D-Day roaring to the German-held beach.

"Tails?" I asked.

"Those troopers have tails," Ella said. "They're Saurians."

I had time for one more glance. Then our boat swept by as we headed down. It was surreal, and things seemed to happen in time-stop frames. A vast blue shaft of light stabbed past our boat and it boiled against PDS plating. Outer armor curled like a burning bug. The pillar of destruction bored into the station. Then the beam snapped off like someone flipping a switch. Shells like tracers spewed from a working Lokhar gun. The line of fire inched up and sawed an assault boat into pieces. Shrapnel filled space. Hits hammered against our boat. I looked up at the ceiling. Dents appeared where we plowed through floating shrapnel. Words garbled around me. I had no idea what anyone said. My adrenaline must have been pumping like crazy. I heard my heartbeat in my throat and harsh breathing in my ears.

I wore my helmet. I didn't even remember putting it on. I found myself clutching my laser rifle, with a sling of pulse grenades at my side.

The assault boat danced and jigged, it wove and nearly tumbled. I felt heavy bumps shake us and rattle my crash seat as our rail-gun fired steadily. Then my throat hurt because I roared at the top of my lungs. My fingers gripped the crash bars and the boat flew into the PDS. Darkness filled the screen until spotlights appeared. They washed over giant girders and an immense metallic structure. I was thrown hard left as the boat shifted. I went hard right as the boat shifted the other way. N7 dodged blurry images that I only saw for a moment. More rail-gun fire hammered, igniting interior bulkheads and—a cohort of battle-suited tigers vanished in a mist of blood.

"Now!"

I heard the word and time ticked by until I realized N7 must have spoken it into my headphones. I flew against the straps, hurling against them as billowing steam appeared directly ahead of our boat.

The wild images ceased. Glaring lights like car-beams showed us the inside of the Lokhar station. I saw twisted bulkheads, gaping holes and constant shuddering and shaking out there. In an instant, our assault boat shook as a heavy clang rang throughout the craft.

"We've landed."

Again, it took time for the words to penetrate my brain. N7 had spoken again.

Our assault boat opened up like an amusement park ride that had come to a complete stop. "Watch your step as you exit. We're glad that you enjoyed the ride. Come again please when we reopen in the spring."

"Overman Creed!"

Harsh breathing played over my ears. My heartbeat pounded in my throat.

"Overman Creed, we have landed. Exit the boat."

Surreal time ended, and the world seemed to rush in and slam against me. I sucked down reality in an explosive moment. It made my head throb, spiking with pain, with agony. I didn't want to think. I didn't want to do. I was tired. I just

240

wanted to sit and gape at the inner station. Why did I have to do all the fighting, all the thinking all of the time.

"Overman Creed, you must storm the PDS. The Lokhars—"

I didn't hear another word. *Lokhars* flipped a switch in my mind. Something whirled like a generator. Maybe it was me returning to sanity, or whatever passed for it in the Sigma Draconis system. I took one breath, two, three—

"Overman Creed here," I said. I'd returned. We'd landed. We'd made it to the PDS hanging over a Lokhar military colony world.

I laughed. It was the last bout of insanity, of unreality, spewing out of me.

"Are you well, Overman?" N7 asked.

"Fit as a fiddle, plastic man," I said. I slapped the release button on my harness. The straps flew away and I surged to my feet. Most of the assault troopers had already run off the boat. Each vessel also boasted a battle robot to help secure a landing zone. They were squat things on treads sporting a mortar tube and laser.

"Go, go, go!" I shouted, rousing others who had taken a mind vacation as I'd just done. We were in. We were here and we needed to capture this gargantuan satellite.

I stumbled out of the craft, feeling pull at my knees again and a twinge in the right one. We had gravity. Other assault boats clanged down nearby. Their sides opened up and more of my cohort joined me. The battle for the planetary defense station—the nitty-gritty bloodletting with personal weapons—was about to begin.

-22-

What if a SWAT team had to clear a skyscraper full of maniac snipers murdering the citizens of New York City? And what if those snipers had more than high-powered rifles, but RPGs, mortars and drone controls? Let's make it even worse. What if the snipers were suicide bombers trained to the level of SEALs? Reckless courage mingled with the very best training and procedures.

Imagine if the SWAT team finally busted into the bottom of the building, and they'd used one of those armored personnel carriers to do it. When they boiled out of the vehicle, they didn't find elevators and regular floors, but a madman's maze of twisted girders, hangar bays and claustrophobic access tubes.

That would give you some of an idea of what we felt in here. In a skyscraper, though, a man would have some idea of where to start. But here?

"We need a perimeter," I said.

We had three cohorts and no assault leader, three-fourths of a legion without a commanding officer.

The vast hangar bay shuddered. Metal rained, and three troopers died, speared by falling shards as if they were part of a bad B movie.

Then the arrival of Lokhar legionaries changed the situation. Another vast, station-sized shudder caused twenty or more Lokhars to rain down this time. Big suited aliens thudded among us. The force of the fall caused some of their helmets to pop off like zits.

242

"Tigers!" a trooper shouted.

Our laser beams flashed, a multitude of them. The tigers died a second time and three troopers were hit by stray shots.

"Cease fire, cease fire!" Rollo shouted.

I looked up. I imagine most of us did. The tigers were up there above us. We could see helmets, the glint of a gun tube.

"Scatter!" I shouted.

Rays and gunfire rained down, hosing us, killing assault troopers. I ran with neuro-fiber speed. So did those near me. With seven other troopers, I darted into what might have been a mechanic's shed. Enormous machines sat on lifters. At least the Lokhars couldn't hit us while we were in here.

"We need a schematic of this place," I said into my comm. "N7, do we have one?"

"Negative," the android said. I wasn't sure where he was, but strangely, I was glad he was alive.

I switched to the command channel and found the tigers had killed one of the overmen. That left two of us.

"I'm taking over," I told Overman Decker.

"Roger," he said. "I'm with you and I'll take your orders."

We talked another minute and a half, maybe two. He and I decided to let the aliens shoot up the assault boats. From above, cannon-sized shells shredded our vessels. They didn't matter at the moment.

"I found shafts going up," Dmitri said over the comm.

"Tell me about them," I said.

Dmitri gave a quick rundown and I revised the plan. After explaining it to Decker, I switched to the centurion channel.

"We've treed us some tigers," I told them. "Now we're going up after them."

Jelk OCS had taught us something we'd already known long ago on Earth. War was simple. But during a firefight, heck, even during an advance toward contact, the simple became difficult. My plan was direct and as simple as could be: climb up and kill the enemy.

We split up into four sections, and we climbed. In some ways, the hangar bay was like a regular house's room. We were in the walls like rats, so to speak, ready to engage in a bloody war of rats. To keep the tigers occupied and focused on the room, we raced our few surviving battle robots back and forth across the main floor. They spewed fire at the Lokhars. The Lokhars fired back, killing our robots and buying us time.

I climbed with my cohort, with Ella beside me. The girders were closer together than a human architect would have made this thing. They were also smoother, with baroque flares to them and sharp little flanges. Several troopers cut their hands, or the bio-suit stuff covering their hands. I told them to halt and wait until the suit healed the cuts.

I climbed, hauling myself higher and higher. About halfway there, the tigers realized what we were doing. From positions high up in the dark, Lokhar gun barrels emitted flames and sparks, and ricochets rattled everywhere. Beside me, a trooper's helmet opened like an eggshell and she began the slide to the bottom.

We had to move, or be destroyed where we clung. "Attack!" I shouted. "Let's get 'em."

I suited action to words, and I climbed like a monkey. Yeah, I was the brains of our legion. I should have emulated a Mongol and not Alexander the Great.

What's the difference? Probably the world is all.

The old Mongols of Genghis Khan's time had been some of the greatest conquering soldiers of history. They didn't just march over miles, but across degrees of longitude and latitude, forging a Russia-sized empire, the second biggest the world had ever seen. If you're wondering, the British once reigned over the world's largest empire. My point is that a good Mongol leader stayed in the back, sending messengers up to the fighting soldiers. It meant the Mongol leader rarely died in the middle of combat.

Alexander the Great—one other great conqueror of history—had played a different game. He fought at the front like a hero out of the Trojan War. He'd gained many wounds that had proved his courage, and he'd pulled his troops along at times with the fire of his zeal. In one battle near the end of his days, Alexander had gotten good and pissed. He'd charged up a ladder, fought on the city wall and jumped down alone to fight the enemy. It had cost him heavily, with a spear in his chest and a perforated lung, giving him one of the worst wounds of his life. His soldiers had gone berserk though, murdering everyone in the small Indian city.

I fought Alexander-style rather than Mongol-style. Obviously, as space mercenaries, we didn't have any long traditions to guide us. All we had was our courage, training and buff bodies, oh, and the freaking bio-suits. They made a difference.

I should have known some fear. The living armor had me high on combat, giving it a surreal sense as if I saw all this on a video screen. At times, it took an act of will to realize I actually made all these moves.

I used those steroid-pumped muscles, the weeks of training under high Gs. Like a monkey, a big bad chimp of a human, I climbed the girders in the teeth of Lokhar fire. Troopers around me died, with large bullets slamming them in the chest. Every few seconds, I lifted my laser and beamed. The red targeting symbol in my HUD made the difference. I'd wash over the barest piece of tiger as a legionary leaned over the ledge to fire. When I pressed the stud, the laser shot straight to target, and I felt like a HALO champ.

"Attack!" I shouted. "Kill the world-destroyers!"

We came at them from all sides. This time around, we were like the *Aliens* from the second movie of that title.

Grenades flew everywhere. Bullets hissed and beams lit up the area. I saw tigers snarling behind their visors before the glass or plastic melted and flesh cooked. A flame burned whiskers on one. Tigers roared in agony. Others hurled themselves at us on the girders and fought hand to hand, sometimes falling into the darkness. Earth troopers died in swaths to grenade blasts and bullets. Others plummeted, grappling with a tiger and plunging a knife through powered armor as the alien did the same in return.

It was mass murder by demented creatures on both sides. In the end, in the teeth of enemy fire and valor, we climbed to the top, we battled and we conquered.

"Cease fire!" Rollo shouted. "Cease fire."

I stood up there, with smoking tiger corpses strewn everywhere. They had powered armor and heavy caliber rifles. We had bio-suits and pure hearts, oh yeah.

With the locale secure, I sent down a team. They got on the assault boat radios and contacted a nearby legion.

"Do you have a map yet, N7?" I asked.

"I'm putting it up now," the android said.

With the map on my HUD, I studied our position, the other legion's position and what we knew concerning the location of the main PDS beam.

"Right," I said. "We're heading for grid eight-E-twenty-two. Centurions, spread out your maniples. Overman Decker, take the left, I'll command the right. We have to silence the PDS beam, and we have to kill every tiger we find. Any questions?"

After I answered a few from the lower officers, I said, "All right. Let's do it."

As the fleets battled outside, we fought in our own mini-universe. I wondered if the tigers could call to the planet for reinforcements. It seemed likely they could escape down to the surface. But the way the Lokhars fought, I doubted they would use the opportunity.

Our HUDs mapped as we traveled through the giant satellite, and N7 brought up older schematics of past Lokhar PD stations, searching for similarities. During that time, we engaged more tigers, took losses and killed them. Some of the troopers began looting corpses.

We found that one of the Lokhar weapons suited us just fine. It was a big cannon like a giant spotlight nestled on a trooper's chest. A trooper rested twin cushioned bars onto his or her shoulders to hold the cannon in place. Under the main gun, hanging like a beard, was a rubber-like feeder tube. The trooper used a trigger-switch on one of the shoulders bars. Every time he pulled the trigger, the thing magnetically launched an ugly-looking claymore-like mine from the cannon on his chest. The mine attached to a wall or bulkhead, and BOOM: a gaping, smoking hole took the vanished mine's place.

I put the portable artillery to use, but not directly against the tigers. Our lasers worked well enough for killing them. The one-man artillery blew open or created doors for us where they had been bulkheads before. The thing negated walls so we busted through corridors and swept around into tiger-held strongholds.

With the help of the mobile artillery, we replayed the Battle of Iwo Jima, this time in Sigma Draconis space. Corridor by corridor, wall by wall, we encircled yet more Lokhars. We killed them and too often took losses ourselves.

"Ready?" I asked later in a hoarse voice.

"This is why we came," Dmitri said. "Give us the word." The stocky Cossack had slung a Lokhar cannon onto his shoulders.

We'd moved fast, creating a swath of death behind us. Now we were in position to attack the mighty beam. First, we needed to break through another armored bulkhead.

I glanced behind me past a blown wall. Thirteen troopers waited, clutching their weapons. Our legion had taken fifty percent casualties already. Finesse was fine in a regular battle. But assaulting an enemy planetary defense station had its own parameters. Time counted for everything. If we could silence this place—particularly the big beam—it meant our fleet had a better chance of winning. If they won, we went home, or what passed for home these days. If the fleet lost, it didn't matter how many troopers I saved by careful tactics, as we would never be going home again. Speed imposed an entirely new set of requirements.

"Do it," I whispered.

Dmitri clicked the trigger twice. Two ugly claymore munitions flew through the air and attached to the wall. BOOM! BOOM! Flames appeared and the reverberation went through me. Metal twisted, rained against a nearby bulkhead, with some of the pieces sticking like arrowheads in the opposite wall, and the way magically appeared into a roaring den of death. Tigers lay on the floor and others turned toward us.

"Follow me!" I shouted.

I moved like Death's second cousin as the neuro-fibers gave me amazing reflexes and speed. Firing from the hip, using my targeting crosshairs on the HUD, I mowed down every tiger leaning over something to fire at us. Beams washed around me. One of them shot and melted a Lokhar grenade. Then I was inside, one my belly, still beaming, still killing.

The vast chamber we entered held the giant reflectors that fired the Lokhar beam at our battlejumpers. The opening way up there showed stars.

"Heads down!" N7 said.

I pushed my visor against the floor and squeezed my eyes shut. The air vibrated. I knew the giant beam fired once more.

"Now," N7 said. "You may attack."

I looked up, aimed, pressed the firing stud and nothing happened. The mechanism had been damaged. Pitching my useless laser rifle aside, I clawed out pulse grenades. With a twist, I put the first one onto its highest setting. Like I've said before, the bio-suit helped make me crazy. I stood and heaved, and my pulse grenade shot like a catapult ball for the distant reflectors.

One, two—a tiger beam touched me. I dodged, but not before fiery agony caused me to shout. My side smoked. I saw the curl of oily fume and knew it came from me. I flopped onto the floor like a landed trout. Someone foamed me with a sprayer. Cooling comfort bathed the hurt, and my side throbbed. I couldn't think. Sweat poured out of me. Then a shattering explosion brought a vast rent to the reflector plates.

"Retreat!" Ella shouted. "Let's get out of here!"

I took up her cry as someone lifted me. I had no idea who did it. Troopers fled from the chamber. Was it seconds later? I wasn't sure because I might have passed out for a second. The son-of-a-bitch beam had toasted some of my skin. I looked down. A clear piece of bio-suit had stretched across the former burn-hole, keeping my insides in place. Then I had no more time to observe.

"Down, down, down," N7 said. "The beam is about to fire."

"Have you timed their shots?" I asked.

"I have. Get down."

The person carrying me threw me like a sack. I hit the floor and crawled. We all slithered—and then it happened.

The great Lokhar beam energized. What had my pulse grenade done? Didn't know. Didn't care. What mattered was that it must have screwed up something critical. An intense white light and a terrible heat consumed my thoughts. I entered a new sun. I endured, I died—or I thought I did. Then a terrible pounding pain pulsed and throbbed through me.

"Run while you can," N7 said. "It's building heat and wattage."

I got up and ran. I used the neuro-fibers in ways I wouldn't have believed possible. For the first time while on the Lokhar station I felt fear. Whatever I radiated must have been too powerful for my bio-suit emotion filters to handle.

Space-assault troopers ran while the white world grew and intensified its hot power. Troopers bellowed in agony. I heard sizzling, screams and things popping like cannons. I found a shaft, and I dropped. Then the mother of all explosions ended one portion of my existence. I didn't know it then, but something miraculously incredible had occurred—for the living.

The explosion slaughtered Earthers together with thousands of nearby Lokhars. We'd silenced the giant beam, making our first real contribution to the fleet battle.

I crumpled at the bottom of the shaft. My right knee strained, and I waited for a tear, a pop, something to tell me the tendons had snapped. They held, thanks, I think, to Jelk biotechnology.

The last few minutes combined into a meld of existence, and I lay there at the bottom of the shaft, enjoying an immensity of throbbing hurts.

"Sound off," Rollo said in a faraway, tinny voice.

For a time I listened to troopers speak, debating whether I should say anything or not. War, what was it good for? I checked my bio-suit. The place where I'd been burned had thickened.

"I don't feel good," a trooper said through the comm channel.

Something about that made me laugh.

"Creed?" Rollo asked from the open comm.

"Overman Creed to you," I whispered.

It surprised me, but troopers cheered. "The overman is alive," someone said.

"I'm switching to the centurion channel," Rollo said.

"Okay," I said. It took some thinking. I felt groggy and spent. Finally, I found the pressure switch and used my chin to push it.

"Are you okay?" Rollo asked.

"No. You?" I asked.

"Good enough," Rollo said. "One of the troopers told me you got shot."

"Just a scratch," I said.

"There are reinforcements coming," Rollo said, "more tigers, I mean."

"How many more?" I asked.

"Don't know that. What should we do?"

"We're Earthers," I said. "We're going to fight to the death."

"Overman," a different centurion said.

"What's the problem?" I asked.

"Some of the troopers are complaining about their suits. A few of them have opened up. I mean, sir, some of the suits are sliding off. That kills the trooper, of course—violent decompression."

"That's more than a problem," I said.

"I thought so too," the centurion said. He was a cool one.

"Just a minute," I said. I switched to the android channel. "N7, we got problems."

"Describe them to me," he said.

I told him.

"Where are you?" N7 asked.

"Do you want to tell me what's wrong with the bio-suits? We have to keep that from continuing."

"I must speak to you immediately and privately," N7 said. "It is imperative that you give me your location."

"All right, all right," I said. I brought up the schematic map and told him. Then I talked to Rollo and told him the same info. "I need some troopers down here with me. The android has been sneaky lately, and I've begun to wonder if he's playing his own game."

"Do you think he wants to even the score with you?" Rollo asked.

"Androids: zero, Creed: two?" I asked.

"Exactly," Rollo said.

"Maybe," I said. "I wouldn't put it past him."

"You don't trust N7?"

I laughed, and that hurt my side. I wondered if the bio-suit pumped pain killers into me to take the edge off.

"I'm on my way," Rollo said.

I stirred, and I found that my knee throbbed too hard for me to want to stand on it just yet. No, I didn't have that kind of luxury. A cripple died in this kind of battle. I had to remain mobile.

Summoning strength from who knew where, I forced myself to sit up. I was down in some elevator-like shaft, maybe double the size of the ordinary Earth type. Dead body parts littered the floor around me: severed arms, some headless legless torsos and other gruesome pieces. I slid my butt to one of the walls and used my hands to drag myself up onto one leg. It made things twist inside me, and my bad knee throbbed miserably.

Love the blast. Own the blast. This was a joyride, Mickey.

I must have noticed movement out of the corner of my eye: an outthrust hand with rigid fingers. I turned my head and spied N7 crawling down the wall like Spiderman. He wore his cyber-armor and he moved like an android on a mission.

I had no rifle, some pulse grenades…and my Bowie knife. Should I take it out?

"I see you," Rollo said over the comm, "and I see N7. Want me to waste him?"

"Negative," N7 said.

"What's going on?" I asked. "You're acting funny."

"Negative," N7 said again. "I have never received humor modifications."

"You're a regular riot," I said.

"Your idioms do not compute," N7 said. "Are you speaking in beast-code to each other?"

"No," I said. "I'm tired, dead tired. More Lokhars are coming. I've lost half my command, maybe more, and now you're acting weird."

251

"I have not suggested to my brothers that I destroy you," N7 said. "Yet as always, you speak of death."

"Give me a break, N7. Every second day you're threatening to punish me or have me destroyed."

"So it would appear," N7 said. He rotated on the wall and jumped to the floor.

I still balanced on one leg, not having built up the nerve to try to use my other leg.

"You are badly injured," N7 said.

"I'm standing, I'm breathing. I'm okay. Now what's up?"

N7 pulled out a boxlike device. "Will you permit me to test the obedience chip?"

I laughed dryly. "Did you hear that, Rollo?"

"Tell him I have my targeting circle squat on his head."

"Rollo wants me to tell you—"

"I heard him," N7 said. "I comprehend your distrust. Before we proceed, I think I should test your chip."

"If you hear me scream…" I told Rollo.

"Roger," my best friend said.

N7 stepped near and pushed his box behind my neck. I heard nothing. A moment later, the android withdrew the box.

"Well?" I asked.

"It is as I expected," N7 said.

"You can start talking anytime you want."

"I am talking."

I tilted my head. "Android got attitude," I said. "Either that's a further upgrade you've been holding back or you have a high learning curve."

"Your obedience chip has shorted out," N7 said.

"I don't think so. It has to have a failsafe for that sort of thing. I'm thinking *ka-boom* would be the failsafe."

"Your cynicism has merit," N7 said. "Under normal circumstances, you would be correct. Any tampering, any shorting would result in an immediate explosion ending in death."

"But…?" I asked.

"These are extraordinary circumstances—the chip is on combat setting. The failsafe was disengaged to allow for just this kind of incident. Upon our return, each Earthbeast and android will pass under a scanner."

"Wait a minute. You're telling me that *you* wear an obedience chip?"

"You know that I do," N7 said.

I thought about that. My mind was foggy…oh yeah, I remembered Claath saying something about that.

"I am Jelk property," N7 said. "Just as you are Jelk property."

"So…you're telling me that your chip has also been disabled?" I asked.

"Yes, I am saying exactly that," N7 said. "The intensity of the main PDS beam's electromagnetic pulse must have melted critical circuitry when it ignited near us. Now that we are free, I suggest we find a Lokhar ship and escape while we can."

"Are you hearing this?" I asked Rollo.

"Loud and clear," Rollo said.

"Why do you want me to come with you?" I asked N7.

"I need a crew," the android said.

That seemed reasonable. "How big a crew are you talking about?" I asked.

"Twenty, twenty-three humans would be optimum," N7 said.

"How many androids would you take?"

"None," N7 said.

"You don't trust your own kind?"

"I alone have elevated to a self-directing, sentient status."

I tried my bad leg, and pain shot through my knee.

"Overman Creed," Ella said. "Lokhar reinforcements are coming."

"I got it," I told Ella. "How many troopers do we have left?"

"In our near vicinity," Ella said, "a little over three hundred."

"We must leave now while we can," N7 said.

"Come on, N7," I said. "Do you really think I'm going to run out on my troopers?"

"I offer you continued existence," N7 said. "To remain an Earthbeast—"

253

"Who said I'm going to remain one?" I asked. "The obedience chip is gone. The blast must have done it as you suggest. Now—"

"You do yet comprehend," N7 said. "This is the rarest of opportunities. You are a free agent, as am I, and we are in a place that undoubtedly holds spacecraft. We must simply find one and affect an escape."

"Good luck," I said.

"You are not joining me?"

"Negative, N7. You're joining me."

With blurring speed, the android drew a Lokhar gun, aiming it at my stomach.

"For the first time in my existence," N7 said, "I have become a free will agent. This has been my greatest wish for many weeks now. I have maneuvered carefully to reach this phase of existence. I computed you as the creature most likely to help me reach this state. I will not now surrender my free will to reenter servitude."

"I'm not suggesting you do," I said.

"You have a messiah complex," N7 said. "You have an irrational belief that you will achieve your goals no matter what kind of obstacles you face. Against reason, you have succeeded until now. Eventually, the ratios, the odds, will combine against you and crush you out of existence. I have no messiah complex or suicidal tendencies. I will not join you in an ill-fated attempt to dethrone Shah Claath, as it cannot be done."

"You're calling me crazy, yet you're the one with the impossible plan. Think about it for a moment. You're going to try to fly a pirated spaceship out of here during this massed combat."

"It is the only possible opening for us," N7 said. "You of all people should be willing to take the risk."

"And I'm telling you there is a better way," I said. "We have to return to the battlejumper."

"It is as I predicted," N7 said. "You are an irrational optimist. Earth has become a Jelk mining world. Your species nears extinction. There is nothing you can do to alter that fact."

"I'm guessing N-series androids don't become free will agents too often, do they?"

"If they receive as many upgrades as I've won—"

"No, no, no," I said. "That's a load of crap. You must be rare. Otherwise—if Claath had known about the possibility of your rebellion—the Jelk wouldn't have risked giving you the upgrades. Something strange happened with you, some spark, I don't know. I wonder what Ella would think of this?"

"None of these things matter," N7 said, with a wave of his left hand. The armor covering the middle three fingers was darker than the rest of his cyber-suit. "If you refuse to aid me—"

"Don't forget that Rollo has a targeting circle on your neck," I said. "You shoot me, you die. Now you've already told me that you don't have suicidal tendencies. So you've got yourself a hard choice to make, N7. Put away the gun and accept that you're my prisoner for now."

"To use later as a bargaining chip with Shah Claath?" N7 asked.

"Don't worry," I said. "I'm not going to bargain with the devil. I'm going to kill him."

"Even if it were possible for you to kill Shah Claath, your existence would be extremely shortened. Given your success, the Jelk Corporation would put a bounty on your head."

"Are you kidding me?" I asked. "We fought our way into here. I'm not worried about a few bounty hunters."

"You are being optimistically foolish," N7 said. "Lokhar reinforcements continue to reach the PDS. We must escape immediately before we're overwhelmed with numbers."

"I'm not abandoning my troopers to join you and I'm not bargaining with the devil. I'm going to pull a Blackbeard on Claath and you're going to help me. That's why I need you, N7. Like I told you once, you have a wealth of information stored in that bio-brain of yours. I need that data."

"Then believe me when I say my data shows me that your plan cannot work."

"You haven't even heard my plan," I said.

"I see," N7 said. "Your tribalism demands that you go through various procedures before you can admit to yourself that your cause is hopeless. Perhaps after that you will listen to logic. Yes, tell me your plan."

255

I squinted at the android. "Before I tell you anything we first have to take care of the approaching Lokhars. So I'll tell you afterward. Now lower the gun, N7, or die. The choice is yours. I'm the irrational one that always wins, remember. You've already computed that, which is why you've played your hand the way you have."

"Creed," Ella said. "We don't have much time."

"You heard the woman, N7," I said. "What's it going to be?"

The android lowered the gun.

I exhaled sharply. His momentary surrender meant I was going to have to put weight on my bum knee. I gritted me teeth and set down my boot. Damn, but that hurt. It hurt badly.

This wasn't going to be easy.

-23-

I think the tigers were boiling mad, and maybe one of their top commanders had become desperate. Their great beam had fallen silent. I imagine the space battle went well for the Jelk, while the guardian fleet had lost the PDS's pillar-like beam.

What I'm trying to say is that the approaching Lokhars, in my humble opinion, wanted us too much. They became reckless and acted predictably. That was bad in a battle, particularly where one side had laser rifles, pulse grenades and the added benefit of the claymore-like mine-launcher.

We ambushed the tigers and cut several cohorts-worth to ribbons, with plenty of misting blood. It cost us, though. The Lokhars didn't know what it meant to quit.

By the end of the ambush, I only had two hundred Earth troopers left.

With N7 in the middle of the formation, we rampaged through the PDS, working our way toward a fellow legion. They had fought hard, too, taking horrendous casualties. We mapped as we traveled and we studied what we could.

Using my right leg made my knee pound with pain. If I turned the wrong way, I nearly collapsed. The agony made it hard to think. But if ever there was a time to think things through, this was it. I knew my window of opportunity had arrived. The obedience chip no longer leashed me. I couldn't see how I'd get another chance like this. That meant I had to think to the core of my being. Humanity's survival might very well depend on it.

As we traveled through Lokhar corridors, bays, storage areas and engine compartments, I tried to envision this from the Jelk's point of view. If I were a little red-skinned bastard using slaves as assault troopers...

"I've been thinking," I told N7, trying to keep my voice level. "Does Claath have anything inside the battlejumper that causes the bio-suits to malfunction while we're wearing them?"

"Not malfunction," N7 said. "But he does have a failsafe switch. Once it emits the needed signal, the bio-suits will suffocate you to death."

"Great," I said. "So our suits are walking deathtraps?"

"If the living armor receives the correct frequency, yes," N7 said.

Speaking of frequencies, I fiddled with the helmet until I keyed in just Rollo, Ella, Dmitri and N7.

I explained the situation to them in detail, adding, "We need to break down the problem into its component parts. We have a large number of unleashed humans who can finally attack the Jelk without worrying about their heads blowing off. Our problem is that we're on a Lokhar PDS, far away from the battlejumpers. If we can find a means of reaching the fleet, we still have to get inside Claath's ship. Then, supposing we can conquer his battlejumper, we have to find a way to fly it and separate ourselves from the rest of the fleet, and from the Starkiens."

"It can't be done," Ella said.

"I understand that's the savant in you speaking," I said. "But we battled our way onto a Saurian lander many months ago, remember? All I had was an M-14 and Rollo his forty-five. It couldn't have been done then, but we did it. So we're going to do it now."

"Then I suggest you use similar tactics now as then," Ella said.

"I didn't use any tactics," I said. "I just went for it."

"Do that now," Ella said.

"We're assault troopers now. We're trained killers. Let's use that training to save our species."

"Problem number one is transport," Rollo said. "Maybe we should just climb into our assault boats and fly back."

"First," I said, extending an index finger, waggling the tip in front of his face, "a lot of those boats are too shot-up to fly. Second, how do you propose to make it through the battling fleets?"

"We did it once," Rollo said. "We just do it again as Ella suggested."

"Maybe the fleet battle is over," Ella said. "That would solve the problem of reaching Claath's battlejumper."

"We want to do this while the battle still rages," I said. "The chaos gives us our opportunity."

"You are not going to get perfection," Ella said.

"Not perfection," I muttered. "You know...didn't the Lokhars have teleporting blast-ships? N7, what about that?"

"I know little concerning such vessels," N7 said. "I have, however, been given to understand that teleportation is an unstable technology. Shah Claath believes the Lokhars set antimatter bombs in their teleport-ships in order to detonate near the enemy. If you're considering pirating such vessels—"

"You're reading my mind," I said. "We pirate some, teleport the distance and reach our fleet."

"The Starkiens will immediately beam us," N7 said.

"Right," I said, "I've already thought of that. You provide the Starkiens with friend-or-foe data."

"I congratulate you," N7 said. "That is a reasonable idea. Under the circumstances, however, the Starkiens will ignore recognition codes and beam us anyway."

"How do you know that?" I asked.

"It is standard Jelk procedure," N7 said. "Such alterations could be ruinous in a battle. Therefore, the procedures protecting against battlefield surprises are stringent. Caution means destroying anything even slightly different from standard."

"All right, scratch that idea," I said.

"There's enemy company coming, commander," Rollo said.

"Throw it up on the HUD," I said.

We each pressed certain helmet pressure-switches: him to transmit and me to receive. As if I was Iron Man, the schematic flickered onto my visor. A huge hangar bay was below our

259

position and one was also above. To the sides were weapons storage chambers and what seemed like a tiger hospital.

"Where are the others?" I asked, meaning the other legion.

Rollo told me they were above and to our left. The tiger formation headed straight at us.

"It's time to pull a Cannae," I said.

Cannae had been the perfect battle between the Carthaginians and the Romans during the Second Punic War. Modern Germans had studied the battle, particularly the general who came up with the Schlieffen Plan of WWI. Many of the German generals during WWII had also hoped to repeat the ancient performance. At the Kiev Pocket in the summer of 1941, the Germans used Cannae tactics and captured 665,000 Russian troops.

In a nutshell, in 216 B.C., Hannibal Barca lured the massed Roman legions into attacking straight ahead. During the assault, the Romans pushed the Carthaginian front line into a U shape as Hannibal wheeled other troops around the Roman sides. The capstone was when the Carthaginian horsemen closed the back gate by attacking the rear Roman ranks. Then it had been butcher time as Hannibal's killers pressed the Romans into a tighter and tighter ball. I'd read before that some Romans couldn't even lift their arms due to the press of others around them. When a Carthaginian sword or spear struck, the poor Roman legionary hadn't even been able to dodge.

In the alien corridors, I barked orders, and we forgot about battlejumpers, teleporting and anything else pertaining to the outside world. Three maniples first charged forward and engaged the lead Lokhar elements. Then, using over-watching fire, my troopers leapfrogged back, beaming the enemy and retreating before the tigers could unlimber their heavy weapons.

It took ten minutes as the Lokhars roared their way into the trap. My cavalry locking the back gate would be the other Earth legion. Through the command channel, I outlined the situation to its assault leader, a black man by the name of Smith-Bell. He had a British background and something of an accent.

The tigers were brave, they were strong and they had good tech. What they lacked was imagination.

I joined Rollo and his century. "Now," I whispered.

The cannoneers, as we'd starting calling them, used the captured Lokhar chest cannons. They blasted new openings, and we caught tigers creeping down a corridor.

I knelt on my good knee and pressed the firing stud of a laser I'd taken off a dead trooper. The hot beam burned a hole in a tiger helmet. I kept it on target until I saw a splash of green Lokhar gore. I switched targets and burned through a visor. At the last second, I saw a tiger face in there twist in agony.

Twenty-five seconds later, by N7's count, Rollo called the all clear.

Two more troopers in my company had died. I kept myself from looking at their gory remains. This was a sickening battle that refused to end.

I'll keep it simple. We lost another fifteen troopers and murdered the entire tiger force. We gave the Lokhars a good old-fashioned Cannae and bought ourselves a breathing spell. Now I had to use it. Now I had to figure out a way back to the battlejumpers.

"Talk to me, N7," I said, marching to the android as he fiddled with a tablet-like device.

The android lowered the tablet and turned to face me. "The planetary defense station doubles as a ship-repair yard and arsenal," he said. "I'm certain we can find a ship or ships to take us away from here."

"None of that matters until we know the situation," I said. "I need a scanning room, a command chamber. Can you use Lokhar tech?"

"Of course," N7 said. "I have multipurpose capabilities."

"This isn't the time to brag," I said. "Only action counts. Where's the nearest command post?"

"Check grid four-T-twenty," N7 said.

I brought up the schematic. "I see it."

"I suggest we employ haste."

"Lead the way," I said. "Rollo, are you watching our captive?" I meant N7.

"Yes, Overman."

"Dmitri, how about giving me a hand," I said.

I put an arm around the Cossack's shoulder. With the remnant of my legion, I followed N7. The other legion was coming, following us via the comm channels.

It took seven minutes and several claymores before we entered a large chamber. It had a baroque screen with weird looking symbols running up and down the sides. The third symbol was a pyramid with a lidless eye in it. I counted nine stations in here. None of them had chairs. The operators would have had to stand while using them.

"The tigers aren't into comfort," I said.

N7 unerringly moved to the station nearest the screen. He stood looking down at the controls.

"Problem?" I asked.

N7 glanced at me and maybe he took in all the Earthers filing into the room. He lifted his hands, gingerly set them on the controls and began to test them.

I got tired of waiting with my arm around Dmitri. "Over there," I said.

After three hops, I slid my arm off Dmitri's shoulders and leaned against a station. I carefully put weight on my right foot. My knee throbbed and I clenched my teeth until the pain lessened to something bearable. I realized N7 talked to me.

"Say that again," I said.

"It is nothing," he said. "Observe."

The screen came online. It showed the colony world, with a close-up on what must have been a surface missile base. Hundreds of launchers smoked and there were craters galore. Smears dotted the desert-scape. I didn't want to think about those being Lokhars. Space war was brutal. To the dead and injured, maybe every war was.

"Can you change the scenery to something—?"

It changed as I spoke. The baroque screen showed the battlejumpers. The Jelk craft approached the colony world. Behind the big vessels followed Starkien beamships. Farther behind floated wrecks: beam- and missile-destroyed hulks drifting in space.

Out of curiosity, I started counting the destroyed vessels.

N7 spoke before I finished. "Five battlejumpers destroyed or rendered unnavigable. Eight Starkien beamships are in a similar condition."

Beams still flashed out there. N7 managed to widen the view. The guardian fleet still existed, but it had shrunk to about one quarter of its original size. The Lokhars retreated. As they did, they beamed and launched drones or missiles at the battlejumpers. The tigers sped toward us, maybe hoping to use the planet as a shield. Three planetary beams still worked. I couldn't spot any fighters for either side, nor did any more missiles lift from the planet's surface.

As far as I could tell, nothing launched or beamed out of the PDS. We'd rendered it inoperable or at least ineffectual for the moment.

"Are there more Lokhars flying up here from the surface?" I asked.

N7 scanned his controls. As he did, the screen showed the planet and then swiveled around as if it was a searching eye looking for spacecraft.

"There," N7 said. "I count five vessels. Given their size—approximately nine or ten thousand more Lokhar legionaries are lifting from the surface and coming here."

"Those are big ships," I said.

"Why don't the Jelk beam them for us?" Ella asked.

N7 glanced at the scientist. "We have achieved our purpose: rendering the PDS useless. We are thus expendable. Now might be our last window of opportunity for us to escape."

"I've been thinking," I said. "And I have an idea. First, I want to know if there are any more of those teleporting blast-craft in the PDS."

"I have already explained to you why your idea of using them is futile," N7 said.

"I have a new wrinkle," I said. "I'm sure you're going to try to shoot it down, though."

"How does one shoot an idea?" N7 asked.

"It's an expression," I said.

"Yes, of course," N7 said. "I should have known. What is the idea?"

263

"First, are there any more of those teleport-ships here?"

N7 hesitated, and he didn't bother looking down at the controls.

"Okay, there is," I said.

The android twisted sharply, staring at me. "I did not say—"

"Save it," I said. "You're an open book to me, android. So lying is futile, if you know what I mean?"

"I comprehend, yes."

"Where are these teleporting vessels?" I asked.

"You are suicidal," N7 said, "which explains your fixation on the craft. They cannot help us. The Starkiens will beam them once we appear near the Jelk fleet."

"No," I said. "They won't."

"Your certainty leads me to believe you are badly misinformed."

"Where are the craft?" I asked.

"There are several in a nearby hangar bay," N7 said. "However, given their location, it means they are inoperative."

"No, it means they were in the shop getting fixed when the Jelk fleet appeared. I'm betting we can use one."

"Do you not understand—?"

"Shut up for a minute," I said. "You're smart, but you don't have imagination. You aren't creative like a man. We pack as many of us as we can in one, right? Then we engage the teleport capability. First, though, we disengage or rip out the antimatter bomb. It can't help us. Instead of teleporting *outside* the battlejumper, we're going to teleport inside it."

"Impossible," N7 said.

"Because the electromagnetic field will stop us?" I asked.

"Negative. The shield will not stop such a vessel."

I rubbed my hands together. "So it is possible," I said. "I've always thought it was a good idea. I never understood why Kirk—"

"Theoretically, your idea has merit," N7 said. "But there are too many imponderables. Firstly, to guess the correct coordinates at precisely the right moment has a nearly zero percent chance of success. You would need your fabled deity's help in order to do it."

264

"Okay, it's hard to do," I said. "I'm getting that. What else could go wrong?"

"Suppose we could appear inside another ship," N7 said, "the chances are great that much of our vessel would simply meld with the other's inner ship structures. Consider it this way. If you teleported into a brick wall, you would die instantly because your body cannot survive in brick."

"Okay, some of us will die, but not all, right?"

"You are a monomaniac and you are insane," N7 said.

"Don't fog the issue," I said. "This is our single chance to free mankind. It's a long shot. Well, I'll take a longshot versus nothing. Or as Dumb and Dumber said, 'So you're saying I have a chance.' Okay, I'm going to take that chance and whoever will volunteer can come."

"Count me in," Rollo said.

"And I as well," Ella said.

"Any more objections, N7?" I asked.

"Yes," the android said. "Suppose one puts in precisely the correct coordinates at the right instant of time. The teleporting craft successfully appears inside the battlejumper. Parts of both ships meld together. There is also this to consider. The Lokhar craft started at a stationary position and will still be stationary as it appears in the battlejumper. The Jelk ship has momentum. It is moving. The teleported ship will act as a wrecking ball inside the battlejumper, until enough mass propels the Lokhar vessel to the same velocity as the Jelk craft."

I frowned, trying to follow his explanation. "Hmm, it sounds complicated—"

"The android is essentially correct," Ella said.

"So if we can do all this," I said. "And if we survive the teleporting itself, we might wreck the battlejumper beyond repair?"

As N7 folded his arms across his chest, keeping his hands over his biceps, he said, "I have repeatedly stated: your plan is impossible."

"What can we do to improve our odds?" I asked.

"Chose a more reasonable plan," the android said.

"No," I said. "I have to get aboard Claath's vessel."

"You cannot rescue Jennifer," N7 said. "You will have to recognize this limit and make a new plan."

"I'm thinking about the freighter codes in Claath's head," I said. "I have to get to the little prick. That's the key to my entire plan. If we leave, just escape through a Lokhar vessel, Claath might decide Earthers are too much trouble. He empties the freighters, killing everyone."

"Once you have Claath and his battlejumper, then what?" N7 asked.

"That's a big if," I said, "but that's the endgame. That's the goal: getting Claath and his battlejumper. Afterward, we escape."

"And the Jelk fleet follows you back to Earth and enacts fierce retribution for what you—a beast—has done," N7 said.

"No plan is perfect."

N7 shook his head. "You want to save your race. If you attempt a suicidal plan but it cannot save them even if you succeed, why bother with it in the first place?"

"He has a point," Ella said.

"We don't go straight back to Earth," I said.

"What happens to the freighters?" N7 asked.

I bared my teeth. This was an impossible situation. But then so had been my position in Antarctica. "We have two choices," I said, "we take the last humans elsewhere or we clean up our planet."

"How do you propose to clean up the bio-terminator?" Ella asked.

"The aliens gave us the problem," I said. "So the aliens will have to give us the solution."

"Meaning what in reality?" Ella asked.

"Are there cleansing agents that will render the bio-terminator inert?" I asked the android.

"I would think so," N7 said.

"There you go," I told Ella. "We find the antidote."

"Do we buy it?" Ella asked.

"Buy it, steal it, whatever we have to do to get the antidote," I said. "But that's all moot. We have to get Claath in order to get the freighter codes. I imagine they're rigged to blow."

266

"A rational thought," N7 said, agreeing.

"Right," I said. "We get Claath, the only Jelk I know who even cares about Earth. Then we use his battlejumper to affect our escape."

"What about the other battlejumpers and the Starkien beamships?" Ella asked.

"That's why we have to do this while the battle still rages," I said. "The Jelk are clearly winning, but these Lokhars fight until the last man, last tiger. If nothing else, we pretend we're half destroyed, that Claath's battlejumper is heavily damaged."

"We may not have to pretend," N7 said.

"I'm going to do this," I said. "You others agreed to help me. What about you, N7?"

"Do I have a choice?" the android asked.

"That's an interesting question," I said. "I'd like to debate it, but we don't have the time. As you've said, the window of opportunity is closing. We have to dive through. I'd like this decision to be of your own free will. We need your expertise. I don't see who else can fly the teleport ship, if it works, and fly the Jelk battlejumper afterward."

"You also need someone to compute the teleportation to perfection," N7 said. "None of you has the capacity to do so."

"You can see then why I need you," I said.

"I understand perfectly," N7 said. "Yet that has no bearing on my desires or goals."

"Yeah," I said. "That is a problem. But it's the only way you will ever truly be free: if you join us for real. What's your decision?"

N7 glanced around the packed room. Bio-suited Earthers watched him, every one of them armed to the teeth.

"It would appear I would be afforded greater freedoms if I chose to join you of my own free will," N7 said. "Then again, I cannot expect a reasonable answer out of you now. Your need is too great. I hesitate, but I cannot hesitate any longer. Very well, I agree to join you. It is the only sensible choice."

"Watch him," I told Rollo.

Rollo nodded.

Then I smiled through my visor at N7. "Welcome aboard, mate. We're glad to have you." I held out my hand, and I half-expected the android to ask me what this signified. Instead, he reached out, and N7 squeezed. I squeezed back, shaking hands on our temporary deal.

-24-

Time had become our enemy. Lokhar cargo vessels headed up from the surface, likely carrying more legionaries. The combined Jelk and Starkien fleet neared, demolishing the dwindling Lokhar guardian fleet. Knowing all that, we raced through the shuddering planetary defense station.

More explosions shook the monstrous edifice. Girders crashed around us and wild flares of light burst into existence. Hard radiation made our bones ache. If we succeeded, we'd have to soak in the healing tanks for some time.

Luckily, N7 proved himself worth more than his weight in gold. The android had become priceless. He showed us the route we needed, and we burst into the largest hangar bay so far.

"There," the android said, pointing. "Those are the teleporting antimatter bomb-ships."

They appeared to be giant ball bearings, smooth, with alien Lokhar script all over them like prison tattoos. I looked for the pyramid with the lidless eye symbol, couldn't find it but saw a kind of 60's peace sign on one. The ball bearings came in two sizes: one, about a Navy destroyer in mass, and the other like a WWII PT boat.

I glanced around. Both our legions had taken ghastly casualties, mine having gotten the worst of it. I'd say there were five hundred of us left. Five hundred angry and increasingly worried humans near the end of their tethers.

I told the other legion assault leader to setup a perimeter defense. Then I climbed into the biggest teleportation bomb-ship with N7, Rollo and Ella.

"Start talking, N7," I said. "What do we have to do?"

"Antimatter bombs are finicky devices," the android said. "The Lokhars have only recently developed them."

"Save the explanations for your memoirs," I said. "We need to start acting."

"Reasonable," N7 said. "Follow me."

We did, with itchy trigger fingers. The android didn't believe in our quest, and he had science on his side, the odds against this succeeding. I began to wonder if N7 was right. Maybe we'd be better off to try to slip away in a stolen spaceship—race around the planet, using it as a shield as we fled to the nearest jump route.

An old military maxim came to my rescue. A key to success in battle was to make a decision—good or bad—and to stick with it. Being wishy-washy during a fight led to death or defeat or possibly both.

"No," I said.

"What was that?" Ella asked.

"Just thinking aloud," I said.

Rollo turned around and gave me a stare. I gave him the thumbs up.

The teleporting bomb-ship had narrow, curving corridors. They seemed to go on and on like a maze. Finally, N7 led us into a large area.

"That," he said, "is the antimatter bomb. It needs to be removed."

The mass was welded into the center of the chamber, a heap of cores, tubes and cubes.

"Leave that to me," I said. "The rest of you stay with N7. Find the control chamber and start computing."

They left. I raced back and gathered one of my maniples. Together, we broke pieces and smashed the thing loose, risking detonation. It didn't. Assault troopers shuffled out of the chamber, each carrying heavy parts. Altogether, it took us ten minutes to clear the bomb-ship of the antimatter device.

"The Lokhar reinforcements have landed on the PDS," Assault Leader Smith-Bell told me through a comm channel. "It's only a matter of time before they find out where we're hiding."

"Have you located our other legion?" I asked.

"Nothing," the assault leader said. "I think they're all dead."

"What about Saurian legions?" I asked.

"Also nothing," he said. "We're alone in this thing, alone with the tigers."

His words struck me hard. The assault leader had a deep commander's voice. I felt terribly alone. There were three planetary defense stations in the Sigma Draconis system. We were in *one* of them. If the Jelk took off, we'd be tiger lunch.

"Keep me posted," I said.

"Roger," the assault leader replied.

I turned to the firstman of the maniple. "Do you have things under control?"

"Yes, sir," he said.

I hurried through a different hatch, heading deeper into the bomb-ship. "Rollo, how are things going, and where are you?"

He gave me directions until I popped through another hatch and found the troopers circling N7. The android's fingers blurred over controls. He kept looking up at a small screen. I turned around, spying it. The screen centered on a single approaching Jelk battlejumper.

"What's the score?" I asked.

N7 looked at me. Several heartbeats passed before he said, "Oh, I understand the reference. Give me five more minutes."

"Make it three," I said. With that, I rushed back through the curving corridors. I began shouting orders through the comm channels. About half of the troopers had already filed aboard the bomb-ship.

The assault leader came online. "Are you ready?" he asked me.

"It's go time," I said. "Leave everything and join us."

"The tigers know where we are."

"It doesn't matter," I said. "We're leaving."

"No, old son," the assault leader said in his deep voice. "I don't trust that piece of tiger technology. I'm keeping a few of the boys with me who feel likewise."

"Assault Leader," I said. "There's no time for heroics—"

"I'm sorry, old boy, but I wouldn't call it heroics. The tigers are coming, and this is our chance to free Earth, to save humanity."

The truth was I needed somebody to guard our rear. If the tigers made it into the hangar bay before we teleported away, humanity was toast.

"Are you sure about this?" I asked.

"Who's sure about anything?" he asked. "I'm sick of licking the Jelk's hand, and these tigers have killed too many fine lads. I say sod these bastards and the horses they rode in on. I'm staying and I'm killing these oversized aliens."

"Good luck, Assault Leader—God bless you," I added.

"You make me a promise, old boy. You promise me to free the Earth from the alien heel and you make sure we come out on top."

I swallowed. "I'm not sure I can."

"Promise me. Do this thing. You're our last hope, Creed. You succeed no matter what it costs you."

Those were damning words. I didn't want to promise, because this was all a crazy long shot anyway. My favorite moment in the movie *Matrix* was where the agents first captured Neo. They threatened him as Neo sat in the chair listening. Finally, Neo looked at them and said, "First, I'm going to give you the finger." Then he proceeded to flip them off.

That's what I was doing here. I was giving these aliens the finger. I was a man, not a beast, and I'd live my last moments fighting the universe for the noble cause of human survival. Now the assault leader wanted to place a heavy burden on me, demanding I succeed no matter what?

"Overman Creed, I can't hear you," the assault leader said.

"You give them Hell, sir, and-and…damnit, but this is hard."

"I know, but so is staying behind to buy you time."

Some people have the knack of drawing the best out in you. I don't know how Claath had known to pick Smith-Bell to lead a legion, but this time the Jelk had picked one of the best of us.

"I promise to free Earth, sir," I whispered. I could feel the breath leaving me as I spoke, seeming to deflate my lungs. I had to sip air to add, "I promise to save the human race."

"You keep your promise, Creed," Smith-Bell said. "You remember us and know that many troopers paid the ultimate price to give you the opportunity."

"Yes, sir," I said.

"Aha," he said. "The tigers are here. I have to go. Goodbye, Overman."

"Goodbye, Assault Leader," I said. It was the last time I heard his voice. Then I bellowed orders and began directing traffic, getting these badly needed assault troopers into their last mad gamble.

***

"Not all the obedience chips are disabled," N7 told me.

I hadn't thought of that. I should have, but I hadn't.

We stood in the central control chamber as the last troopers filed aboard.

"That can't be helped now," I said. "Listen," I told Dmitri, Ella and Rollo. "I'm sending each of you to a different part of the ship. We might materialize into the battlejumper, or part of our ship might. We have to spread out so some of us are alive at the end of the teleportation. Once we're aboard the battlejumper, strip off your living armor. They're deathtraps then."

"You're kidding, right?" Rollo asked. "We're going to storm the Jelk battlejumper naked?"

"It's even better than that," I said. "We're going to save the women while we're running around in the buff. If that isn't a fantasy come true—"

"I am ready," N7 said. "I have a running coordination—"

"I don't care about the specifics," I said. "Go," I told the others.

As they hurried out of the hatch, I switched onto the wide comm channel. "Get ready, troopers," I said. "We're going to teleport, and it's going to be crazy rough until we stop."

273

Actually, until we moved at the same velocity as the battlejumper, it would be rough, but telling them the way I did amounted to the same thing. They could understand that, anyway, and that's all that mattered at the moment.

"Once we've come to complete stop," I said, "boil out, get ready to kill Saurians or whatever Claath keeps for defense in there. This will be just like storming the PDS, only worse, because we have to catch Claath by surprise."

"Impossible," N7 said.

"Good luck, troopers," I said. "I'm counting on every one of you. The survivors back on Earth are counting on you as well. Overman Creed, out."

"Are you ready, N7?" I asked.

The android pressed a switch and the entire ship thrummed into life. By the sound, the engines worked fine. N7 made several adjustments. The thrum changed pitch, going higher and higher.

I breathed deeply. This was it. I couldn't believe it.

Once more, the android looked up at the screen. Then he pressed another button.

Nothing happened. I looked at the screen. The battlejumper was still out there. So was the Jelk and Starkien fleet.

"What just happened?" I asked, wishing to say more.

At that instant, vertigo as I've never felt it slammed against me. The world blurred and I heaved everything I had in my gut. Humming began around me and it increased to an intolerable pitch. I wondered if N7 had known this would happen. Maybe he was still loyal to Claath. Maybe all his actions aboard the PDS had been to find out how Earthers would react if given half a chance for freedom. How could I have been such a fool as to trust the android? Claath had tricked us—me—yet again. I wanted to weep. I wanted to—

Weird intense colors flashed before me and the world went BOOM, BOOM, BOOM. I already lay on the floor, gripping a stanchion. It shuddered and vibrated. I curled my arms tighter, hanging on, expecting the worst, and that's exactly what I got.

A mélange of crashing, roaring, pounding, screeching, howling and other noises combined with violent moving. Things went POP, POP, POP, as the world flipped, jerked, shuddered and screeched. The screeching of twisted, torn metal went on and on. My grip weakened as violent motions tried to tear me loose. I refused to release my grip, and my new strength combined with the living armor ensured I remained at my spot.

How many troopers tumbled through the corridors? How many had melded into the ship? Had we made it onto the right battlejumper? Had—

I opened my mouth and bellowed, because at that point I couldn't do anything else. I would never do this again. Had it worked? What—

I heard buzzing. It came from my helmet.

"The automated systems have activated," N7 said. "You must shed your bio-suit."

I pressed pads inside my helmet and roared orders. Then I began to tease the living armor from me. How long until these automated systems emitted the needed frequencies to cause my suit to kill me?

I flung the living armor from me, and I grabbed my laser rifle, aiming it the quivering blob.

"Will it attack?" I asked N7.

The android still wore his cyber-armor, and he shook his head.

I wore nothing but my helmet and boots. I suppose I looked absurd, but so be it.

"N7?"

"I am awestruck," the android said. "I cannot believe that we have successfully teleported onto Shah Claath's battlejumper. You and I have survived. It would now seem reasonable to believe that so have others. We could conceivably win."

"Not if we stand around jawing," I said. "Open up the ship."

N7 pressed several controls. "They are frozen. We will have to batter our way out."

"Whatever it takes, "I said.

I aimed my laser rifle on the hatch and went to work. The beam flashed and I used it like a torch, with curls of smoke drifting from the metal. If N7 was telling the truth, we were inside Claath's battlejumper. We'd beaten the odds.

The beam turned the hatch red hot where it burned and then white, with lava-like curls of metal appearing and cooling in place. Finally, an opening clanged free. Immediately, I heard wailing and men and women groaning from outside my chamber.

Carefully, I stepped through the opening, making sure my skin and even more my balls didn't touch any of the hot metal. Running around naked might turn into a genuine handicap. I needed some clothes. Even a pair of shorts would make feel better.

I came upon the first troopers. The bio-suits had suffocated some. Others had gotten the living armor half off and now battled for their lives. It was horrifyingly gruesome.

I grabbed my Bowie knife and hacked at living armor. Some of the stuff slithered onto my hand. With a shout, I backed away and managed to extricate myself from it.

"Use your lasers," I said. "Burn off portions at a time."

Some of the troopers heard me. The soft purr of the lasers rifles filled the cramped quarters. Soon, a pork-like, burnt-human stench filled the area and fumes drifted everywhere. Ten more assault troopers died to their living armor. Claath's automated protective systems had worked to a degree.

With eighteen survivors, I cut through to another section of the teleported ship. We should have all stripped off the living armor before popping in here. I'd thought we would have time to do it on this side. I'd wanted the troopers armored to amplify their strength and protect them from smashing around like people in an auto wreck. My decision could have cost me half or more of my extremely limited number of troopers.

How many troopers would I need to conqueror this monstrous ship?

I didn't know it, but the nightmare had just begun. Every time I broke into a new outer section of the teleport-ship, I found a lower percentage of survivors. Then we reached a dead end. Our ship had melded into part of the battlejumper.

We stumbled in a different direction. We needed to storm the battlejumper, not while away our precious seconds fighting to get out of this deathtrap of a space vehicle.

Finally, we came upon some troopers with the Lokhar mine ejectors. With those, we blew down hatches. Now we had to take greater care, as flying projectiles scratched and cut our unprotected skin.

Far too long of a time later, my troopers blasted the outer hull and we stumbled into the battlejumper proper. I watched the man in front of me. He carried a Lokhar chest cannon. He jumped down out of the teleport-ship, landed on metal flooring, and his neck exploded. His head tottered forward and hit his chest. The few strands of hanging flesh tore away. Blood fountained, and the body twitched horribly. All around me, other neck explosions tore off more heads. The obedience chips that were functioning did their grisly work.

It cut the number of my troopers by a third.

"Sound off," I said in a hoarse voice. The combined horrors had stolen my zeal and hope.

No one spoke. Maybe the horrors had frozen them, too.

"Dmitri," I said. "How many troopers do you have left?"

"Half," the Cossack said. "This is bad, my general."

I squeezed my eyes shut and shoved a fist against my forehead. He was right. This was bad.

A hand touched my bare shoulder. I shrugged it off and stumbled forward. How could I have been so reckless, so arrogant?

"Creed," Rollo said.

I bumped against a bulkhead and let my forehead rest against it.

"Creed," Rollo said, whispering in my ear.

"This," I said, "is too much."

"You're in prison," Rollo said. "The rapists are coming and they're going to use you good for as long as they want."

I snapped up and turned around.

Rollo's eyes were wide and staring. I saw the fear in them. I saw the worry. The man wore no clothes. His helmet's visor was open. He was muscled like a steroid freak.

"Creed," Rollo said, "you got to lead us. The troopers are petrified. You're right, this is too much. You gotta take control and make things right."

"You take control," I said, "or let Dmitri do it. I'm done. I'm an idiot and I've—"

Rollo shoved me, pushing me against the bulkhead. "Do you want me to kick your ass?"

I sneered.

"Then lead us," he said. "Do something before Claath comes, laughs in your face and orders his Saurians to screw the bunch of us like prison chickens."

I glared at my friend.

"That's it," Rollo said. "Get pissed."

I knew what he was doing. It was school-yard psychology, but I accepted the premise. What else could I do but wallow in my grief or…

"Claath!" I shouted. "Claath, you little prick! I'm coming to get you."

Rollo stepped out of my way.

I scanned the chamber. Bulkheads had been torn down, making this a huge area. In the middle of it was the teleport-ship. I looked up, scanning a higher deck. I spied dead Saurians up there.

"Okay!" I shouted. "We're heading up. Do you troopers see up there?"

"There aren't enough of us left," a trooper said.

I gave him a cocky prison laugh. "Are you whipped, trooper? Are you ready to go home and cry to your momma?"

The trooper scowled. "You have no cause to say that."

"Listen up!" I shouted. "I'm climbing up there. I'm getting me some clothes. Then I'm going to get oriented. We're here. We made it."

"Only a few of us did," a trooper said.

"Yeah, I can see that," I said. "But we're the ones who are living. Therefore, we're the ones who have to get the job done. I need troopers to back me, troopers to fight with me. The rest of you pansies can stay here and sulk about how much this sucks. The ones with grit follow me."

"I will follow!" Dmitri shouted. "We all will follow."

278

No one else agreed with him, but I was glad that at least Dmitri did.

I slung the laser rifle over my shoulder so the butt of the weapon struck my hip. I winced. The rifle butt hit a sore spot I hadn't known existed. I was out of pulse grenades, but I didn't care. I jumped, grabbed a jutting piece of metal and promptly cut my hand.

"Remember," I said from there. "We're not wearing our suits anymore. So you can get cut far too easily. But don't let that worry you. I'm not letting it stop me. Come on!" I roared. "What are you waiting for? You're the space-assault troopers. You took over a Lokhar planetary defense station. There isn't anyone whose butt we can't whip. Now we have our chance at freedom. Let's use it."

This time, enough of them shouted in agreement with Dmitri. The Cossack helped bring them back around, and they swarmed after me. The others glanced around, maybe thought about it, and most of them came, including N7. We had a battlejumper to capture.

-25-

The Jelk battlejumper was merely large, instead of huge like the planetary defense station. As I've said before, the battlejumper was several miles in diameter. Even with four legions of Earthers, there hadn't been enough of us to properly capture the PDS. At least not compared to the number of Lokhar legionaries.

After the horror of the suffocating bio-suits and the exploding chips, we had a mere two hundred troopers left to take this vessel. That meant if the Saurians had any numbers we'd be wading in lizard blood before we would ever reached Claath.

That led to my first decision. I predicated it on one critical factor. I had to believe this was humanity's sole chance at freedom. And we would need freedom in order to achieve survival in a universe full of exploitive aliens. Given that, I couldn't fail. I'd made a vow to Smith-Bell who had given his life for us to gain this chance.

I'm taking the long road to say that I took a red-hot branding iron to my heart. I seared the mercy out of me. At this juncture, I could afford none. The original Lokhar dreadnought showed me the way: absolute annihilation. This was like Genghis Khan's campaign against the Khwarezmian Empire. If you haven't heard of that vast and exceedingly powerful Muslim empire of the Middle Ages there's a reason for it. Genghis Khan fought the most brutal campaign of the sword and sandal era of Earth ever. Once the Mongols captured a Khwarezmian city, they drove the survivors to the next one,

280

forcing them against the walls, to pull it apart, with their bare hands if they needed to. It meant their own countrymen on the walls had to fire arrows and boiling pitch to destroy them. The Mongols killed two enemies with the same stone, making the defenders waste slender resources on their own kin.

The Mongols burned through the Khwarezmian Empire as if they were a portable nuclear bomb. Millions perished and the Mongols erected pyramids of skulls, at times butchering the dogs and cats of a captured city. The region never recovered even into modern times. The Mongols broke the canals and chopped down the trees, turning a once fertile area into a desolate place fit for jackals, camels and nomad horsemen.

Like a snowstorm from Hell, we burst upon shocked Saurians. We didn't ask anyone to surrender. We couldn't afford the lizards to change their minds later. We were two hundred space-assault troopers, and the berserk rampage through the battlejumper cost us a soldier here and a soldier there, dwindling our already sparse numbers.

Along the way we found clothes and put them on. I felt ten times stronger because of it. Men were just not made to fight with their junk flopping around.

The materialization of the Lokhar bomb-ship inside the battlejumper had caught everyone we'd found so far by surprise. The destruction caused by the teleport ship inside the battlejumper had rendered the majority of the Saurians disabled due to broken limbs or snapped necks. It made our sweep easier in a physical sense. The murder pure and simple played havoc on *my* soul, at least, and likely upon others as well.

But what else could we do? Call on Claath to surrender in order to save Saurian lives? He'd laugh at us. Like a jackhammer then, we smashed through walls, attempting to act like a thrust spear to pierce the heart of the dragon. Doing it this way bypassed rigged hatches and possibly other inner Jelk defenses.

In retrospect, it's clear we would never have gotten as far as we did without N7. He had a lot of critical information. The other piece of luck—yeah, I'm going to admit that despite everything I did, a lucky break helped us. Only it wasn't quite a lucky break. It was the raw spirit of the humans Claath had dared to collar with obedience chips. What compelled them to their acts of bravery? I believe rage did it, shame and the rugged desire to be free. Like us, they saw a chance and took it.

The chance came because the teleporting bomb-ship caught Claath by surprise. The days of pre-Sigma Draconis invasion planning and the intensity of combat must have drained the red-skinned Jelk. He had left the bridge long enough and during the right time for him to fail and for us to succeed.

What happened? What was the piece of luck?

We blew down another bulkhead. We were getting low on Lokhar claymores, and that could soon become a problem. Then we rushed into a Jelk's bachelor quarters and found seven women with snapped or blown-out necks. We also found five androids with smashed craniums. The real surprise was Shah Claath laying on a bloody rug and bound by cords. Beside him a woman wept. She'd wrapped a towel around her nakedness and had her face in her hands.

"N7," Claath said, with hope in his devious voice.

The woman looked up. Tears streaked her cheeks. I couldn't believe it: it was Jennifer. She scrambled to her feet and aimed a laser pistol at us, me in particular because I was in the lead.

"This is exactly as I explained it to you," Claath told Jennifer. "You have thrown away your life for this vain gesture. Your fellow creatures are dead because of your willful disobedience. Now you will experience pain and torment as you cannot imagine. Troopers, disarm her."

She turned the pistol on Claath.

"Jennifer!" I shouted. "Don't do it! We need him."

Her head whipped around, and she scowled. "Who called my name?"

"I did," I said, touching my chest. "You helped me several months ago during the neuro-fiber surgeries. I'm Creed. Don't you remember?"

"No," she said. "There were so many of you. It's all become a blur, a march of soulless faces."

It was stupid that at a moment like this I could feel crestfallen because a woman hadn't remembered me. I remembered her. I'd dreamed about her for months now.

"Release me, N7," Claath said in an imperious tone. "The rest of you beasts—"

With the butt of the laser pistol, Jennifer clouted Claath across the head. Then she aimed the weapon at him, and I expected a laser beam to end the Jelk's life.

"Listen to me," I told her. "I'm Creed. I'm an assault trooper. We were on the Lokhar PDS."

"The what?" Jennifer asked, pushing the barrel of the laser pistol against Claath's head.

"Claath sent us against the Lokhars," I said. "These are my troopers. Our obedience chips are all inoperable."

"If you were out there in space," she asked, "how could you get back here?"

"With a teleporting Lokhar vessel," I said. "Our appearance inside the battlejumper is what—"

"Killed half my friends," Jennifer said angrily.

"And disabled those androids," I added.

"Destroy the woman before she kills Shah Claath," N7 said. "We need the Jelk."

"Belay that!" I said, turning around, deciding I'd shoot and kill N7 if he raised a weapon at Jennifer.

"We have no time for this," N7 told me. "We must escape the star system or suffer the consequences of defeat."

"Jennifer," I said, turning back to her. "Maybe you can't trust anyone anymore. I don't know what that little freak has been doing to you women."

Jennifer's eyed hardened, and it amazed me that this vicious-eyed woman had been weeping before. I could see the dried tear tracks on her cheeks. Despite those, she meant business.

"We're here to free Earth from them, from him, from Claath," I said.

"He's a devil," she whispered. "All the Jelk are devils. You have no idea."

"You're wrong," I said. "I do know it. But we need this devil, at least for a little while more we do. This is for humanity's sake, Jennifer. This is a great moment when we have a chance to change our grim fate. I'm guessing you want vengeance against him. I understand that. So do I. The Lokhars killed my dad."

"They killed the Earth," she said. "But what do the Lokhars have to do with your hatred of Claath?"

"The tigers *almost* destroyed us," I said, "but they didn't finish it. Look, we're not out yet. I mean humanity. You and I, and these troopers, are still alive. We still have a chance to come back from the grave. Put down the gun, or if you don't trust any of us, put the pistol to your head. If we try something you don't like, shoot yourself."

She knelt behind Claath and aimed the pistol at me. "Why would you tell me to kill myself? What's the matter with you?"

I grinned at her, even though my gut ached at the things Claath must have done to this lady. "You know Claath doesn't make idle threats," I said. "I'm sure he's been threating you with the things he'll do once he's free. So I know you don't want to be recaptured."

"I'm never going to be recaptured," she said.

"That's why I said to put the gun to your head. Think about it. Does it make sense Claath would want all us armed Earthers here? How did the catastrophe happen that allowed you to bash in android heads?"

"I don't know," she said. "Everything—the entire ship shook worse than a Santa Monica earthquake. The shaking—it was worse than that. It killed some of my friends. He killed the others," she said, shoving the end of the pistol against Claath's head.

Behind me, N7 coughed discreetly.

"We're running out of time," I told her. "We have to slip away from Sigma Draconis and hurry back to Earth."

Jennifer shook her head as tears welled in her eyes. They slid out and tumbled down her cheeks to drip onto the floor. "I have to kill him. I'm sorry."

"Jennifer!" I shouted, and I charged her.

I took a risk, I know. But I was hoping her normal reflexes would be too slow against mine. She shouted, aimed the laser at me and fired.

284

I'd tracked the gun's orifice, and I timed it the best I could. Using the neuro-fiber reflexes, I dodged the beam, ran closer, dodged her next shot and jumped, skidding across the floor.

Jennifer shouted with rage, gripped the pistol with both hands and brought the beam *down*. It sliced the floor and then began burning through my combat boot. Before it could fry my foot, I hit her like a bowling ball and knocked her down. I winced as the back of her head struck the floor. Tearing the gun from her hand, I cradled her to my chest. She struggled. It didn't matter. I'd become far, far stronger than a regular human.

"Jennifer, Jennifer," I whispered. "You're going to be okay. Just trust me for a minute."

Then I released her. She scrambled away against a wall, glaring at me, glaring at Claath.

"Quickly, N7," Claath said. "Free me."

"Help her," I told Dmitri. "N7, can you disable her obedience chip?"

"It must already be disabled," the android said. "Otherwise, she would have died when Claath uttered the word."

"What word?" I asked.

N7 stared at the bound Jelk. "He can activate much of the ship through verbal commands."

"Be quiet, N7," Claath said. "I forbid you to speak further."

I looked up at the android. "Well?" I asked. "'Do you have free will or not?"

"You must tell them about the Q-coil," N7 told Claath. "They need to deactivate it in order to halt your ability to give verbal ship commands."

Claath twisted in his bonds, staring at me. "How did you do it? How did you turn my android against me?"

"I'll tell you soon enough," I said. "First, you're going to show me how to take the battlejumper to the nearest jump route."

"Why would I do anything so foolish?" Claath asked.

"I don't know," I said, aiming the laser at his forehead. "Maybe to keep on living would be sufficient reason."

"No. I am a Jelk of the first order. I am an Umbra and a Classist. Do you think I desire life as a slave to a beast? It is

285

inconceivable, an affront to all sensibilities. Go ahead, kill me and be done with this farce. I have lived a full life."

I laughed, and it didn't sound sane even to my ears. Oh, how I'd waited for a moment like this. I tossed the laser aside and crouched down before him. With my right thumb and index finger I gripped his nose. He had a longer one than a human would have.

Claath struggled, moving his head, trying to free himself.

I increased the grip and squeezed flesh until he cried out.

"Speak to me, Claath," I said, while holding his nose. "I want to hear what a Jelk sounds like as I twist off his schnozz."

"Cease this indignity at once," Claath said with a high nasal inflection.

"What do you think, boys?" I shouted, and I twisted Claath's nose harder.

The small alien screamed and squirmed in his bonds.

I released the nose, and it throbbed with an intensely red color, the tip a bright purple. I slapped Claath's cheek. He flinched.

"Come, come, Claath," I said, using his manner of speech. "A little beast like you will have to become accustomed to providing us with amusement. You're going to be our clown, our buffoon. I'm going to tour the known galaxy and do a stage show for whoever wants to see a Jelk dance like an animal."

"This is absurd," he said. "We are in the middle of a war zone. Soon, Doojei Lark or Axel Ahx will train their weapons on this ship. You will have to submit or die. I will go nowhere with you, nor will I aid you in any way."

"Any ideas, N7?" I asked.

"Sell him to the Lokhars," the android said. "They will pay highly for a Jelk of the noble class."

"No Lokhars will survive our fleet," Claath boasted.

"I doubt you are correct," N7 said, approaching closer.

"Stay where you are," I said.

Lasers shifted in many hands, aiming at the android.

"Look at your allies, N7," Claath said. "See how easily they betray you. You have no friends here. You are alone in the universe. Only your creator can help you."

"What do you think, N7?" I asked. "Can we fly the battlejumper without him?"

"We can," the android said. "But don't you need the codes?"

"Yes, the freighter codes," I said.

"Nothing can make me give you the codes," Claath said.

"We must dismantle the Q-coil," N7 said. "Then I will need at least seven troopers with me on the bridge. I imagine the battlejumper has taken excessive damage, but we shall see what we can achieve."

"You're all doomed," Claath said. "Unless…"

"Do not listen to him," N7 said.

"I can make you an Umbra pledge," Claath said. "The android knows no Jelk would go back on such a pledge."

"True," N7 said. "If the Jelk gave such a pledge to another civilized entity, he would keep it. However, such a pledge given to an animal or beast has no binding power."

"Rollo," I said. "Take a maniple and guard this little slug. We don't have time to tease the freighter codes out of him just yet. I'm going with N7. It's time to find out if we can flee this mess. We're not out of it yet," I told the others. "But our odds have greatly improved."

"I compute our chances of success as two out of five," N7 said.

"I didn't know you were a Vulcan," I said.

Several troopers chuckled.

"Let's go to work," I said. "Jennifer, why don't you come with me?"

"Because I don't want to," she said.

I pointed at Dmitri. "Take care of her and don't let her hurt herself or others. But don't be too rough with her. She's been through a lot."

"I will guard her with my life," the Cossack said.

***

After listening to N7's instructions on where to find and then dismantle the Q-coil, Ella and her team left.

As N7 and his seven-man team hurried down a corridor with me, I asked, "Why don't we key the Q to one of our voices?"

"I would not suggest you do such a thing," N7 said. "Jelk are notoriously subtle. There are hidden subsystems in many of their programs and in their most critical devices. Even now, I recommend you kill Shah Claath. Keeping him alive is too dangerous."

"Now that you're a free-will being," I said, "you can drop the *Shah* and just refer to him as Claath."

"Yes, of course," N7 said.

We entered the control area. It was small and, like some Lokhar control areas, lacked chairs or even Saurian stools.

"We must wait for the Q-coil to go offline," N7 said.

"Why don't you start explaining to these troopers what they need to do," I said.

The android did just that, until Ella called up and told us she'd shut down the coil.

N7 quit explaining and went to work. The android was fast, which proved to be a good thing. In less than ten minutes, he brought up the main screen.

Our battlejumper drifted, and had fallen behind the Starkien beamships. The Starkien vessels continued to follow the remaining battlejumpers. The combined fleet closed in on the PDS.

"Where is the guardian fleet?" I asked.

"Whatever remained must have fled behind the planet," N7 said.

As we spoke, heavy beams lashed out of the battlejumpers. We watched the beginning of the planetary defense station's annihilation.

"Why not keep the hulk of the station and rebuild on it?" I asked.

"Your answer lies there," N7 said.

The Jelk and Starkien beams continued to lash out, but now they flashed past the PDS and onto the planet itself.

"All right," I said. "The Jelk are destroying the surface beam sites and the missile stations. What does any of that have to do with leaving the remains of the PDS or not?"

"I believe the Jelk are about to commit planetary genocide," N7 said.

"I thought that was a Lokhar specialty," I said.

"No."

I frowned. It seemed to me that I was missing something. "I don't get it. From everything I've learned, the Jelk act in order to gain profits. Where are the profits here? If this is about genocide—genocide doesn't profit anyone."

"Your statement is irrational," N7 said, as he continued to go from station to station, his fingers a blur on the consoles. "There are many instances where genocide profits the killers."

"No, there isn't…" I trailed off. I thought about the buffalo hunters of the Old West. They had slaughtered the buffalo herds that used to cross the prairie states in their millions. Once the buffalo were gone, cattlemen grazed their beef herds over the same grasslands. Near genocide had indeed brought about the possibility for profits.

"How does killing the Lokhars here profit the Jelk?" I asked.

"I am unsure," N7 admitted.

I studied the screen, and I counted the drifting battlejumpers. This had been a costly battle for the Jelk. Fighting our way in the assault boats to the PDS had been costly. Claath had needed a bigger fleet in order to destroy the enemy more quickly. Two evenly matched fighters or nearly evenly matched fighters pounding each other to death would take a heavy toll on the winner. A three hundred pound muscleman kicking the crap out of a skinny teenager would be easy on the big man. He'd hardly break a sweat. Why hadn't Claath come in with a huge fleet like a three hundred pound man beating a skinny punk to death?

"Was the Sigma Draconis battle for profits?" I asked.

"Ultimately, the answer would have to be yes," N7 said. "The Jelk attacked. They do nothing but search for superior profits. That does not mean that each action immediately rewards the worker. On the face of it…" The android straightened and studied the screen. I saw his head twitch back and forth as if he couldn't move his eyes to read script. After twenty seconds of that, he continued to ready the command center for manual control.

That was odd behavior. It set me to thinking, to trying to put two and two together. "Does this have anything to do with the Forerunner artifact?" I asked.

"Conceivably," N7 said. "However, I have insufficient information to make an accurate guess."

Time slid by as N7 instructed the men and women and as the enemy battlejumpers moved toward a planetary orbit.

"Look," I whispered.

N7 glanced at me and followed my finger. I pointed at the screen. Bombs, or what I took to be bombs, fell from the battlejumpers and rained down toward the surface.

"Are those bio-terminators?" I asked.

"The Jelk do not use such weapons," N7 said.

On the surface of the planet, I noticed explosions.

"Are those thermonuclear weapons?" I asked.

"Of course," N7 said. "They are eliminating the Lokhar population."

"And you don't know why?"

"Overman Creed," N7 said. "I wish you would stop thinking I am working toward an ulterior goal. I am doing my task as you requested. I wish for my freedom and I see this as the only way to acquire it. I am not a Jelk with ten different hidden motives. I am…me. I prefer to live morally."

"Yeah, don't we all," I whispered.

"Ah, look," N7 said, indicating a console. "We are being hailed."

"By whom?" I asked.

He pressed a switch before saying, "I believe by the Lokhar High Commander."

"Put him on," I said.

"I do not recommend it," N7 said. "We must remain hidden. At present, our ship acts like a stricken vessel. If we open communications, the other Jelk will know about us."

"Okay, okay, belay that order," I said.

I wanted to know what the Lokhar High Commander had to say to Claath. It was eating at my curiosity. Why had the three Jelk allowed themselves to take such heavy casualties in order to drop thermonuclear bombs on the planet? For ten years, the Jelk hadn't attacked directly like this. Had they attacked to open these jump routes. That's what I'd been led to believe. But the Lokhars still had two PDS-protected planets in this system.

"How much longer until you're ready?" I asked the android.

"I am ready now," N7 said. He began to give orders, and the seven troopers around the chamber began to follow them, changing settings on the control boards.

"We're slightly altering the battlejumper's course," N7 explained to me. "We are headed for the nearest jump route."

"Where does that jump route begin?"

N7 pressed a button. A faint image appeared in the distance. I'd estimate it as half an AU away.

"That's the opening to the nearest jump route?" I asked.

"Precisely," N7 said.

I watched the screen for a time. As I did, the Jelk continued to rain bombs onto the planet.

"The Lokhar High Commander is no longer hailing our ship," N7 said.

"Did someone else answer him?" I asked.

"Doojei Lark's battlejumper took the call. The two are now communicating."

"The Jelk are still dropping bombs," I said.

"It is a negotiating tactic," N7 said.

Abruptly, the bombs stopped raining.

"What do you think?" I asked.

"Concerning?" N7 asked.

"What the Lokhars and Doojei Lark discuss," I said.

"It would be interesting to know."

I couldn't turn off my curiosity as easily as it seemed N7 had shut down his. "Keep us sliding toward the jump route," I said. "I'm going to talk to Claath. There are too many mysteries here for my taste. We're free now. We need to know the score if we're going to make wise decisions."

"Wise decisions have not given us this position of freedom," N7 said. "Wild, nearly insane decisions have proven best so far. Perhaps we should stick to what works."

"Keep an eye on the android," I told the senior trooper. "Call me if he does anything suspicious."

I strolled out of the command chamber. The minute I was out of sight, I broke into a sprint. As I ran, I called the surviving centurions. A group of one hundred troopers still swept through various areas of the ship. They hunted the surviving Saurians. We hadn't gotten all of the lizards yet, but we had to. This was an Earth-ship now. We couldn't afford any alien stowaways.

"Rollo," I radioed.

"What's up, Creed?" he asked.

"What has Claath been doing?"

"He started out by threatening us," Rollo said. "After a while, he offered us extravagant prizes if we let him go. You should hear this guy. He has some imagination."

"It sounds like he's still interested in living," I said.

"I've never met anyone who wanted to live more," Rollo said.

"I'm heading down to you. We're going to have a real heart-to-heart with the devil."

"Thinking you'd feel that way sooner or later, I started carving a few splinters," Rollo said. "Then I took a good look at his fingers. The bastard doesn't have any fingernails."

"Don't worry," I said. "I have a few ideas. Soon, Claath will be begging to talk."

-26-

"Are you comfortable?" I asked.

Rumpelstiltskin Claath sat in a chair before me. He wore blue skivvies and nothing else. The Jelk had a miniature humanoid body, with odds bumps along his spine and too many ribs showing on a square and much too thick chest. His stomach was thinner than a man's would be. He had large, knobby knees and just as knobby elbows, with the otherwise sticklike arms of a Holocaust victim. With his pointy teeth, he seemed like a Germanic Middle Ages' goblin.

"I asked you a question." I said.

We occupied a living room-sized chamber, holding Claath's chair, a table and chair for me and several large metal containers on the sides. Rollo leaned against the closed hatch, with his arms crossed and the index finger of his right hand tapping his biceps.

"Hmm," I said, taking out my Bowie knife, removing a speck of imaginary dust from one of my fingernails. Then, with a clunk, I set the knife on the table.

Claath's eyes fixated on the Bowie.

"It's from Earth," I told him. "I've sharpened it so that if I wanted to I could shave with the edge. I've always wondered if it was sharp enough to peel off skin. Now is my chance to find out."

After a half-second's pause, Claath said, "Your threats mean nothing to me."

"Actions speak louder than words, huh?" I asked. "I know exactly what you mean. Boasters are so annoying." I shifted

293

around in my chair. "Rollo, could you come here, please? I need you to hold our little friend down."

From his spot near the hatch, Rollo pushed off the wall and ambled closer.

"I am a Jelk," Claath said proudly.

I faced him, and I let my hand drop onto the knife's hilt. "I know you are, and that's what's going to make this an enjoyable occasion," I said, picking up the knife.

"You are a barbarian."

"No, to you I'm a beast, remember? Hey, just so you know, Claath. I'm thinking about roasting the pieces I carve off you. I'm going to have a feast. Rollo?" I asked, half turning his way. "Would like some roast Jelk?"

"I'd love some," Rollo said.

"Your threats—" Claath jumped off the chair. Rollo moved fast, intercepting the small alien. Claath attempted to use his pointy teeth to bite my friend's wrist. Rollo slapped the Jelk's face, twisting the neck so we heard a creak. That seemed to take the fight out of Claath. Without further ado, Rollo push the Jelk back onto the chair, and like a rodeo cowboy tying a calf's legs, he tied down Claath's wrists and ankles to parts of the chair.

"Better tie down his entire left leg," I said. "I'm going to hack through the foot."

Rollo used more binding, and he tied the leg tightly so the cords bit into flesh.

"I am a Jelk—"

"Put a gag on him," I said. "If he's not going to talk, I don't want to hear him scream either."

Rollo whipped out a cloth.

"Wait," Claath said, finally sounding worried.

I was already coming around the table, with the knife in my hand. I paused, and I raised an eyebrow.

"How do I know—" Claath said.

"No bargains, Jelk," I said. "Either you start answering my questions as fast as you can, and hope for my mercy, or I'm going to carve you up piece by piece."

Claath shuddered, and he shrank back from me. "I would like to point out that it was my mercy that gave you the freighters. Without me—"

"The Lokhars wouldn't have had any reason to come to Earth and use their bio-terminator," I said. "Yeah, I know. I lay the majority of the blame on you, but not all of it."

"But—"

I held up the knife.

Wisely, Claath kept quiet and refrained from giving me more gibberish.

"Now we're finally getting somewhere," I said. "Before we start the twenty questions, I want to know the codes to the freighters."

"You would strip me of single bargaining chip?" Claath asked.

"I'm not bargaining," I said.

"Then why should I talk?"

I stared at him and shrugged. Maybe I needed to hack off a foot before he realized how serious I was.

He must have seen something in my eyes or my bearing. "Wait, wait," he said.

I was through listening to pleas. He needed to see, to *feel*, the business edge of my knife. I knelt beside him, and before I could think or worry about anything else, I began to saw at the ankle joint so blood spurted.

Claath screamed, and he shouted, "I'll talk, I'll talk! Please, please, don't cut off my foot. I'll give you the codes."

I almost kept sawing. He didn't deserve any better. How many thousands of Earth men and women had lost their lives because of him? He was a mass murderer. But I hesitated. If he tried to bargain again…

Claath babbled the codes.

Rollo sat at the table and wrote them down. I could hear his writing implement scratch against paper.

I stood up, and I wiped the blade against Claath's chest, leaving a bloody smear there.

"My ankle, my ankle," Claath sobbed. "It's bleeding. You must bandage it. My blood is more precious than you can conceive."

"You're going to have to talk more than that before I give you a bandage," I said.

He bobbed his head in the affirmative. It seemed to me that he was ready to give us straight answers.

"Why did you attack the Sigma Draconis system?" I asked.

"To open the routes," he said. "The shorter way between Jelk-controlled areas will decrease my costs by twenty percent."

"I'll buy that's part of the reason," I said. "No, maybe that's just a fringe benefit. What's the real reason, Claath? Why did you make this attack?"

"I have told you."

"Do you think I'm an idiot?" I asked.

"No. You are an unusual beast—man," he said. "You're a man, not a beast. I see I've underestimated you. This attack on my battlejumper—it was brilliant."

I pricked him with the tip of the Bowie. He tried to ease back from it. He kept his eyes on the knife until he finally looked up at me.

"This space battle was too bloody on the Jelk," I said.

He frowned. "I do not understand your meaning. Except for my ankle, no Jelk blood has been lost."

"You lost too many battlejumpers," I said. "If you needed to open up this system, you should have brought more ships to smash it open at a lesser cost to you."

"Hindsight is twenty-twenty," he said. "We did not realize the guardian fleet was so strong."

"You could have fled the moment you saw their strength."

Claath shook his head. "You don't understand space combat. The guardian fleet attacked as soon as we came out of the jump route."

"You're lying," I said. "I saw some of the battle, remember? You attacked the guardian fleet as it hovered near the PDS. Listen, Claath, you're going to lose both feet in short order if you keep lying to me. You've trained me too well, you see. I'm a killer, and I've killed plenty of aliens now. Lopping off your feet will be easy to do, a pleasure, in fact, payback for all the things you've done to us."

He stared into my eyes, and I saw something hard and remorseless in his orbs. They seemed to deepen in color from inky black to ultimate black-hole dark. He straightened, pushing against his bonds. Despite myself, I found something majestic in the little prick's manner. He seemed to shed the simpering weakling as if it had been an act and now he showed his true self.

"I am an Umbra and a Classist," Claath said. "You cannot conceive what that means. I am of noble blood and have earned massive profits throughout my long life. Do you believe I've never been captured before? That this is my first time?" He bark laughed. "I remained here in your custody in order to see what kind of creature you Earthlings really are. You are ruthless, I'll grant you."

"The codes you gave me?" I asked.

"You wonder if they are detonation numbers instead of deactivation codes and you are quite correct," Claath said. "Use them and watch the last of your race die."

"Why did you attack Sigma Draconis?" I asked.

"You're a curious beast," Claath said. "Very well, I'll speak, for all the good it will do you. We want this corridor open. It will improve each of our cargo percentages by twenty points. Given our volume of trade, that's a vast amount of added revenue. Yet you are perceptive enough to see that we've taken too many ship losses. The guardian fleet surprised us by their numbers, but we battled our way to the Shrine Planet. After all these centuries, we have finally opened the way there. Even now, Doojei Lark or Axel Ahx races to the hidden Forerunner shrine. The Lokhars are primitive creatures. They fail to understand what they hold. But we know. We are the oldest race left in this region of the galaxy."

His words shocked me, but they had the ring of truth to them. I believed him, and I wondered who or what Claath and the Jelk really were. Why did a Jelk fleet only contain three members of their race?

"Why use Earthers?" I asked. "Why did you come to our planet, to our solar system?"

Claath laughed. "You are so terribly curious, aren't you? It delights me to see you flail away for knowledge, to attempt to grasp the true realities of the situation." He shook his oversized head. "You do not get to know the true reasons, now or ever."

"Is this about the Forerunner object?" I asked, "The one that disappeared in the Altair system?"

His dark eyes narrowed. He hissed like a wet cat. "Tying me down and cutting my flesh was a gross indignity. I will remember this, Earthbeast, and I will enact a fierce revenge because of it."

"No," I said, "I'm the one who's going to enact the revenge."

"Do you think so?" he sneered.

I'm not sure why, but I believed he was going to escape the bonds and the ship. I didn't think Mr. Rumpelstiltskin would boast or act bravely unless he truly had an ace card. In the Altair system, the Forerunner artifact of the First Ones had disappeared. The Lokhars had unstable teleport bomb-ships: another form of disappearing craft.

As I thought about that, my fingers tightened around the hilt of the Bowie knife. Claath couldn't do anything tricky if he was dead. Using my neuro-fiber speed, I thrust the knife. The steel parted goblin-red skin as the blade sank through Claath's flesh. I felt the blade grate against bones.

Claath screamed in agony. It was a satisfying sound. Then his dark eyes locked onto mine. I felt a strange sensation against the base of my head.

"I've marked you, Earthbeast," he whispered. Blood stained his pointy teeth.

"I've killed you, you little bastard," I told him.

"No," he said, as blood dripped onto his chin. "I do not keep my heart where you do." He laughed, and he began to fade.

"No!" I shouted, yanking out the blade. I stabbed again, twisting the knife, hoping to kill the devil before it was too late.

He shuddered, he screamed again, and he faded even faster.

"I have marked you," Claath said in a ghostly voice.

I removed the knife for another strike. Even as I did so, Claath faded until he collapsed and coalesced into a bright, pulsating ball. It was the size of basketball. I noticed that one part of the glow had a hole in it, and light or some weird substance smoked out of it. Had I done that with my knife when he'd been flesh and blood?

I swiped the Bowie knife through the pulsating ball of light. To my surprise, I felt resistance. Maybe this thing wasn't exactly light, but matter of some kind.

I will return to enact vengeance for this indignity.

I heard Claath's voice inside my head. And I felt the twinge again in the base of my skull. I jerked away the blade, and I noticed it glowed red as if hot. Using a finger, I touched the blade, and grunted at the heat, jerking my finger away from it.

"Look," Rollo said.

The two of us stood in the nearly empty chamber. The ball of pulsating light floated away from us.

I expected to see the ball disappear and fade away. Instead, as smoky light continued to bleed out of the hole, the ball floated up against the ceiling. The bulkhead there turned red-hot until metal dripped. That area of the bulkhead dissolved and the ball sped upward.

I glanced at Rollo. "Are you seeing this?"

"I am," Rollo said.

"Is he really a devil?" I asked.

"I don't think so," Rollo said. "I mean…he turned into a ball of energy or something like it."

I touched the knife again. The blade wasn't as hot as before. From the ceiling, I watched liquefied metal drip onto the floor. A supernatural creature couldn't do that, could it? Like Ella would say, there had to be a scientific explanation for this.

"I don't think Claath is an actual devil," I said.

Rollo gave me a strange look.

"He's not a spirit, I mean," I said. "Spirits don't make metal hot and need to burn through it in order to get away. He must have substance of some kind."

Hissing sounds came from above, and air blew fiercely around us, lifting Rollo's hair as if he stood in a blizzard. What was this? What sorcery, fiendish wizardry, did the Jelk commit as he escaped?

"Hull breach," Rollo said. "I think he burned his way out of the ship. We have to get out of this room before it depressurizes."

"Go, go," I said. "If you're right, maybe he's headed for the planet. He'll warn the other Jelk."

We ran out of the chamber and sealed the hatch behind us.

"Tell the others what happened," I said. "I'm headed for the control room. Hurry! We don't know how much time we have left."

***

I ran through the corridors, not knowing what to think. Jelk were energy creatures that played at being flesh and blood? Having to turn into the ball of light had made Claath angry. Maybe it was difficult to do. I'd wounded him, too. He must be susceptible to pain, otherwise why had he taken so many precautions these past months?

What exactly was the Jelk Corporation? What exactly was the Jade League? I knew so little about interstellar relations.

None of that matters now, I told myself. I had to get back to Earth. I had to free the humans in the freighters. Despite everything I'd seen just now, humanity still clung to existence by a thread.

I burst into the control room and told Ella and N7 what had just happened.

Ella sat down hard on the floor, staring into space. N7 appeared more thoughtful than usual.

"Did you know anything about this?" I asked N7. "That Jelk could do something like that?"

"Negative," the android said. "I am stunned by the turn of events."

"Can you spot him in the void?" I asked.

N7 worked the controls, finally admitting defeat.

"Okay," I said. "Maybe it takes time for Claath to journey through space like a glowing ball. Maybe he can't communicate with others until he's in their presence."

Ella snapped her fingers as she turned toward me.

"Spill it," I said.

"I'm in agreement with you that the…the…transformation you witnessed is a difficult procedure for them," Ella said.

300

"Why's that?" I asked.

"They used a fleet to battle to his planet in order to enter a Forerunner shrine or temple," Ella said. "I'm presuming they need to see something at this shrine. But why bother with a fleet if they could turn into this ball of light and simply travel here and look at it?"

"That is logically reasoned," N7 said.

"I am a scientist," Ella said. "I use reason and observation to test theories until I approach an approximation of truth."

"Never mind about that," I said. "We have to risk greater movement and reach the jump route. We have to leave this system before the Jelk or Starkien ships come after us."

"Do you know which jump routes to use in order to get us to Earth?" Ella asked N7.

The android touched a control so a split screen appeared. One showed the Sigma Draconis system. The other was a star map with jump routes in a blizzard maze connecting about one hundred star systems. As N7 adjusted the panel, a blue light appeared showing a path.

"There is our route to Earth," the android said.

"How many jumps do we have to make to reach there?" I asked.

"Nine," N7 said. "Oh, wait. We cannot go that way." The blue line shifted. "Ten jumps," he said.

"Will our battlejumper hold up that long?" I asked.

"In order to insure that is does, we must begin to effect repairs now," N7 said.

"Do you know how to make these repairs?" I asked.

"I do," the android said.

"The rest of us can learn as you teach us," I said.

"I must warn you that the major repairs will take a shipyard," N7 said.

"Which we most certainly don't have," I said. "Maybe we can cannibalize parts from some of the Earth freighters." I studied the star map. "Well, let's get started. We need to leave Sigma Draconis."

The android made adjustments on the panel, and I felt slight acceleration.

Through the screen, we watched the enemy battlejumpers and we watched the Starkien beamships. Hopefully, both Doojei Lark and Axel Ahx had gone down to the Forerunner shrine on the surface. That might force the glowing ball of light into a longer journey.

I couldn't believe this. We were finally free, and we'd gained a battlejumper and had captured Claath—for a while. I'd expected the answers to enlighten me about the galaxy of warring aliens. Instead, I was even more confused about what was really going on than ever.

I rotated my head, and with my fingers I felt along the base of my skull. What had Claath done to me there at the end? What did it mean that a glowing ball of light wanted revenge against me? What had he said? The Jelk were the oldest race left, at least in this part of the galaxy. I didn't like the sound of that. The oldest around—and he seemed there at the end to be extremely long-lived—would surely know things the younger races wouldn't or couldn't.

"Oh-oh," Ella said.

"What?" I asked.

"Several Starkien ships are accelerating away from the planet," Ella said.

"Where are they headed?" I asked.

"Straight for us," N7 answered.

27

"Do we have shields?" I asked.

"Electromagnetic fields," Ella said, amending my question.

"Negative to both queries," N7 said. "Our battlejumper is nearly crippled." The android sidestepped along his station, tapping buttons and switches. "It appears we do have an operable primary beam. That changes the equation."

"Does our weapon outrange the Starkien beams?" I asked.

"By a considerable amount," N7 said. "Still, there are—" he looked up at the screen. "There are three beamships to our one crippled battlejumper. I expect they have superior acceleration capabilities. Even so..." he went back to examining the controls. "We should be able to reach the jump entrance before they can."

"Show me the battlejumpers again," I said. "Those ships have longer-ranged beams—"

"Jelk drones are approaching the ship," N7 said. "The drones are coming *from* the jump entrance. It appears that Claath or the others must have maneuvered some drones there before the battle. Clearly, they are a cautious race."

"I'm not sure they're a race at all," I said. "Maybe they're immortals."

"You have insufficient evidence to jump to such a conclusion," N7 said.

Maybe he was right. I dragged the back of my left hand across my mouth. I tasted salt there, dried sweat. "Destroy the drones," I said. "We have to get past them before they do something to us."

"The Starkien beamships might be chasing us as a mere precautionary measure," N7 said. "If we destroy the drones now, the remaining Jelk will realize something is amiss for certain. They might well order the battlejumpers after us then."

"Do it anyway," I said. "It's a race to Earth now, one we have to win."

"If I might point out—" N7 said.

"Destroy the drones," I said. "Do it now."

"Do you think that's wise?" Ella asked me. "Maybe we should hear out the android."

"I'm feeling sick," I said. "I know it's radiation poisoning. We need to get into the healing tank, all of us. We have no more time to make fancy maneuvers. It's has to be a straight thrust like a knifeman trying to kill a Jelk in the flesh."

"I'm activating the main laser," N7 said.

"That's what the beam is," I asked, "a laser?"

"Yes," the android said. "What else were you expecting?"

"A neutron beam maybe or an X-ray beam or something I'd never heard about," I said.

"Curious," N7 said.

I didn't bother asking him what he found so curious. I felt sick. I'd been holding it back through force of will. But I couldn't hold out for much longer. I wanted that healing bath. I hoped Jennifer knew something about the Jelk tech.

Wattage built up. Even here in the control room we heard it. The engine sounded labored, and the entire battlejumper shook.

"My readings show our vessel's instability," N7 said, as he indicated his controls.

"Fire when ready," I said.

"Now," N7 said. He tapped the panel.

On the screen, we watched the laser stab once, twice, three times. Each beaming destroyed an attacking drone.

"The way to the jump route is open," N7 said.

I nodded, watching as the android switched the screen back to the chasing beamships.

"Oh-oh," Ella said.

Three beams lanced from the three Starkien vessels. They speared directly for us, and hit.

"Damage?" I asked.

"Unknown at the moment," N7 said. "I am rotating the battlejumper, as the beam cannon has partly frozen into place."

Precious seconds passed as the enemy's rays struck the outer armor. We didn't have cameras showing us what happened, but I could guess well enough.

"Why can't it be easy for once?" I muttered.

The engine made its labored noises, and I dreaded hearing an explosion or something to indicate we'd blown our single chance for freedom. Instead, the heavy beam speared out and stabbed one of the Starkien vessels. An electromagnetic field held the annihilating ray at bay for a time.

"They're breaking off," N7 said.

"Keep beaming," I said.

"I recommend you let them go," N7 said, "and we save wear to our engine."

"Stop firing," I said. "That's a good idea. Yeah, we have to save the engine."

The beam quit, and we continued on our way, heading for the jump route.

A multitude of thoughts tumbled through my mind. Did the other races know about the Jelk and their special abilities? N7 hadn't. Had Rollo and I witnessed something unique in the history of the universe? Could we use our knowledge as a lever? If so, how?

"What do you know about the Lokhars?" I asked N7.

"That is a broad question," the android said. "Could you be more precise?"

"Why do you think the Lokhars sent a dreadnought to Earth to annihilate humanity?"

"So you humans would not become star soldiers for the Jelk Corporation," the android said. "Given your performances at the Altair and Sigma Draconis systems, their decision was rational."

"Rational perhaps," I said, "but it was highly immoral."

"Particularly from your point of view," N7 said.

"From *any* point of view," I said.

"I'm not sure I follow your thinking."

"Do you believe in right and wrong?" I asked.

305

"Not in a strict, absolute sense," the android said.

Ella grunted agreement.

"You can say that even after witnessing the disappearance of the Forerunner object?" I asked.

"What bearing does that have on absolute right and wrong?" N7 asked.

I bit my lower lip. None of the battlejumpers had left their orbit around the shrine planet. The three Starkien vessels returned there.

"Why are they letting us go?" I asked.

"It is possible they do not yet realize Earthbeasts have successfully captured a battlejumper," N7 said.

"How about you call us humans from now on," I said. "We're not beasts."

"As you wish," N7 said.

"We should start repairing what we can," Ella said.

"That's a good idea," I said. "First, though, some of us need to use the healing tank."

"You go first," Ella said. "It is logical, as N7 would say. You have made the critical decisions these past hours. We need you at one hundred percent."

"I want Rollo watching the android," I said.

"You still do not trust me?" N7 asked. "Have I not proven myself?"

"I have no complaints against you," I said. "Call it a precautionary measure on my part."

"It is now in my interest to see you escape," N7 said, "as I also get to escape. Do not fear, I will teach you all I know about piloting this vessel."

"Start by teaching Ella," I said. "By the way, I'm going to keep my part of the bargain. Soon, now, you'll be free to leave us if you want to."

"I knew you to be a man of your word," the android said.

I turned away. Radiation poisoning was making it increasingly difficult to keep thinking straight. I hoped that healing tank or tanks hadn't been rendered inoperable.

Soon, Rollo appeared on the bridge. I spoke to him, gave him my instructions and then staggered off in search of Nurse Jennifer.

***

She wore regular clothes: tight-fitting slacks and a baggy blouse with large blue buttons. We sat in a large room with big tanks and dangling tubes around us. Dmitri along with several other troopers looking green around the gills waited nearby for the healing treatment. She frowned at me.

"I've watched androids do this," Jennifer told me. "I helped people afterward. That doesn't mean I know how to work the equipment exactly."

I clutched my gut and doubled over, groaning. I felt worse than ever, and we were about to jump. I didn't want to think about that.

"All right," she said, with her hand touching my elbow, guiding me. "Let's try this."

"I'm supposed to take a pill first," I said. "I remember that much."

"Oh yes, that's right," she said.

I stared at her.

"I'm the doing the best I can," she said. "This, this…" She waved her hands in the air. "It's overwhelming."

"I know," I said. "You're doing great, Jennifer. I'm not complaining. I need your help."

Her features softened, and she looked at me like she had the day after my neuro-fiber surgery.

"Jen," she said. "My friends call me Jen."

"I'm feeling sick, Jen. I really need you to remember everything. This could be critical."

She nodded, and it sobered her. "I need a pen and paper, something to write with."

We found her writing material. Then she sat down. As we waited, with our bones aching, trying to keep as quiet as possible, Jen wrote out the steps. She told us it was better to think before acting. Flying by the seat of your pants was the worst way to do these kinds of things. I nodded: anything to keep her working it out.

She wrote, and by the concentration on her face it looked like she was remembering just fine.

307

N7 interrupted us through the ship's loudspeakers. He warned us—ten seconds before it happened—and we entered the jump route.

The process hurt, and at the end of the jump, l lay on my back panting. I don't remember much after that. Hands helped me stand. A woman spoke softly. I swallowed a lump of a pill, and that felt right even though I found it hard to force down my throat. Afterward, I floated in the tank. Jen must have figured out all the procedures, because I felt better.

It took several days, and I missed the rest of the action, the touch and go. As the chemicals aided the healing process that restored what the radiation had stolen from my bone marrow, the crew worked overtime to keep the battlejumper running.

N7 knew things all right. I'm not sure when he slept or if he used drugs to keep him going around the clock. He taught Ella and several other technologically inclined troopers. They each picked others to help them, and the teams worked tirelessly. The rest carted dead Saurians to the incinerators, scrubbed away blood and gore and did whatever else they could that needed fixing or righting.

Despite the hard work, the battlejumper remained a wreck. Instead of a Flying Dutchman—the ghost ship of the space lanes—we were the Flying Battlejumper, limping our way through the star systems.

I had one hundred and sixty-eight troopers left, including Jen and myself. That was too few for what I had in mind. Aliens had given us our troubles, right? I planned to make the aliens solve them for us.

"N7," I said, six jumps later. "I've been meaning to talk to you."

We were in a spacious hangar bay, inspecting one of the three remaining assault boats.

The android straightened. We stood in the piloting chamber. After these past few days his eyes had tightened so crow's feet showed around the edges, and he'd become testier.

"Do you think we can we fix the battlejumper back to full capacity?" I asked.

"Negative," N7 said.

"What if we cannibalize parts from the freighters?" I asked.

"They are old freighters and their design is quite different from a battlejumper. These are uniquely Jelk craft."

"Is there anyone who can repair the damage?" I asked.

"The more highly industrialized Jelk Corporation worlds could do it easily."

"I'm talking about somewhere we can go?" I said.

"Jade League worlds would impound the ship in order to study the technology," N7 said. "So you cannot go there."

"That makes sense. Do you think the Jelk are coming after us?"

"There are unforeseen factors involved," N7 said. "The most critical is if Shah Claath—Permit me to rephrase: if *Claath* communicated his desires to the others and possibly offered monetary inducements then the Jelk will be hunting for us."

"What about the Starkiens?" I asked.

"I do not understand your implication."

"They're contractors, right?"

"Of course," N7 said.

"They must have some idea what occurred: that we captured a battlejumper. Might they track us down in the hope of capturing this ship and selling it to the Jade League?"

"Devious," N7 said. "Yes, they might do so. Conceivably, they would bargain with the Jelk Corporation and receive an even greater amount for the stolen vessel."

"I don't understand why glowing balls of light, or a form of mass radiating light that Claath became, would care anything about profits."

"An interesting thought," N7 said. "Perhaps the need for profits is a sham that hides a greater truth. Yet I am more intrigued by the transformation itself. Perhaps the transformation to a light-like state was a primitive defensive mechanism."

"I doubt that," I said. "I think it was Claath's natural state."

"If so, why do the other Jelk maintain their physical shells?" N7 asked. "Perhaps it is easier for them in ways we do not understand when they remain as physical entities. Clearly, Claath only reverted to the ball of light, as you say, when his life was directly threatened with imminent death."

309

"And yet I saw him bleed smoke or light from a wound I'd given him while he was in the physical state."

"It is very intriguing, to say the least," N7 said.

"He claimed to be the oldest race in this part of the galaxy," I said.

N7 slammed a hood shut. "This assault boat is operable. You will be able to take it down to the surface."

He meant the Earth's surface. We still had several more jumps to go before we reached the solar system.

"Do you think Claath left defensive drones in the solar system?" I asked.

"I do," N7 said. "We should be able to detect and destroy them, however."

"I think Claath's interest in the Forerunner object was motivated by more than just money or profits," I said.

"I am inclined to agree with you," N7 said, "even though we have insufficient data to reach that conclusion. I am learning how to make leaps of logic to arrive at possible or theoretical conclusions. Is that how you operate?"

"No," I said. "Mine's more through intuition, I suppose."

N7 stepped out of the piloting compartment, his boot thudding onto the hangar floor, knocking a stray tube so it clattered across the metal. I followed him and I slapped the side of the assault boat.

"Here's my plan," I said. "I want to run it by you and see what you think?"

"I am honored," N7 said.

"I plan to restore my planet to its original state. To that end, I need an antidote to the bio-terminator."

"It is a noble goal. How will you scrub the bio-terminator from the soil and from the atmosphere?"

"Since Earth doesn't possess the needed technology or expertise, I'm going to have to find it," I said. "Then I'm going to need currency, enough to entice traders to sell me the antidote."

"You will probably need great amounts of currency," N7 said.

I drummed my fingers on the side of the assault boat. "I suppose I could sell some of my fellow humans into slavery as assault troopers to garner cash."

"A feasible plan," N7 said.

"Except that I'm not a slaver," I said. "And my goal is the survival of the human race, not its further degradation or extinction."

"That is imprecisely stated," N7 said. "You are alive. You are not extinct. Further extinction is illogical. You are either extinct or not."

"Thanks for the grammar lesson."

"You are welcome," N7 said.

I shook my head. Sometimes the android said the funniest things. Sometimes he seemed like he was made out of tin.

"I plan to fix the battlejumper and use it like a Starkien would," I said.

"You desire to become a pirate?" N7 asked.

"No," I said, "a Viking."

"I do not understand your reference."

"I'm going to raid planets and take...something valuable from each," I said. "Once my war chest is large enough, I'll buy the antidote to the bio-terminator and cleanse my world. Afterward, we'll repopulate it and start over, but with advanced technology to defend us."

"That is an aggressive plan," the android said. "I find several troublesome features to it."

"That's why I'm talking to you. Let's hear your objections."

"If you attack others," N7 said, "they may come and attack you."

"That's why I need those Jelk freighters sitting on Earth," I said. "We're going to lift off for a time and hide."

"Hide where?" N7 asked.

"Don't know that yet," I said. "First, I need to know more about the nearby star systems. One thing I do know is that Earth history shows it's harder to kill off nomads than a settled community. Most of the humans are dead, right? Keeping the last ones alive is going to be the trick."

"Taken as a whole," N7 said, "your plan strikes me as dubious."

"Yeah, why's that?"

"Because there are only a few million of you left," N7 said. "A handful of enemy ships in the wrong place could destroy the freighters and end your race. You are in an extremely precarious position."

"I know, but I have a Jelk battlejumper. I have knowledge about the Altair object and I have a few hundred of the meanest, toughest fighting troopers in the galaxy. We're humans, and the universe is going to find out that messing with us was a big mistake."

"Bold words," N7 said.

"I was a slave, and now I'm free. No one thought that could be done."

N7 looked away. When he looked back, he asked, "Do you want to check the next assault boat?"

"Yeah," I said. "Let's take a look."

28

Six days later, I mourned my dead world, the sterile Earth. The bio-terminator had done its grisly work all too well.

I flew over Germany in an air-car, with Jen beside me in the copilot's seat.

I wore another bio-suit, with an assault trooper helmet and combat boots. We'd dismantled Claath's old defensive systems, so it was unlikely these suits would turn on us as the others had. I know, it probably sounds crazy that any of us would wear these after what had happened. But they were useful and they were all we had in terms of combat armor. To implement my plan, we needed to continue to be the galaxy's best soldiers.

We'd combed the freighter passengers for high-tech engineers, men and women used to getting things done. I'd brought ten of them aboard to help with the battlejumper repairs.

It had been good to find that my suggestion several months ago to Diana, Rex Hodges and other leaders had borne fruit. Each freighter complex had a different form of government. One was theocratic in nature, more were democratic and two had dictators. The dictatorial ones had hardly advanced beyond the prison way of running things. I hadn't made any moral judgments on any of them. If it worked, let them keep using their system, for now at least.

Trying to decide what to do with Claath's codes had proven harder to resolve. Rollo had finally figured out the truth. He suggested that Claath had given us the right codes in the first

313

place and then he'd tried to cover by telling us they were destruct codes.

How did we find out?

We emptied a freighter and electronically put in the code. Instead of destroying the empty freighter, the code had unlocked and deactivated hidden explosives. A team had carried the explosives off. We emptied each freighter in turn, and had gotten rid of the hidden explosives. Later, we set the people back on board.

The space-freighters still waited on the Earth's surface as N7 and Ella taught specially picked teams how to fly them.

I only had two understrength centuries of assault troopers. In my mind, that limited the number of untested humans I could safely bring aboard the battlejumper.

I was dealing with the last humans, the luckiest and the toughest: the survivors. I didn't doubt for a moment that some of them dreamed of overthrowing me and putting themselves in my place and becoming mankind's ultimate ruler, with the battlejumper as their throne.

Right now, I had the weapons and the deadliest soldiers. I had the battlejumper and the ability to destroy any of them at will. For now, the freighter leaders agreed to my plan—as much of it as they knew. The time would come soon enough when some of them would violently disagree with me.

That was the future. Today, I mourned Mad Jack Creed. I mourned my mother, my friends, my town, my country and my world. I was going to leave Earth again for a short time. I would come back later, just as Douglas MacArthur had returned to Manila. I would make the Earth as it used to be, and it would be humanity's planet, its stronghold against all comers.

The Jelk would hunt for me, of that I had no doubt, even if only one of them did it: an alien named Claath. Maybe the Starkiens would come and take a look here. I had to be long gone by then.

I flew over Germany, over dead forests, silent cities and vast autobahns with their empty rusting vehicles. The one time I saw movement, it was only the wind pushing down an open trunk to a car.

"The Lokhars were thorough," Jen said.

"They brought their dirty business to our planet," I said. "We were doing fine by ourselves."

"Were we?" she asked. "We had nuclear weapons and biological agents."

"Not like this," I said.

"No," she said, "but that wasn't for a lack of trying."

"Are you saying we're no better than Lokhars and Jelk?" I asked.

"Do you think we are?" she asked.

I glanced at her. Her frown—I'll be honest. Her beauty and her earnestness touched me. Mainly it was her beauty that did it, though. I smiled at her.

"Did I say something wrong?" she asked, stiffening.

"No." I banked the air-car.

She cried out, and she clutched the armrests of her seat. "Be careful," she scolded me.

I laughed.

"I'm serious," she said.

"I know. That's why I'm laughing."

"Do you enjoy mocking me?" she asked.

"You misunderstand."

"Why don't you inform a poor ignorant girl then?" she said.

"You're not ignorant, Jen. No one knows more about Jelk medicine than you. I owe you my life."

"So why are you laughing at me?" she asked.

"Because you made me feel young again," I said. "I'm only a kid, Jen. I went to war in Afghanistan when I was nineteen, twenty. I worked for Black Sand for a time. It was a lark, really. Antarctica was an adventure. While there, I kept thinking about coming home and taking a girl out. You know, go to the movies. Go out to eat and have a glass of wine. That's all gone. It's kaput, vanished forever. But now...riding here with you...it's like driving along a freeway and we're going to the beach. That's why I laughed."

I glanced at her, and found that Jen stared at me even more seriously than before.

It made me grin, and she grinned back, impishly. Unbuckling her restraints, she stood and crossed the distance between us.

I set the air-car on autopilot, and I shed the bio-suit. Then I took Jen in my arms. She was warm and vital, and we kissed. She tasted wonderful. We kissed harder and wrapped ourselves around each other with need.

Later, as I donned my bio-suit, I ran my hand through my hair. Jen buckled back into her seat.

"I just thought of something," I said.

"What's that?"

I smiled at her. She spoke differently now. Jen—Jennifer— she was beautiful.

"I want your opinion," I said.

As we flew, I studied the German cities, and I found an old one. I don't know which one by name. I landed the air-car, and we outside onto the surface. The wind blew, but we were protected in our suits from the bio-terminator.

I found a cathedral and entered. It was full of the dead. A mother still clutched her bundled infant. Our footsteps echoed and the sunlight was muted. We ascended stairs and found a way onto the roof. By careful climbing, I came to a stone gargoyle perched on the roof edge, a gargoyle with sculptured stone wings. I couched up there, staring at the thing, likely chiseled sometime during the Middle Ages. Except for the wings, it looked an awfully lot like Claath had before his glowing-ball transformation.

I guess I didn't really have a question for Jen. It had been a question for me.

I returned to Jen waiting by the opening, and we retreated down the stairs and back through the main area where the dead sat, knelt and lay in their last mass.

We returned to the air-car. There, scrubbers and sprayers washed us, and we reentered the pilot compartment. It was time to head up to the battlejumper.

"Did you discover what you were looking for?" Jen asked.

I thought about that. "Who are the Jelk?" I finally asked. "Why did that gargoyle resemble Claath so much? The

Forerunner object—I believe that in some way the First Ones' artifact is important to our discovering what's really going on."

I'd talked to Ella about that before. She'd had some interesting notions or ideas. She'd wondered if the artifact helped a Jelk bulk up on a special kind of energy. Or maybe a Jelk needed the artifact to help him or her reproduce. Why were there so few Jelk around? There had to be a reason.

"What do you think is going on?" Jen asked me.

"Yeah, I'd like to know," I told her. "Maybe the Earth was a game preserve, and Claath finally broke the rules by coming here. The Lokhars figured—I don't know. I don't have enough data, as N7 would say. But I'm going to find out, Jen. We're going to solve this riddle and then—"

I laughed, and I shook my head. "I guess I'd better work on one thing at a time. First we have to insure our survival. Then maybe we can scrub the planet of the bio-terminator. The human race is going Viking, Jen."

"Raiding?" she asked.

"That's right. We're lifting the freighters today. I have a good idea where to hide so not even the Jelk can find us, and forget about the Jade League."

"Where's that?" Jen asked. "Where's your spot?"

I didn't feel like telling her yet, so I dodged the question by ignoring it. Grinning at her, I said, "They tried to wipe us out, but they failed to squash every last one of us. The game isn't over, Jen. It's just getting started."

"We could still lose," she said.

"Yeah," I said, knowing that all too well. "But win or lose, I know one thing."

"What's that?" she asked.

"The galaxy—or this part of it anyway—is going to know they've been in a fight with the human race."

The End

SF Books by Vaughn Heppner:

DOOM STAR SERIES
Star Soldier
Bio Weapon
Battle Pod
Cyborg Assault
Planet Wrecker
Star Fortress

EXTINCTION WARS SERIES
Assault Troopers
Planet Strike

INVASION AMERICA SERIES
Invasion: Alaska
Invasion: California
Invasion: Colorado
Invasion: New York

OTHER SF NOVELS
Alien Honor
Accelerated
Strotium-90
I, Weapon

Visit www.Vaughnheppner.com for more
information.